1788 and all that...

WHEN TIMES WERE
TOUGH

As a first-time author/publisher, I have found working on this historical novel a real challenge on the one hand and providing a wonderful sense of satisfaction on the other.

I was born in England at the beginning of the Second World War and moved to four different countries before settling in Australia for the last thirty-five years. My twenty years living on Norfolk Island have provided much of the insight necessary to write the last few chapters of this book.

I currently live some one hundred and fifty kilometres from Brisbane, Australia, in a small country town called Yarraman, an Aboriginal word meaning "wild horse".

When Times Were Tough

Phil Page

Phil.Page Publications

WHEN TIMES WERE TOUGH

Preface

This historical adventure novel, set in 1787-88, travels from one side of the world to the other. Times were indeed "tough" in those days, and the four main characters in this story experience everything you can imagine.

The book is based on the trials, tribulations, and adventures of a fictional young Marine and a girl who travel from one side of the world to another to finally meet on Norfolk Island. How they get there, why they get there, what happens on the way, and when they finally arrive form the central part of this story. It involves sailing ships, convicts, sailors, prisons, soldiers, adventure, family relationships, home life, conflict, and love. I have tried to use enough historical facts so that the reader can appreciate what life was like in the late 18th century, although I have not been afraid to stray from time to time.

The story in this book is predominately set in Portsmouth, England, on board two ships travelling to the other side of the world and on Norfolk Island, an island in the South Pacific Ocean, where I lived for nearly 20 years.

The fascinating history of their destination in this story, and its involvement with Australia's early history, makes everything to do with Norfolk Island's early history both intriguing and, in a few cases, unique and violent at the same time.

I have also tried to use authentic historical timelines, people, places, and actual events that I have weaved into this fictional tale with the view of combining both fiction and non-fiction into one story. Some of my fictional characters in this story held actual historical positions, and any storyline I have used does not reflect those who held those positions. Actual historical figures have been included in this historical novel to assist the reader in understanding important figures of the time, places, events and dates. While the fictional events could have taken place, to my knowledge, they did not, and are entirely of my imagination. This is, after all, a historical novel!

Chapter 1

Elizabeth Johnson and her mother, Ann, stood outside their stone Tudor-style house and gazed with wonderment at the shapes and movement of the various sailing vessels within their view. There was a strong south-easterly running that provided each vessel in sight with the power to surge through the water, leaving white froth in their wake.

Both Ann and Elizabeth stood there facing the bay, each enjoying the view and the strong wind on their face and in their hair. The freshness of it all was something they had both enjoyed for quite a few years now and although they did not do it as often as they used to, it was always an invigorating experience. This handy viewing site was just across the road from their house, which made it that much more enjoyable. The added fact that Elizabeth could see the bay and all the ships from her bedroom window made her feel very much a part of it.

While the wind was fresh, the sky was cloudless, and it was not cold considering the time of year. Standing there, taking it all in, both Ann and her daughter considered themselves to be very lucky to be living in such a pleasant part of the south coast of England, Portsmouth.

Elizabeth finally turned to her mother and asked the question, "Have you ever been on a ship like that big one over there?" pointing to a vessel about to enter Portsmouth's inner harbour.

Ann, not wanting to brag or anything like that, replied, "Yes, in fact, I have."

"Really, you mean you have actually sailed on a ship? Like that one over there?"

Wanting to lead her daughter on and make a joke of it, Ann turned on her heel, crossed the road, and started to go back inside the house.

Elizabeth, while wanting to know the answer to her question, hesitated for a few moments as she eyed a handsome young man walking along the other side of the road. Wondering who he was, she followed her mother through the doorway, eager to continue the conversation. She glanced up the street one more time and then closed the front door.

Stopping at the end of the hallway, Ann turned to her daughter and said, "Well, I have been aboard a ship like that."

"Oh! For goodness' sake, you are not telling me the truth!"

"Yes, I have. You asked me if I had ever been on a ship like that. I have! I have been on a ship like that, but it was tied up at the wharf at the time, and I think it was in 1766," Ann replied while laughing at the same time. She had fooled Elizabeth once again, which she always enjoyed, particularly when getting one over on her daughter.

Elizabeth, fully understanding her mother's weird sense of humour, laughed with her mother as they both moved into the kitchen. On the other hand, Elizabeth often tried to get one up on her mother, but to this point, she had never really achieved it to her full satisfaction.

They both appreciated living within reach of such an exciting harbour, and it was a sight that neither of them ever got tired of. They often wondered where in the world those tall two and three-masted sailing vessels were coming from. Many were vessels of the Royal Navy coming and going into England's major naval port from who knows where, while others were trading vessels bringing a wide range of exotic goods from all over the world. One could only imagine.

Elizabeth was only a gangly teenager, as she had just turned fifteen a couple of months ago. She was truly fortunate in many ways, being an only child and having a father who had a regular and reasonable level of income. This allowed Ann to educate Elizabeth at home, as her mother was very protective of her, and she thought that a dependable governess was the safest and most effective way of learning.

Elizabeth noticed that it was nearly 10 o'clock in the morning by this time, and her regular governess, Mrs Williams, was about to arrive.

Elizabeth's formal education was about to finish, and Mrs. Williams was only coming to the house today to let her know how well she had done on her recent test. A knock on the door, right on time! Elizabeth ran to the door.

A callout from the other side of the door, "Are you there, Elizabeth?" emphasising that it was Mrs. Williams at the door and not an unwanted intruder.

"I'm coming," called out Elizabeth.

Opening the door with a flourish, she ushered Mrs. Williams inside with a welcoming gesture. Elizabeth not only recognised her tutor's talents, but she also considered her a friend as she had been regularly coming to the house for five years now. Rearranging her hair, as it was very windy outside, Mrs. Williams went with Elizabeth to a small reception room just past the front door, where they both sat down.

"Well," said Mrs. Williams, "I was nearly blown away as I came around the corner into your street."

"Yes, I know, Mother and I were outside watching the ships in the harbour earlier on, and it was quite windy then."

"Now," Mrs. Williams said with a wide smile on her face, "I have good news for you. You got most of the questions correct in that letter-writing test I gave you last week. It means that you have now passed everything you need to and can now consider this part of your education complete."

"Great, that means I can now do more work down at the local hospital. I love doing that work. So many come in with extremely complicated diseases and accidents, and I don't know how the doctors know where to start. I like to help where I can."

Mrs. Williams got out of her chair, commenting at the same time, "That is great, but remember you will only be able to go when it is convenient for your mother to go with you."

"Yes, I understand."

Mrs. Williams continued, "Before I forget. Here is a letter describing what you have learned over the last few years, which might help you later."

Feeling rather awkward, Elizabeth gave Mrs. Williams a half hug as she thanked her for everything. They both quietly walked to the front door.

"Thanks once again," said Elizabeth, "I do appreciate what you have done for me, and I will remember you fondly."

Mrs. Williams thanked Elizabeth for being such a good student, walked to the front door, looked back, smiled at Elizabeth, and promptly left the house.

Later in the day, Elizabeth noticed that she was not feeling very well as she helped her mother clean the largest room in the house, the main parlour. She had not slept well for the last couple of nights, and every movement of her arms and legs was now becoming an effort. Her mother, Ann, always appreciated the help that her daughter volunteered to do, and, at the same time, she knew that her daughter did not usually pretend to be unwell. If Elizabeth said she was not feeling well, that indeed was the case.

"Mother," Elizabeth cried out, "What is the matter with me? I feel really ill. I have trouble standing now."

Ann knew that the meat they had eaten the night before had smelt awful, but she had decided to cook it anyway due to the shortage of good meat. She thought it strange that neither she nor her husband had been affected. Maybe the meat was the problem?

"Elizabeth, I think I know what the problem could be. It was probably the meat you ate last night, but I do not know what I can do about it. Leave the cleaning to me and go to bed; you might feel better in the morning."

As Elizabeth was an only child, Ann was inclined to spoil her but resisted the urge to do so as much as she could. She thought that her daughter had to make her own way in the world, particularly understanding that she would not always be around to help.

Ann was always grateful for her daughter's work around the house, but she did not want Elizabeth to get dangerously unwell by forcing her to continue working. "Off you go, dear; I shall finish here."

Elizabeth reluctantly left the room and trudged up the long flight of stairs to her bedroom. Her progress was a real effort, and her legs did not want to take that next step, but she slowly managed to make it to the top, walk down the hallway, push open the door, and then staggered into her bedroom.

Falling onto her bed, she wrapped the bedding around her and fell back onto the pillow, completely exhausted. Elizabeth also had a violent headache, her stomach hurt, and her body was starting to ache all over. "I feel like I am going to die," Elizabeth moaned to herself, and that was the last thing she remembered before she fell asleep.

Meanwhile, her mother continued cleaning up the parlour as she was expecting her husband, William, who was likely to arrive home at any moment. Her husband was a big burly man with a temper to match, and he was always in a bad mood when he first entered the house after a tiring day. He worked long hours, and sometimes it was hectic as a surgeon in his practice, which was just a short walk away from their house. Keeping the house neat and tidy was something that William was a stickler about, and Ann knew what the result would be if his rigid standards were not maintained. She continued tidying up the parlour when she heard a strange noise coming from upstairs.

Elizabeth had woken up with a start, and in her confused state, she did not know what was happening. The noise sounded like broken glass, but her sense of what was going on and what made the sound eluded her. In her half-awake state, and at the same time not feeling well, she tried to focus on what was happening. Hoping the whole thing was only a dream, she tried to relax, but in the back of her confused mind, she was confident she had heard an unusual noise. Finally, after waiting a minute or two without any further noise or disturbances, she drifted off to sleep.

Bang! More tinkling of broken glass and then a rolling sound. It sounded really close this time, and Elizabeth sat up instantly, trying to figure out what was going on. She then heard voices coming from outside her window, and within a couple of seconds a loud bang from downstairs, and then her dad yelled out, "Get away, you bastards, leave my family out of this."

Ann had also heard both the banging noises and the excited voices as she rushed into the hall to find William trying to hold the door closed with his back hard against it. After being chased by a small crowd down the street, he just managed to close the door behind him and draw the latch. Voices were calling through the door, but, in the commotion, she could not make out what they were saying. Then, without even thinking about it, Ann let out a piercing scream.

6

Meanwhile, Elizabeth, being upstairs in her bedroom, could not hear what was being said, but she began to realize that several people outside were violently venting their frustration. Looking around her bedroom, she saw a large rock on the wooden floor and fully understood what had made the noise that woke her up. What was going on? And then she heard her mother let out that scream.

With extreme difficulty, feeling half asleep and fuzzy-headed, Elizabeth slowly dropped her feet over the side of the bed and tried to stand up, but that proved impossible as the world around her spun round and round. It sounded like Mother needed help, but that thought would be impossible unless she could get downstairs.

Ann eventually found her voice and yelled back at those outside, "Leave my husband alone; he has not done anything wrong."

There was an instant reply from the other side of the door, "Your husband nearly killed my child – he should be strung up!"

There was more banging on the door as William struggled to hold it firmly shut, thinking that the door could come off its hinges at any moment.

"You call yourself a surgeon; I have seen butchers do a better job," a woman yelled from outside. "Have you no sense of right from wrong?" she continued. "Come out here and face the music, you coward!"

By this stage, William had got his breath back from his earlier sprint down the street and into the house and replied, "Let's just talk about this; we can talk through the door right now if you want." No direct answer, just the sound of voices talking to one another. William finally managed to add the other lock to the door.

Eventually, a man's voice called out, "What have you got to say?" "Have you got some sort of solution?"

William paused before answering as he knew the correct answer here might get that angry mob away from the house.

William remembered the woman coming into his surgery a few months ago with her son, who had a bad knife wound on the top part of his leg. Thinking that the injury was not significant, although it looked large and bloody, he had decided to pull the edges together, bind it with a bandage, and thought that would do. The woman, whose name he could not remember, had returned to see him a couple of weeks later, complaining the wound was not healing. "It was continuously oozing, which would not stop," she said. William recommended that she remove the bandages, add the compound he gave her, and re-wrap it. He had not heard anything further until today.

"Hurry up," came a male voice from the other side of the door. "We need an answer; we can't wait here all day."

"All right, I think I have the answer to the problem. I will come to your house first thing in the morning and look at he boy's leg. I am sure I can fix him up. I will not be charging you anything; it will be free. Is that all right with you?"

"You bloody well will fix him up, or we will be back again tomorrow demanding justice."

William finally drew a breath as he felt extremely uncomfortable defending his house and family like this. It could have turned out ugly, but at least now it looked like he had resolved the immediate problem with some quick thinking.

Answering back through the door, William, in a very calm voice, assured the family, "I promise I will be at your house just after sun-up in the morning, and I will see what I can do. All right?"

"We will be waiting. You had better be there!"

With a sigh of relief, William paused for a little while and then moved away from the front door. He slowly walked back to Ann, who was still shaking with fear, and who had, by this stage, retreated several yards back down the hallway.

"That was close! I never want to be in a situation like that again," Ann whispered in a trembling voice, "I am glad that you managed to satisfy that angry mob, as it could have been far more dangerous. I can't hear any more voices, so I think they have gone."

While all this was going on, Elizabeth had managed to crawl out of bed, open her bedroom door, lean on the door frame, and then try to listen to what was happening downstairs. While voices had obviously been raised, she eventually realized that the immediate physical danger had passed. She then staggered back into her room and flopped down on her bed, still as unwell as ever.

Elizabeth had a very fitful night as she had to get up and empty her stomach several times into the wash bowl on the dresser. Finally, after a couple of trips to the bowl, she had nothing left in her stomach, and as a result, things settled down, and she finally drifted into an uninterrupted sleep.

Ann quietly opened Elizabeth's door the next day just before the sun rose and found her daughter quietly sleeping, so she crept back out of the room. After leaving, Ann decided it would be best to let her daughter sleep for as long as she liked, as there was no real reason for her to get out of bed. Ann had heard noises coming from Elizabeth's room on a few occasions during the night and understood precisely what was happening. By the time Ann got up, William had left the house to travel to that poor boy's home, hoping he could treat the wound and not have any more problems.

It was nearly time for the usual mid-day meal when Elizabeth finally stirred, simultaneously realizing that this debilitating headache was finally gone. Her mouth felt parched and tasted terrible, so a drink of water made things that much better. Then she became aware of an awful smell in the room and, upon looking around, realized that she had forgotten to cover the wash bowl during the night. Elizabeth grabbed a cloth and took care of that problem, quick smart.

Hearing movement noises from upstairs, Ann climbed the stairs and was pleased to find her daughter sitting on the side of the bed, looking much better.

"Elizabeth, how are you feeling?"

"A lot better, thanks; at least I feel alive."

"When you are ready, come downstairs. You might feel like something light to eat after that terrible night."

"All right, Mother, I won't be long."

After about 10 minutes, Ann heard Elizabeth coming down the stairs and entering the kitchen cautiously. The kitchen itself was a separate building connected to the main house by a short, covered walkway. That kept cooking smells out of the house and certainly made things much safer if any unwanted fire erupted in the kitchen. Another advantage of having a separate room from the rest of the house is that it had a fire of its own, which created a distinctly warm and cosy atmosphere, which was a real advantage on a freezing cold day.

"Look what I have here, Elizabeth; it is a nice broth, and a little bit will make you feel better and help you get your strength back."

Elizabeth sat down very slowly as she still felt fragile and did not feel like talking. She sipped the broth, and while her mouth had not as fresh as she would have liked, she enjoyed the warm and familiar taste.

While she knew the kitchen well, she glanced around the kitchen in a new light which made her appreciate the large fireplace and the warm fire in the hearth. Various kitchen cooking pots and utensils surrounded this, which greatly added to the homely atmosphere. Off towards one side was a large cast iron pot full of hot water that looked like, by the amount of steam, it was about to boil. Elizabeth had noticed many times that it was always there, and she understood the importance of having hot water available for all kinds of cleaning jobs, including bathing. On the other side of the fire was another smaller pot with a lid, and knowing her mother, she assumed it was some form of stew, probably with plenty of vegetables.

After having a little broth and now feeling far warmer and more comfortable, Elizabeth started nodding off in the chair. She suddenly came to her senses at the sound of a loud bang. It sounded like the front door slamming. Next came her father's heavy footsteps as he called out in a thunderous and frustrating voice, "Who the hell do these people think they are, making ridiculous demands? Ann, where are you?"

Ann at once knew that things had not gone smoothly this morning and it looked like she was about to receive the brunt of it all. "I am in the kitchen," replied Ann in a reluctant tone, "I have some nice warm broth here for you." All she got was a grunt in reply before William angrily swept into the kitchen.

Elizabeth quickly came to her senses and swung around to face her father, not knowing what to expect. "Father, are you all right? You have not been injured or anything, have you?"

The look on her father's face told a story. He was seething with rage, and it was obvious that the atmosphere in the kitchen would not be so warm and cosy as it was before his arrival.

William said, "Some people don't want to accept your help and only criticise you when you try. I went around to that boy's house early this morning and fixed up his leg without too much trouble, but that was not good enough. Even though I had to put stitches in it to hold it together this time, all for free, they were still not happy. They caught up with me a little while ago while I was walking home, and they verbally assaulted me once again, and in the main street."

"Is the boy's leg going to be all right?" Elisabeth replied, hoping to change the subject.

"He will be fine, providing they do what they were told!"

"That's good," she replied hopefully, "Things will probably get better now."

The slight change of subject made a small difference to the atmosphere in the room as William, who looked somewhat defeated, slumped down in one of the kitchen chairs.

Thinking it was now safe to say something, Ann suggested, "I have some lovely broth here, and I think you will enjoy it. Shall I get you a bowl?"

All Ann got in reply was a grunt. Knowing her husband as well as she did, she knew what that meant, so she turned around and ladled several spoonsful of the hot soup into a bowl. "Here you are, dear; sip it slowly as it is still very hot. I would hate for you to burn your mouth."

With loud slurping sounds, William started to eat his soup, that is, after roughly tearing a piece of bread off the loaf that was on the end of the table. "I can't stay long, as I must get back into the surgery as soon as possible," he angrily said, "Leave me be. I will be all right!"

Ann and Elizabeth left the kitchen, deliberately leaving William in a bad mood and with his thoughts. He felt he had done the right thing by the injured boy and his family, so he thought it would now be best to forget about it and get on with his daily role as a surgeon. William finished his soup and promptly left the house, hurriedly walking down the road and returning to his surgery.

Elizabeth soon found that sitting in the kitchen chair was uncomfortable, and although she felt better from eating something, she decided to return to her bedroom. She spent the next day doing very little, but by the middle of the day, she was starting to feel somewhat normal. Most of the morning she sat in the parlour, sometimes reading and sometimes dozing, but now feeling much better. Finally, she thought it best to go up to her bedroom and give it the necessary clean and tidy. The room looked a mess, and as everything she did took real effort, it took considerable time to get things back into place.

Elizabeth found that the effort taken to clean up the mess had taken its toll, so she sat down for a breather. Without realizing it, she dozed off.

Elizabeth woke up and immediately glanced out of the broken window onto the street below. She was obviously feeling better after her short sleep, and she found herself thinking about that young man whom she saw walking down the road. Who was he? What is his name? Does he live around here? I have not seen him before. I wonder where he was going. She had no idea what the answers to any of these questions might be, but she enjoyed the entire thought process. She had noticed that her thoughts were moving increasingly to the opposite sex as she grew older, and while she did not fully understand what was going on, it was, nevertheless, a rather interesting and pleasant feeling.

Now that Elizabeth had finished her formal schooling, she felt it was time to find an interest that would occupy her time. She used to attend the local hospital from time to time with her mother, but she felt that maybe she could find something else. Her mother had spoken to her on several occasions, but nothing had come to mind upon which they both agreed. Ann was hoping that Elizabeth would learn a great deal more about what she considered to be necessary for her daughter's long-term happiness. Skills such as: how to buy well at the markets, how to make and repair one's own clothes, the best ways to keep a house, and other useful skills necessary for a competent wife and mother. While she knew that Elizabeth was quite capable with a great number of these required skills, she hoped that her daughter would become proficient enough so she could finally marry well and happily settle down in her own home and have a family.

Elizabeth had other ideas on how to improve her chances of being happy, and she was, in fact, thinking about her future as she heard her mother call out, "Elizabeth, are you doing anything important?" Waiting for a couple of seconds and with no answer forthcoming, she called out once again, "Elizabeth, can you hear me?"

Thinking that it would be wise not to ignore her mother any further, Elizabeth replied, "Yes, Mother, I can hear you. What do you want?"

"If you are not doing anything important, please come down here."

A quiet and remote-sounding answer came back, "Coming, Mother, I will be right down."

Elizabeth had no idea what her mother wanted to talk to her about, but by the tone of her mother's voice, it sounded important. She descended the stairs and followed her mother into the front parlour.

"Are you feeling all right?" asked her mother.

"Yes, I feel much better now."

"Good. I know we have spoken about how important it is for you to be more familiar with how a family household works, but we have not yet come up with any real answers. I was thinking about a finishing school. Have you thought any more about your future?"

"Not really mother, there is time to learn such matters, but I want to experience a few exciting adventures before those things become important. I have no idea what; I am just not ready to think about settling down yet."

Ann sighed deeply, knowing just how deeply her daughter wanted to do more with her life, so she replied, "I see. All right, that's enough for now, but we must discuss this again before long. It is important, you know. All right with you?

Reluctantly, Elizabeth replied, "I will think about it," as she turned and walked out into the hallway. Elizabeth returned to the parlour and sat down, thinking about what her future might hold.

After sitting there thinking for some time, she decided to go into the little alcove at one end of the parlour, which held a painting on an easel. The half-finished watercolour of the sea view outside the window had not been touched for some time. Elizabeth had recently lost interest in painting, but recently watching the comings and goings of ships on the sea outside the window was perking up her interest. Looking at the painting and then the view outside the window, she said to herself, "Maybe I should try and finish it."

Ann stood in the middle of the kitchen, wondering what she had done wrong to bring up such a headstrong girl who did not want to acknowledge reality. Girls of her age should not have such grand ideas or even think about such things - it was not safe; it was not right or proper.

While all this was going on at home, William was at work discussing with his assistant, Thomas, the best way to deal with patients' families that irrationally became irate and violent. He understood their concerns, but threatening behaviour was not the answer, so he said,

"Maybe I should explain things more clearly so that relatives know what to expect. Maybe I'll try that next time."

Thomas, not having any other solutions himself, replied, "I think you could be right. I don't know what else you could do."

While they were talking to one another, William and Thomas were feeling quite comfortable standing opposite each other across a very bloody operating table. They had just removed a bullet from the hip of a sailor who nearly bled to death before he even got to the surgery. The bullet had damaged a main blood vessel and smashed part of the pelvis. William forced a quantity of whiskey down his patient's throat, hoping it would deaden the pain. They had managed to remove the bullet but could not do a great deal about the broken bone other than to remove the small pieces that had splintered off. They both doubted that the patient would ever be able to walk properly again as the chip was right at the hip joint. They were not even sure that he would live past the next 24 hours, as he had lost a considerable amount of blood before and during the operation.

He was currently moaning with pain in the other room, awaiting his family to come and pick him up as William's surgery had no long-term after-surgery facilities. Naval patients either went to the local hospital, returned to their ship or shore base, or were taken home – there were just no other options.

While William did not regularly treat navy hospital patients, sometimes the navy could not manage the number of injuries sustained themselves, and he offered to help in such situations. This patient had been checking several muskets on board a ship and somehow, one had been left loaded, and it had accidentally discharged. In extreme agony, the patient was rushed to William's surgery as the naval surgeons were just too busy to take on another major operation.

While the operation had gone reasonably well, they were not confident of the patient's active future.

William and Thomas cleaned up the surgery, including the operating table and the floor, both a bloody mess. A bucket of water was finally splashed across the floor, and the red water was swept out the door. The family of the patient in the other room finally came with a handcart, and then, with a little help from all present, they managed to lift and roll the groaning man onto the cart. It was now time for the poor fella's family to look after him the best way they could. By the time the patient and his family had left, William and Thomas had enough for the day, and as there were no other patients expected, they decided to shut up shop. Tomorrow was another day, and they could never ever guess what may turn up!

"Thanks for helping today, Thomas. You did well. I will see you in the morning!

"Thanks. I'll see you tomorrow."

William closed the front door and started off down the road toward home. He had every intention of going straight there, but temptation got in the way. Close to his surgery was the local inn, the Cock and Hen, which beckoned every time William walked past. He was not now a big drinker, but he did not mind a pint or two of ale or the occasional whisky, now usually taken at home. There was, however, one big problem that he always needed to remember. About ten years ago, William used to go into this inn, and others like it, on a regular basis, often not leaving until closing time. Once again, he resisted temptation, walking past the front door while at the same time remembering his early pledge to Ann not to frequent such places. He continued his way home.

Historically, he had proven to himself that he could not have just a couple of drinks and then go straight home. He had always found that incredibly hard to do and usually stayed drinking for far too many hours, and then eventually arrived home dead drunk.

His earlier habit was something that Ann was not willing to accept any more, and she had put her foot down. It took every bit of courage on Ann's part to lay down the ultimatum, and she had said, "If you continue down this path, I will walk out of this house and take Elizabeth with me. I am not putting up with this anymore!" William, knowing "which side of the bread was buttered on," finally and reluctantly gave up the hard-drinking lifestyle, bringing a sense of order and peace back into the family home.

By the time William reached his house, he was not feeling his usual self and found it difficult to climb up the front stairs. He had just got to the door when it burst open in front of him. Not expecting this, he suddenly stepped back in an automatic defensive reaction. Missing the next step down, William yelled out, "What the hell?" as he tumbled backwards down the next three steps.

"Father. Are you hurt?" called out Elizabeth, suddenly feeling very guilty to have opened the door in her father's face and realizing that she was the reason for her father falling.

Gathering himself together, and at the same time trying to work out what damage he may have incurred, William let out a torrid string of swear words, "Bloody hell! What the shit are you thinking of? You could have killed me."

Feeling surprised by the sudden bad language, and at the same time, concerned for her father's welfare, Elizabeth rushed down the steps and tried to help her father to his feet.

Wrenching his arm out of Elizabeth's grasp, William struggled to his feet and angrily spat out the words, "I am quite capable of looking after myself, thank you! Where did you think you were going in such a hurry?"

Not wanting to give anything away, Elizabeth replied, "I was just coming outside to get some sea air," at the same time trying to sound very casual.

What Elizabeth did not want her father to know was that she was hoping to see the young man she had seen walking past the house a day or two before. She had looked out of the upstairs window earlier in the day, and she had seen him walk back up the street. She then thought to herself, "Yes, it would be interesting to meet him! Maybe I can just "accidentally" bump into him somehow?"

Jolting Elizabeth out of her dream, her father yelled, "Get out of my way! You have done enough damage for today," as he pushed past her up the steps and into the house.

Elizabeth sheepishly followed and quickly ran up the stairs into her bedroom. She was not sure what to think, as she felt very sorry for knocking her father down the steps on the one hand, but then, she had not seen the young man she went outside hoping to see on the other. Either way, she felt this had not been a good day.

Ann had heard most of her husband's outbursts, and she thought it best to keep well out of it. She knew that when William was in such a bad mood, it was best not to complicate things by making any comments or otherwise getting involved. That just made things worse. As she heard William enter the parlour, probably to get a stiff drink, she thought of her motto, "When things go wrong, just keep out of the way", and then decided to leave him be. Thinking further, she thought that he would probably feel better in an hour or so and that serving the evening meal would just have to wait till then.

Chapter 2

Not very far from where Elizabeth and her family lived, was Sergeant Richard Clarke, a member of the local Portsmouth Naval Detachment. While he had been on board various ships over the five years he had been in the Navy; he was now based as a Marine on shore, aiding in the defence of one of the Royal Navies' major harbours, Portsmouth, located on the south coast of England. He joined the Navy when he was only 14 years of age to get away from his violent family and everything that went with it. He could remember having to leave the house when the atmosphere became too heated, and he just had to get out of there. He left exiting the family home far too late on one occasion, and he got caught up in the violence which resulted in him being knocked unconscious. As he was a quick learner, he left home far earlier in any future violence after learning what that earlier episode meant, but things still did not get any better. He pitied his mother, but there was little he could do about it. When living at home became more than he could take, joining the Navy proved to be the best decision he had ever made. The ability he had learnt to think quickly on his feet at home became an asset once he became the youngest crew member on board one of His Majesty's ships.

Noticing the differences in the types of work that Naval Marines did on board ship and on shore, he thought that that would suit him more, so he applied for a transfer from the Navy into the Marines. After considerable Navy protest and procrastination, he finally managed to join the Marines five years ago. He thought that his world had now changed for the better. The number of years he had spent in the two services had provided him with a certain sense of confidence and satisfaction in a job well done.

"Sergeant Clarke," a voice called out as he was getting dressed to attend the usual early morning muster, "The Captain wants to speak to you right away."

Quickly getting dressed, and making sure that he looked ship-shape, he crossed the parade ground and entered his unit's headquarters. Stepping just inside the front archway, he was promptly bought up short, "Sergeant, where do you think you are going? You can't just barge in here anytime you like?" someone bellowed.

The guard on duty was just out of sight in the shadows, and as Richard had just come in from the bright sunshine, he did not see him. "Sorry, I did not see you. I am Sergeant Clarke, and I have been given orders to see Captain Evans."

The guard at once lowered his guard as he knew Sergeant Clarke and that he could trust what the sergeant was saying. "I see. Go ahead, turn right at the next corridor and the captain is normally in the last office."

Arriving at the end of the corridor, Sergeant Clarke stopped for a couple of seconds as he tugged at his uniform, ensuring everything was in the right place. He knocked on the door.

"Come in," called out a voice from inside. It was a voice he recognized, but somehow it seemed different, and he wondered who else could be inside the office with the captain.

Richard entered the office, took two steps, stood to attention, and said, "Sir."

"Yes, Sergeant, I did want to see you. Relax, you have done nothing wrong, I just want to ask you a question. I know the work you are currently doing, but I think I have something else that would suit you better. How about working as a building consultant on defence walls and bastions?"

Richard hesitated for a couple of seconds while pondering his answer, wondering, more than anything, where all this was heading. "Well. Ah. Sir, I am quite happy where I am."

"Sergeant, according to this file, you have been in the Marines for about five years. I also know that you served as a regular sailor before you joined the Marines. Is that correct?"

"Yes, Sir."

"As you have had a wide range of experience in both offensive and defensive tactics on board a ship and on land, you would have extensive knowledge of both sides in any conflict, particularly where cannons are concerned. Would you agree?"

"Yes, Sir."

"Well, I have a new assignment for you. I think that you could be ready for this type of change, and for a new challenge."

Richard did not reply as he was not sure what his response should be. Was he going to be transferred to another unit? Will I be staying in Portsmouth? Surely, they are not asking me to go overseas. There were just far too many unanswered questions to be able to make an on-the-spot decision.

Captain Evans, understanding the sergeant's hesitancy, continued, "This is what I am proposing, Sergeant. You would be aware that Fort Cumberland is being improved and that a great deal of work is going on there.

"I have heard about that, Sir."

"Well, they have asked us to find an experienced sergeant with wide experience to help them with certain construction decisions. You would be helping them to understand what is needed to make such a fort defendable. You have the experience that is needed in both gunnery and sailing. Are you interested?"

"Sorry, Sir, but you have given me an awful lot to think about, and I am not sure what to say."

"Well, this may help. You will be billeted with a local family, as there is very little suitable accommodation anywhere near there, so that will take you out of the barracks. In a sense, you would be a free agent but, ultimately, still reportable to me."

"Put that way, sir, and as it would be different and something of a challenge, I accept."

"Thank you, Sergeant; I will put everything in order so that you can start there next week. Dismissed, Sergeant.

Richard at once stiffened and replied, "Sir." He then swung around on his heels and marched out of the room.

By the end of the day, written orders had been received by the Lieutenant, and Richard was excused from attending his current unit from that point on. He could now prepare for the transfer to Fort Cumberland.

As Fort Cumberland was only some 5 miles away, and as Richard had to take all his worldly possessions with him, as little as they were, he was advised that he would be provided with a horse and cart, including a driver.

He was to report to the front gate first thing in the morning and that there would be transport waiting for him.

Early the next morning, he lugged what he could carry to the gate. Seeing a horse and cart with a rather sad-looking driver just outside, he asked, "Are you waiting for someone to drive to Fort Cumberland?"

A strange bumbling voice that was hard to understand replied, "That's right, are you going there?"

"Yes, that's me. Wait here, as I have a couple of other things."

Richard was not sure how sensible it was to go back inside the gate and lose sight of the horse and cart with most of his personal goods. Taking a chance, he rushed inside, grabbed the rest of his belongings, and hurried back. The man, his cart, and his kit were still there. He quickly threw everything in the back of the cart and jumped up alongside the driver. Richard's nose at once caught the smell of someone who had not only not washed for some time but had also probably slept somewhere closely alongside his horse. Richard moved as far away as the small bench seat would allow.

"Are we ready to go, Sergeant?"

At least the driver understood the sergeant's insignia on his marine uniform, which was at least a start. Richard, thinking to himself, thought, "Maybe we will get there in one piece."

Richard replied, "Yes, Fort Cumberland. Do you know how to get there?"

"Yea, no problem. I have been there before."

The horse suddenly shot forward as though it had been asleep when the reins were shaken over its back. It then settled into a slow trot, although Richard doubted that the mangy steed could keep up that pace all the way there. Sure enough, after about ten minutes, the horse slowed to a walk, and that is about as fast as it got for the rest of the journey. Richard tried to start up a conversation, but that was just too hard and turned to nothing, so they travelled the rest of the way in silence.

Richard had been told to find the worksite boss, Mr. Smithers, who, he was informed, was easy to find as he usually had several others following him around the building site, and he also had a full head of grey hair. Richard had also been told that Fort Cumberland had been originally built in 1747, and as that was 40 years ago, it was thought necessary that it be upgraded and enlarged. His part in the project was to consider each construction phase as it happened and supply informed comments as to its suitability from a defensive point of view. It was felt that an on-the-spot evaluation by somebody who had both naval and heavy gun knowledge would be an advantage. He was advised that he could not suggest major changes to the plan, but he could advise on minor improvements as construction progressed.

Suddenly, the cart came to a stop. They were there, catching Richard by surprise as he was in his own world, thinking about what was ahead of him. Coming to his senses, he realizes that this was the start of something new and that he had better create a positive first impression. Richard promptly jumped off the cart, went around the back and removed his few belongings, including his kit bag. "Thanks for that. I suppose you have been paid?"

"I already got paid all right."

As Fort Cumberland was not in use as an active fortification, there were no guards on the gate, so Richard walked right in hoping to easily find the worksite boss. He asked the leader of the first group of workers he came across where Mr. Smithers could be found. "I think he is over there near that wall with the holes in it," came a voice with a strong accent he was not familiar with.

Richard dropped his baggage off just inside the door of a building he assumed was part of the original fort. He then noticed that the convicts he could see loading carts looked somewhat different from those he was familiar with, but in the first instance, he could not put his finger on why that was so. Other than one lieutenant he saw on the other side of the compound, everyone else seemed to be civilians. Looking everywhere, he eventually came across the wall with the holes in it and thought to himself, "Oh well, I guess I will eventually find out what is going on."

He noticed an older man with partially grey hair amongst a small group who looked like they were inspecting a wooden foundation, so he stopped and waited to be recognised. Waiting 2 or 3 minutes, and without any acknowledgements, he moved slightly closer just in case he had not been seen. Suddenly a loud voice demanded, "What are you doing here, Sergeant?"

He first wondered where the voice was coming from, as the man he thought was Mr. Smithers was still looking down the hole, so it could not have been him. Turning to his left, where he thought the voice had come from, Richard noticed a small grey-haired man looking straight at him in a rather menacing manner.

"I am Sergeant Clarke, and I have been told to report to Mr Smithers," he replied as he stood to attention.

The sound of Richard's voice made everyone in the group turn towards him, all wondering what was going on. He repeated his earlier remarks, "Am I addressing Mr Smithers?"

"Yes, you are indeed, and I assume you are Sergeant Clarke, correct?"

"Yes, Sir."

"I have been expecting you, but I was not sure when you would arrive. Wait here, and I will be with you shortly."

Richard stood easy and then looked around at the others in the group and the area they were all standing in. It looked like some large structure had been here at some stage, but it had either fallen or had been partially knocked down. Not understanding anything to do with this type of construction, he did not pay much attention to what they seemed to be inspecting. Looking at the rest of the work site, he could see that there was not much left of the original fort other than a couple of rather substantial brick buildings and much earlier earthworks. Most of the old outside walls seemed to have been demolished.

Richard had never been to Fort Cumberland before, but he had heard of the enormous fortification and why it had been originally positioned there in the first place. He also knew that the fort covered some 24 acres and had been mildly upgraded until relatively recently when it was decided it needed improving and updating. That required nearly all the original structures to be dismantled over the last year or so and then built anew. So, while some of the old buildings had yet to be removed, many new fort structures were now being constructed.

After what seemed like hours, but it was probably only a few minutes, Mr. Smithers said, "Sergeant, come with me, and you will then have some idea as to your role. As you can see, I am rather busy now, so I will need to discuss the details with you tomorrow morning."

"Yes, Sir," was all Richard felt he could say as the whole party moved off to another part of the construction site.

As the group moved around, he kept looking at the various workers, and he could see there seemed to be two separate groups doing the work, with one group appearing to have more oversight than the other.

Not being able to keep quiet, Richard asked one of the men in the inspection team, "Sir, there seem to be two different groups of workers here. Why is that?"

"Ah," he replied, "some workers are convicts serving part of their sentence; the others are contract workers."

"Ah. That explains it. Thanks."

By this stage, Mr. Smithers turned his attention to Richard, "If I understand correctly, you have served in both the Navy and the Marines for about ten years. Is that correct?"

"Yes, Sir."

"You have been transferred here to help me to understand the requirements of defending this fort from both an attack and defence point of view. You have actively done both, and your experience will aid us in making this fort far more secure. Can you appreciate where I am coming from?"

"Yes, Sir."

"That's good, have a look around here today and familiarise yourself with what is going on, and I will see you at my office over there at seven tomorrow morning."

"Sir."

Richard moved away from the inspection team and gazed at the tremendous scope of the work around him. He was impressed at what he had seen so far, as he had always been good at coming to logical conclusions about complex problems. However, he thought that this was going to be a far more challenging job than he was led to believe.

Suddenly, loud voices were coming from the other side of the compound, and as they were some distance away, they must be shouting at the top of their voices. He could not hear what was being said, but the tone was enough. As he got closer, the shouting got louder, and the expletives became clearer. The din continued and got noisier the closer he came. Then, out of the blue, he heard one loud shot! Then another! Then all went quiet.

In the meantime, a few soldiers came into view, running around the corner of what looked like a guardhouse, all armed. They headed off toward the area where the shots had come from.

Still in his marine uniform, Richard thought he could not stand there looking obvious and not doing anything, so he took off in the same direction. By the time he arrived, all was quiet, other than a considerable discussion between the overseers and the soldiers. Richard scanned the scene and noticed a body lying crumpled in a doorway. Not wanting to get involved in what was not his direct responsibility, and as he was very new on the job and did not yet know who managed what, he stood back and watched.

No one was close to the body when he first arrived, so Richard assumed that the person was dead as blood slowly seeped into the ground from under his chest. Whatever happened to cause the violent argument was now defused by the shooting. Within seconds, Richard's deadly thoughts proved to be the case, as two burly workers grabbed the body and half lifted and half dragged it onto a pushcart, usually used for moving around the soil. Two other men grabbed the handles and took off towards the front gate, seemingly to get the body out of sight as soon as possible.

By this time, the confusion diminished, and everything started returning to normal, while Richard wondered what it was about. He started wondering whether this post would be as interesting as he first thought or if it would be one drama after another. "Oh, well, I guess I will have to wait and see," he said to himself. Everyone else seemed to be taking this incident in their stride, but he felt he had to understand what type of awkward situations could develop on the site by finding out what had just occurred.

Seeing the soldiers returning to the guardhouse, he wandered over to one of them to find out a little more. "Corporal, I am new here, so could you please tell me what just happened?".

Questioning what a marine sergeant was doing at the fort, he replied, "It is none of your business, and what are you doing here anyway?"

"I have been appointed to help Mr. Smithers and have just arrived. Was that a convict that just died?"

"Yes, it was. It is not uncommon when things get overheated. Something had to be done to keep discipline. Sometimes you can't trust the bastards," replied the Corporal as he rushed off to join his departing comrades.

Richard had seen many deaths in his years in the Navy and the Marines, but he never got used to them, and this death seemed so unnecessary. He found that each such occasion gets pushed to the back of his mind and only surfaces occasionally, usually at the wrong time. So, Richard decided to put this incident out of his mind as he returned to where he had been with Mr Smithers and his team earlier, while also reminding himself at the same time, not to take too much notice of such incidents in the future.

"Sergeant, such situations do occur from time to time, especially when there are several hundred convicts working on the site. Stay with us for a while, and you may find out a little more," recommended Mr Smithers.

Richard, not yet fully understanding what was planned, thought this was probably the best way of getting to know what the fort would be like when it was finished, so he tagged along, staying in the background. Watching and listening to what was going on, he concluded that the team seemed to know what they were doing. He, therefore, kept any thoughts or ideas to himself, thinking that his time would come.

By the time the inspection was completed, Richard had assumed that the working day was nearly over, and then he remembered he did not know where he was going to sleep that night. He was initially told he would be staying with a family in a nearby house, so he asked one of those in the inspection party whom he should ask to find out more. It was suggested that he see the clerk in the office, who should be able to point him in the right direction.

Walking into the office, he first saw Mr. Smithers with his back to him in the rear office and then noticed the clerk putting things away from a desk in the right-hand corner of the room. "Sir, I am Sergeant Clarke. I will be helping Mr. Smithers, and I was told that I will be billeted with a local family. Do you know anything about it?"

"Um, Ah yes, I remember. I have details here somewhere," replied the clerk, rummaging through papers on his desk. Finally finding a piece of paper, he read it aloud: "Sergeant Clarke billeted at Mrs. Jackson's, 3 King Street. I know where that is; it is about five minutes' walk away. Just turn right outside the main gate and keep going; you can't miss it because it is nearly at the end of the street."

Remembering his baggage, he left the office, turned into the small next-door building, and thankfully, his belongings were still there. Luckily, it all appeared that nothing was missing. Thinking about the large number of convicts on the site, he reminded himself not to leave things lying around in the future. With considerable difficulty, Richard loaded himself up with all his kit, left the fort site, and headed up the road. "Only 5 minutes away," I think he said.

After rearranging his load several times, he continued to trudge up the street, reminding himself to travel with considerably less gear next time. The load was getting heavier and heavier, and he reminded himself that he could have left half of his belongings at the barracks if he had thought of it. "Never mind, it shouldn't be too far," he thought.

As the houses were so close to the fort, he assumed that they were originally used as married officer quarters, or maybe for civilian contractors. He counted two homes back from the last one, finally realizing that no actual numbers were showing on any of them. Richard paused outside the third house, wondering what kind of family lived in this one. Then, gathering courage, he walked to the door and knocked. No answer. So, he knocked again.

Waiting for someone to answer the door, he noticed movement out of the corner of his eye in one of the upstairs windows. By the time he looked up, the curtain was back in place. Then he heard a female voice call out, "There is someone at the door." About ten seconds later, the door was opened by a middle-aged woman who stood there for a few moments, saying nothing.

"I'm Sergeant Clarke. I have been sent here by Mr. Smithers from the fort. I believe I am to be billeted here. Are you Mrs. Jackson?"

For a second, the woman hesitated before answering, "Ah, yes, someone from his office told me you were coming, but I thought it was not till next week. Never mind. Come in."

Richard awkwardly moved with all his gear through the narrow doorway into the hall. At that moment, he glanced upward and noticed movement at the top of the stairs. Was that the bottom hem of a dress he saw as it quickly disappeared out of sight? Pushing the thought out of his mind, he concentrated on what was being said, "We have a spare room on the ground floor at the back. Follow me."

Richard followed Mrs. Jackson down the hallway to the last door on the right, which she opened. "There you are. This should do.".

"Thanks very much. Yes, it will be fine," as he bundled his belongings through the door, dumping them on the floor.

"We will be having a small supper shortly if you are hungry. The kitchen is just on the other side of the hall from here, and it will be ready in about 15 minutes," explained the woman as she closed his door.

Richard slumped onto the bed. "Hmm," he thought, "it seems hard, but I have slept on worst." His thoughts then turned to that bottom hem of a skirt he saw disappearing out of view, wondering who it could be. No doubt, the answer to that question will be known in due course.

Although the room was tiny, it did have a dresser on one wall with a washing bowl, and hopefully, that jug had some water in it. He thought it would be wise to clean up somewhat, so he washed his hands and face. A tiny mirror over the wash basin was so small that one could not see their entire face at any one time. Examining what he could see, "That'll do, I suppose."

The dresser had sufficient draws to hold most of his clothes, although his uniform, which he was still wearing, was the most important. Unfortunately, he only had one uniform, so he would have to look after it the best way he could.

No sooner had he finished washing and putting his clothes away when there was a knock at the door, and the woman said, "Supper is ready if you want some."

"Coming."

Richard opened the door, moved across the hall, through the doorway, and into the kitchen. He noticed that for the size of the house, the kitchen seemed quite large, with a big fireplace on one side and a large table on the other. However, there were only two chairs on the ends of the table and one on either side. "That's interesting." he thought, "I wonder how many are in the family?"

A large, rough-looking man entered the kitchen, and in reaction to seeing a stranger, he stopped in his tracks and exclaimed. "Who do we have here?"

Mrs. Jackson quickly explained, "This is Sergeant Clarke; he will stay here for a while. Remember, I mentioned this last night!"

"Oh, yes, I remember. My name is Stuart Jackson," offering his large and rough hand, which Richard duly took. "Take a seat. That chair over there will do."

Richard sat down and, as he did so, casually looked around. This family was not well off, but it looked like the essentials were all there. "I wonder what they are having for supper?" he thought, thinking at the same time, "I wonder who is going to sit in the fourth chair."

He then heard light footsteps and the swishing of material as a striking young woman entered the kitchen. She stopped suddenly, not sure what to say or do, as she was not expecting a stranger to be in their kitchen.

Richard stopped breathing for a second or two as he gazed at this apparition. "So, this is the owner of that skirt hem I saw," he thought. He quickly stood up and then looked away as he realized it was rude to stare, but he tried to look casually without it being too obvious. The owner of the skirt did not move as though she was rooted to the spot.

After what seemed to be a very long time, Mrs. Jackson said, "Emily, this is Sergeant Clarke. He will be staying in the spare room for a while."

Not knowing where to look, Emily whispered, "Hello", still not looking directly at Richard.

Not knowing quite what he should say, he also replied, "Hello," which, under the circumstances, did not seem enough, but his tongue was tied in a knot so that he could say no more.

"Hey, you two! You can relax now and take a seat. Sit down, Richard," said Mrs. Jackson, full-well realizing what she had just witnessed. "This could be a problem," she thought, thinking ahead.

Stuart thought it best to join the conversation and asked Richard, "Sergeant, what is your job at the fort?"

Richard, not wanting to be rude but thinking it was not wise to say too much, said, "I am helping Mr. Smithers on some technical matters, and I am not sure how long it is going to take."

"On the reconstruction?"

"Yes, that's right," thinking it would probably not be wise to say too much.

At that moment, Mrs. Jackson moved over to the table with four bowls, followed by a cast iron pot half-full of soup. "This should fill you up. It has both meat and vegetables in it."

Both Richard and Emily sat in silence, not knowing what to say or do, other than to eat their soup. The impact that they were having on one another was something that Emily's mother was aware of, and she was not sure what she should do about it, if anything. Everyone finished their soup, and a strange silence seemed to embrace all four of them.

Mrs. Jackson thought it wise to break that silence with the words, "Hey, you two! You cannot carry on ignoring each other like this forever, so who is going to make a start?"

Both feeling embarrassed, neither Emily nor Richard looked up from their empty soup bowls.

Concerned about the unhealthy silence continuing for much longer, Mrs. Jackson decided to restart the conversation. "Sergeant, how long do you think your work at the fort will last?"

"A few months, I expect, although I have not been officially advised."

"Do you expect to stay here with us for the entire time?"

"Well, yes."

"No problem," she replied, looking at her husband as she did so, and then at her daughter. "Sergeant, perhaps it would be a good idea for us to use our first names while we are in this house. Is that all right with you?"

"That would be fine. My name is Richard."

"Fine, Richard, my name is Molly, and my husband's first name is Stuart. And of course, I introduced Emily to you earlier," looking from Emily to Richard and back again, wondering if there would be any reaction. "That was not hard, was it?" she said.

Emily, feeling very awkward and not knowing what to say, excused herself as she got up from the table, "I am sorry, but I do not feel very well, so if you excuse me, I will go up to my room."

Richard stood up and, for an unknown reason, noticed the decorated hem of Emily's skirt as she quickly left the room. "Interesting," he thought, turning his gaze back to the table.

At that moment, Stuart interrupted Richard's train of thought and asked, "How long have you been in the Marines?"

"About five years now, Sir, um, I, I mean Stuart."

"That's quite a long time. Do you still enjoy it?"

"Yes, particularly if I get to do something different, like this job, for example."

Stuart, remembering that Richard was somewhat reluctant to say too much when spoken about his job earlier, just nodded and then went on to say, "I suppose you will be starting fairly early in the morning?"

"That's correct. I start at 7 am. Is that a problem?"

"No, that will be fine. Molly will have breakfast available from 6 am. Does that suit you?"

"That's fine. Thanks very much for the soup; it was delicious. I think I will turn in now if that is all right with you?"

"Fine, see you in the morning."

Richard got out of his chair, exited the kitchen, and moved to his bedroom door. He heard the floorboards creak above him, and it reminded him of Emily, which was indeed a pleasant thought. However, as he entered his room, he realized how exhausted he was, so without doing anything further, he promptly flopped onto the bed. He awoke a couple of hours later, remembering that he was still in his uniform. "Damn," he said to himself, "I had better get out of this and into bed properly."

Before Richard knew it, it was about time to get up. He quickly washed his hands and face and looked into the tiny mirror. "Well, you fool, this is the first day of a new life, so I had better make the best of it," he thought. He could hear noises coming from elsewhere in the house and knew it must be nearly 6 am, so after putting on his uniform and brushing it down, he opened the bedroom door and stepped across the hallway into the kitchen.

The only person there was Molly, and she was busy stirring something while standing over the fire. Richard then noticed it was quite a large pot and guessed it was probably some porridge. It was not his favourite first meal of the day, but it usually lasted a long time and always kept the wolf from the door till dinner. He noticed that the table was not laid out as though anyone else would be present, so he sat on one of the seats with a spoon in front of it.

By this time, Molly said, "Good morning. It is good to see you are up bright and early. How did you sleep?"

"Good, thanks. No problem."

"I see you have found yourself a spoon, so sit tight, and I will bring over the porridge," said Molly as she turned around with a large bowl in her hands, obviously very hot, as it was giving off a large plume of steam.

"Thanks," is all Richard said as he tucked into his breakfast.

Richard wondered where Emily was as he hoped she would have come downstairs for breakfast. He had thought about her for quite a while last night before he finally got to sleep, and he hoped he would have the opportunity to get to know her better, and that thought stirred his inner emotions. Knowing, however, he could not afford to be late for his first day on the job; he quickly remembered he had more immediate things to think about, so he promptly finished his breakfast and grabbed a cup of tea as he left the table.

"Thanks for that, Molly; that was great," he mumbled as he left the kitchen for his bedroom.

Standing there in the middle of his room, not doing anything, he started to think about Emily again, but then his sense of duty came to the fore, and he temporarily put her out of his mind. He checked his uniform, grabbed his hat, and headed for the front door.

No sooner had Richard opened the door when he heard a faint female voice, "See you at supper time, Richard."

Richard at once swung around, but by the time he looked back and then up the stairs, he only noticed a tiny bit of that hemmed skirt again, and then it was gone. He closed the door slowly, reluctantly left the house, and headed toward Fort Cumberland. He envisaged it would be a long day, at least until he knew what Molly really meant by her parting words.

Chapter 3

Elizabeth still felt both annoyed and sorry that she had knocked her father down the stairs and was glad that no lasting damage had been done. She reminded herself that her father could often overreact to such incidents, and, from her earlier experiences, she knew it would soon blow over. She had gone to her room and, after a bit of reflection, decided to read a book, although she had difficulty getting right into it. Just as well, as it was not long before her mother called her to come downstairs.

Elizabeth slowly climbed down the stairs, not sure how she would be welcomed, or even welcomed at all.

Her mother, Ann, called out from the kitchen, "I am in here, dear. I want to talk to you about what happened earlier."

Elizabeth walked into the kitchen, not sure how all this was going to end. Finally, feeling unsure, she murmured, "I am here; what do you want to talk to me about?"

Ann, understanding how her daughter might be feeling, gave her some assurance by saying, "Don't worry, I am not mad at you; I just want to go over what happened with your father."

Relaxing somewhat, Elizabeth sat down at the kitchen table, wondering why all this was necessary. She knew her father sometimes could display his short temper, but she had not heard any ranting and raving, so she had assumed all was now well.

"Your father was first very annoyed with you, and it took some time for him to settle down. However, he finally accepted it was just an accident, and you had done nothing wrong, so he eventually calmed down."

"That's good."

"He was originally feeling a little dazed, but I think that has now passed. He is not holding you responsible, so don't worry. I don't think he will hold any grudge."

Elizabeth uttered a sigh of relief and replied, "I am glad that he accepted what happened was an accident, as I was somewhat concerned that he would blame me."

"That's all right; I suggest you be a bit more careful about opening doors in such a forceful manner in the future."

"Thanks, Mother; I do feel better now."

Elizabeth had only just finished speaking when her father entered the kitchen and in a somewhat cheerful voice while trying to show some concern, said, "How are you feeling, Elizabeth?"

"Fine thank you, Father; I am glad you are now feeling well."

"Yes, thanks. I just want to forget about it."

Not knowing what more could be said, and with a sense of relief, Elizabeth replied, "Yes," as she turned on her heel and left the kitchen.

She was glad there were no repercussions from what had occurred, but she still felt somewhat guilty as she slowly climbed the stairs back to her bedroom. Elizabeth lay down on her bed, and, with considerable difficulty, tried to think of other things. Once she got the whole episode of the father falling down the front steps of their house out of her mind, other more interesting things came to the fore.

She remembered the young man that she had seen walking down the road the other day and wondered where he was now. Elizabeth made a positive decision that she should really make a real effort to meet him sometime. But how, without looking too forward? She accepted that it was not easy to meet a person in the right circumstances, particularly when you have only seen them once on the street. "This is going to take a measure of careful planning if I am to be successful," she thought. "I don't feel like doing anything now, so I will sleep on it and take some positive steps in the morning."

Elizabeth woke up early the following day, and, shortly after that, had worked out a plan, as she had taken considerable time going over the options before she went to sleep. She decided that watching from up here in my bedroom would not work because he would be gone by the time I got downstairs. Pacing up and down the street hoping to catch him going by would also be just too obvious. She finally settled on a plan that she felt should work, provided her mother and father did not catch on as to what was going on. As she often went across the road to take in the view over the bay, looking at all the large ships coming and going, she thought that her parents would probably not guess what her real plan was, particularly if she took a chair across the road and sat there looking out to sea for a while.

"Now to put that plan in action," she thought as she dressed in a pretty dress, hoping she would not be questioned about it at breakfast time. Finally finding a dress that she hoped would be suitable but not too obvious, she went downstairs and into the kitchen.

"Elizabeth, you look nice today," her mother quickly commented.

"I just thought I would try something different for a change," she replied, trying to sound very casual.

Elizabeth thought, "It looks like I overcame the first hurdle." Then she said, "What's for breakfast, Mother?"

"I have managed to find several fresh eggs, so we are having them boiled this morning. They are hard to get, so enjoy it," Ann replied. "Take a seat, and I can put one on for you."

While her egg was being cooked, Elizabeth reviewed her plan and realized that it would not be that easy getting a small chair across the road. She had never attempted such a daring stunt before, so she guessed the trick would be to get it there without being seen. Then she remembered the old chair at the back of the small room just off the hall. "Ah, that will do," she thought.

After eating her egg with a piece of stale bread, Elizabeth quickly got up from the table, hoping that her mother would probably stay in the kitchen for a little while. Moving swiftly to the small room off the front hall, she opened the door, hoping the old chair was still there. It was. "Now, to get my timing right," she thought. She was not sure where her father was, or even if he was home at all, so she decided it would be best to find out before doing anything reckless.

Rather than checking out the whole house, she yelled, "Mother, is Father here, or has he gone to work?"

Thankfully, a favourable reply came back, "No, he is not here; he is at work."

Elizabeth looked at the big grandfather clock in the parlour, and as it was only 9 am, she thought that now may be a good chance of seeing that young man. Gathering her composure and the chair, she opened the front door quietly and slipped out. No person in sight. "That's good," she thought as she scurried across the road, chair in hand. Looking up and down the street for a handy but not too obvious place, she noticed a slight grass rise over to her left. Awkwardly holding the chair as she walked up the road a short way, she found a spot and positioned it as though she was using it to watch the ships in the harbour.

Now to sit down and keep a weather eye out for that passing stranger – very casually, of course. A slight breeze blew from a different direction from when she was out here with her mother a few days ago, making the boats lean over at a different angle. "Now I must pretend that I am looking out to sea," she thought, casting a rapid and casual eye over her shoulder. Still, no one was in sight.

Elizabeth continued watching the various boats, large and small, all with their sails pulling them strongly through the choppy water. It was not easy turning to one side and then the other, and, at the same time, making it look like she was more interested in what was happening out on the bay. "This is a lot harder than I expected," she thought, so she stood up and decided to stand beside the chair for a while. Then, after about 15 minutes, she saw movement out of the corner of her eye. Deciding it best to slowly, very slowly, turn her head further in that direction. "Damn," she mouthed; it was not the young man she was hoping for; it was an old lady, probably off to the local market.

There was very little foot traffic walking up and down the street, so Elizabeth spent more time looking at the boats in the harbour than anything else. Her patience was running relatively thin by this stage, particularly as her mother may be somewhat concerned about her absence; Elizabeth stood on one foot impatiently and then the other while she waited. Then came footsteps. Casually looking over her left shoulder, she noticed a figure walking down the other side of the road in her direction. She wasn't sure whether he was the young man she was waiting for, as he seemed to be dressed somewhat differently. Elizabeth decided that now was the time to pick up the chair and walk back across the road.

Grabbing the chair in her right hand, she swung around and started to cross the road, but by then, the figure was nowhere in sight. Looking up and down the street once again, she realized that the unknown figure had turned around and was heading back from whence he had come. "Damn," she muttered louder than what she thought was wise, putting her left hand in front of her mouth. She stood in the middle of the road in amazement as the unknown person disappeared back around the corner. "Maybe I should follow him," she fleetingly thought, putting the silly idea out of her head as quickly as she had first thought of it.

Elizabeth then realized that she was bringing attention to herself standing in the middle of the road, so she quickly scampered over to her house. She quietly opened the front door and crept inside, expecting a strident voice to call out at any moment. Not a peep came from anywhere, so she dropped the chair off into the small front room and swiftly and quietly ran up the stairs. "Whew," she thought, "that was lucky."

Elizabeth found she was breathing heavily but was not sure why. Though on reflection, she guessed one reason was that this type of deception was all new to her, and she had never done anything like that before. Sitting on the one chair in her room, she reflected on what had just happened. Was the whole episode worth doing considering what her mother and father would think of her, or do, for that matter? Could I get away with doing it again? Is it worth the risk? She was not even sure that the figure she saw was the same young man she had seen before. "Maybe I could try meeting him another way," Elizabeth mused.

It was getting closer to dinner time, and Elizabeth thought it would be wise to check in with her mother, so she left her bedroom and headed downstairs. She heard a noise coming from one of the rooms at the back of the house, so she headed off in that direction. Then a loud bang. "What the hell is that?" she thought. Turning into the room, further down the hallway from the kitchen entrance, Elizabeth could not see her mother, although she could still hear rustling sounds coming from somewhere in the room.

"Mother, are you in here somewhere?" questioned Elizabeth, still unsure where her mother was.

A faint voice replied, "I am over here, under an old iron bed in the corner."

"What are you doing under there?"

"You know we mainly use this room to store big stuff, but I was looking for a metal bowl that was on that shelf over there, and then I dropped it. It rolled under the bed, and as I had nothing to get it out with, here I am."

"Oh, Mother, you do strange things sometimes. Have you got it?"

"Yes, I've got it now."

Ann carefully climbed out from under the bed and awkwardly stood up.

Elizabeth asked, "What I was wondering is. Do you want me to do something for dinner?"

Straightening her dress and hair, Ann explained, "No, that's not necessary; I have everything under control."

With the iron bowl in one hand, she quietly slipped her other hand into Elizabeth's as they walked towards the kitchen.

"So, Elizabeth, what have you been doing this morning?"

"Nothing really," was the only response she could think of, and as her mother did not press her any further, she thankfully left the whole matter there.

Elizabeth was trying to find a way to get her mother to help her with her problem without explaining any details. Maybe if I asked her details about her when she was of a similar age, I might get a clue or two.

Elizabeth, in a quiet voice, asked, "Mother, I know this is a strange question, but at what age did you have anything to do with young men?"

Ann was unsure whether she heard the question correctly, as this subject had never come up before, so she questioned, "Did you say something about young men?"

Elizabeth was unsure where to look or what to say, so she said nothing.

Looking closely at her daughter and unsure she had heard the question correctly, her mother waited for a response. She repeated, "Did you ask me a question about men?"

Wishing she had not asked the question and still looking down at the floor, Elizabeth replied tentatively, "Ah, Yes, I did," wondering what was coming next.

"That's fine. We would have to have this conversation sometime, so why not now? To answer your question, I was a little older than you are now before I had anything to do with young men other than my older brothers. As you do not have brothers, it is a little harder for you to know anything about young men."

Elizabeth held her breath while waiting for an answer but finally breathed again as it looked like her mother was agreeable to discussing this personal matter in more detail. "Thanks, Mother. I am glad that you are happy talking about such things."

Ann struggled to know where to start this first-time conversation, so she thought a little history might be the safest way to get things rolling. "We have a little time before dinner, so I will keep things simple. I will tell you about how your father and I met, which took place when I was not that much older than you are now. As you know, your father is about four years older than me, and we first saw each other outside an inn. Both our parents were inside at an unknown meeting, and because of our young age, we were awkwardly waiting outside. Neither of us felt very comfortable just standing there, although children hanging around outside an inn waiting for one of their parents was not that unusual. I had not seen him before then, as he and his family had just moved to Portsmouth. He was waiting just along the road on one side of the inn, and I was waiting on the other side. I think we kept glancing down the street at one another, trying not to be too obvious about it. Finally, after time, your father decided to walk down the road to where I was, and while I would not usually talk to a stranger like that, I could not resist his cheeky grin. We started to talk to one another while standing a little distance apart. Obviously, we did not want other people to think wrongly of either of us, so we tried to make it look very casual. Anyway, to cut a long story short, our parents came out of the inn shortly after that, and we were formally introduced to each other."

"Mother, so romantic!"

"I don't know about that, but that is how we first met."

"What happened after that? I mean, when did you next meet?"

"I don't want to go into any further details now, but we will discuss this again sometime if you are interested."

"Yes, Mother, I find this really interesting. So, you met each other strictly by chance?"

"True, but it is not how it should be, although I have no real issues with how it turned out. Anyway, it is nearly dinner time, and I need to get things moving, so let me get on with it, and I will call you when it is ready."

Elizabeth, thrilled about knowing how her mother first met her father, rushed out of the kitchen and into the parlour and flopped down on one of the chairs. Thinking out loud, she said, "So, that means I should be able to try something similar."

At the same time, Elizabeth's father, William, was in his surgery about to see another patient, this time a rubbish cart driver who had accidentally been run over by another heavy cart. A good Samaritan bought him in, and he was cursing and screaming in pain in the next room. Thomas, his assistant, was holding the patient down on the table where he had been left. This was proving increasingly difficult as the patient was a big, strong man and was making it difficult for Thomas, regardless of what he did. Thomas decided that he needed immediate help if they were going to do anything with the man's bloody and now misshaped arm. Thomas thought the arm would probably have to be amputated, as it was barely hanging in place, probably only by flesh and skin.

Thomas yelled through the patient's screams, "William, come here quickly. I can't hold this man still, and blood is going everywhere."

William rushed into the other room and grabbed the shoulders of the writhing man. "I think we will have to do this here. Get me a couple of straps. They are over there," pointing to several loose straps on the top shelf.

Grabbing two straps from the pile, Thomas rushed back to the table and started to wrap the straps, which looked like very long belts, around the tabletop and over the patient.

"One over his shoulders and another around his waist, including the good arm," William yelled over the turmoil.

With extreme difficulty, the two straps were finally put into place. Thomas was pleased that the patient was no longer thrashing around and now not likely to fall off the table.

The patient was still writhing in agony, so Thomas tried to subdue him further by pinning his legs to the table.

"Another strap for the legs," yelled William.

He then unwrapped the bloody towel that had been wrapped around the misshaped arm. William knew that it was necessary to quickly find out exactly where the break in the arm was exactly located so he could decide what the next step would be.

Thomas, who had helped William with such accidents in the past, knew that speed was essential if the patient was to live. He also knew that the patient's teeth might suffer from the grinding caused by the pain, so he grabbed a piece of thick leather from off the shelf and forced it between the patient's teeth. At least the screams were less, but the groaning continued.

William examined the mangled arm and realized that the lower part of the arm was beyond saving as the bone was cleanly broken at an angle. Therefore, the arm would need to be amputated cleanly well above the elbow. He rushed next door, grabbed a scalpel and a bone saw, and at the same time, positioned a cauterizing iron into the fire.

"Hold the upper arm still and put your thumb on that artery. Quick, I need to move fast," instructed William.

With that, William quickly stabbed the scalpel deeply into the patient's arm and ran it around to the other side. The patient made even more noise, but William had to finish the job. Pulling back the flesh, William grabbed the bone saw and frantically sawed away. It took a couple of minutes for all this to occur, and even with Thomas blocking the artery, there was blood everywhere. Finally, the amputated arm fell away onto the table. While Thomas held onto the artery tightly, there was not too much blood, but the problem needed to be permanently solved. With that in mind, William ran next door to grab the now red-hot cauterizing iron.

William returned with the red-hot iron in his hand and was just about to cauterize the butt of the upper arm when he realized the patient was not making any noises. He quickly put the hot iron down on the stone floor and examined the patient. At first, he thought the patient had fainted, a not uncommon result when a patient was trying to deal with such extreme pain, but then William realized that the patient was not even breathing. He put his ear to his chest and could find no heartbeat. The patient had died, probably from the combination of shock and the lack of blood. William just stood there, somewhat in shock at losing another patient.

"Poor fella, we tried, but we could not have done any more," said Thomas, now somewhat concerned about the patient's relatives, who were expected to arrive at the surgery at any time.

While agreeing with Thomas' comments, William always felt a sense of failure when a patient died before they even had a chance to finish the surgery. He knew it was not his fault, but fingers were always pointed when a patient died on the table, regardless of the reasons. In this case, he believed the patient had lost much blood before he even arrived, and therefore the shock of it all and the amount of blood he lost during the operation was the last straw. William knew that his chances of living after such an operation were probably no more than 10%, regardless of what he had done. It did not make him feel any better.

By the time the family arrived, and the arrangements were made for the body to be returned to his home, both William and Thomas had had more than enough. It was the end of a day that neither thought was very successful nor productive.

Thomas suggested," Let's go to the local and have a drink. I could surely use one."

While William was always aware of his earlier long-ago history with drink, he hesitated and replied, "Why not, after we have cleaned up a bit more here."

Neither liked the job now at hand, but each grabbed an old cloth hanging over the sink and roughly wiped most of the blood, now somewhat half dry and sticky, from the table and floor.

Thomas was keen to get out of the place, so he said, "That will do; let's get out of here!" as he hung his still bloody apron on the nail on the back of the door.

William followed Thomas out the door, who locked it, and they both walked up the street toward the inn. It was only a couple of hundred yards away, so they arrived in a few minutes and then paused outside. William hesitated a second or two longer before following Thomas across the threshold. Once inside, William was still not feeling very confident about being in the inn, and he was still not sure whether he should stay or not. His early drinking history came flooding back to him, adding more doubts. It just did not feel right!

Swinging back towards the door, William carefully informed Thomas of the situation. "I don't think it would be wise for me to stay here as I have too much to lose if I go off the rails. Here is some money to have one on me. Sorry. I could do with a drink, but it is not wise for me to drink here."

William reluctantly left Thomas at the inn and started the walk home. Keen to get there, he picked up speed while thinking about the stiff drink he would enjoy when he finally arrived.

William could already taste the whisky as he opened the front door of his house and went inside. He rushed into the parlour, then straight to the whisky decanter.

Ann heard her husband come in the door and waited for him to enter the kitchen, which he usually did as soon as he arrived home. Ann hesitated for a few seconds, waiting to see what was going to happen. Nothing, not a sound. "I had better go and find out what is going on," thought Ann as she scampered out of the kitchen into the hallway.

"William are you there?" she called out. No answer.

A little louder, "William, is that you?"

After waiting a little longer, and as there was no answer, Ann wondered if someone else had entered the house.

She was just about to call out again when she heard William's somewhat muffled voice coming from the parlour, "I am in here."

Thinking that something must be wrong, Ann rushed into the parlour, only to find William standing near the whisky decanter with a glass in his hand. "What's wrong? Why did you not answer me?" gushed Ann.

Turning towards his wife, he replied, "Nothing is wrong. I just wanted a quick drink, that's all."

"You scared the hell out of me. How could you do that?" she demanded.

William spat out, "Sorry, but we had a really bad day at the surgery today, and I just had to have a stiff drink. Somebody died on the table again today, and I am getting sick of it. For some reason or other, I don't feel very confident about carrying on like this unless my luck improves."

Feeling that she overreacted somewhat, Ann replied, "That's fine. I am sorry that I spoke to you like that and that things did not go well today."

"I nearly went into the inn a little while ago, but I changed my mind. Thank goodness I came home. That's one good thing."

Ann fully understood how hard it is for William to limit his drinking and appreciated that he had managed to resist the temptation. "Well, enjoy your drink," she said.

Walking back to the kitchen, Ann was concerned that her husband was not coping well with all the death and destruction that seemed to be dogging him. Maybe it is time for a change.

Elizabeth had heard her mother calling out earlier but relaxed once she heard both her parents talking.

Chapter 4

Less than 5 miles away from where Elizabeth and her family lived in Portsmouth was Fort Cumberland, and Richard had woken up that morning thinking about his new job. He had thought of it for most of the previous evening as well, all while lying flat on his back on his bed. Finally, he accepted that would be very different from what he was used to and that much of what he had learnt over the last ten years would not necessarily apply.

Striding out towards Fort the following morning, Richard wondered how the system would work in practice.

Fort Cumberland was not an actively manned defence position while it was being upgraded, but there were still a few soldiers on site to keep convict and site security. He understood that they were bunked down in the old guardhouse, which would be retained as part of the refurbished fort. Richard thought it wise to start the day by making himself known to the office building where Mr. Smithers was located, and hopefully finding out exactly where he would start and with whom.

Walking through the unguarded front gate, although there were a few workers and soldiers around the area, Richard walked into the office area he had previously visited. The clerk he had spoken to yesterday was leaning over a pile of significant papers, probably building plans; he looked up and recognised Richard.

"Morning, Sergeant, I see you are bright and early. Mr. Smithers is not in yet. He should be here shortly."

"I see you have some plans there. May I look at them, because you know why I am here at the fort?"

"That should be all right, although Mr. Smithers has not said anything about you looking at plans."

Richard walked over to the plans and started to quickly thumb through them, trying to get an overall idea of what was planned. He found it difficult as many of the plans included a considerable quantity of detail that Richard was unfamiliar with. Still, as he got to the bottom of the pile a general outline seemed to emerge. It was undoubtedly an enormous undertaking and something that he was now even keener to get stuck into. The fact that his schooling had been minimal, and he was not very good at it made the examination process that much more difficult.

After about 15 minutes, Mr. Smithers arrived, understood precisely what was at hand, and said, "I see you have already started by looking at those plans. Are they something with which you are familiar?"

"Not completely, sir, I can understand what the basic structures will look like, but the detail is well over my head."

"That's fine, Sergeant; you will be able to pick up what you need to know in time. You know that your role is to consider each structure from both an attack and defence point of view and make any improvement suggestions. Are there any problems with that?"

"No sir, that is my understanding."

"Good, you can come with me later this morning."

"Sir," Richard replied, drawing up a chair and going back to looking at the plans, but looking at each page a little closer this time.

Mr. Smithers was good as his word as he called Richard into his office about an hour later. "Sergeant, here is the plan of the southern side of the fort on which I am currently working. Have a quick look, and you may be able to see what I am talking about. Take it to that table over there."

Taking the plan, Richard sat down and examined the plan in more detail. At first, it seemed like nothing but lines, angles, and numbers, with a few named areas thrown in. After about 15 minutes, things started to take shape in Richard's mind, and he got a rough idea of what was planned. "Sir, I think I have an idea of what this is all about, so what do I do now?"

"Come with me, Sergeant. We will go and have a look at it now. Roll up the plan and bring it with you."

They left the office and quickly walked to the southern side of the compound, with Mr. Smithers stopping to talk to a couple of supervisors on the way. Arriving in the relevant area on the plan, Mr. Smithers asked Richard to spread the plan on top of a pile of stone blocks. "I will turn the plan around so it is facing the right way, and you will see the outline of the foundations on both. This is the question. From your experience as a Navy man, who has been involved in firing many cannons over the years, if an attacking ship was offshore in that direction, how secure do you feel any defender would be behind a thick wall here?" pointing to the dug foundation trench.

"Could you give me a minute, Sir? I would like to get my bearings as though I was on the ship, but I will need to go over in that direction and look back."

"Fine."

Richard moved over towards the south about fifty yards and looked back. He tried to imagine himself on board a ship that was offshore and about to shoot at the fort from this angle. Richard thought through the onboard evaluation process on an attacking ship, "Was it a good target? Did it look as though it could be damaged easily? What about the range and angle of the shot? What defences do they have? Is this the best option?"

Then he thought about the safety of the defending soldiers on the inside of the wall, "Is it defendable? Was this a safe place to be? Could the fort itself be improved?" These were just some questions that raced through his mind as he stood there imagining both sides involved in this potential conflict.

Richard returned to Mr. Smithers, not in a hurry to get back as he took the time to consider the entire bombardment process from both an offence and defence point of view. By the time he returned to the plans, Mr. Smithers was nowhere in sight. He studied the plan some more and could see where slight improvements could be made from a defender's point of view.

Mr. Struthers came back from behind a pile of rocks to where Richard was standing.

"Ah, you are back, Sergeant. Have you managed to come up with any improvement, or is it all right as shown on the plan?"

"Sir, it would be best if this wall was angled a little more in that direction and the wall strengthened by being thicker. It is well within the range of any decent gun."

"I can see what you mean. I will recommend that the necessary changes are made. Thanks for that. That is exactly the reason you are here."

Now pleased that his evaluation had been accepted, Richard relaxed as he looked over more of the vast expanse of the building site. When finished, the fort was going to encompass some 24 acres of land and be at a slightly different angle than the old fort, which meant that a large quantity of earth needed to be moved. That was primarily the role of the on-site convict labourers. The plan of the completed fort showed it was to be pentagonal in shape, with five bastions and a ravelin on the western side. It was an enormous task, but Richard felt confident he could achieve what was required.

Richard suddenly realized that Mr. Smithers was no longer near him, so he went looking for him. He eventually saw him about a hundred yards away, discussing something with one of the team supervisors. Richard walked over to see what was happening, ready to add his knowledge if necessary. He listened for a while and heard them talking about the height of the new block walls and their immediate lack of any temporary support. They were concerned that they could come crashing down should a strong wind arrive while the new mortar between the blocks was still fresh and, therefore, weak. The mortar needed to set for about one week to have any real strength, and therefore it was agreed that a few extra timber supports were required. It was suggested that support at a forty-five-degree angle would hold the wall up, at least until additional backing was added when the next inside wall was built.

The discussions only took a few more minutes, and then Mr. Smithers returned to the main office, with Richard moving quickly to catch up. However, it was becoming evident that he would have to keep his wits about him if he was to appear interested in what Mr. Smithers was doing.

Catching up, Richard just caught the beginning of Mr. Smithers talking to a supervisor about other areas that needed further evaluation from both offensive and defensive perspectives. "Sergeant, I will get you to look at these areas tomorrow, and in the meantime, I suggest that you have a good look around for the rest of the day, and you can let me know what you have found later this afternoon."

"Yes, sir. Is it all right if I have another look at those plans as I now feel a little more comfortable with what I am looking at?"

"That's fine."

They both walked back to the office in silence, each with their own thoughts.

Mr. Smithers was thinking carefully about how and where he could best use Richard's skills and experience to make the fort as impregnable as possible. That was, after all, why he was here.

Richard's mind turned back to the flash of a skirt hem he had seen out the corner of his eye earlier that morning, and the words he clearly remembered, "See you at suppertime Richard." It was a pleasant thought that lingered, and he decided to keep that at the back of his mind until he returned to the house at the end of the day.

Richard settled down at the office table and examined the plans of the fort, and after a short time, it became apparent just how much work was still needed to complete the project. Part of the problem, from Richard's point of view, was that he found reading the plans difficult as his schooling was limited. He had only learned the basics of reading at school, so he could never consider himself a good reader. His ability to understand the meaning of numbers was much greater. In many respects, he felt he had learned far more over the years since completing school, which proved the case with this job. Luckily, time had proved him to be a quick learner.

Richard inspected, in conjunction with Mr. Smithers, a couple of other parts of the fort, but he could not see any achievable improvements. However, he felt he had achieved more than enough by the end of his first day on the job as he was not used to all this plan reading. He said goodnight to Mr Smithers and the clerk and then headed out of the fort's front gate.

Strolling down the road towards his lodgings, his mind once again focused on the comments that Emily had made as he left the house for the fort earlier that morning. "See you at suppertime Richard" is what she had said, and he could not figure out exactly what was behind those words. In anticipation of discovering what she meant, he walked a little faster as he got closer to the house.

Arriving at the front door, Richard, realizing that he had no key to the front door and, without thinking, knocked. He waited, then knocked again. Then he heard a faint voice, "Is that you, Sergeant? If so, come in; the door is not locked." Richard tried the door handle; it was indeed unlocked, so, feeling something of a fool, he went inside.

Mrs. Jackson came out of the kitchen with a tea towel in her hand and said, "We do not normally lock the front door during the day around here; just let yourself in next time."

"Oh, all right," replied Richard as he glanced up to the top of the stairs. Disappointingly, there was nobody there.

He walked into the kitchen, and Molly was now sitting at the table darning socks, something she hated doing, but it was just one of those jobs that needed to be done. She thought socks were too expensive to replace just because a small hole suddenly appeared in the heel.

"How was your day, Sergeant?"

"It went quite well, considering that that was my first day."

Richard noted that it looked like Molly was going to cook something different for supper tonight as the stewing post was not on the fire. "Whatever it is, I am hungry," he thought, sitting down at one of the kitchen chairs.

His thoughts then turned to Emily, but as he had not seen or heard anything upstairs, he wondered where she was. He was not sure if it was the right thing to do to ask Molly where her daughter was. Would she consider it none of my business? Can I ask the question without any repercussions? These and many other questions sped through his mind without any obvious answers.

Not knowing what to do or say, Richard decided to go into his room and relax for a while. "I will be in my room when you need me," he advised as he got up from the table. There was no reply. Mrs. Jackson was obviously thinking of other things.

Richard flopped on the bed as soon as he entered his room, and before he knew it, he had drifted off to sleep. A knock on the door suddenly awakened him, and he was just about to respond when he heard a female voice say, "It is supper time Richard."

Richard at once sat up, now wide awake. "That was not Molly's voice," he suddenly realized. Assuming it was Emily's voice, he quickly replied, "Thanks. I will be right there."

Richard hurriedly washed his hands and face, checked that his uniform was neat and tidy, opened the door of his room, and entered the kitchen. Sitting at the table was Emily, while her mother was busy cooking over the fire.

"Hello," he said casually, "how is everybody this evening?" Then, not waiting for any answers, he walked up to the table and called her name, "Emily," hoping to get her attention.

"Hello, Sergeant, I mean, Richard."

At this moment, Molly turned from the fire and said, "Take a seat, Richard. Supper is ready."

Richard sat down in his usual spot and looked at Emily, who, at this point, was looking down, playing with her fork.

Richard was about to say something when Stuart entered the kitchen and immediately sat down, and in a very straightforward manner and while looking directly at Richard, said, "I see you made it through the day."

"Yes, everything went well, and I learned a great deal."

Richard was not sure what Stuart did for a job, so he was unsure if he should say any more. No one said anything until Molly walked over to the table with a large tray of fish pieces and slices of bread and said, "Help yourselves. I think it is good fish. Which is hard to get these days."

Nobody said anything for the next few minutes as all were busy eating fish, which was indeed very tasty, although a little chewy.

Richard regularly glanced at Emily, but she seemed busy eating and not looking in his direction. Eventually, Richard could no longer stand the silence, so he asked, "Emily, how did your day go?"

Emily quickly looked up, but as she was not expecting any questions, she hesitated for a few seconds while Richard patiently waited for an answer.

"Sorry Richard, I was miles away; what was that you said?"

"I wondered how your day went."

Nervously she responded, "Fine, thank you, I went to my Auntie's house."

Although he did not know where it was heading, Richard wanted to keep the conversation going and asked, "What do you usually do when you are at your Auntie's house?"

"Nothing much, usually some needlework, which I really enjoy doing."

Stuart at once commented, "Emily, I don't think Richard is interested in needlework. Is that so, Richard?"

Richard felt he was being put in an awkward situation, so he quickly replied, "I am interested in whatever Emily is doing," wondering, as he said it, if that was the best reply he could come up with.

In a coy voice, Emily quickly said, "Thank you, Richard."

Stuart said no more, finished his fish, excused himself and left the room. At this point, Richard was unsure what to say, so silence again fell around the kitchen table.

When everyone had finished eating their fish Molly was the first to break the silence, "How was the fish? I liked it."

Emily and Richard agreed with Molly as she cleared the dishes off the table, "Why don't you two go into the parlour and continue your conversation?"

Richard, not sure what that meant, slowly rose from the table, watching to see what Emily might say or do. She quietly got up from her seat and tentatively walked towards the door. Now realizing that she was probably doing exactly what her mother suggested, Richard quickly followed.

Both Emily and Richard walked into the parlour, unsure where to sit. Looking at each other in a quandary, they hesitated as Richard pointed to a chair on the other side of the room and then turned and stood in front of the chair right behind him. Emily at once sat down where Richard had suggested. Richard sat down as casually as he could, although he was not feeling very comfortable.

Both were thinking the same thing. Who should speak first, and what would they say? After a couple of seconds of thought, Richard offered out his hand, palm side up in the direction of Emily, showing that it was her turn to speak.

Emily quickly apologised, "Sorry, Richard, for my father being so rude; he is not always like that."

"That's fine with me; I didn't take it personally. Anyway, I was asking how your day went. All good, I presume?"

"Yes, I always enjoy visiting my aunt as she is always doing interesting things. She is also going to teach me how to ride a horse, something I have always wanted to do but have never had the opportunity."

"Really, have you never been on a horse?"

"I have sat on a horse a couple of times, but I never actually ridden one."

Richard, thinking that this may be an opportunity too good to miss, asked, "I know your aunt has promised to teach you to ride, but would you consider me helping you to learn? All I would need is access to a suitable horse, but I think you could probably organise that."

Emily hesitated, not sure if she should accept his offer or not, because, after all, she had only known Richard for a couple of days.

Richard could see by the look on her face that the wheels were turning and how unsure of herself she was. He paused because he realized that her hesitation meant that she was at least thinking about the offer.

Eventually, Emily spoke in a faltering voice, "Thanks for that, Richard, but I will need to talk to my aunt before I can give you an answer."

"I can understand that. Please let me know.

"Yes, I will. It is a very generous offer," she said while getting out of her chair.

Richard quickly stood up and acknowledged the comments with a nod. He watched Emily leave the room. He could not help but notice how tall she was, and how her long dress accentuated her tiny waist. He stood still, rooted to the spot and simultaneously thinking about how all this may turn out. He was looking forward to the possibilities. All he had to do now is wait for an answer and be careful how he managed the situation from then on.

Until this moment, Richard had not realized how tired he was, but thinking about it, it had been an exceedingly tiring and eventful day. He promptly went to his room, got into bed, and with the picture of Emily in his head, quickly fell asleep.

Chapter 5

About 3 miles away on the other side of town, Elizabeth woke early, rolled over, and looked out of one eye, trying to get an idea of the time by how strong the light was that came around the edges of the curtains. It seemed about half light, so she guessed it was about 7 am, about time to get out of bed and start this specially planned day. She had thought about this a great deal over the last few days and was looking forward to what could be a successful scheme. The young man she had seen a couple of times going down the street outside her house remained a mystery, although she had discovered a little more by discretely asking around her neighbours. She had found out that he lived on the street which ran parallel to her own, not more than a quarter of a mile away. She had no idea why he walked down her street, but that was not important at this stage as she planned to learn more about him.

Elizabeth had not heard any noises from downstairs, so she assumed that her father was either still in bed or had already gone out. She quietly opened her door, looked up and down the hallway, and slipped down the stairs. She expected to find her mother in the kitchen, as that is where she usually is at this time of the morning. Arriving at the kitchen door, Elizabeth was ready to say something to her mother when she realized she was not there. Swinging around, she walked back into the hall, trying to guess where she could possibly be.

"Where are you, Mother?" she called out, not getting any reply.

She waited a few seconds and called out again, this time a little louder. Still no answer. Elizabeth was starting to be concerned as this had never happened before. She always found her mother easily every morning, and for some reason or other, the silence did not feel right. She quickly checked all the downstairs rooms, even the small room near the front door. Nothing! She quickly ran upstairs, calling out to her mother as she went. The last room upstairs was her parents' bedroom. The door was closed. She hesitated, then decided to knock. No answer. "What do I do now?" she thought while waiting patiently and expecting an answer. But nothing! She knocked again. Still nothing. She quietly turned the doorknob and slowly opened the door. The room was empty, and the bed was still unmade.

Elizabeth stood in the middle of her parent's bedroom, wondering what was going on. It seemed that the house, except for herself, was completely empty.

"Now what?" she said to herself out loud.

Not coming up with any answers, Elizabeth suddenly remembered that she had not looked outside the back door yet, so she ran down the stairs, down the hall, and out the back door. Looking around the small, paved area only proved that both her parents were not in the house anywhere. She sat down on the top doorstep with her head in both hands as tears started to form in her eyes. A million and one things buzzed through her mind, but nothing made any sense. She felt vulnerable and did not know what to do next.

After several minutes of pondering the whole question and not coming up with any answers, Elizabeth wiped her eyes on the back of her hands, got up, and walked back into the house. In anger, she slammed the back door so hard that the catch did not hold, and the door swung back open. Realizing her mistake, she slowly closed the door this time and locked the door.

Walking back down the hall towards the kitchen, Elizabeth heard a knock on the front door. "That can't be them," she thought, "they would just walk right in!" She ran to the door and quickly opened it, not knowing who or what would be outside. Standing on the doorstep were an older man and a woman, whom she recognised as a couple from the local markets.

"Can I help you?" asked Elizabeth.

"Sorry, dear, but we have some bad news. Your father has been in an accident, and your mother asked us to come and get you."

"Oh no! What's happened?"

"Your father has been injured rather badly. Just come with us, and we will tell you what we know on the way."

Elizabeth looked on the backside of the door for the key that was usually there, but the keyhole was empty. Quickly looking around, she saw the key on the hall floor; she picked it up, slammed the door, locked it, and walked down the front steps as the couple started to walk off. Hurrying to catch up, she called out, "Hang on a moment; I had to lock the door. Now tell me what you know."

"I don't know the full story, but your father has been in an accident, and I think he is hurt. He and your mother are down at that building site near the harbour entrance."

Elizabeth began to pick up speed and leave the women behind, "I know where that is. I will run from here," she thought. She hoped things were not that bad, although the woman had given her some good news. All this apprehension only made her run that much faster, and the bystanders she ran past looked surprised, wondering what was going on. This was not something that a young lady usually did, and the surprised look on their faces proved that to be the case.

Running around the last corner, Elizabeth could see a large crowd gathered in front of the new, large warehouse building site. She pushed her way forward hoping to find her mother, and found her bending over in front of a person lying on the ground. It looked like a man, at least that was how he was dressed, lying there with blood seeping from his ears and mouth.

Elizabeth gasped! "Oh no," stepping up beside her mother. Ann at once turned to her daughter and tried to stand between her and the man's body. Elizabeth was keen to look past her mother, trying to see the person, whomever it was. "Thank goodness," she thought, noticing that the body was of a much smaller man, "It is not Father!"

Ann noticed the colour of her daughter's face change to a ghostly white, so she grabbed Elizabeth's arm and dragged her a couple of yards away from the horrific scene.

"That's obviously not your father, he has just been taken to the hospital with a broken arm, and while it hurts a lot, he should get over it."

Elizabeth sighed with relief, "Well, at least he is still alive. When I first arrived, I thought that was father lying on the ground. Thank goodness it wasn't. What happened?"

"Well, that man was working at the top of that large building over there when one of those huge beams came loose and fell on him. His leg was jammed between that and one of the other large beams, and the workers were afraid to move either the beam or the man as they did not know what would then happen. They asked Father to come and have a look as they thought they might have to amputate his leg to move him safely. Your father climbed up to have a look, and his extra weight dislodged one of the beams. It hit your father's arm as it fell, but he was able to hang onto the other beam, but the man fell all the way to the ground."

"That's awful," was about as much as Elizabeth could say, while physically shaking just thinking about what might have been.

Ann, understanding the shock the whole episode had on her daughter, quietly escorted Elizabeth away from the ghastly scene and down the road toward the hospital.

Elizabeth's colour was slowly returning to her face as she followed her mother, saying nothing, as both were immersed in their own thoughts.

Arriving at the hospital, Ann asked the man at the door, "Where is the man who just came in with a damaged arm?"

"Oh, that one! He was complaining about his rotten luck as he went up those stairs over there," pointing to the stairs over the right. "I think he will be down at the end of the hall."

Elizabeth sprinted up the stairs, leaving her mother well behind.

All the while trying to catch up, Ann exclaimed, "Hang on a minute, I am also here, you know!"

"Sorry, I just want to see if Father is all right."

Half walking and half running, Elizabeth quickly moved down the hall dodging others coming in the opposite direction. Then, with blood smeared across her left cheek, a woman came rushing around the corner and caught Elizabeth's shoulder, half knocking her to the floor. Barely noticing what had just occurred, Elizabeth gathered herself up and continued into the room. In front of her was her father, sitting on a chair with his legs outstretched and clutching his right arm to his body with his left arm.

"Father, are you all right?"

"Of course, I am!" was his curt reply. "I thought I may have broken my leg, and my arm is sore. The leg is all right. It just hurts. I can survive that."

71

"I..., I was afraid that you were really hurt!"

Looking at his wife, William retorted, "No, I am tougher than that, but I am just sick and tired of things going wrong."

Wanting to change the subject, Ann asked, "Have they looked at your arm yet?"

"No, they haven't, and at the speed that things happen around here, I am not sure when that will be. If I could, I would fix my own arm, but that is not possible with only one good arm."

Ann and Elizabeth both sat down in chairs on the other side of the room and looked at each other, both not sure what could or should be said.

All three were sitting in silence when a man came into the room and asked, "Who thinks they have a broken arm?

"I don't think, I know!" exclaimed William, looking at the man as though he had rudely insulted him, "I am a surgeon. I know!"

"Come with me," came the curt reply.

William, with the help of the doctor, entered the next room.

Elizabeth and Ann looked at each other with all-knowing looks and shrugged their shoulders. They had seen such interactions before, and it was getting worse. They had discussed the problem before, but they had not come up with any answers.

They waited silently for a couple of minutes, trying to hear what was going on in the other room, but they could only hear muffled voices and could not tell what they were saying.

Then, suddenly, a thunderous voice, "Give me that bandage; I can do better with only one arm! Do you have any idea what you are doing?"

There was no response, just silence.

It was not more than ten minutes later when William came bursting through the doorway, hobbling on his sore leg, turned back towards the doctor's room, and in an accusing voice said, "I will never come and see you again; you are not fit to do anything!"

With that, William hobbled out of the waiting room clutching his arm, with Ann and Elizabeth in hot pursuit.

William was muttering and cursing under his breath as they all carefully left the doctor's rooms. He understood that the bone in his arm had not broken cleanly and that with care, it would heal in its own time. With Ann's help, he would rebandage it when he got home and learn to keep it as still as possible until it healed. The doctor thought that the bone was split lengthways and that it would heal with rest. The doctor also thought the break was not the main reason for the pain but was probably made worse by a torn muscle. William had difficulty walking as the pain in his leg seemed just as bad as that in his arm, so Elizabeth took his good arm in hers and slowly walked the short distance to the hospital's front door.

At that stage, William realized he would not be able to walk all the way home, and fortunately, a hire cart arrived at the front door while dropping off a patient. The driver was more than pleased that he had found another customer so quickly. The cart slowly took the three of them home, with William complaining about the roughness of the ride all the way there.

Chapter 6

The following day, after a restless night, Richard woke up feeling exceedingly seedy, so he was not sure what time it was, but by the light coming into his bedroom, it looked like it was later than he had hoped. He quickly got out of bed and dressed in his uniform, noticing it was dirty and needed washing. "No time for that now!" he thought as he rushed towards the door.

He opened the front door, then noticed that the sun was far higher in the sky than he thought, which meant he would be late for work. Richard nearly ran down the road in his haste to get to the fort as he knew that his lateness would not be well accepted.

Rushing into the work site office, Richard looked to see if Mr. Smithers was in his office. Just as he was about to look away, a recognisable voice said in a sarcastic manner, "Sergeant, I see you have finally decided to grace us with your presence."

Quickly swinging around, he replied, "Sorry, Mr. Smithers, time stood still this morning, and I apologize. It won't happen again."

"I bloody well hope not! It is just not good enough."

"I fully realize that Sir."

"We have already done one early inspection, and I wanted you there. You will just have to go and look at it yourself. It was alongside the same area we were in yesterday. The local site supervisor will explain what we were looking at. Now hop to it!"

"Yes Sir," Richard quickly replied, as he rushed out the door to the relevant work site. "Damn", he thought, running a couple of hundred yards to the earlier visited area. He arrived well out of breath, and looking around, could not see the same site boss that he had seen the day before. He was not in a habit of being late, and the whole exercise, and the subsequent dressing down, made him feel very uncomfortable.

"Stop thinking about it and get back to work," he told himself.

As it was obvious that those working on the shovels were convicts, and as they could not help him, he looked for the usual soldiers who are normally not far away. The nearest one was sitting on a wooden box eating an apple, so he walked across and asked, "Do you know where the boss has gone?"

"Nope, don't have a clue."

Richard, in a stern voice, "Private, you do understand that I am a sergeant, don't you!"

"Sorry, Sergeant, I am so used to being here with the convicts that I forgot my place. I do know where the boss is. He just went through that door over there."

Richard decided to have a quick look over part of the site while he waited. He particularly noticed that the convicts were not very enthusiastic workers, and it looked like it would take forever for them to achieve anything of consequence. The two soldiers appointed to this gang of convicts also seemed to be as uninterested in their jobs as the convicts themselves. But Richard guessed that providing none of the convicts escaped, no one would care anyway.

A couple of minutes later, the local site supervisor returned, and on seeing Richard smiled, and then said, "Oh, you have finally turned up, have you? The boss was here earlier and asked me if I had seen you. Obviously, I told him the truth."

"Thanks, that's just what I needed."

"You're welcome," he replied with as much sarcasm as he could muster.

"Mr. Smithers and his crew were looking at something earlier. I need to look at it. What is it?"

"If you remember, we were discussing the angle of that wall which you suggested we change. Well, we should have also discussed the angle of that adjoining wall."

"Ah, I see what you mean. Let me think about it for a minute."

With that, Richard walked away from the wall about 50 yards towards the sea to get a better overall view. Then, looking to the adjoining inlet, and then out to sea, he tried to envisage how an attacking ship would go about its job and whether that other wall would be in the direct firing line. Finally, thinking from both an aggressor's and defender's point of view, he decided that this other wall would be fine where it was originally going to be built.

Richard wandered back to the site boss and asked, "What did Mr. Smithers think?"

"He thought that it could be changed slightly, but he was not convinced that was necessary. That is why he wanted your opinion."

"Yes, I agree. I don't think it is important, so I suggest it stay as the plans indicate."

"That makes my life easier. He said I should go with whatever you say as long it did not vary greatly from what he thought. Thanks for that."

"That's it then?"

"Thanks."

With that, Richard wandered off towards the site office when he noticed a couple of convicts on top of an elevated work platform. The top deck looked like it was only held up by a rickety bunch of undersized sticks tied together with rope, all with very little diagonal bracing. It looked rather dangerous to him so he headed off in that direction while thinking that the whole thing could collapse before he even got there.

Richard got close enough to call out to the convicts, "That platform you are standing on does not look very safe. Are you happy being up there?"

"What was that? I can't hear you," was the reply.

Richard continued walking until he stopped alongside the platform and its support structure, as he yelled, "That platform does not look very safe. I would come down from there if I were you."

No sooner had Richard uttered these words when the whole structure started to lean to one side, coming towards him, just to where he was standing. The movement of the platform caused the two convicts to lose their footing as they struggled to stay on their feet as the tip worsened. Richard was about to move back away from the obvious danger when the whole structure started to make strange noises; then, it crumbled and plunged toward him. Richard could see it coming, but conditions underfoot were muddy, and his feet could not get a grip. He at once bent down and put his hands down on the dirt, hoping that this would help him get extra traction. Unfortunately, he had only moved a couple of feet in his frantic effort to get away when the platform edge clipped him on the side of his head as it crashed to the ground. Richard hit the muddy ground, which was his last memory of the incident.

Richard slowly opened his eyes and looked upward towards a group of unknown faces, at the same time trying to remember what had just happened. Then it dawned on him where he was. Richard turned his head towards the now pile of timber that used to be the elevated platform. He noticed a group of people looking down at the ground on the other side of the timber. Even though he felt groggy, his curiosity got the better of him, so he tried to sit up to have a better look when somebody put a hand on his shoulder and said, "Don't get up. You have a damaged arm and a bump on your head. It is best you lie down." Richard reluctantly did as he was told.

Then the whole painful episode hit him! He tried to get into a more comfortable position, but that movement caused excruciating pain that ran right up his left arm, at which he yelled, "Bloody hell! That hurts." He noticed that not only did his arm look to be at a strange angle, but it was also bleeding, so he carefully rearranged his arm into a more comfortable position, wrapped his ripped sleeve around the bleeding area, and just lay there feeling somewhat helpless. His vision was blurred from the blow to his head, and the world was spinning around before him.

Then he heard a commanding voice call out, "Attention, everyone, this is not a holiday camp. Everyone back to work. Soldier, make sure it happens!"

"Yes sir," came the reply, neither voice familiar to Richard.

Laying there quietly seemed the only thing he could do under the circumstances, but upon hearing the excited voices coming from the other side of the now-damaged platform, he tried to see what the excitement was all about. "What the hell is going on over there?" he thought. Then he remembered the two convicts that were on the platform when it fell. So, to no one in particular, he called out, "What has happened?" pointing in the general direction with his good arm. There was no response, so he tried again, "Can anyone tell me what is happening over there?"

Then that same commanding voice again, "It's all right, Sergeant, don't worry about that. You have your own problems to deal with."

Richard turned his head to see an army officer in uniform, but he could not see his rank from where he was lying, so he just replied, "Yes, Sir."

The pain made it difficult for Richard to concentrate on what was happening, so he lay back, closed his eyes, and waited. He obviously had a damaged arm, which would have to be looked at, but his major concern now was what he believed to be a far worse accident on the other side of the platform. In that regard, he opened his eyes, hoping to find someone whom he could ask what all the noise was about. Not expecting to see anyone he knew, he was surprised to discover that he was now looking directly into the eyes of Mr. Smithers, who said, "Richard, what have you got yourself into this time? It looks like we need to get someone to look at that arm of yours."

"Yes, Sir, it does hurt, but that is not what I am really worried about. What happened over there?" he asked, nodding his head in the direction of the commotion.

"It is not your concern. I believe one of the men on the platform broke his neck in the fall and died. The other one was a lot luckier."

The first thing that came to Richard's mind was whether he could have been responsible for the platform toppling over. Thinking about it for a second or two did not help him resolve that question, as he still had difficulty concentrating.

Mr. Smithers bought him back to thinking about his own condition when he said, "I have ordered a cart to take you to the guardhouse, where they have a doctor. They regularly deal with such accidents as there are hundreds of workers here at any one time."

As Mr. Smithers spoke, a cart pulled up beside Richard. The driver helped him to lay down in the back, which luckily carried a half load of straw that helped him get reasonably comfortable. Mr. Smithers gave the driver the necessary instructions, and the cart slowly moved away from the deadly accident scene.

Richard tried to look back at the incident, but the cart moved around the corner of a half-completed wall blocking his view. The whole area was very uneven, so the cart bounced around considerably as the driver slowly picked his way toward the guardhouse. Richard tried to reposition himself while clutching his damaged arm to his chest, hoping to lessen the pain, all to no avail. It felt like someone was jabbing a knife into his arm with every movement of the cart. The large bruise on his head did not help.

The cart eventually reached its destination and came to a halt outside the main entrance, upon which the driver, with the help of another man, helped Richard to climb down. He slowly made his way inside. The pain was still making his head swim.

He was shown into a room on the right-hand side of the long and dark hallway, where a couple of patients were waiting, one sitting, one standing. Unfortunately, there were no chairs available, so Richard moved over to the opposite blank wall and leaned against it. The arm was still very painful and swollen, but unfortunately, it looked like it would be a long wait.

The surgeon's assistant went over to each patient and tried to find out what was wrong, and several patients then disappeared into the next room. At other times, they were simply treated right then and there.

After about an hour, at least that is what it felt like, it was Richard's turn to be looked at by the doctor. He was asked to sit on the edge of the low bench, upon which the surgeon said, "Now, let's have a look at that arm."

The doctor examined his arm and said, "I think we can solve this problem quite easily, although it will be very uncomfortable. I want you to hang onto the edge of this bench with your good arm because I am going to pull and twist your dislocated arm back into position. Are you ready?"

With that, the doctor grabbed the lower arm with both hands, pulled back with weight, and quickly twisted the arm back to the correct position. Although expecting the pain, Richard heard a loud snap, and although he tried, he could not help himself from swearing. He suddenly felt faint, and for some reason, he found himself fighting to stay conscious. After a couple of minutes composing himself, Richard looked down on what was a badly twisted arm. He was thankful that the arm now looked to be at the correct angle. It was still bleeding, and the pain was still intense, but nowhere near what it was like earlier when the joint snapped back into position. The surgeon cleaned the blood off the cut on the elbow and wrapped a bit of cloth around it, saying, "That is going to be very painful for some time, and you will not be able to do much with it, so I suggest you find a wide strap which will help to keep it still."

By now, bathed in sweat, Richard acknowledged the suggestion with a grunt and then managed to find the word "Thanks."

Still groggy from the entire experience, Richard stood up, holding his damaged arm with his good one gingerly walked out of the room. He made his way slowly toward the front door. Fortunately, the cart driver was hanging around the doorway, so he came over and said, "I will take you home; that is what Mr. Struthers wanted."

Gritting his teeth with the persistent pain, Richard finally found a reasonably comfortable position as the cart trundled off towards his lodgings. Thinking about the whole episode and accepting that the pain was not quite as bad as it was, Richard was thankful that his injury was not as permanent as he initially thought, "At least I should be able to get around if I take it easy."

Arriving at his lodging, the driver helped Richard get down from the cart and eventually to the front door. Finding the door unlocked, Richard asked the driver to help him into his room, as he was once again feeling unsteady on his feet. Walking down the hall towards his bedroom, he expected to hear Molly, but nothing! He called out several times, but there were no answers.

 Reaching the end of the hall, he opened the door and with the aid of the driver, made it to the edge of the unmade bed. "Thanks for that. I owe you something. Just a minute, I think I have something in my tunic." With that, Richard pulled out a shilling that he had been saving for just such an emergency.

"Thanks very much," replied the driver, who quickly slank out of the room as though he was expecting to be told to return the coin.

Richard carefully lifted his legs onto the bed and lay back, and although the arm was still painful and the bump on his head still hurt, he managed to find a reasonably comfortable position. He then remembered it was important to hold his arm still for some days, so he got off the bed and found a scarf that could function as a supporting bandage. Finally, with considerable effort and more pain, he managed to wrap his damaged arm close to his body. Not ideal, but it would do for now.

He lay there thinking over the eventful day. "Things are certainly not going my way. I wonder what the future holds. Hopefully, tomorrow will be better."

Chapter 7

Elizabeth and her parents finally arrived home from the hospital, although it took considerable time as William was finding it extremely difficult to walk after his accident. At times, his wife and Elizabeth took each arm to help, but William made it noticeably clear that he did not want to be assisted. After a while, he soon realized he had no real alternative. While he had not broken his leg, the muscles in his broken arm were extremely sore, which cramped from time to time during the journey home.

As William hobbled through the front door, he called out in frustration to no one in particular, "I am going upstairs to lie down, and I do not want to be disturbed." In silence, his wife and daughter helped him upstairs and onto his bed.

Elizabeth and her mother came downstairs and then moved into the kitchen, neither talking, both deep in their own thoughts and their own world. They sat down at the kitchen table without saying a word. After a while, Ann said, "Your father is not a very happy man, but I am not completely sure why things are getting to him. He has had his fair share of bad luck recently, but anybody can have that."

Elizabeth was quickly brought back to the present by her mother's comments, but as she was unsure of the answers to the questions, she said nothing.

After a couple of minutes, which seemed a lot longer, Elizabeth finally said, "Mother, I am not sure anybody in this family is thrilled with how things are at the moment. So maybe we should think of doing something completely different. Maybe even going to a new place? In other words, a fresh start."

"Where did those ideas come from? Have you been speaking to your father?"

"No, I haven't! Although if we could catch him in the right mood, he might consider it."

"Elizabeth, I don't know where you get these ideas from. Certainly not from me."

"I have been thinking of doing something different for some time, and now seems the right time."

Ann did not respond. She got up from the table and walked over to the kitchen fire, which had virtually gone out by now. She rustled up a few sticks of firewood, and after a bit of coaxing, the fire sprang back into life. While all this was going on, Ann was in deep thought at what her daughter had just said and was amazed at her coming up with such a ridiculous suggestion. Move to another place! Where did that idea come from?

Elizabeth kept quiet as she knew that her mother was trying to take in what she had just said. "I probably should have suggested the idea at a better time and in a more delicate manner," she thought.

After putting a pot on the fire to heat the water, Ann turned to her daughter and said, "You have surprised me with your strange idea. I will have to give that suggestion some thought if you are serious."

"Yes, Mother. I have been thinking about that for a while now, and I think we should all take the time to talk about the idea. Father is not very happy at the moment, and I am not sure how you are feeling."

With that said Elizabeth left the kitchen and went up to her bedroom, unsure what her mother thought of the idea. She flopped down on her bed and lay there looking at the ceiling and wondering if she had suggested the idea at the right time. While lying on her bed, Elizabeth went over and over what she had just said to her mother and, for many reasons, kicked herself for bringing the subject up when she did. Knowing her mother, she will probably now speak to her father, and the whole idea will get scuttled before it gets going. "Oh well, better luck next time," she thought.

Down in the kitchen, Ann was busy preparing the evening meal and, at the same time, mulling over what Elizabeth had said. Her thoughts ranged wildly from the absolute logic of the idea to the sheer fantasy, but every time coming back to the question of how William would react to such a suggestion. She knew he was often in a bad mood recently and thought that maybe a change would be for the better. However, she fully realized that introducing such a wild idea to William would have to be at an ideal time, and under the current circumstances, judging the right timing would not be easy.

William, who by this time had been asleep for a couple of hours, found that he had been sleeping in a somewhat awkward position, and while his leg had not suffered, his back had. He rearranged his position in bed, relaxed a little, and started thinking about what had happened that day. "I will definitely not be climbing up so high in the future," he thought. "It was a stupid thing to do."

William started to worry about what would happen at the surgery and wondered if his offsider, Thomas, could cope without him. He realized that Thomas could look after minor illnesses and accidents but thought that if any major incidents did come up, he might not be able to cope. What really concerned William was how long it would take him to get well enough to return to work. Realizing that the accident had affected him far more than he first thought, William deliberately kept very still and slowly drifted off to sleep.

After what seemed like no time, William heard his wife call out as she climbed the stairs. "William, do you realize that it is after 7 o'clock and dark outside?"

He awoke somewhat startled and replied, "I did not know it was that late. Can you help me get downstairs?

Coming into the bedroom, Ann went over to the bed and helped her husband get his feet on the floor, with some difficulty, as William was a much bigger person. William hobbled to the top of the stairs and slowly climbed down with the help of the balustrade on one side and Ann on the other. By the time he had reached the bottom, he was starting to sweat from the exertion.

"This is impossible!" he exclaimed, stopping to get his breath back, "I don't know how I am going to cope. Get me that walking stick that is in the front room. That might help."

Rummaging around the storage room, she asked, "Where is the walking stick?"

"I think it is the back right-hand corner leaning against the wall."

With those instructions, Ann climbed over the old carpet, around broken chairs, and other rubbish and eventually found it. She grabbed it, found an easier way back to the door, closed it, and called, "I've got it."

With the cane on one side and Ann on the other, William slowly hobbled into the kitchen, where he noticed that supper was about to be served. He carefully sat down.

"Where is Elizabeth?"

"I think she has been asleep like you were. I will go and get her."

Ann had just got to the top of the stairs when she heard a door opening, and Elizabeth appeared in the doorway, looking somewhat sleepy.

She was surprised to see her mother and said in a slow and measured voice while rubbing her eyes, "Oh, mother. I was just about to come down. Sorry, but I could not wake up."

Both climbed downstairs and entered the kitchen without saying anything more. Then, seeing her father and remembering the accident, Elizabeth enquired, "Father, how is your arm, and your leg?"

"Bloody terrible!" snapped her father.

Thinking of no reasonable answer, Elizabeth sat down at the table while her mother promptly filled three bowls with stew from the pot hanging over the fire. No one spoke as they emptied their bowls, although William found the process difficult.

"That stew was beautiful, even if I say so myself," quipped Ann, wanting to break the silence carefully.

It is evident that William was feeling better by now, so he answered, "Yes, Ann, I did enjoy that. That was one of your better ones," trying hard to supply a compliment.

"That's good. What did you think, Elizabeth?"

"Yes, Mother, it was nice."

Taking note that her mother and father seemed to be in a positive mood now that they had both eaten, she thought now might be the ideal time to bring up the question of them moving. With that in mind, and thinking it would be best not to raise the question directly or too quickly, she asked, "Father, are you quite happy living here in Portsmouth?"

Surprised at the question itself and not knowing where it was coming from, her father replied, "Why do you ask?"

Knowing where all this was leading, Ann decided to keep out of it and watch the proceedings.

Elizabeth hesitated before answering, "I don't know, but I have noticed that you have not been very happy recently, and I believe that some form of change might be good for you."

William wondered what had prompted his daughter to ask such a question, as that had never entered his mind. "Well, it is true. I have not been very lucky recently but have never considered that."

"Well, Father, I was thinking that a change might give us a new start, and from there, things could only get better."

With a look of puzzlement on his face, William said, "Ann, do you know anything about this?"

"Well, Elizabeth has mentioned it, but I did not know how serious she was, so I have not thought about it much," answered Ann, trying to minimise the impact.

Not knowing precisely what Elizabeth was talking about, William said, "As you know, this is all very new to me, and I am sure what you really mean. Elizabeth, are you suggesting that we move away from here?

"Ah. Well, yes. I am."

"Let me get my head around this. Are you suggesting that we move away from this house? There would be many things to think about before making a decision such as that."

"That is what I was thinking about," replied Elizabeth in a tentative voice.

With that, both Ann and Elizabeth thought it best to say nothing further for a few minutes, upon which her father finally said, "Could you both help me to get upstairs? My head is swimming as all this is too much for me."

With one on each arm, Elizabeth and Ann helped William upstairs and into bed. Even after lying down, William could not get this ridiculous idea of moving out of his head. Where to and what would I do? It was just all too much to think about.

Returning to the kitchen, Ann said, "I was not expecting you to mention anything to your father so soon. Your timing may be a problem. Have you thought about it anymore?"

"Not a great deal. The idea is not new to me, so I do have a few ideas."

"Yes, I understand that, but this may take some time for me and your father to think through. I am not fully convinced myself, so I need more time."

With that, Elizabeth left the kitchen, went into the parlour, and decided it would be best to forget the moving idea and just read for a while. However, Elizabeth realized that the question of moving would take considerable time to resolve, and in the end, nothing would happen until both her parents agreed.

Ann went to bed that evening and could not get the whole idea out of her head. There was just so much to consider that various thoughts kept going around and around in her head, usually with no conclusion. What concerned her most was where they would go and would that place be better for the entire family in the long run. After considerable thought and pondering from every angle, Ann finally managed to get to sleep after making at least one decision – she would enquire in the morning about places they could move to.

Ann did not sleep very well, often waking up, usually with thoughts in her head that were difficult to shake. Finally, the dawn broke, and after checking on her husband, she went downstairs to the kitchen, the place where she felt the most comfortable. She believed that should they move, William and Elizabeth were more than capable of making new friends and settling into new environments, but to her, the thought of starting afresh was more than daunting.

Ann had eaten her breakfast early this morning, as she always thought best with a full stomach. So far, she had not yet seen or heard from either her husband or daughter. She was just about ready to go upstairs to see what the story was when she heard a knock on the front door. "Who the hell can that be?" was her immediate reaction.

As the kitchen was at the back of the house, walking from there to the front door took a little time, which resulted in another knock. This time a little louder. Not wanting to wake those upstairs, Ann quickened her pace and then opened the door.

"Hello, Ann. Sorry to come so early, but I was passing and thought I would catch up with you before you headed out."

"That's all right, Mrs. Williams; I have been up for a while. Please come in."

Ann ushered Mrs. Williams into the front parlour and pointed to a seat opposite her own, simultaneously wondering why Elizabeth's former tutor was calling.

"I know it is very unusual for me to come here unannounced, but I believe I have some important news. I heard about your husband's unfortunate accident, and I thought you should know that his assistant at the surgery has been taken ill and can't get to work. I don't know what is wrong with him, but I thought it best to inform you. By the way, how is your husband?"

"His arm is only partially broken. It is bandaged and should come right in time, but it is still very painful. His leg is also very sore, which does not help matters.

"Sorry to have to give you the bad news, but I thought it best that you were told."

"Yes, thank you for that. I will let William know. Was there anything else?"

"No, that is all the bad news I have, and anyway, I think I had better be going."

Mrs. Williams rose from her seat and moved towards the front door, apologising for the intrusion so early in the morning.

As Ann opened the front door, she said, "Thank you for that. It is not good news, but at least we know the story."

No sooner had Ann closed the door when she heard her husband. "Who was that?" came a croaky voice.

"It was just Mrs. Williams. I will tell you about it when you come down."

Knowing that her husband was awake before he called downstairs, Ann rushed upstairs, seeing how well William had spent the night with both a painful leg and arm. She was pleasantly surprised when he said, "Good morning. Sorry for sleeping in so late, but I could not wake up any earlier."

"That is all right. How are the arm and leg now?"

"They are still sore, but they are getting better. I hope the leg will hold up when I put more pressure on it."

As he said that, William slowly lifted his body over the side of the bed and started exerting his total weight on his leg.

"Ow! That hurts," he yelled as he dropped back on the bed. "This is going to be more challenging than I thought. I don't know what is wrong with it, as neither the doctor nor myself believe it is broken. Luckily my arm does not hurt as much."

"That's fine, dear, I did not expect you could walk on it all by yourself, so you will just have to take it easy for a while."

"Damn! I was hoping that I could at least walk on it with the help of a walking stick."

Although William was still feeling somewhat sorry for himself, Ann decided it was essential to bring the matter of Thomas not being at the surgery to his attention.

"Sorry to have to tell you this, William, but Thomas is not very well and will not be at the surgery today. Hopefully, he will be back at work in a day or two. What do you want me to do?"

"I think we left a closed sign on the front door, but anyway, the message will soon get around that neither of us is there. There is not much more you can do anyway."

"All right, you stay right there, and I will bring you up something light to eat."

Ann returned to the kitchen and started to review all the happenings going on in their lives right now. Is it possible that Elizabeth's crazy idea of moving may make some sense after all? The oats that Ann had made earlier had gone cold by now, so she put the pot back on the fire, all the while trying to make sense of what was happening in their lives. "It is all too much!" she thought.

Elizabeth had slept in way past her usual time and felt better for it. She first remembered the discussions she had with her mother and wondered if anything would come of it. Thinking out loud, she said, "I will just have to play it smart from here on in and see what happens." She got out of bed, washed her face and hands in the bowl, brushed her hair, and got partially dressed, although she could not remember getting out of her clothes the night before.

Leaving her bedroom and walking into the hall in somewhat of a daze, she saw something out of the corner of her eye; she suddenly shrieked, "Heaven forbid!" She was not expecting anyone outside her door, and the surprise got the better of her.

Her father, concentrating on trying to walk reasonably well with a walking stick, did not see Elizabeth, so he jumped back in surprise when he heard the shriek. He lost his balance, but Elizabeth managed to grab hold of him and keep him on his feet.

In complete agony, William yelled out, "Bloody hell!" while at the same time clutching his leg.

Eventually, Elizabeth came to her senses and said, "Father, I am sorry about that, but I did not see you."

William, in pain but now understanding what had just happened, buttoned his lips the best way he could and cursed under his breath.

Elizabeth, now aware of what she had just done, said, "I am truly sorry for doing that to you." Feeling terrible, she just stood there, not knowing what more she could say.

Ann, who had heard the cursing, was now at the bottom of the stairs, but she could not see exactly what was happening. Rushing up the stairs, she called out, "What's happened?" Before getting any reply, she got to the top of the stairs and could see her daughter and husband standing there.

"For goodness' sake, are you two all right?"

"This bloody leg hurts like hell," was the only answer she received.

Ann and Elizabeth helped William get back to his bed, where he lay down on his good side while trying to adjust the angle of his leg to minimise the pain. A few groans and moans went with the whole painful process.

"I don't think I have done any more damage, so I will just lay here for a while."

Elizabeth was still stunned by the fact that she had knocked over her father once before and scared him to death this time. Even though she felt sorry for him, she realized both were pure accidents. She and her mother left the room without saying anything and silently returned to the kitchen.

William stayed in his bed for most of the day and tried walking around his bedroom with the aid of the walking stick a couple of times, but every time he tried, he collapsed on his bed in agony. Eventually, he gave up.

The following day, William woke up after a fitful night trying to get comfortable enough to get some decent sleep. By daybreak, he had finally found a reasonably comfortable position, so he slept on.

He finally woke up long after his usual time, but at least his leg felt a little better, so he decided to remain in this comfortable position for a little longer. Then, feeling somewhat sorry for himself, he started thinking about that change Elizabeth had discussed. After mulling the whole idea around in his head and acknowledging that they had lived in Portsmouth for many years, Elizabeth's suggestion might have merit. A fresh start may be just what the doctor ordered.

As no unusual noises were coming from either Elizabeth's or William's room, Ann decided it would be best to just let them sleep. It also gave her more time to consider Elizabeth's idea of selling up and moving. She had never considered such an idea before, but the idea of bettering themselves by moving had some appeal.

Ann had just finished sweeping out the kitchen when Elizabeth appeared in the doorway, looking very sleepy and not dressed in her usual tasteful manner.

In a soft tone, Elizabeth said, "Mother, sorry about being so late. It looks like I slept in. Have you seen Father yet?"

"No, I decided to leave him be if he is comfortable. You look like you are still half asleep."

"Is it all right if I go back upstairs and finish dressing?"

"That will be fine, and we can talk later if you like."

Elizabeth returned upstairs and finished dressing as her mother would expect, and then returned to the kitchen, understanding her mother probably wanted to talk more about the possibility of moving.

Sure enough, Ann at once began speaking before Elizabeth even had time to sit down. "I know I have not been particularly interested in your suggestion that we move house, but I have thought a little more about it. I think it might have some merit. I will obviously have to talk to your father about the whole idea, and I think he may agree, particularly considering his recent bad luck."

"That's great, Mother. I know he has not been very happy recently, so let me know what he thinks."

"I will go up to see how he is getting on, and if he is in a good mood, I will raise the subject later."

"Thanks, Mother."

Not particularly hungry, Elizabeth felt like going outside and getting the feel of that appealing breeze that freely blows from across the bay. She left the table, opened the front door, and walked across the street. There was only a light wind blowing, but the fresh, clean feel of the wind on her face gave her a sense of renewal and freedom.

While enjoying the pleasant sensation the breeze was providing, she noticed a large sailing ship leaving the shelter of the harbour and venturing out into the open sea. "Going overseas. That would be a real change. That is something worth thinking about." she said to herself.

After about thirty minutes of enjoying the wind in her face and watching the ships sailing in and out of the harbour and the odd horse and carriage driving up and down the street, she turned around and headed back to her house. As she did so, the wind suddenly changed direction, and a gust of wind blew sufficiently strong to blow up the edge of her skirt, which she quickly held down with one hand. At the same time, a sheet of newspaper came out of nowhere, and with the force of the wind, it stuck to her other arm. Still holding on to her skirt, she finished crossing the road, finally reaching the calmness of her front door. Once out of the wind, the sheet of newspaper then fell to her feet.

Thinking it would be handy for her mother to light the fire, she picked it up and glanced at the headline as she did so; it read, "FLEET OFF TO NEW SOUTH WALES." Smoothing out the page so she could read more of the article, she soon gathered what it was all about. A fleet of ships was being assembled with the object of creating a new colony on the other side of the world.

Immediately thinking this might be an idea worthy of a family discussion, Elizabeth folded the newspaper neatly and went inside. She sat on the small chair in the hall and read the rest of the article. Her interest at once heightened when she read the list of the skills of people whom they were looking for to join the fleet. They were looking for, amongst others, a ship's surgeon.

Elizabeth rushed into the kitchen, hoping to find her mother, but she was not there. After hunting high and low, she finally found her outside the back door hanging out clothes to dry.

Rushing down the stairs and into the garden, Elizabeth shouted as she went, "Mother, look what I have found!"

"Heavens forbid, what is all the excitement about?"

Flourishing the newspaper page in front of her mother's face, she said, "Look at this. It could be what we are looking for."

Ann stopped what she was doing and started to read the paper, first noticing the headline and dismissing it, then she began to read the rest of the article. Getting to the end, she paused before saying anything.

"Are you suggesting what I think you are suggesting?" questioned Ann.

"Did you see the bit about them wanting a surgeon?"

"I did. So, I suppose that you think this is a good idea?"

"Well, if you think about it, it is a possibility that does not come up every day, and the trip out there would be free. I think it is worth thinking about, don't you?"

"What you are talking about is a huge step, even for you, and I am not sure what your father will think of the idea. Let me think about it a little more because it will not be that simple."

Elizabeth was amazed that her mother had not unthinkingly knocked the idea and that she was actually willing to think about it. "That is a good start," she thought. She realized the hardest person to convince of the idea's merit would probably be her father. Thinking about it further, she believed she might be able to persuade him as her passionate pleas sometimes swayed him. She took the piece of newspaper and decided to work on a plan.

Elizabeth walked back to the kitchen and put the sheet of newspaper on the table, ensuring that her mother would see it again.

Later, Elizabeth saw her mother leave the kitchen with something in her hands, which Elizabeth assumed was something to eat for her father. She then noticed that the piece of newspaper was no longer on the kitchen table. "That's good," she thought, "it would be best to give them some time to discuss the possible move to New South Wales". In the meantime, Elizabeth decided to go into the front parlour and think this whole matter through, and then, if time, read the book on the sideboard. She remembered she had started reading it some weeks ago. The trouble with leaving a book so long was that she could not even remember what it was all about.

Elizabeth did not spend much time working on her plan to convince her parents to join the fleet sailing to New South Wales because she concluded that she would probably have to play it by ear. She settled down for a good read, although it was difficult to concentrate on her reading. Her mind was elsewhere.

It would have been nearly an hour before she heard any movement or voices from upstairs when she heard the creaking boards as her mother descended the stairs. Putting down the book, Elizabeth left the front parlour and headed for the kitchen.

Elizabeth rushed into the kitchen with a sense of anticipation on the one hand and dread on the other. Her mother was sitting at the table at this stage, and the look on her face gave nothing away, so she was unsure what to say. She paused once inside and then noticed that her mother had her head in her hands and was in deep thought. She hesitated a few seconds before addressing her mother.

"Mother, how did it go?"

Suddenly aware of her daughter's presence, Ann lifted her head, paused, and said, "Your father was surprised at your suggestion, but after a little time, he warmed somewhat to the idea. He agreed to think about everything involved in such a move before making any further decisions. However, he was not dead against it, which means it could happen."

Elizabeth did not raise the question with either her mother or father for days after that, as she did not want to be seen to push the point.

Her father's leg was better by this time, so he had managed to hobble into his surgery. He found it difficult to stand for very long, which made any work nearly impossible, so he returned home early most days. Amazingly, his arm seemed to be healing well, and he could use it for light work. A colleague of his dropped into the surgery earlier, allowing him to discuss the whole idea of sailing to New South Wales. His fellow surgeon was more aware of what was planned than William, and after some discussion, they both thought the whole idea had merit, particularly the way life, in general, had been going for William. They both thought it was a real opportunity for a fresh start if that is what was required.

That evening, Ann and William discussed the matter and eventually came to a decision, upon which time they asked Elizabeth to join them. She hesitatingly sat opposite them at the kitchen table, not knowing what to think, so saying nothing seemed the best.

William, with his wife sitting alongside him, got straight to the point, "Elizabeth, we have both been discussing your idea of taking a ship to New South Wales, and we have decided that providing there are no adverse reasons that we have not yet thought of, we think your idea has merit."

"Oh, Mother, Father, that is tremendous!" replied Elizabeth as she rushed around the table, stood between them, put an arm around each of them, and gave them a big hug. Her parents looked at each other and said in unison, "Thank you."

Her father went on to say, "This whole idea may not be possible."

"Yes, I understand. I will just have to wait and see," Elizabeth replied.

Chapter 8

Richard managed to get through the following day without too much difficulty, but dressing was not that easy with one good arm. He also noticed that Emily was not at breakfast and wondered why, but he did not feel he should ask her mother. Molly helped him wrap the long scarf over his arm and around his body underneath his uniform tunic. While it looked like he only had one arm, it looked better and was far more comfortable.

As he walked to the Fort Richard was amazed at how walking with only one arm took far more effort than with two. Swinging only one arm seemed to put one off balance. Finally arriving at the fort, Richard was walking into the office when he was stopped by the clerk coming out of the front door.

"Sergeant, what have you done there?" he asked, pointing to Richard's empty sleeve.

"I twisted it when that platform collapsed."

"Ah, yes, that was unfortunate, but then accidents are always happening around here. Sometimes people never learn. How is the arm anyway?"

"Fine now. It will not take long to improve and should not affect my work here." With that, Richard entered the office to find Mr. Smithers searching through the pile of plans on the table.

"I know it is here somewhere!" he muttered, not realizing Richard was standing there watching the proceedings.

Richard then remembered he had left one of the plans he was looking at the day before on another table. Not knowing which plan Mr. Smithers was looking for, Richard thought it best to come clean. He walked over to the other table, found the plan lying there, and bought it back to where Mr. Smithers was by now making a mess of the pile of plans. He was getting very irate and was increasing the volume and number of swear words.

Finally getting Mr. Smithers's attention, Richard handed over the plan and said, "Sorry, Sir, but is this the plan you are looking for?"

"Where the hell did you find it?"

Feeling it was best to tell the truth, Richard pointed to the other table and said, "It was over there."

"How did it get over there?"

"I am very sorry Mr. Smithers, but I left it over there last time I looked at it."

"God damn! I thought you knew better than that. I have been looking for that plan for ages!"

"Sorry about that; I just forgot to put it back on the pile."

"Never mind now, Sergeant. You need to come with me, and we will look at the other end of the wall we looked at before."

Mr. Smithers angrily stomped out the door and headed across the building site, with Richard in hot pursuit. Richard soon realized that one's balance is severely limited when crossing rough terrain with only one arm. He nearly fell a couple of times trying to maintain the pace.

Arriving at the area of concern, Mr. Smithers laid out the plan on the ground and pointed to the landward side of the bastion they had looked at earlier.

"Now, Sergeant, you remember you looked at the other side last time? Well, you must now consider this other wall on the same bastion from the possibility of attack from the landward side."

Richard, saying nothing and still smarting from the earlier rebuke, quickly moved off to view the other wall. He walked around from one angle to another, returned to where the new wall would be constructed, and then looked away from the fort.

After careful consideration, Richard could not see any weaknesses in the angle and position of the proposed wall, so he commented, "I think that everything looks good to me. I think the position as shown on the plan is fine."

By this stage, Mr. Smithers had calmed down, and his earlier red face had disappeared. "If it's fine with you, it is fine with me," he said.

By the time Richard had turned around to say something, Mr. Smithers had already turned his back and was heading back to the office. Richard's first thoughts were negative, and he was unsure how this episode would influence their relationship. This posting was not quite how he would have liked it, but he hoped things would improve.

Richard's arm was still inside his tunic, and as it felt reasonably comfortable, he decided to withdraw it from the sling while he walked back to the office. However, once the total weight of his arm was no longer supported, he winced, which made it clear that it would take a little longer to heal than he thought. So, he returned his arm into the sling and inside his tunic.

Arriving back at the office, he found Mr. Smithers sitting at his desk, so he knocked on the door, but to his surprise, he was told, "Stay out there; I will be there shortly."

Richard waited outside the door, thinking about what Mr Smithers had just said because it seemed contrary to his earlier, more friendly relationship. He could not put his finger on it, but the tone was just different.

Mr. Smithers finally came out of the office, stood before Richard, and said, "Sergeant, do you feel that your obvious experience in both the Navy and the Marines is fully taken advantage of here at the fort?"

"Well, I have not done much work so far."

"In any event, the powers-at-be have decided to send an engineer here instead of yourself, as they feel he would have wider knowledge and experience that I could put to better use. Maybe your talents could best be used elsewhere."

"I beg your pardon, Sir. Are you suggesting that I am not needed here?"

"Well, to be quite honest, yes, I am. Under the circumstances, I contacted your commanding officer yesterday and told him as much. I should get his reply either later today or tomorrow, and as I have not got any further sites for you to inspect right now, I suggest you find something to do, and I will talk to you again before you go home tonight."

Richard just stood there with a look of absolute surprise as Mr. Smithers turned and returned to his office. While he appreciated that his knowledge was of limited use on the site, he had felt that he had the first-hand experience with ships and forts that should be useful. Richard thought out loud, "What the hell would engineers know about canons anyway?" The higher-ups obviously thought otherwise.

Richard was aware he had not completed that many inspections, but he thought that things would get busier in time and that his skills could then be put to good use. He left the office not knowing what to do next, but it looked like the first decision had already been made.

Having visited the guardhouse earlier, he decided to walk over there and have a yarn with whoever was on duty. He reasoned that at least they were fellow soldiers, meaning they should understand his position. Every soldier knew and understood that a transfer could occur at any time, and usually, as it had just now, it happens quickly and without any consultation.

Walking up to the front door, he was just about to enter when he heard a loud and heated discussion taking place, which sounded like something that he should stay well clear of. He spun around and walked a few yards away. The argument settled down after a few minutes, and then a soldier angrily stormed out of the door and took off towards the barracks.

Richard waited a couple of minutes before he entered the door while at the same time looking around, making sure it was wise to continue. Everything seemed in order, although the only person present, a sergeant, looked somewhat perturbed, although he looked busy sorting out something on the table. Not wanting to interrupt rudely, Richard stood still for a while, thinking it was not wise to break the silence.

A couple of minutes passed before the sergeant suddenly looked up, and with a look of surprise, he asked, "What the hell are you doing here, Sergeant?"

"Sorry! Wrong time?"

"No, not a problem. What do you want?" he replied in an annoyed voice.

"Well, this has nothing to do with you directly, but I have just been told that I am no longer needed here at the fort, which has come as a bit of a surprise, to be honest. So that means I will now be posted elsewhere."

"Oh, that was not expected. I thought that Mr. Smithers could have used your knowledge. Never mind, we do not decide these things. I see you have hurt your arm."

"Yes, nothing really; I'm just resting it so it will heal quicker."

"Now, what have you really come here for?"

"Well. As my commanding officer will probably want to post me to the West Indies or somewhere like that, I thought it might be a good idea to find a preferred posting and apply for that quick smart. It just might work."

"I can't think of anything. But, hey, hang on a moment. This may interest you. Somebody told me the other day that quite a large fleet of ships is heading off to create a new colony in New South Wales. I believe there will be Marines going. That may be an idea?"

"I have not heard of that. That is something different. I might investigate that. It could be interesting. Thanks for that. I will now leave you to whatever you were doing."

"Nothing much. Just the usual rubbish one must do."

"Thanks for that."

After that exchange, Richard left the guardhouse and strolled around the entire fort building site, reinforcing his earlier view of just how big a job it was and how his knowledge could have been used. "Never mind," he thought, "it does not look like it will involve me."

The afternoon was ending, and groups of convicts started to leave the site on their way to their nightly imprisonment on one of the old prison hulks moored in Langstone Harbour. It was nearly time for Richard to return to the office and see Mr. Smithers, although he was not looking forward to it, so he did not exactly rush to get there.

He tentatively entered the office to find that Mr. Smithers was nowhere to be found, so he asked the clerk, "Do you know where Mr. Smithers is? He wanted to see me before I went home."

"He had to leave the office in a hurry about an hour ago. He said he would not be that long. I suggest you wait."

As there were no chairs in this outer part of the building, Richard decided to take a seat outside, where a bench was situated along the front wall. Not sure from which direction Mr. Smithers would come or how long he would be, he decided to lean back against the wall, close his eyes, and think about the last week. Several unfortunate situations had occurred, and he was unsure why things had gone the way they had. However, he also did not feel he was to blame for any of them. It was just plain unfortunate circumstances.

He must have dosed off in the warm sun as he was suddenly awakened by the sound of Mr. Smithers's voice, "Sorry about that, Sergeant, but something urgent came up."

Coming too with a start, Richard promptly stood up and hesitated for a second or two before answering, "You wanted to see me, sir."

"I am sorry, but I have some bad news. I have received a reply from your commanding officer, who agreed with me that your time here is wasted, so you are to report to him first thing in the morning. I thought I could use your knowledge and experience far more than I have, meaning your talents are somewhat wasted here. I have found an engineer with knowledge and experience in building forts, and that wider experience will be very useful in those other areas. I appreciate what you have done, and it is a pity it has not worked out for you. I will arrange for a cart to pick you up at 7 a.m." Upon which, he promptly disappeared back through the door into the site office.

Richard, stunned, just stood there. Not sure what to think, but fully realizing that these things happen when you are in one of His

Majesty's armed services. It is always difficult to plan anything long-term, and your future is entirely out of your own hands. Resigned to the unfortunate news, he quickly left the office and walked out of Cumberland Fort for the last time, disappointingly looking around at what might have been.

Although the walk to his lodging was short, it gave Richard the time to think about what the army sergeant had said earlier about the fleet that is going to the new colony of New South Wales. "That would be a big change," he thought. "Maybe I should consider that!"

Richard arrived at the house and went straight to the kitchen to inform Molly that he would be leaving first thing in the morning. For some reason or other, she was not that surprised. He also looked around, hoping to see Emily, but he could not see her and was unsure whether to ask Molly where she was. Deciding not to make any enquiries, he entered his room and started to gather his belongings and stuff them into his kit bag. In his hurry, he thought that his bag was either getting smaller or he now had more belongings, as they did not seem to fit in the bag. He emptied the bag and started again, taking more care this time.

After breakfast the following day and after a fitful night, Richard was not feeling that well and was disappointed he had not seen Emily, which did not help how he felt. Not being able to ignore Emily's absence anymore, Richard asked Molly, "I have not seen Emily since I got here last night. Is she well?"

"Yes, she is fine. She is at her auntie's place again."

"Oh, I see. I just wanted to say goodbye before I head off. Would you please give her my regards? Oh, tell her I am sorry I cannot now teach her how to ride," Richard said, simultaneously trying to hide the disappointment from his voice, "Not a problem, Richard, I'll do that."

At that, Richard heard the big grandfather clock in the hallway chime seven times, which meant he had better hurry as the cart should now be outside.

He rushed from the table, thanking Molly for her kindness as he went, grabbed his bag out of his old room and rushed to the front door. He was just about to open it when he heard someone knock, "Timing just right," he thought, opening the door to find the cart driver standing on the doorstep.

"Thanks, Molly," he yelled out as Molly came into the hall, "Thanks for everything."

His ride back to his old unit at Four House Barracks was slow, and it seemed to take forever, although it would not have been more than three-quarters of an hour. He was not sure how his fellow marines would treat him after returning so soon from what they would have thought to be an easy job. He decided to learn more about the fleet sailing in a few months' time to New South Wales.

As the day was still early when he arrived, he thought it best to report directly to his commanding officer, Captain Evans. So, he went straight to the captain's office, and luckily, he had not passed any of his fellow Marines, as he was still not looking forward to that prospect. While the situation was somewhat embarrassing, he realized it was not his fault, but his comrades may not see it that way.

Arriving at the office, Richard asked the corporal sitting outside, "Corporal, I am Sergeant Clarke, reporting to Captain Evans."

"Please wait, Sergeant." The corporal quietly knocked on the office door and went inside. He was in the office for a couple of minutes with considerable discussion taking place, although Richard could not hear what was being said. Finally, he exited the office, closed the door, and explained to Richard, "He will see you shortly."

Richard settled down in a chair and started to think more about the possibilities of joining the fleet. He thought it best to breach the subject with the captain as soon as possible, as this possibility would only be available to him before he got formally posted elsewhere. Nevertheless, the idea was certainly appealing, and he thought it would be a tremendous adventure and challenging at the same time.

Then, catching Richard by surprise and jolting him out of his current thinking, the door to the office suddenly opened, and Captain Evans appeared. Richard at once rose from his seat and snapped to attention, and said, "Sergeant Clarke reporting, sir."

He replied, "Just a minute, Sergeant; I will be with you shortly." as he walked over to a cupboard, opened the door, and removed a document.

"Send this with that letter, Corporal," as he dropped both on his desk.

"Sergeant, come into the office."

Richard quickly entered the office and asked, "Close the door, sir?"

"Yes, that would be best. Now, Sergeant, things did not go as we both thought they would at Fort Cumberland, but that is no real problem, although your old position has now been filled. Unfortunately, I have not had time to think of other options as to where you should be posted, but I should have time later today."

"Sir, seeing as I do not have an immediate posting, would you consider me putting my name forward to join the fleet sailing to New South Wales? I don't know much about it yet, but I am interested.

The captain stared at Richard for a moment or two, then replied, "There has been talk that there will be a detachment of marines attached to that fleet, but I am not sure what unit they will be coming from. Are you really interested in being a part of this expedition? If so, I can make some inquiries."

"Yes, sir."

"Very well, I will see what I can find out. I suggest you stay here with the rest of the headquarters staff until I can find out more. Is that all, Sergeant?"

"Yes, sir."

Richard was extremely thankful that there were no ramifications of having to leave his last post after such a short period, and the captain was going to find out if he could join the fleet.

After leaving the captain's office, Richard asked the corporal where he would find the headquarters' staff living quarters. He was given directions, and the corporal suggested, "Seek out Sergeant Pearce; he is in charge."

The following day saw Richard trying to find out from any sailor or marine just what the real story was about the fleet and what marine units were expected to board. He heard that Captain Arthur Phillip had been appointed the Governor of the new colony and that HMS Sirius was the fleet flagship. Much of the other information was minor and only rumour, so he needed to find someone directly involved to get the facts.

Early on his second day, and as the captain had not yet got back to him, he decided to ask further afield in his quest for more information on the proposed fleet. Thinking further, he decided to ask those in the Navy rather than his fellow marines, as it was, after all, a fleet of ships that would be assembled, and they may know more. As the Navy's Gun Wharf was only a couple of miles away on the other side of town, he decided to walk there to see if he could find someone who had any more information.

As Richard was in his marine uniform, he was not challenged as he walked onto Gun Wharf, wondering who would have the most reliable information as he entered the gates. He did not have to go far because a ship was tied up at the wharf loading guns and ammunition. "Someone aboard should know what it is all about," he thought. However, it was unnecessary to go onboard as an older midshipman on the wharf was supervising the loading, who, luckily, was handily sitting on a gun carriage.

Rich walked over and stood to attention close by, expecting to be recognised, but the midshipman took no notice as he was studying some form of document.

After feeling like a fool standing there for so long, Richard said, "Excuse me, sir."

Looking up, surprised at seeing a Marine standing to attention in front of him, he replied, "Yes, Sergeant."

"Have you got a minute to answer a personal question, sir?"

"What do you mean by personal?"

"I am considering my future, and you may be able to help."

"Yes, if you are quick."

"Sir, I am looking for information about the fleet of ships planning to go to New South Wales. Unfortunately, I am having difficulty finding any facts."

"I have not seen or been told much about it, but I can tell you this. A fleet of over ten ships is expected, and I believe the Sirius is the flagship. There will be convicts aboard, both men and women. If you are thinking of putting your name down, you may be lucky, as I believe most ships will have Marines on board. Your commanding officer should know how to apply for the transfer. I am not sure I can help you any more than that. That is all I know. Is that it, Sergeant?"

"Sir."

With that, William left Gun Wharf and walked back to his barracks. It took a while as he thought long and hard about the risks of taking such a long voyage into the unknown. So many unanswered questions remained, but he was warming to the idea of such a life-changing adventure. Later in the afternoon, he returned and went straight to his bunk, only to find a note on the pillow.

Firstly, he looked at the sender's name. It was as he suspected, from Captain Evans, and he read on:

"Sergeant, I have found out the following:

1/ There is an 11-ship fleet now being assembled for the voyage to New South Wales

2/ HMS Sirius is the flagship, accompanied by HMS Supply

3/ Captain Arthur Phillip has been appointed governor

4/ Over 200 marines will be embarking

5/ Over 800 convicts are expected to board

6/ The fleet is planning to leave in April or May

7/ They are looking for more marines

If you wish to join the fleet, I suggest you report to Captain Jones, who can be found on the top floor of the same building as my office. Please keep me informed as to the outcome of any inquiries."

While the note did not add much to what he already had found out, at least he had now been given a contact name.

Although Richard was ribbed by some of his old comrades that evening, he had managed to hold his head high, particularly when he mentioned that he intended to join the assembling fleet. A few had heard of it, but none had any more knowledge over and above what he now already knew.

Richard arrived at Captain Jones's office early the following day, surprised to find no one in the outer office. There was no sign or name anywhere. He had only managed to find the correct office by asking a rating when he arrived at the top floor.

Looking around and wondering what the procedure should be, he knocked on the inner office door and waited. Then waited some more, so he knocked again. Still no answer. He carefully tried the door handle. It was locked, so he assumed the captain was out. Finding a chair in the corner, he sat down, hoping the captain would return shortly. Fortunately, he arrived within about 10 minutes.

"Captain, I would like to speak to you if possible."

"I assume it has something to do with the fleet?"

"Yes, sir."

The captain opened the door with a key and said, "Right, come in."

The captain supplied further information during the next quarter hour or so with most answers to his liking. It seemed to Richard that joining the fleet would undoubtedly be a challenge and very different from his role at Fort Cumberland. He decided then and there to volunteer to join the fleet travelling to New South Wales in a few months.

Chapter 9

It became clear that Elizabeth and her family could, now that William's application had been accepted, take steps to join the fleet travelling to New South Wales. He was told that he would be helping a Mr. John White, the appointed Surgeon General of the fleet and the new colony and that he would be attached to one of the fleet's ships. The appointment was made in early February 1787, and William was informed they could expect to sail sometime in April or May that year.

While Elizabeth had never been on a boat or ship of any kind, she was extremely keen to take the voyage. Her mother was far more practical about the whole thing, still with doubts but understanding that they were now committed. She then began to sort out her personal and family belongings seriously. They had been told that space was extremely limited and only items that could be packed into a trunk could be taken on the ship.

While continuing to function as a surgeon for the local area, William slowly arranged his affairs so that he could leave the practice. This included introducing Thomas, who had acted as his assistant for some time, and who was now going to take over the practice, on how everything worked. One of the significant worries for William was their two-story stone house, which he had owned for some time and was worth considerable money. He had offered the house to a few people he knew, but they either could not afford it or already had a house they were happy with.

As soon as her mother agreed she could make the move public, Elizabeth had several discussions with those she knew. A number were horrified by such an idea, while others were envious of her participating in such a marvellous adventure. Once she knew she would be joining the fleet, she became even more interested in ships, so she regularly crossed the road outside her house and watched the large sailing vessels coming and going. She pictured herself standing on the foredeck of a ship with the wind and the sea spray blowing on her face. She could nearly feel it. She also watched the waves disappear under the bow of each ship as they moved in and out of the harbour. Her anticipation heightened with every over-the-road visit.

Her father, William, who also wanted to know as much about the trip as possible, started to speak to those around him to find out as much as he could about the fleet going to the new colony. While a few had read or heard something about Captain James Cook's voyages to the Pacific Ocean, in the main, they were very ignorant of the area or its history. This lack of knowledge was somewhat concerning, but it proved that the expedition would be a true adventure and a test of strength of character and spirit. He was getting increasingly interested as time went by, imagining the exciting challenges it would provide.

As the time for the fleet to begin collecting in the area had now arrived, William was advised to report directly to Mr. John White, the Surgeon General, who would then outline his fleet duties. As Mr. White spent much of his time visiting the various vessels as they arrived in turn at the anchorage, finding the exact time to speak to William was difficult. Eventually, the call came late on a Monday afternoon.

William arrived at Commissioner's House, where he was to meet Mr. White, early on Tuesday morning. Arriving at the front entrance, a pair of naval ratings greeted him, "Please state your business, sir," piped up one of them.

"I am William Johnson, a surgeon applying to join the fleet sailing to New South Wales. I have an appointment with the Surgeon General, Mr. White."

"Thank you, sir," he promptly swung on his heels and disappeared into Commissioner's House.

After several minutes, he returned and said, "Follow me, sir."

The rating sprinted up the two flights of stairs, with William hurrying to keep up with him. They arrived at the landing and took a hard right turn along a long hallway to an open office door. Popping his head into the office, the rating spoke, "Sir, here is Mr. Johnson."

"Thanks. Please show him in."

William entered the room, which he noticed was an outer office, upon which a voice said, "Please sit down, Mr. Johnson." Looking around the room, William saw it was quite large, but it was sparsely furnished; the walls were bare, and there were no pictures or other adornments. He sat down as directed.

The door to the inner office was closed, and he could hear voices coming from inside, but what was being said could not be understood. Suddenly, the door opened, and a naval officer, a midshipman, came hurrying out the door and left the outer office quickly, not looking right or left as he went. This action not only surprised William but also gave him reason for concern. "I wonder what that was all about?" he thought.

William waited for some time, all the while staring through the open door as it had not been closed properly, although from where he was sitting, he could not see anybody inside. The waiting was starting to get to him as he impatiently moved around on the hard seat, straightening one leg, then the other, and then alternate bum cheeks. His damaged leg was still sore, and although he could at least walk with a limp, sitting on this hard seat was becoming difficult. He was unsure that he would have continued to sit on this uncomfortable seat for so long if he had not committed his family and told everyone else that they were joining the fleet. Eventually, he heard the noise of a chair scraping on the hard wooden floor from inside the office, which immediately heightened his expectation.

Then a voice from the doorway, "Mr. Johnson, please come in."

William went into the office and looked around as he assumed that there must have been someone else present.   There was not. "Strange, he thought."

"Please sit down. I understand you wish to join the fleet going to New South Wales as an assistant surgeon. Is that correct?"

Understanding the importance of the position of Surgeon General of a complete fleet, William formally replied, "Yes sir, that is correct."

"It says here that you have owned and operated your own surgery in Portsmouth for over ten years."

"That is true."

"Would you be travelling alone, or would someone be accompanying you?"

Hesitating, William replied, "I have a wife and a daughter who will be coming with me."

"That is possible, particularly accompanying a person with your skills."

"If I may, sir, what duties could I expect?"

"Most ships will have a qualified medical person on board, and you would be one of them. You would have to look after the entire crew, the marines on board, the convicts, and any other passengers. In other words, everyone on board. When you arrive in New South Wales, you will have to apply your knowledge and skills for the benefit of the whole settlement for a minimum of 3 years. What you did after that would be up to you. The trip will take about 6 or 7 months, so it is a long sea voyage, which will be a real challenge in itself. You would, of course, be paid for your services, and all the transport costs for you and your family to the new colony would be paid for. How does that sound?"

"That seems fair and reasonable, sir. I am certainly interested in taking up the challenge."

"Well, you are lucky. We thought we had enough for the trip, but one surgeon had to pull out, so a position is available that needs to be filled at once. Several ships in this area already have convicts aboard, and they and their guards need immediate medical attention. Can you start as early as next Monday?"

Although feeling somewhat unsure of himself, William thought he was expected to answer the question there and then, so he replied, "I would have liked to discuss this with my family, but as I have to make a prompt decision, I accept your proposal."

With that acceptance, Mr. White replied, "That is very kind of you. I will write out your appointment now and include what is expected of you. As you would know by now, the fleet is starting to arrive here in Portsmouth, and it should be fully assembled by the end of March. In the meantime, a couple of ships carrying convicts have already arrived, and those aboard will require attention. I will visit the individual ships as they arrive and again before the fleet sails. Any questions?"

"No sir, not at this stage."

"If you wait for about half an hour, I should have written out your appointment document by then, and you can start next week. I will also supply details of what I would like you to do over the next few weeks. So, you can pick everything up from the corporal outside when I have finished?"

"Thank you, sir; I appreciate your confidence."

With that said, William left the office, walked around outside for a while, and waited for the documents to be prepared. The walking helped him accept the enormity of what he had just done. He eventually sat down on the doorstep and started thinking about what Ann and Elizabeth would think and say and what he had just committed them to. The whole idea was more than daunting, and while he accepted the challenge, he was apprehensive at the same time. It would be scary, challenging, and somewhat wild, and he was unsure which of these he should be most concerned about. William was still having difficulty taking it all in as his head was swimming with many concerns, thoughts, and ideas.

A little later, and after reasonably accepting the appointment in his mind, William picked up the documents, and there were quite a few. After a quick scan of the documents, he decided not to read them in detail until he got home and broke the news to Ann and Elizabeth. He also pondered on the best way to introduce what an extreme and challenging undertaking the whole trip and experience would be. Finally, thinking aloud, he said to himself, "What have I got myself and my family into?"

William's leg gave him twinges as he walked home, but his thoughts were on other, more important things, so it was not overly troubling. He arrived home, carefully unlocked the front door, opened it, and gingerly entered the house. He deliberately wanted to convey a sense of calmness and control, although, within himself, that was far from the case. Knowing that Ann was probably in the kitchen, he immediately headed there. He got halfway down the hall when Ann called out, "Is that you, William?" but the voice did not sound like it was coming from the kitchen.

"Yes, it's me. Where are you?"

"Upstairs, cleaning the bedrooms."

"Is Elizabeth here?"

"Yes, she is outside hanging out some bedding."

"Well, could you both come into the front parlour as I have something important to tell you."

William entered the parlour, spread out the documents he received from Mr. White, and sat down in one of the padded chairs. He thought that either Ann or Elizabeth would first ask what all those documents were about, allowing him to start the somewhat delicate conversation. He was not wrong; as soon as Elizabeth came into the room, she noticed the paperwork and at once said, "What is all that about?"

"Ah, that is what I wanted to talk to you about. Take a seat over there, as this may take a while to explain fully."

Ann, not sure what this was all about and not wanting to make things awkward for William, saw all the papers, sat down, and said nothing.

On the other hand, Elizabeth was usually very inquisitive, at once wanting to know more and said, "Is this about what we have been talking about? Moving, that is."

"Yes, it is. I will tell you about my visit to the Surgeon General of the new settlement of New South Wales, who is also the head surgeon of the fleet. I will tell you everything I know, so please do not interrupt me." William went on to explain nearly everything that had happened during his discussion with the Surgeon General. As he continued, he could see that Ann and Elizabeth were becoming somewhat impatient as he would not allow them to interrupt him and ask questions.

No sooner had William paused for a couple of seconds when Elizabeth, in her enthusiasm, jumped out of her seat and blurted out,

"Goodness gracious me! Does all that mean we are actually going? What are all those documents about?"

"Well, there is one thing I have not told you. As I have committed to join the fleet, I will start working on a ship next Monday. One of these papers is my authority to work on convict prison ships in this area. The object is to ensure that as many convicts as possible are in the best physical condition before the fleet sails."

More concerned about her home and possessions, Ann asked, "So we must sell this house and all the furniture? How long have we got to organise all that?"

"Don't worry too much about that, Ann; we have about 2 or 3 months to sort that out, and it should be possible over that time. Now, Elizabeth, the documents you see on the table are, well, come over here, and I will show you."

Ann came over to the table with Elizabeth, and William went through them one by one, which seemed to satisfy them both, at least from the formal appointment and subsequent responsibilities point of view. Elizabeth showed her usual enthusiasm about the whole trip, while her mother was more inclined to ask what was needed to pack up and get aboard a ship.

As none of them had ever been aboard a sailing vessel before, they started to surmise what it would be like and how they would cope. There were also many unanswered questions to this whole exercise, so the entire family agreed to get answers to their own questions from anyone they could. They lived in a Royal Navy town, so there should be plenty of people able to answer some of their questions. However, the more they talked, the more it became apparent to all three that they had much more to learn before they would feel comfortable and confident of taking a ship to the other side of the world.

Chapter 10

After Richard had heard his application to join the fleet was successful, he was informed by Captain Jones that his services would be needed on board one of the ships that were starting to congregate in the Portsmouth area. First, he would need permission from his current commanding officer to get a transfer, and then he was to report to a Captain Martin for his next posting. He had no difficulty getting his existing commanding officer's permission.

The next morning, Richard, even though he had been told where to find Captain Martin, found it necessary to ask various ratings on the dock before eventually finding him. He was a relatively small man, at least in height, but as Richard approached, he could hear a strong and confident voice giving instructions to a Lieutenant. Slowing his walk somewhat, Richard judged his arrival just as the captain finished speaking, so, catching the corner of his eye, he stood to attention and said, "Sergeant Clarke reporting for duty, Sir."

Looking up, the captain hesitated for a couple of seconds before he said, "Sergeant, your name or face is not familiar, so why are you talking to me?"

"Captain Jones ordered me to, sir."

"Ah, yes, and I assume you will be joining the fleet. What were his instructions?"

"To report to you, sir."

"That's fine. Lieutenant Jenkins, whom I was just speaking to, will be your superior, and I suggest you try and find him and advise him that you have spoken to me. As you can see, we are starting to load these two ships, and you will be assisting in keeping the ships and the cargo secure. Any questions?"

"No, sir."

Richard saluted, turned, and walked back along the wharf, looking for the lieutenant. He noticed a few marines, both on the ship's decks and on the wharf, so he assumed that the lieutenant would not be far away.

Richard noted that the ships were not of the Navy, and their names were the Golden Grove and the Fishburn. Then, taking note of what was being loaded, he assumed they were the fleet's store and supply vessels. As the lieutenant was not on the wharf, Richard approached the loading ramp of the Fishburn and spoke to the private marine standing there, "Private, I am looking for the lieutenant. Can you help?"

"Yes, Sergeant, he is below deck at the stern."

With that direction, Richard climbed up the loading ramp and onto the deck of the vessel, then turned aft towards the rear hatch. While Richard was not familiar with the layout of this type of ship, he did know that most of the interior of the ship, the hold, was just a large open storage area. He also realized there would be space for the crew and passengers to sleep, working spaces, and general storage space for ship stores, but over 80% of the interior space would be for cargo.

Richard kept away from those workers loading cargo, and it appeared that they were all convicts, except for those giving the orders. Then, arriving at the rear hatch, he looked over the edge and called out into the empty void, "Is Lieutenant Jenkins there?"

A faint voice replied from the blackness, "Who wants to know?"

Richard replied, "Sergeant Clarke reporting for duty, sir."

"All right, Sergeant, wait there. I will be on deck shortly."

"Sir."

While Richard had served on a few ships during his time in the Navy and the Marines, he was unfamiliar with this type of vessel, so he decided to look around while he had the opportunity. The deck was not as cluttered as a fighting ship, which seemed to make it roomier, although the overall length and width were not as large. There were two holds, the main one in the middle and another smaller one in the stern. He fully realized that it was not only essential to secure the cargo from theft during the time it left the wharf until it was placed in the hold, but that the convicts themselves also needed oversight. He was also trying to note all the differences this ship had against the naval ships he was familiar with.

Richard was quickly bought to his senses and surprised when he realized that the lieutenant was trying to get his attention, "Sergeant, over here. I assume Captain Martin has directed you.

"That is correct, sir."

"As you can see, we are loading general cargo that goes on continuously for about 10 hours every day. We are short a sergeant, so you will oversee the eight men on this detail. You will be responsible for ensuring there is no cargo theft and that no harm comes of it, plus ensuring that the convicts are on the job and do not escape. I am usually around the dock area if you need me. Any questions?"

"Not really, sir. When do you want me to start?"

"Right away. Well, as soon as possible as I have been doing your job up to now. I suggest you quickly check out the cargo on the wharf, what is in the hold, and where it is being stored, and at the same time, see who is doing what. I will stay here for the next few hours, and then you can take over. Understand?"

Richard replied, "Yes sir," upon which he turned and went down the gangway to inspect the cargo on the wharf, thinking this would be the best place to start. He noticed a continuous stream of carts and large wheelbarrows arriving with a wide variety of goods and stores. Most were not very big and therefore did not hold a great deal, so a constant flow was necessary to keep the convict gangs busy and maintain a reasonable flow of cargo. Richard also noted that most of the goods were either in wooden crates, trunks, or tied together in bundles, which meant that many were quite heavy, and they sometimes required two convicts on each ship's hand cart to get them up the gangway. Smaller heavy items were usually loaded onto a wheelbarrow and manhandled onto the ship by a single convict.

Richard decided to return to the hold and continue his exploratory rounds, this time hoping to look at the type of cargo on board and how it was being stored. He had been told that there were three special store vessels with the fleet and that two of the ships now on this wharf, out of the three, would be his responsibility, although he would only work one at a time. He noticed the huge variety and number of goods already loaded, including spades, hoes, axes, nails, ploughs, iron pots, spinning wheels, chisels, knives, material, leather, bedding, etc. plus a huge variety of non-perishable food and clothing. He realized that everything needed for a community to live in a new country, which now had absolutely nothing, was being loaded. He also understood that it was essential that they all arrived in good order. Lives depended on it.

Each vessel in the fleet would also need to carry enough food and other stores for their own use until it arrived at their next port of call. The organisation required to buy, transport, and load such a huge quantity of goods was more than Richard could envisage. The scope and variety of the supplies that he could see coming aboard were beyond his imagination.

By the time Richard had had a good look around, it was time to catch up with the lieutenant and get his final orders. He found him on the top deck.

"Sir, I have had a look around and I now have an idea as to what is needed to load these two ships. I assume the Golden Grove is just like this one?"

"Yes, Sergeant, it is, although the actual goods loaded may vary. I have informed the other ranks that you will be taking over from me as of now, and I suggest you make yourself known to each of them as you go about your business. You can make your way back to the barracks with them, and they will point out the sergeant's quarters. Any questions?"

"No sir, I can handle it from here." Richard came to attention and saluted, upon which the lieutenant went ashore. After his recent experience at Cumberland Fort, he immediately thought, "I had better not mess this job up!"

Richard soon became used to the routine of watching the carts unload on the wharf, making sure all was correctly loaded aboard the ship, and ensuring the convicts did their jobs and, at the same time, they did not leave the area. It was a job that required him to keep his wits about him and not to stay too long in any one place, as such routine would allow a convict to take advantage of that fact.

The entire process went well for a couple of weeks until one convict thought he could get away with, what he thought, was a cunning plan.

The carts would often line up in a long queue, with as many as 10 of various sizes, one behind the other. As most of the items were in smaller lots, they were soon dispatched up the gangway and into the holds, allowing each cart to move off quickly. Sometimes the cargo would build up on the wharf if the unloading of carts was quicker than loading the ship. At the end of the day, the aim was for no cargo to be left on the wharf.

One day, while Richard watched the process, he became aware of what seemed like unusual behaviour from a particular driver and one of the convicts unloading a cart. The actions of these two individuals were unusual in that both spoke to each other far more than usual. This was not typical, as nearly all cart drivers and convicts were unknown to each other, so it caught Richard's eye. He walked over to the cart just before it started to move off.

"Hey, you," he called to the driver, "Pull over there," pointing to a place away from the others. "I want to have a look in your cart."

Immediately after that, Richard ran over to the convict, who was starting to climb the loading ramp with a sack from the same cart on his shoulder.

"Come with me, now!"

"What me?" replied the convict.

"Yes, you! Come with me and bring that sack with you."

The convict reluctantly followed Richard to the stopped cart, dropped the sack on the ground, and stood there. "Somethings not right here," thought Richard.

The cart driver suddenly said, "You can't do this to me; I have another load to do today. I don't have time!"

"Yes, I can. You can go in a minute if everything is as it should be. I want to look in the back," upon which Richard moved around and looked more closely into the back of the cart.

He could see what looked like an empty sack in the front corner, and it looked a bit larger and bumpier than it should have been. Richard climbed into the back, stepped over to the sack, and lifted it. Immediately he did that, the convict, standing alongside the cart, quickly looked around to see who else was watching and then took off running back down the wharf.

Richard, wondering how to manage both men simultaneously, remembered a marine near the gangway; he called out, "Marine, chase that running convict and get him back here quick, smart."

The marine looked up and took off in pursuit while calling out for the convict to stop. The convict was wearing a light pair of leg irons, which hampered his ability to run very fast, so the marine soon caught up with him. He grabbed him by the scruff of the neck and half dragged him back towards the cart and Richard. The convict was cursing under his breath all the way, occasionally struggling to escape, but the marine had him in a firm hold.

While all that was going on, Richard started to examine the uncovered sack once again when he then remembered the driver, "Stay there. Don't move!"

The sack was not just an empty sack thrown in the corner of the cart, as it was lumpy and heavy.

"Don't worry about that, Sergeant, that sack's mine!" called out the driver.

"I will have a look inside anyway."

Richard untied the rope around the neck of the sack and peered inside.

"You did say this was yours, did you not? Well, what would you be doing with a sack full of files? These are not yours, and I believe they belong on board the ship."

"They really are mine, Sergeant."

"Well, I will let the lieutenant decide that."

By this time, the marine had returned the escaping convict to the cart. Richard told him to take the driver and the convict to the base of the gangway and await instructions. The marine grabbed two powerful handfuls of collars and marched them to the gangway.

Richard half dragged the sack of files off the cart to where other items were awaiting loading. He left the sack there with the neck open. Richard was unsure where the lieutenant was, or, for that matter, what to do with the suspect thieves. He could not see the lieutenant on the wharf, so he climbed back on board the ship to find the senior private marine he knew was there.

Finding him near the aft hatch, he asked, "I have caught two suspected thieves of the ship's cargo, and I need to advise the lieutenant. Do you know where I could find him?"

Pointing to a building on the wharf's edge, the marine replied, "Yes, Sergeant, he has an office in that building over there."

"Thanks."

Richard left the ship and walked across the wharf and into the building. He saw the lieutenant sitting at a desk in an office on the right. "Sorry to interrupt you, sir, but something important has come up. I have caught a cart driver and one convict stealing a sack of files. What do you want me to do with them?"

"Oh! I see. Let's go and have a look."

Richard and the lieutenant crossed the wharf to where the two suspects sat—neither looked very happy at being caught because they both realized the punishment for stealing. Seven years in jail at the minimum, or even hanging, was not an impossibility.

The lieutenant ordered the private, "Take them both to the forecastle, shackle them so they cannot get away, and come back here. I will get to them later."

Richard asked the lieutenant, "Is there anything else you want me to do?"

"Can you write, Sergeant?"

"Somewhat, sir."

"Well, to make things easier and save you from going to court, write up what you found in the cart and who the two suspects are. Leave it in that office where you found me earlier."

"Yes, sir. Anything else?"

"No, continue what you were doing after that."

After writing his very minimal report, Richard returned to the wharf to observe what was happening between the other cart drivers and convicts. He assumed others could be involved in a similar racket, so a close eye was needed. The carts kept on coming, sometimes singly, sometimes in groups. This ship seemed to be loading many smaller items, so the carts were inclined to be smaller, while the other ship was loading bigger items from much larger carts. Every cart seemed to be unloading correctly, at least according to the relevant paperwork. The supervisor on this loading ramp took the papers from each driver, had a quick look at what was coming aboard, and waved the waiting convicts to the cart with little time to do much else.

What amazed Richard more than anything else was the variety of drivers, some old, some young, some sullen, some cheerful, some cooperative, some not, and on and on the various types went. Occasionally, drivers would argue about who should go first, particularly if they arrived at the unloading spot at the same time. The supervisor usually sorted that out, except for one occasion.

Richard had just returned from getting a drink of water and walking back down the ramp when he heard loud voices from further up the wharf.

An argument had become heated as the volume of voices increased to the point that Richard clearly heard what was being said.

"You bastard, what the hell do you think you are doing?" came a hysterical male voice.

"None of your bloody business, you shithead," replied a squeaky voice.

"Don't call me a shithead. I'll knock your bloody head off," upon which the speaker grabbed the other driver by the arm, who promptly fell off the cart and landed heavily on the ground. The driver struggled to his feet, and although smaller than his assailant, he charged at him with all his might. The bigger man was not expecting such a violent reaction, so he caught the full force of the charge and fell backwards onto the ground.

Picking himself up, shaking his head to clear his thoughts, he yelled, "That is enough of that; I am going to twist that ignorant head right off your bloody shoulders."

Raising himself to his maximum height, he approached the much less intimidating driver with a furious look. Although his intention was clear, it was also apparent to Richard that this would not end well.

By this stage, Richard had reached the two men, and he soon realized that the situation would become deadly unless he intervened in the fight quickly. He yelled out, "Stop that immediately," fully understanding that neither man was interested in what he was saying or even heard him for that matter. While the assailant was a larger man, he was no bigger than Richard, which gave him the confidence to move in between the two fighting men.

Both combatants were surprised to find a red-coated marine in their midst, so they paused for a second or two before continuing to attack each other by going around each side of Richard. Richard looked like a maypole as they danced around him to reach their opponent. Thinking how ridiculous this situation was, Richard reached out and luckily grabbed both by their clothing. Holding on with all his strength, he swung them both around in the same direction they were already travelling. Unfortunately, this caused both to gather speed and lose their footing, at which point Richard released his grip. Completely off balance, they were both flung outward.

The larger of the two men could not keep on his feet as he headed toward the driver's cart, entirely out of control. He put his hands out in front of him, but his hands missed the edge of the cart, which meant he could not stop himself from hitting his head on the corner. He let out a blood-curdling scream and then slowly slumped to the ground.

The other driver also fell heavily to the ground and then decided to stay there for several seconds while he gathered his wits about him. He said nothing as he stumbled to his feet, noticing that his attacker was no longer a danger as he was lying in a crumpled heap alongside the cart.

Assuming the larger man was not likely to get up anytime soon, Richard went over to the other man and said, "You stay right there. I will be back for you in a minute." He went over to the slumped figure, looked at his face, and at the same time checked for a pulse in his neck There was none. He checked again by testing the man's wrist. Still no pulse. The blow to the head had been fatal, and, unfortunately, the man had died on the spot.

By this time, a few cart drivers and bystanders had gathered closely around the scene, and Richard yelled at them to stand back. He wanted to keep a clear head without any further distractions.

A young boy of perhaps eight stood in the small crowd and seemed very interested in the proceedings. Not wanting to leave the scene, Richard, pointing to the office on the landward side of the wharf, asked the boy to report what had just occurred to the lieutenant and ask him to attend. The young boy sprinted off towards the office.

Richard returned to the driver, still standing quietly where he initially landed, and said, "What was that all about?"

Although looking like he was not injured, the driver spoke with a slow slur in this reply, "Nothing much. He just wanted to look at what was in my cart."

Richard became somewhat suspicious and said, "Well, just so I know there are no other problems, I am going to look in your cart. Come with me."

Both the driver and Richard inspected the cart's contents, and although Richard could not see what was in the secure crates, everything else looked as it should be.

Richard had seen the fight himself and accepted that the driver did not cause the accident that killed the other man, so he let the driver get back on his cart and in line.

The lieutenant arrived shortly after this, and Richard explained the circumstances leading up to how the dead man had died and why he had let the driver go. The lieutenant accepted the story, recommended that Richard return to his usual duties, and said he would organise what needed to be done. Richard then returned to where the ships were being loaded and to his regular job, overseeing the security of the fleet's valuable cargo.

Richard continued checking the loading operation on both the Fishburn and the Golden Grove for the next couple of weeks, and luckily, there were very few significant loading difficulties during that time. Richard thought the word had gotten around that it did not pay to buck the system. By then, the date of the fleet's departure was not that far away, and the excitement around the place grew. This only made Richard think about the future and look even more toward a new, exciting, and adventurous chapter in his life.

Chapter 11

As soon as Elizabeth and her family had decided to join the fleet sailing to New South Wales, they all pitched in as a family into whatever needed to be done.

Elizabeth started to ask questions of everybody she met about what was involved with sailing on such a long voyage, beginning a new life in a new country, and what life may be like with convicts aboard. Most had no knowledge or idea of any kind other than to say what a tremendous adventure it would be. However, they were all pleased for Elizabeth in what they thought would be a new and challenging experience. While Elizabeth became excited about such an adventure, she was also scared and anxious about the unknowns. Some of her friends were concerned about her taking such a trip to the other side of the world, while others were somewhat envious of her opportunity to experience the bigger, wide, wide world.

Ann, Elizabeth's mother, was far more concerned about all the planning and actions necessary to get ready to sail on such a long sea voyage. Not only that, but she had to arrange to sell her many more oversized personal items. She also knew that she could only take a limited number of small household items as space was very limited on the ship. The same applied to each of the family's things. The main question was what to take and what to leave behind, which she found difficult as she had never moved further than a couple of miles before.

On the other hand, William was more concerned about the sale of the house, as the market for such a house was not that large. Some of his friends had mentioned they could be interested in buying his home, but that was years ago. So, he began his sale journey by asking friends and neighbours if they knew of anyone interested in buying it, but this always ended up with him having to explain in detail why he was selling. The fact that he could not find anyone interested made the explanations they always demanded frustrating. It was proving far more complicated than he first thought.

One day, Elizabeth suddenly thought of her tutor, Mrs. Williams, as she had often made complimentary comments about the house. Elizabeth thought it best to inquire herself, and accordingly, because she only lived a short distance away, she decided to walk to her house and broach the subject.

Elizabeth mentioned her intention to talk to Mrs. Williams to her mother, who thought it unwise for her to walk that far by herself. The next day, Ann and Elizabeth arrived at the house and knocked on the front door, which just happened to have one of those strange, complicated-shaped knockers that made it difficult to decide where to grab it. Elizabeth's first choice did not work. The second one did.

Elizabeth was happy that Mrs. Williams answered the door herself, as Elizabeth always found it difficult to first explain to a 3rd party who you were and what you wanted.

"Oh, hello, Elizabeth and Mrs. Johnson! I was not expecting you, but you are always welcome. So, what do I owe the pleasure?"

Elizabeth took the lead, "Sorry to interrupt you Mrs. Williams, but if you have a minute to spare, I wish to ask you an important question."

"Of course, dear, please come inside and sit down. Over there, will do," pointing to a pair of overly stuffed chairs, "I won't be a minute."

Elizabeth and her mother sat on the two chairs just along the entryway, not far from the front door. Looking around as she waited, Elizabeth noted that this house was completely different from hers in that there was no long hallway, and she could not see any stairs. She had not noticed earlier what the outside of the house looked like, so maybe there was not an upstairs.

Mrs. Williams returned in about 5 minutes and explained, "Sorry for taking so long, but I was just in the middle of a complicated design on my weaving loom, and I did not want to forget where I was with the pattern. Now, what did you want to ask me?"

Elizabeth was unsure how to broach the question, even though she had thought about it earnestly since she left home. She hesitated, thinking it may not be wise to blurt the question immediately, so she politely asked, "How have you been Mrs. Williams since I last saw you? All well, I trust?"

"Thank you for starting the small talk. It is appreciated, but I would prefer you get straight to the question. I won't be offended if you are direct." Mrs. Williams smiled at Elizabeth as she said it, which put Elizabeth at ease enough to put the question more directly.

"Mrs. Williams, you know you have made several compliments over the years regarding our house; well, I thought you may be interested in it."

"Oh, I see. Why is that so? Are you moving?"

"Ah, well, you could call it moving, although not in the usual sense. We are all sailing to New South Wales, all part of a large fleet that will take many people there and create a new colony."

"Well, you too, Mrs. Johnson? That is certainly interesting. Are you both keen to go?"

"Yes, I am, and Father is confident, but Mother is not so sure. It will be an exciting adventure that will work out fine once we get there."

"That's good. I am glad to see you are happy. Now, what is that about the house again?"

Elizabeth said, "Father is trying to sell the house, and I thought that you may be interested in buying it."

"Now, that is an interesting question. We have not considered moving or buying another house, so this will need some serious thought. We will come over and talk to your father if we are interested, and I cannot give you any definite answer on that, one way or the other. Happy with that?"

"Thank you, Mrs. Williams. I am glad that you are willing to at least think about it. Sorry to disturb you. Thank you once again."

Ann, who had felt quite comfortable with Elizabeth taking the lead in asking the original question, added, "It is appreciated that you will at least consider purchasing the house. Thank you."

"Thank you both for coming here. We will see what comes of it, and I will let you know."

Elizabeth and her mother left Mrs. Williams's house knowing that the matter would be seriously considered, and they were both sure that William would at least be pleased about that.

Upon arriving home, Ann, while slightly looking forward to the challenge of moving to the other side of the world, was still somewhat apprehensive about what the future might hold. It was a vast undertaking full of potential dangers, not only during the actual voyage but when finally arriving in New South Wales. She went over and over everything in her mind on what needed to be sorted out before they left, and the stress of that, and the sale of the house, kept her awake at night. There was so much to do and not enough time to do it.

Ann eventually found out exactly what space would be allowed on board the ship for the family's personal effects, and that was not very much. It amounted to three large travelling trunks for personal effects and one large one for household items. This meant there would be no space for furniture or other such larger items. It also meant what Ann had feared the most, which was that all such things would need to be either sold or given away.

Knowing exactly what space she had available, Ann wandered around the house, writing down what items she thought she should take on the voyage. The first list was getting too large, but it would be challenging to decide what could or could not fit, and at the same time, trying to prioritize their many smaller precious items. Thinking about that, Ann realized that she needed to be extremely sensible and not be overly sentimental when making such decisions. She finally concluded that she would need some help making the extremely tough decisions on what to take and leave behind.

Considering the whole process and accepting that William was not particularly interested in household items, Ann decided to get Elizabeth's views on the subject.

One morning, after William had gone out to enquire further as to who may be interested in buying the house, Ann caught Elizabeth just as she returned from her regular visits to the other side of the road.

"Elizabeth," she said as she entered the front door, "Can you come into the parlour? I have something to show you."

"What is it?"

"Just come in here, and I will show you," Ann said as she guided Elizabeth to sit beside her on the settee.

"You are being very secretive, Mother. What's going on?"

"I just want your opinion on something."

"Oh, all right then," as Elizabeth relaxed and settled comfortably on the settee.

Ann, not wanting to put forward too big a problem at once, handed Elizabeth only one sheet of paper showing a list of items she thought could be taken on board the ship. Then, she said, "Have a look at that list. What do you think it is?"

"I don't know. It looks like a list of items that are from around here. What does it mean?

Ann explained to her daughter the type of smaller items that could be taken on the ship and, once again, stressed the minimal space available for even those. "This is my first effort trying to decide what we should take," she said. "Understanding what I have just told you, you can appreciate that one large trunk would not hold very much. You would know that only a fraction of what we own would fit into that small space. My problem is deciding exactly what we should take with us and what to leave behind."

With a quizzical look, Elizabeth asked, "But there is not much on that list you have there. Is that the entire list?"

Grabbing the rest of the papers, Ann said, "These other lists are also items I thought I would like to take. The trouble is, there is far too much to fit in one trunk. So, I need to weed out many things, and that is where you come in."

"Me, what can I do about it?"

"Help me sort out what we should take, of course."

"Goodness gracious me! How do you expect me to answer that question?"

"Well, I thought we could find some answers if we put our two heads together. At least, most of the answers."

"Oh, I see. That may work. Let me see what you have on those other lists."

With that, they went through the lists, agonising over every item. It proved far more complicated than Elizabeth first thought, but things were scratched off each list one by one. The hardest part was guessing what they would most likely need when they landed in New South Wales. Looking at what was scratched off and what was left on the various lists, Ann and Elizabeth felt they had done a reasonable job. However, they were also unsure what was left on the list would fit in a large trunk. Not knowing exactly what size the large trunk would be, they decided to leave that decision until packing it and then leaving behind what would not fit.

While Ann and her daughter were trying to sort out what household items to take, William kept moving around Portsmouth, visiting as many persons as possible who he thought may be interested in buying the house. Unfortunately, while there was interest in the place, none were interested in buying it. They had either bought a house recently, were very happy with the place they were already in, or they were not in a financial position to purchase it. Other times, they thought the house was just not suitable for them. The situation was becoming increasingly frustrating, with William unsure who else to contact or where to turn next.

Then he had an idea. He was surprised that it had not occurred to him earlier. Why not approach the Navy? After all, Portsmouth was a prominent naval port. Such ports had high-ranking officers and sub-contractors who may just be interested and able to, purchase a house. Even the navy itself may be interested! William decided to go to Commissioners House and make inquiries as soon as possible.

William arrived at Commissioners House early the following day and approached the guard at the front door, "Excuse me, but I need to talk to someone about purchasing a property. Do you know who that would be?"

The corporal hesitated for a few seconds as this was rather an unusual question, "I am not sure, but I think that the best person to ask would be the lieutenant, whose office is just inside the front door on that side," pointing to the right-hand side.

Moving into the building and then to the right, William noticed that the office door was open, so he carefully entered, although he could not see anybody inside. He stood there looking around when another door at the rear of the room suddenly burst open, and a young man rushed past William and into the hallway. No words were spoken.

Somewhat taken aback, William paused, waiting for someone else to come through the same door. He waited for a few minutes, wondering what to do next. While looking around, he noticed that the walls in the outer office were covered with street maps. "Obviously, I am in the right place," he thought.

Eventually, a lieutenant came through the open doorway, saw William, and said, "Oh, I did not know you were here. Can I help you?"

William noticed the lieutenant had a red face and looked somewhat flustered and bothered by him entering the office. William asked, "Is this an opportune moment, or should I return later?"

"No, no, no. Now would be fine. Please excuse the drama, but that was my son leaving after an argument. Now, what can I do for you?"

"My name is William Johnson, and I am a surgeon who has been taken on to sail with the fleet now preparing to sail to New South Wales. As you know, it sails shortly, so I am trying to sell my house. My problem is that I am currently having difficulty finding a buyer, and as you appreciate, time is of the essence. Do you think that the Navy or anyone else connected with the Navy would be interested?"

"Ah, you certainly have a problem there. You will need to tell me exactly what kind of house you have and where it is. I cannot think of a need right now, but we sometimes are in the market for ourselves or somebody who works with us."

Picking up a pen, the lieutenant started to write something down and then asked for all the relevant details., which William willingly supplied.

The lieutenant said to William, "That is enough detail for now. I will consider it and ask a few questions over the next few days. You can come back on Friday, and hopefully, I have some good news for you. You appreciate that I cannot guarantee anything, but you never know."

Although somewhat disappointed that nothing more definite eventuated, William felt better as there was at least a possibility, "Thanks for that. I will return on Friday, and hopefully, you will have some good news."

Arriving home, William, now somewhat keen to tell Ann some good news, went straight to the kitchen hoping to find Ann, but she was not there, even though that is where he usually found her at this time of day. He left the kitchen and called, "Ann, where are you?"

He heard what he thought was a faint reply, although he had no idea where the voice was coming from, so he called again, "Ann, where are you?"

By this time, Ann had poked her head out of the storage room that was near the front door and replied, "I am here; I need to show you something." Richard just saw the top of her head as she disappeared back into the room.

Arriving at the open door, William could not see Ann, so he called out again, this time in an agitated voice, "Where the hell are you? I am not chasing after you all over the house!"

Ann was behind the door on the other side of a large empty bookcase, so she popped her head around it and said, "Sorry to run you all over the place, but it is important that you see this. I had forgotten all about it."

William then saw what he first thought was an empty sizeable wooden storage box, but looking down at the bottom, he saw what looked like an old, broken, tattered, flat box.

Now somewhat annoyed at what he thought was of no great importance, William said, "Why are you showing me that junk?"

Ann quickly said, "I picked it up, and the box started falling apart, and then I realized what it was. It is that ancient chess set that your father gave you many years ago. I was looking through these boxes, and I had forgotten we even had it, but there it is."

In the first instance, William was still unsure what he was looking at, but then it came to him. This was from a long time ago, and it had completely escaped his memory. Then it dawned on him, "Oh, I had completely forgotten about that old chess set; it was originally my grandfathers'."

Ann replied, "Yes, you know about those lists I have and how many items I have had to remove because of the lack of room in the trunk. Well, this was not on my list, and we will have to decide if it goes with us on not. There is very little room, and we must decide how important this chess set is. It is certainly not an essential item."

"Oh, I see what you mean. They will not be necessary over there, that's for sure. Maybe we should find a place to store such items. What do you think?"

"That's a good idea, but we must find someone we can trust to leave it with. This whole process is getting harder and harder and is far more difficult than I originally thought. In the short term, I will just put such items aside. You happy with that?"

Suddenly feeling weighted down by the work involved, William moaned and said, "Yeh, that will be fine." Unfortunately, the tough decisions necessary to reduce years of accumulated household items were getting the better of him, to the point that he forgot to tell Ann about his trip to Commissioners House.

Ann reluctantly returned to her sorting other various items that had been in that room for many years. Many proved smelly, dusty, and in such poor condition that one could not even consider taking them. Those never made it onto any list.

William still went into the surgery occasionally to help his earlier assistant, Thomas, mainly when he needed a second hand or another opinion. It appeared that Thomas was handling the role well, and William now felt happy to sign over the whole practice to him just before they leave Portsmouth.

With one thing and another, William forgot which day was what, so he was surprised to realize it was Friday when he promised to return to see the lieutenant at Commissioners House. It was a little later than initially indicated, so he walked across town as quickly as possible.

After going through the check-in process, he arrived at the lieutenant's office to find it closed. He knocked and waited. Within seconds he heard a voice from inside the office that said, "Just a moment."

William took his hand off the doorknob and stepped away from the door, wondering what the holdup was about. Whatever the issue was, it did not affect the lieutenant finally opening the door, who said, "Oh, it is you. I was hoping to see you sometime today. I may have some good news for you."

Entering the office, William quickly replied, "That's good. What have you found out?"

"There is a naval officer currently in Portsmouth with his family who wants to live well away from this base itself. He may or may not buy a home, but the Navy wants to keep him happy, so they may arrange something that could involve your house. Can we arrange for some form of inspection?"

"That would be fine, and I would like a couple of days' notice."

"Well, I assumed that something like that would be preferable, so I tentatively organised the visit for Friday at the end of this coming week if that suits you."

"Friday will be fine. Any idea as to the time?"

"I suggested mid-morning.

"That's fine. Thank you very much, lieutenant. I hope it all works out to everyone's advantage."

William left the office feeling like a great weight had been lifted from his shoulders, even though any formal arrangement had not yet been completed. To a certain extent, it would depend on whether the officer concerned was happy with the house, but William was reasonably confident something could be worked out. He left Commissioners House with a spring in his step and was looking forward to telling Ann and Elizabeth what to expect. He fully appreciated that it was important that the price put on the house would significantly affect the chance of a sale. He also thought an inspection was a good start.

Over the next few weeks, Elizabeth and her mother and father were extremely busy sorting out what would fit in the four trunks, which had by now arrived. They had found buyers for much of their furniture and other belongings, and hopefully, the first step in selling their house. Subject to the house sale, the only difficulty now was trying to organise temporary accommodation until they boarded the ship. The actual sailing date was still not definite. It had already been postponed once, significantly adding to the whole family's apprehension.

Chapter 12

In March 1787, the fleet began to assemble off the Isle of Wight as it prepared to sail to New South Wales. It included eleven vessels, two ships of the Royal Navy, six convict transporters, and three supply vessels. HMS Sirius was selected as the fleet's flagship, with HMS Supply the other naval ship in support. The six convict transporters included the Alexander, Charlotte, Friendship, Lady Penryn, Prince of Wales, and the Scarborough. Accompanying these eight vessels were the three supply/store vessels, the Golden Grove, Fishburn, and the Borrowdale.

The trip was expected to take six to eight months, and it planned to travel via Teneriffe in the Canary Islands, Rio de Janeiro in South America, and Cape Hope in South Africa. Their destination was Botany Bay, New South Wales, a trip of nearly 15,000 miles (24,000klms), crossing the Atlantic and Indian Oceans on the way. The ships were to carry about 1,420 persons, including approximately 800 male and female convicts; the rest comprised the ship's crew, officials, marines, and all their families.

The fleet was under the command of Captain Arthur Phillip, who would assume the position of Governor of the new colony of New South Wales upon their arrival.

Sergeant Richard Clarke was named to be a part of the New South Wales marine detachment after helping with loading two supply vessels for some seven weeks. He was then informed he would be a part of a detachment of 41 marines on the Alexander, which was due to load some 200 convicts. Richard continued to be a part of the security contingent overseeing the two ships he had been working on for some time. As most of the cargo had now been loaded, the usual large number of delivery carts were no longer needed, except for those carrying extra food, water, and other stores for the actual voyage.

Richard received his orders to proceed to the Portsmouth marine headquarters so that the arranged transport could take him and a small contingent of his fellow marines to the Alexander, now moored at Mother Bank, off the Isle of Wight, on the South Coast of England.

The Alexander had already been moored there for some months with most of the expected convicts and many of the marine contingent already on board. Accordingly, Richard joined a few of his compatriots at the wharf in Portsmouth to be taken to Mother Bank, which lies about 5 miles (8klms) south of Portsmouth and off the Isle of White. He travelled in a cart with five other marines, all privates, destined for the Alexander, which was the beginning of the adventure itself, giving them a taste of what they were all looking forward to.

"We are nearly there!" exclaimed one of the privates as the cart came to a halt.

"Don't get overly excited private; we have not even started yet," replied Richard.

Each marine gathered their gear, which, because of the length of the trip, included an extra duffle bag that allowed a few additional long voyage essentials and comforts. They noticed a small sailing vessel tied up alongside the wharf, which they assumed was waiting for them.

Richard, the senior present, ordered, "Gather all your belongings and put them at the top of those loading steps. Stay here, and I will go on board and check if everything is ready."

With that said Richard descended the steps and stepped aboard the vessel. No sooner had he done that when he heard a voice, although he could not see where it was coming from. A sailor popped up from under one of the boat's seats and said, "I was expecting you, Sergeant; where are the rest of you?"

"Up there," said Richard, pointing to the top of the stone steps. "Are you ready for us now?"

"Yes, bring them down. We must wait for a few sailors to return to the same ship."

Richard bounded back up the steps and ordered the marines, "All right you, lot, grab your stuff and climb aboard."

"Yes, Sergeant," was the common response, upon which they climbed down the stone steps and boarded the vessel. It was not very big and had no cabin or enclosed space, but it could carry about a dozen people on bench seats. There were also provisions for oars, if necessary, but today it looked like the wind was favourable.

The marines found seats in the bow while they waited for the Alexander's sailors to arrive. Because this was the beginning of a tremendous adventure for everyone present, much excitable discussion took place, most with no actual knowledge of what they were likely to see or what may occur. Richard included himself in the banter by putting the usual rank formalities to one side as he felt this was allowable under the circumstances. He reminded himself that once on board, all lower ranks would have to respect his authority and the rules of the Marines, as they all had an important job to do.

About 10 minutes after the marines boarded the vessel, the sailors arrived, looking like they had been drinking as a couple were unsteady on their feet. Richard had no direct jurisdiction over them, even though they were all ordinary seamen, so he just kept his mouth shut, at the same time telling himself to watch out for this problem with his men.

Richard had been on many ships over the years, so while the Alexander was new to him, the general layout and procedures were familiar, at least as far as his fellow marines were concerned. The sails were hoisted, and the cutter took off towards the Alexander.

Arriving at the base of a rope ladder hanging down from the ship's side, Richard gave the order, "Climb aboard and wait for me on deck." They all arrived on board, although some carried too much over and above their standard equipment, so they struggled to climb the rope ladder. Richard made a mental note to do something about it if the extra proved to be a real storage problem once on board.

As Richard climbed over the rail, one of the marines already aboard commented, "Welcome aboard, Sergeant, as we travel to the other end of the world!"

"That's enough of that! We are now aboard a ship, and I will now demand the required respect. Wait here, and I will find your quarters."

"Yes, Sergeant," they replied in unison.

Before Richard had time to turn around, a voice called out, "Over here, Sergeant," as the lieutenant made himself known by waving his hand over his head.

Richard replied, "Yes sir," as he to walked over to the other side of the vessel.

The lieutenant peered at Richard as he came closer. He thought he knew him from somewhere but could not remember where.

Richard saluted the lieutenant without recognising him and said, "Sergeant Clarke reporting, sir."

The lieutenant was sure he knew Richard, so he replied, "At ease, Sergeant. I think I know you, but I can't seem to remember where or when."

Unsure of exactly what the lieutenant was getting at, Richard replied, "To be honest, sir, I don't remember you, although I have worked with many officers over the years."

"Never mind, Sergeant, it will come to me in time. Now, I see you have bought along a few more marines. They will be bunked down right under where I am now standing. There are two cabins for that lot, and they must sort themselves out with those already there. Anything else?"

"Not really, other than to ask where us Sergeants are sleeping?"

"Oh, yes, I forgot. There is one other sergeant on this ship, and you will be in with him, and that room is just astern of the other ranks."

"Thank you, sir," upon which Richard saluted and returned to the ship's opposite rail.

As Richard walked across the deck, he noticed a terrible smell coming from the ship's hold. He then remembered that this was not a Navy Man-of-war, which he was used to, but a privately owned convict ship, a completely different type of vessel. He had been advised that most of the ship's convicts had been on board for some time and that it was, obviously, the cause of the repugnant smell. He thought remembering to stay up-wind whenever possible would be wise.

Speaking to the marines who had come with him onto the Alexander, Richard said, "All right, you lot, gather your stuff and follow me."

They gathered their belongings, moved to the rear hatch, climbed the steep ladder to the lower deck, and moved aft. Checking a couple of cabins on the way, he saw a private marine's uniform in one that clearly showed its use and then said to the privates, "This is yours. You will need to work with the others already here."

Richard left them to sort out their quarters, then decided to find his own, which was supposed to be just behind the privates'. Everything is packed so close together on board a sailing ship, all he needed to do was swing around, and there was a cabin. The door was closed, so he knocked and waited. No answer, so he knocked again. Finally, a sleepy voice called out, "Who is that?"

Richard quickly replied through the door, "It's Sergeant Clarke. Am I in the right place?"

"Yes, come in. The door isn't locked."

He opened the door, peered around the small space and noticed a person sitting on the edge of the lower bunk, who said, "I have been expecting you. Come in. I had a terrible time last night and just had to get some much-needed sleep. I'm Michael Jones. Welcome to the ship from hell."

"Richard is my name. Is the top bunk free?"

Receiving a nod, Richard slung his gear onto the bed and noted how narrow it was and how little room was alongside it. The room would be about 6 feet long and 6 feet wide, which meant he could just stretch out in the bunk, and other living space would be at a premium for the two of them. There was not enough room for furniture besides a few hooks on the walls– just enough room to dress and undress in. If two of them tried to dress at the same time, each would undoubtedly need to keep their elbows well in.

Richard sat down on the edge of the lower bunk and asked, "How long have you been aboard?"

Michael, a fellow sergeant in the Marines, was not feeling very talkative as he was not fully awake, so he hesitated before replying, "About two months."

Seeing how the sergeant looked and sounded, Richard said, "That's all right. I will leave you for a while and catch up later," he stood up, opened the door, and quietly closed the door behind him.

Richard went up to the top deck and saw the marine lieutenant and two privates looking down into the forward hold, so he walked over. When he had originally come aboard, there was little noise coming from the hold, but now a great deal of yelling and screaming was coming from the convicts.

Catching the lieutenant's eye, assuming that he may be of use, Richard said in a loud enough voice to overcome the racket, "Sir, can I be of any assistance?"

Moving away from the hold towards the port rail, the Lieutenant said, "Come over here, sergeant; I need to bring you up to date on what has just happened and what you can expect. Most of the convicts already aboard have been on the Alexander for over four months now, and you can understand they are more than sick and tired of that. They have been causing trouble one way or another for weeks now, and we must keep a lid on everything. It could end up fatal, for either them or us. You will be involved directly and take turns with your fellow sergeant, and he should be able to clue you in on how things work around here. Any questions?"

"That will do for now, sir."

"Well, between the other sergeant and myself, we should quickly bring you up to date. By the way, we usually let a small group of convicts at a time up on deck for some fresh air and a hose down, but that will not be happening today."

"Sir."

With that, Richard walked across the deck and joined the two privates still standing near the hold. The racket from that area had lessened somewhat, so he assumed that no further action would be necessary.

Talking to what looked like the senior of the privates, Richard asked, "Private, do you normally get involved with these types of arguments?"

"Not normally, Sergeant; we only get involved if things get out of hand. It is hard to know who started what, so finding the person responsible is nearly impossible. We normally let them sort out their own problems."

"I see. I will obviously have to use your knowledge, as guarding convicts in this situation is not something I am familiar with. What normally happens now?"

"Nothing really, Sergeant. We will stay here briefly to ensure things don't flare up again."

"By the way, private, how many marines are aboard this ship?"

"There are 41, including yourself."

"And convicts?

"About 200, I believe, although there was great sickness aboard recently and some convicts died. It should be much better from now on, as the bilge is now pumped out regularly."

"Understand."

Richard then turned his attention to the hold, peering into the darkness, trying to get a picture of what it was like. He could see that the bulk of the area had been cut off from the stairway by what looked like cages of wood and iron. Rather than one large cage, it was divided into four smaller sections, and it is evident that this kept the convicts confined below decks. He could see many hammocks hanging from cross beam to cross beam or from the edges of the cages, some in place for immediate use, some hanging down to supply more open space. It certainly looked exceptionally crowded with very little room to move, never mind get any exercise.

Richard was about to leave the edge of the hold when a loud, croaky voice rang out, "What the bloody hell are you looking at?"

Not knowing whether it was wise to respond, Richard noticed a large man with long hair staring at him, so he moved away from the edge of the hold and out of sight. Thinking about the comment, he murmured to himself, "I will have to make sure that I am not seen as weak and not in control."

Richard was not entirely sure what his duties would be on board the Alexander, so he thought it wise to find the lieutenant and get further instructions. He did notice that additional provisions were coming over the side of the vessel and being distributed to various areas, obviously stored for safekeeping. The ship's crew seemed to know what they were doing, and he had to dodge them as they moved around the deck and went about their duties. It was a busy place, but it was good to get aboard a ship again, as his recent experiences were beyond his earlier naval or marine knowledge. The only thing that concerned him was that the vessel was carrying approximately 200 convicts, which would undoubtedly complicate everyday shipboard life. Learning and getting familiar with the day-to-day procedures would also be necessary. He went looking for his commanding officer.

He eventually found the marine lieutenant talking to the captain of the Alexander, Captain Duncan Sinclair, near the stern rail. He waited a few yards away for a couple of minutes. As there was no recognition of him even standing there, he decided to go below to his shared cabin, where, hopefully, Sergeant Jones would now be awake and able to explain the routine from a sergeant's point of view.

He entered the cabin to find the sergeant getting dressed in his uniform, upon which Richard said, "Ah, it looks like I caught you at the right time. I wanted to ask you a few questions."

Startled by Richard suddenly entering the cabin, Sergeant Jones said in a surprised voice, "Oh, I was just going to get something to eat if there is anyone in the galley. Come with me, as my watch starts in less than an hour."

"Lead the way," suggested Richard, as he still did not know where anything of importance was on this ship.

On the way out of the door, Richard noticed a simple wooden slide to lock the cabin door from the inside, but there was no way to lock it from the outside. He followed Sergeant Jones past the other rank's sleeping quarters and across to the port side of the Alexander, where they came upon the galley. As the first dog watch, and therefore mealtime for half the crew would start in a little over an hour, the cooks were busy getting the first sitting of the meal ready.

Putting his head through the doorway, Sergeant Jones asked the nearest cook, whom he appeared to know well, "I have not eaten all day. Is there a chance of something?"

"Not bloody likely; I have heard that one before. Can't you see I am busy?" While saying this so everyone else could hear, he slipped Michael a slice of bread without the others noticing, upon which they both slipped away from the galley doorway.

As the lieutenant would be on duty until eight bells on the afternoon watch, they went up to the main deck and walked over to the port rail that looked across the water toward Portsmouth.

158

Richard started the conversation, "As you would know, I am fully aware of what happens on a naval vessel, but having so many convicts travelling on a transport ship like this is all new to me. What are the most important things that I need to know?"

"This lot has been on board for months now, so the situation is different than what one would normally expect at sea. Many of the convicts have a short fuse, so fighting is widespread, and unless it gets out of hand, we do nothing. They usually sort it out themselves. Us marines must not only keep the peace where necessary, but we must organise much of their daily lives. That includes trying to keep things as clean as the surgeon wants, particularly after the number of recent deaths. Also, supervising feeding times can get nasty at times. They are allowed on deck in small numbers at certain times of the day, but we must watch carefully for any absconders. We also get them to throw water at each other occasionally. Those are the main things I can think of. Does that help?"

"Yes, it does. I will take over from you at the end of the first dog watch. Ah, one more question. Does the lieutenant get involved much or leave it to us?"

Michael hesitated before saying, "He does not like the rough stuff very much, so he usually stays clear of that. He only gets involved when we need the additional authority."

"All right, I will keep that in mind, and thanks for the other information; it will come in handy. By the way, how long have you been in the Marines?"

"About seven years, but only a sergeant for the last two years. And you?"

"Nearly ten years, joined the Navy first and then with the Marines for the last five. A little longer than you!"

The two sergeants continued chatting until eight bells signalled the end of the afternoon watch and the beginning of the first dog watch. Michael walked to the area just aft of the Mizzen mast, where the marines usually formed up at the beginning of each watch. They would then move to relieve those on the earlier watch unless they had been previously advised to go directly to affect an immediate relief.

Richard relaxed as he had the next 2 hours free before he was due to go on duty for the last dog watch. Each dog watch would last for 2 hours, and during that time, each watch was expected to eat its evening meal. Richard keenly moved down to the galley as he was looking forward to a hot meal.

Arriving at the galley, he was surprised at how fast the others on his watch got there. Due to his recent outside postings, the movement reminded him that he had not joined in this type of frenetic activity for quite some time. He hesitated outside the group of nearly 15 junior sailors and marines and watched, as he did not personally know anyone on this watch – his watch. There did not seem to be any seniority involved, whether sailor or marine; they just lined up as they got there. He decided to wait.

While Richard watched, a Marine corporal paused at his shoulder and said, "Sergeant, welcome to the Alexander."

Richard turned and answered, "Thanks, corporal; I am Sergeant Clarke. Are there any rules I should be following here?"

"Not really, Sergeant. You can join in anywhere, although I usually hold back until the mad rush is over."

"I see what you mean. I'll take note of that."

The corporal and Richard stood side by side as they waited for the others to get their food, while a few of those waiting were trying to push in before their turn, with the inevitable results. Occasionally they

160

were pulled back by the scruff of their necks and forced to go to the back of the line. With this group, there were very few "pleases'" or "thankyous".

The hot food was dished out in bowls, and each person was provided with a spoon with which to eat it. As the steaming bowls passed Richard, he noticed that it smelt and looked like meat stew, with vegetables added and a small piece of bread on the side. His mouth started to fill with saliva in anticipation. Many of those present just stood nearby and ate; others sat down wherever they could, while others disappeared to who knows where. Finally, the line shortened, and Richard and the corporal moved forward and joined those waiting. No other words were spoken as each received their meal and moved away from the others.

"Do you mind if I join you, Sergeant?"

"Not a problem, corporal, although we must be careful."

Richard knew and understood that there was a fine line between friendly communication on the one hand and keeping a sense of remoteness that is essential for maintaining discipline on the other. He often had to remind himself of that fact.

The stew was delicious and satisfying at the same time, and Richard hoped that the standard could be kept, although he knew that it was tough to do so once they had been at sea for any length of time.

Richard and the corporal devoured their meal, as that was the norm on board a ship, as there was usually limited time for casual conversation. He thanked the corporal, left the table and returned to his cabin, knowing he was on duty shortly. He needed to get his thoughts in order, ensure his uniform was tidy and prepare himself to get back into the routine necessary on board a ship like the Alexander.

Chapter 13

William and his family continued to work tirelessly towards being ready to board one of the fleet's ships on their adventurous voyage, as they knew that there was now a real sense of urgency as the fleet would be sailing in a couple of weeks.

Elizabeth spent much of her time talking to as many young people as possible, although finding someone with actual knowledge of the subject was difficult. With the help of the young people she knew, she managed to speak to a couple of their parents who had overseas and sailing experience. They were encouraging and recommended that she expect anything and everything when taking such a long, ground-breaking trip.

On the other hand, Ann was still finding it challenging to come to terms with the limited baggage she was allowed to take on board the ship. She had been living in a large house for a considerable time now, and she had gathered many homewares and personal items. Sometimes she found herself sitting on the floor in front of something that she had had for many years, and the tears just seemed to flow, even before she had decided whether to take the item or not. The whole process was overwhelming to the point of desperation, but she somehow managed to hold herself together.

William returned to see the lieutenant at Commissioners House on Friday morning, looking forward to a favourable decision from the Navy on the next step to buying their house.

He arrived at the lieutenant's office a fraction early and walked further up the street to pass the time. Commissioners House was right inside the naval shipyards, and many people were coming and going, some in uniform, some not. There were always a few ships in dock, some returning to port, others getting ready by loading the necessary supplies ready to sail. At times it was a bustling place.

William returned to the House, got approval from the guard and knocked on the lieutenant's door.

"Come in," was the muffled response.

William entered and, looking around, could not see the lieutenant, but a voice called from the room next door, "In here, in the other office."

William entered the other room and noticed the lieutenant was standing on a chair, trying to reach something on the top shelf of a tall bookcase.

The lieutenant peered over his shoulder and said, "I thought it was you. That is why I suggested you come in here. I think you will like the news I have for you."

William's thoughts raced as he replied, "That's good; what can you tell me?"

"Hang on a minute, don't get too excited," said the lieutenant as he climbed from the chair. "Much of what I have to say is good, some not so good. Firstly, you know that they are interested in buying the house, but the price they have offered is even less than what I first indicated and now is well below what you were hoping for."

In the first instance, it was difficult for William to know whether he should be happy or not. Finally, wanting to know exactly what was on offer, he responded, "Don't leave me in suspense. How much!"

"Let's return to the other office, and I will read exactly what has been said."

They both walked back into the main office. The lieutenant offered William a seat and then removed a sheet of paper from a file on his desk.

"Let me see," the lieutenant offered, "it says. Please advise Mr Johnson that we are willing to buy his house, subject to a more detailed inspection, for 350 pounds. I know that is less than you hoped, but that is what they are now offering."

"Heavens forbid! That is a great deal less than I thought."

"Yes, I can understand that, but that is what is being offered. What do you want me to say in my reply?"

"Well, to be quite honest, I have not got many options at this stage, have I? So, I will have to accept the offer.

"They may be interested in renting the house, but that would not give you a lump sum, and negotiating would take time. Do you still want them to go ahead with the offer formally?"

William paused, thinking about all the pros and cons of selling the house at such a discounted price. What would Ann think? Can I forget this offer and keep trying to sell at a better price? Are there any other options?

Finally, he concluded, "While I am not happy with the price, I think it best that I accept the offer under the circumstances. Please make the necessary arrangements; the required inspection can occur at any time. By the way, thanks for your efforts so far."

William left the office with two conflicting thoughts going through his head. One made him quite happy that the house had been sold and he did not have to worry about that anymore, and on the other hand, he was disappointed that the financial transaction had not gone as he had hoped. He left the Commissioners House feeling somewhat down, with his hands stuffed in his pockets, thinking about how he would tell Ann. It was a slow walk home, and it seemed to take forever.

William eventually arrived home, only to find the front door locked. Upon unlocking it, he discovered that neither Ann nor Elizabeth was home, so they must have gone out somewhere. "I wonder where?" he thought.

William went straight into the parlour, slumped into the nearest comfortable chair and lay back, thinking about the next step in this extraordinarily worrying and unknown undertaking. Travelling to the other side of the world gave him a severe headache in more ways than one.

Earlier the same morning, while William was at Commissioners House, Elizabeth and Ann were in their usual places in the kitchen when they heard a loud knocking on the front door. Ann could not think of who it could be, as William would still be at Commissioners House. However, the commanding sounding knock on the door caused her to very cautiously open the front door, unsure who would likely be there.

The first thing she noticed was the size of the man in a bright red uniform, and then she heard a deep voice, "Excuse me, madam, but I need to inform you that there are a couple of escaped convicts in this area, and I wonder if you have seen them. They are both dangerous, so your safety is of concern."

Ann hesitated, as the sight of a marine in full uniform was not something she expected to see on her doorstep. Finally, she replied, "N,n no, I have seen no one this morning."

"Well, they are in this area, and we need to search everywhere, including your house, just in case they could have got in without you knowing. So, these marines will now search. Is there anyone else in the house right now?"

"Yes, my daughter. Shall I go and get her?"

"One of my men will go with you." He turned behind him and said, "Private, go with this lady to get her daughter." And at the same time, he said to the other marines present, "Search this house."

Ann was just about ready to go with the marine upstairs to get Elizabeth when she appeared on the upstairs landing and asked, "What's going on?" Then she noticed several men in red uniforms come streaming through the front door, and she shrieked!!!

Ann immediately said reassuringly, "It's all right; just stay there, and I will come and get you." She then bounded up the stairs with the accompanying marine close behind.

"Don't worry, just come with us," she said as she grabbed her daughter's hand and quickly ran down the stairs.

Elizabeth settled somewhat when she felt her mother's hand in hers and immediately complied.

Upon reaching the front door, the marine Ann first spoke to said, "Take your daughter to the other side of the street with one of my men and stay there until all is well."

Once outside, Ann put her arm around her daughter's shoulders, guided her across the road, and said, "Everything will be fine. They are hunting two escaped convicts, and they say they are around here somewhere."

Elizabeth stood trembling with her mother by her side as she gazed up and down the street, expecting to see a stranger at any moment. Other than a few soldiers, there was no one in sight. A couple of minutes later, one of their older neighbours hobbled across the street, accompanied by a marine.

Ann and Elizabeth waited as their house was being searched, and, finally, a marine lieutenant came over to them and said, "I am afraid that you cannot go back into the house as we think they have been in your back garden. These two are pure evil and very dangerous, so can you go somewhere else safer until we find them?"

Ann, thinking quickly replied, "Yes, we can go up the street to a friend's house."

"That's good. Go there now, and we will watch you as you walk up the street."

Grabbing Elizabeth's hand again, Ann walked up the street, ensuring they stayed on the opposite side of the road from all the houses. Finally, they arrived at their friend's house, and luckily, they were home, and after a short explanation, they were let into the house and made more than welcome.

By the time William arrived home, the two convicts had escaped and were seen crossing a field some distance from the house. The Marines took off in pursuit, allowing the houses in the original search area to return to normal. Unfortunately, Elizabeth and Ann were still at their friend's house, so no one was home when William arrived.

But that all changed shortly after.

No sooner had William settled into his favourite chair when he heard the front door open, and assuming it to be Elizabeth and Ann, he yelled out, "I am in here."

Upon hearing the familiar voice, Elizabeth rushed into the parlour and to her father, who had stood up by this stage. She ran right up to him with her arms outstretched and, surprisingly, right into his waiting arms.

Before he had time to inquire about the upsetting situation, she blurted out, "Father, that was scary!"

Awkwardly hanging on to his daughter, he innocently asked, "What was scary?"

She leant backwards, looked straight into his face, and said, "Don't you know what happened?"

"No! Tell me."

Not understanding why her father knew nothing about the escaped convicts, she told her story.

"Well, earlier today, while you were away, we answered the front door to find a bunch of soldiers outside, and they told us to leave as two dangerous criminals were hiding in our area. They searched the house, and we had to find another place while they continued hunting them down. They were not in our house, and they eventually found them and chased them over the back fields. I was shaking all over, and it was scary. Mother and I spent time with Mrs Simmons while they searched. Father, it was terrible."

Letting go of his daughter William said, "Well, it turned out all right, didn't it? So, we will put all this down to experience and move on, if you know what I mean."

Ann had been standing there listening to father and daughter talking, which she was happy about as that did not occur very often. But at least they are talking! She then decided to change the subject and butt into the conversation, and asked William, "How did your trip to Commissioners House go?"

William hesitated before answering as he did not want to overly discourage Elizabeth, so he only gave a rough outline of what occurred. "The good news is that we, subject to another inspection, have sold the house to the Navy. The not-so-good news is that they did not offer us what we had expected. But the job is done, and we can now move on."

Elizabeth, releasing her hold on her father's hand, suddenly forgot the escaped convict episode and became excited to learn that things were, at last, working out favourably, "That's good, isn't it?" she retorted.

In as confident a voice as he could muster, William replied, "Yes, it is good news."

Ann, thinking that now was a good time to move the subject on and not discuss any unfortunate news, said to Elizabeth and her husband, "Come on, let's go into the kitchen and get something to eat."

Arriving in the kitchen, Ann said, as she started to prepare the meal, "As this has not exactly been a good day, let's have something special for a change. I was going to cook this meat tomorrow, but under the circumstances, we will have it today. It tastes best when fried, so cooking should not take long."

All three of them thoroughly enjoyed their meal and continued to discuss what had to be done in preparation for their long sea voyage. The house had now been sold, as had much of the larger furniture and other household items, although Ann was still apprehensive about the considerable time everything took. William had finally sorted out all outstanding matters with his assistant at the surgery, so he no longer needed to go there. Elizabeth had given many of her items to her girlfriends and had managed to whittle down her clothing to an acceptable level. By the time the meal finished, they all felt reasonably comfortable with where things were at. They were each busy working on what now needed to be done. Excitement levels were rising as the whole family would soon board a ship sailing to the other side of the world.

Later that evening, while Ann and William were tossing and turning in bed trying to get to sleep, Ann decided to get something worrying her off her chest and said, "William, I can't get to sleep, and there is one thing I need to know now. You mentioned earlier that the Navy did not accept what price we had on the house. How much did they offer?"

"Yes, well, not nearly what I hoped for. They only agreed to pay 350 pounds and …."

"What, only 350 pounds!!!!

"Ah, that is all they were willing to pay, so as time is now so limited, I had no choice but to accept the offer."

Ann was starting to see red by this time, so she raised her voice, "You could at least have asked me before agreeing to anything so ridiculous."

"I agree that talking to you would have been best, but I had no real choice, and I felt we had no real alternative. As you know, time is running out; I had no option other than to agree to their terms right then and there."

Understanding how impetuous and headstrong William could be, she slowly lowered her voice when she said, "I understand the time question, so I guess there was not much else you could do. Did you try and improve the price?"

"A little, although I was told that serious negotiations would take considerable time. We do not have that amount of time."

Thinking more about the practical side of selling the house, Ann said, "Well, it is done now. When are they going to do the inspection?"

"Someone will come later in the week, but considering the agreed price, I do not think that will be a problem."

The house inspection took place as planned and proved successful, so the sale progressed. Elizabeth was now happy with how things were going and looked forward to the upcoming adventure. While Ann was still unhappy with the amount of money they received for the house, she understood it was the best they could expect in the circumstances. William was relieved that he could now continue sorting out the other more minor matters that needed to be resolved. He also understood there was still much to be sorted before they finally walked up that ship's gangway.

About a week later, Elizabeth happened to be near the front door when she was surprised by a loud knock. She had been told many times to be very careful when answering the door if alone, but she reasoned that as both her parents were upstairs busy sorting out their things, this time it would be all right. She waited for a second knock. It came, so she carefully and slowly opened the door so that she could slam it shut if necessary. A young man was standing there with a large envelope, which he offered, saying, "Does William Johnson live here?"

"Yes, he is my father."

He passed the envelope to Elizabeth, "Good, please give this to him," and then he was gone.

Elizabeth closed the door while simultaneously wondering what was in the envelope. "Hand delivered. It must be something important," she thought, so she decided to take it upstairs.

Running up the stairs two at a time, she knocked on her parent's door, even though it was half open. She had been reminded to knock many times through the years by her father, regardless of the circumstances.

Her mother called out, "Come in," and not turning around from what she was doing, said, "Is it important?"

"I think so. It has just been hand-delivered."

Both her parents looked up, each with a surprised look on their face, and then her father said, "What has been delivered?" He could not remember ordering anything, but then he noticed the large envelope in Elizabeth's hand and said, "Ah, I think I know what it is."

Taking the envelope from Elizabeth, William tore it open, pulled out a couple of pages of paper, and then said, "Yes, this is what I thought it might be.

Both Elizabeth and Ann stayed quiet as he read the contents carefully. Then he said, "The first one is for the house sale, and the second one informs us of the ship we are to take. It says here that we are to board the Scarborough in two weeks with all our belongings. How's that?"

Elizabeth was the first to react, "That's great. Something is happening at last!"

Still finding the process very difficult, Ann wanted to say something on the one hand but was unsure what she should say on the other. Then she heard Williams asking, "Ann, isn't that good?"

Ann replied, "As Elizabeth has said, we now have some definite information."

Still unsure how she felt, Ann continued, "Yes, I guess it is," although her tone was not very convincing.

William approached Ann, put his arm around her shoulders, and said, "I know all this is very hard for you, but I believe you will be happy with a brand-new start when the voyage ends and we finally get there."

Elizabeth noted how her father had reacted to her mother's feelings, and she could not remember when he showed such kindness. She noticed how her father seemed to have mellowed somewhat since he stopped attending the surgery. It was evident that working in that rough and ready surgery environment had adversely affected him. "Maybe this is the start of a new beginning," she thought.

"Two weeks, you say!" Ann said, acknowledging what William had said earlier. "That means we all need to get moving," smiling at her play-on-words. "Let's sit down right now and sort out what we still have to do and when it needs to be done because time is now against us."

Elizabeth was glad that both her parents were discussing things sensibly and civilly, which gave her confidence that all would end well.

The next couple of weeks went extremely fast, and although the whole family thought they would never be ready in time to catch their ship's sailing, they finally managed to do so. They had to stay at an inn for the last few days as their house was virtually empty.

On the last night before they were to board the Scarborough, Elizabeth found getting to sleep extremely difficult, tossing and turning for several hours until pure exhaustion finally overtook her.

The following day, as the sun supplied a slight glimmer of light to the eastern horizon, Elizabeth found herself wide awake and in anticipation of a momentous day, and unusually for her, she eagerly got out of bed. Upon her feet hitting the floor, she realized just how little sleep she had managed to get. Even though excited about boarding a ship later in the day, Elizabeth realized that the lack of sleep would make it long and tiring.

She quickly dressed in the pale blue dress she had picked out the previous evening, as it was simple in design, had a square neckline, long sleeves, a fitted bodice and a long and full skirt. Ann had warned her always to dress modestly while on board a ship and when around so many men. With the help of her mother, she bought a couple of extra dresses with that cautious note in mind.

173

As they were not due to arrive at the wharf until the afternoon, Elizabeth spent most of her spare time reading a book after packing and repacking the various layers of her trunk. She kept asking herself what goes at the bottom, what goes flat, what you squeeze into the corners and what goes on top. Although the result was not perfect, she was finally happy with how it all turned out. She had to sit on the lid and bounce on it several times to latch the lock.

All three had returned from the Inn to their old home as the four trunks had been stored there that night. The coach and accompanying cart arrived in the early afternoon and, with the drivers' help, loaded their three individual smaller trunks and the one large family one into their places. Looking around her, Elizabeth realized that this would probably be the last time she saw the home she had known since birth and how she would try to remember it. She accepted that pleasant memories of her early years would take over from now on.

Elizabeth and her parents were about to board the coach, but first, William made sure that everything was at hand as they were now committed to board the Scarborough, their home for the next six to eight months. Elizabeth looked at her mother and said in a trembling voice, "I hope we are doing the right thing."

In a reassuring voice, Ann replied, "Yes dear, we are," although she was not as confident as she tried to look and sound.

Sensing the doubting tone of voice in both, William said, "Of course, everything is going to be all right. If I thought otherwise, I would not be taking you both on this trip."

With those last comments, the coach took off with a lurch, making Elizabeth's hat slip back onto the back of her neck. She quickly returned it to its proper place and then remembered what her mother had said about the strength of the wind she could expect on the ship. "I am going to have to find a better way of keeping it on," she thought.

The wharf was about fifteen minutes from their old home, so the trip went quickly, with barely enough time for Elizabeth to get her thoughts in order.

As the coach carrying Elizabeth and her family got close to the wharf, she could see the towering masks of two sailing vessels over the tops of the surrounding buildings. "Which one is the Scarborough," she thought as the coach turned the corner and then along the wharf. The whole area was awash with activity, with people walking all over the place and coaches and carts unloading alongside both vessels. Elizabeth tried to see the name of the first ship they came to, but it was not shown anywhere she could see.

The driver of the coach stopped, asked one of the wharf workers which was the Scarborough, and then drove on to the second vessel and stopped just behind a cart unloading barrels.

Elizabeth had never seen a large sailing ship so close as this before, and she was amazed at the height of the masts and the tremendous amount of rigging hanging down from all three of them. At the same time, she was surprised to see so many people, either on the ship, on the wharf, or climbing up and down the gangway. It was, indeed, a busy place.

William had not thought much about his role as the ship's surgeon, but now that he was right alongside the vessel, it reminded him of what was ahead. He decided it would be best to seek out the captain immediately after getting Elizabeth and Ann safely aboard. They did not have to wait long when he heard the sailor supervising the loading call out, "Next. Hurry up, we have not got all day!" upon which the driver promptly drove them forward.

Upon hearing the command, William stuck his head out of the coach's window and addressed what was obviously a senior sailor, saying,

"My name is William Johnson. I am the surgeon for this ship's voyage and have my family with me."

The sailor walked over to the coach and said, "It is good to meet you, sir. I heard there would be a surgeon coming on board." He turned and appointed two seamen to help with the loading and then said, "I think it would be best for you to stay here for a minute until we unload your baggage."

The three smaller trunks were unloaded from the roof rack, and then the larger one lifted off the rear of the coach. It was evident that it was heavy as they could hear the grunts and groans of those doing the lifting. The large trunk was then loaded onto a wooden cart, with the other three loaded onto a separate one.

Trying to be helpful, William called out, "We will not be needing the large trunk on the voyage, so it need not go in our cabin."

Elizabeth and her family alighted from the coach and followed their baggage up the gangplank, all three trying to take in this extremely foreign environment. Arriving on deck, William looked around for a naval or marine officer who could direct him to the captain, because only he would be completely aware of the terms of his employment.

Elizabeth stood, with her mouth hanging open in utter amazement, studying every part of the ship she could see, as well as taking note of every person on deck.

William waited for a few minutes before he said to Ann and Elizabeth, "Stay here while I look for the captain." He moved towards the stern of the vessel and noticed that his large trunk had disappeared, and the other three were piled on each other. He also noticed that many sailors aboard were not in formal uniform, and then he reminded himself that this was not a naval vessel.

In the meantime, Elizabeth started to look carefully at every person who came within her view, and then it dawned on her that everyone she had seen so far was a man. Standing here in the middle of the deck with her mother, she felt very awkward and embarrassed as every man that came her way stared at her. This made her seriously look around to find a fellow girl or woman, which would at least make her feel a little more comfortable. She hoped that she and her mother were not the only women aboard. With a sigh of relief, Elizabeth noticed a women open a door and disappear in the general direction her father was walking. "That's good. It looks like we are not alone," she said to herself.

Her father was just about to knock on the cabin door when it opened, and a middle-aged man stopped and stood in the doorway. "How can I help you," he said.

Not knowing whether he was talking to the captain, William said, "Sir, my name is William Johnson, and I am the new surgeon assigned to this ship."

"Ah, I have been expecting you. I am Captain Jones. Come in and meet my wife."

The captain glanced up and, noticing Ann and Elizabeth standing in the middle of the deck, said, "I see you have your family with you. Ask them to come this way."

 William turned around and gestured for both to come forward; after gesturing a few times and finally getting their attention, they did. "Captain Jones, I would like to introduce you to my wife, Ann, and my daughter, Elizabeth."

The captain nodded in acknowledgement and said, "Good to meet you both. Please come in and meet my wife, who will, by the way, be travelling with us on this voyage."

Neither Ann nor Elizabeth knew what to say, so they just nodded and followed William and the captain into his cabin. The cabin was not what they expected, as it was larger than they thought and quite well furnished, particularly as this was aboard a ship that generally carried cargo.

Captain Jones gestured to a couple of chairs on the other side of his desk and asked Ann and William to take a seat. Elizabeth did not even realize what was happening because she was busy looking around the cabin and suddenly noticed that both her parents had taken their seats. When she joined them and stood just behind her mother, she heard a woman's voice, "Sorry to intrude. I did not know anyone else was in here. I was in our sleeping cabin through there."

The captain at once said, "This is my wife, Margaret. Margaret, this is William Johnson, our surgeon for the voyage, his wife, Ann, and his daughter, Elizabeth."

Both parties acknowledged the introduction, with William promptly standing up and saying, "It is a pleasure to meet you, madam."

Margaret responded, "I am pleased to meet all three of you. I am sure this will be a very long voyage and a challenge for everyone. Please sit down. I think it would be proper for us not to stand on formality in this cabin when it is just us, so if you have no objections, perhaps we could use our first names when we are alone?"

The captain at once concurred and said, "I have no difficulty with that. Is that idea all right with you? By the way, my first name is Stephen. "

He promptly offered his hand, which William shook and said, "Yes, a good idea, and on behalf of my family, I thank you for the warm welcome."

The captain, who seemed somewhat impatient by this time, said, "I am sorry to rush you, but there are several urgent matters that I must deal with, and I think it would be wise that you get settled into your cabin as soon as possible." He opened the door and called out to a passing sailor, "Boatswain, would you please show the surgeon and his family to their cabin."

"Yes. Captain. Please come this way."

William noticed that their three trunks were no longer on deck, and he assumed, hopefully, that they had been taken to their cabin.

As they followed the boatswain, Elizabeth was still amazed at the situation she was finding herself in, as everything about this ship was very different from anything else she had ever experienced. It made her feel uncomfortable and completely out of her depth.

They climbed down a flight of very steep stairs to the deck below, turned to the left towards the stern of the ship, along a short passage, and stopped in front of a heavy wooden door.

As he opened the door, the boatswain said, "I believe this is your cabin, sir."

William entered what looked like a tiny room, particularly as they were all used to living in quite a large house. Ann and Elizabeth followed, not sure what to think or say. They expected it to be small, but this small.

Finally, after looking around, Ann said, "This is going to be cosy."

The three trunks had been piled up on top of each other against the back wall, with a set of bunks on one side wall and a single bed on the other. There was a small dressing table with a bowl, a small wardrobe at the other end, and nothing else.

All three stood there for a few minutes, trying to imagine themselves living in such a small room for the next few months. It was obvious to Ann that most of the items in their three trunks would have to stay where they were, as there was not enough room to put the contents anywhere else. She thought it would take considerable time and effort to make such a small space work, plus the cooperation of both William and Elizabeth would be essential.

After a short while, William gathered his thoughts, put down his instrument case, and said, "I will sleep in the single bed over there, and you two can sleep in those two beds. Maybe it would be best for Elizabeth to sleep in the top bunk. While you two are sorting out the cabin, I will see if I can talk to the captain and get right to work."

Elizabeth and her mother looked at each other and nodded. William left the cabin, and Elizabeth said, "I will go on the top bunk, Mother. All right?"

"Yes, dear, that will be fine. Let's just sit here for a minute. I think we will need to adjust our thinking and some agreement on how things will work around here before we can try to settle in."

They both sat down on the bed and noticed that the mattress was hard and lumpy, especially compared to those at their old home. Elizabeth and Ann sat silently while looking around the cabin, neither feeling like saying anything until they had sorted out their thoughts. The reality needed time to sink in.

They were both startled by a knock on the door and a voice calling out, "It's Margaret. Have you got a minute?"

Ann hesitated for a second or two and then replied, "Just a moment."

Opening the door, Ann said, "Oh, hello, Margaret.

"Sorry to disturb you, but I am about to have a cup of tea, and I thought you both could do with one."

"Yes, that would be nice. I am a bit thirsty."

"Well, come when you are ready. I am just about to boil the kettle."

"Thanks. We will be right there."

Elizabeth and Ann tidied themselves up a bit and left their cabin, entering the captain's cabin and noticing that Margaret was seated at a table at the back.

"Please sit down," said Margaret, motioning to the two empty chairs.

"Thank you," said both Ann and Elizabeth in one voice.

Margaret poured both a cup of tea and asked, "Just out of curiosity, what made you decide to take this long voyage?"

"We thought it was a time for a change, and this came up. I am not sure why we decided on this one. It is certainly going to be an adventure in any event."

"Yes, it certainly is. My husband had trouble finding the promotion he was looking for, and this one came up. It is more of a career choice for us, but it certainly is an interesting one."

Elizabeth was finding that the conversation was not directly involving her, so she was finding the occasion rather difficult. She politely nodded where she thought she should and said very little,

They eventually finished their tea, and Ann and Elizabeth made their excuses as they were keen to settle into their tiny cabin. They returned to the cabin, looking around again, wondering where they would start and where to put their things in such a confined space.

Elizabeth was finding it difficult to imagine what living on board this ship would be like. Her thoughts raced between the fact that there was absolutely no privacy, no place to wash, not enough space for clothes and very little light due to the cabin only having a tiny, shuttered window. They would need candles or some form of lamp during the evenings, otherwise reading would be impossible.

Once they gathered their thoughts together, they started discussing what they thought life would be like and how they could each contribute to making their temporary world as pleasant as possible. Such a small space would prove challenging to all three of them. Very little else was achieved over the next half an hour or so.

Chapter 14

Richard decided to go up on deck and familiarize himself further with this particular ship, knowing that every ship was different. It would take a while as he was not at all familiar with the layout of the Alexander. He also knew that what would typically be the lower gun deck on a naval vessel was taken up by several wooden and metal cages especially installed to carry convicts. As this area most likely required his involvement over the coming months, he wanted to get to know his way around as soon as possible. He did not go below immediately as he thought it best not to do so by himself, so he wandered around the top deck, passing the odd seaman occasionally before catching up with Sergeant Jones and three privates near the capstan.

Richard, who saw the four of them before they saw him, said, "Sergeant Jones, I think it is nearly time for me to take over."

The sergeant whipped his head around as he was not expecting to hear a voice from that direction and said, "Sergeant, you caught me by surprise. Yes, are you ready to take over?"

Not being that sure of himself but not wanting to sound unsure, Richard replied, "Of course."

No sooner had Richard said that when the squad he was to supervise arrived at the changeover point. Before moving over to them, he asked Sergeant Jones, "Is there anything I should be aware of?"

"No, nothing really, although the scum below seems quiet tonight."

"That's good," Richard replied. "That means everything should go well."

"Never assume that, if I was you."

The ship's bell rang four times, which informed Richard, and the entire crew, that the First Dog Watch was about to finish and the Last Dog Watch was about to start. That meant that it was now 6 pm, and it was time for Richard to begin his watch.

Richard was unsure if or when the lieutenant would come on deck or whether it would be best to continue without him. He moved over to the usual change-over point and noticed that a couple of the privates he had shared on the earlier small boat trip were included in his watch.

He approached the Marines, still considering how he should approach the 12 standing in two rough lines. The problem was his unfamiliarity with the security arrangements and existing protocols on board the Alexander. As most of the others on his watch were familiar with the current routines, Richard thought it wise to forget about rank for a moment and take advantage of their local knowledge and experience.

Stiffening his stance and standing tall, he strode up to the front of the squad, who were standing in a very informal manner, and said, "All right, you lot, let's get yourselves sorted out and in two straight lines."

It was apparent to Richard that this group was not used to such formalities, so it took some time for them to organise themselves. They finally got in line, some came to attention, and some did not. A few uniforms were untidy, others very dirty.

Richard decided that the original soft and informative approach he was going to take would now need to be implemented later. If he was going to project any real authority, now was the time for discipline and military standards.

Richard strode to the front of the squad and, with as much firmness and focus as he could muster, said, "Not good enough. Fall out over there and immediately come back here and line up properly. Now move!"

Some individual members of the squad looked at each other and then started to do as instructed, although with no real urgency. They finally got into line and stood to attention. This lack of real effort was getting under Richard's skin, and he said," I am not sure how things have been in the past, but as far as I am concerned, the beginning of each watch will start properly. It can all be done in less than a minute if you co-operate. Now fall out again and get back here, smartly. Go!"

This time the watch moved with speed and purpose and quickly lined up as ordered, prompting Richard to say, "That's a lot better. You can see that it is not hard."

Richard walked up and down the line, returned to the middle, and then said, "Stand at ease. Now that we have that sorted out, I now need your co-operation. As you all know, I am not familiar with the routines necessary on this ship, especially when there are convicts aboard. I have been a sergeant in the Navy and the Marines for many years, so I am familiar with normal routines. What happens with convicts, and when, is something I must learn, and I am looking for your co-operation."

Noticing that there was a corporal in the squad, Richard said, "Corporal, what normally happens from this point?"

The corporal stepped forward and said, "Sergeant, we normally split up into three groups, one to oversee the convicts, one on deck security and one below."

"That makes sense. You sort out the groups, and I will tag along with your group, corporal."

It was obvious that these groups were already organised as they quickly moved into their groups and moved off to their appointed positions. Richard joined the corporal's group as they headed to the ship's bow. He noted that the lieutenant had not turned up, but then he was unsure if that was the usual routine.

185

Tagging along, Richard wanted to find out the routine, what they should look for, and the perceived threats. He thought he would watch at this stage and ask questions as they went. They moved along the port rail towards the bow, with one of the marines looking over the side occasionally on the way. Richard wondered what they were looking for, so he asked one of the privates, "Private, are you looking for anything in particular?"

The private was reluctant to say anything, so Richard said, "I am not checking on you. I want to understand the routine that you go through. So, what are you looking at?

The other three marines were somewhat wary of their new sergeant, so they came closer to find out what Richard was saying.

Richard, now aware that they had come closer, thought it wise to speak to all of them at the same time, so he said, "As I have just said to this marine, I am just trying to find out exactly what your routine is and why you do it. That's all!"

All four relaxed somewhat when they heard this, so the three others wandered past the bowsprit to the starboard side. The first private stayed back and started to answer Richard's question, "Sergeant, there is one main reason. We are making sure that there are no small boats alongside, as they could be used to help convicts escape or they could be used to bring somebody on board who does not belong. Otherwise, they are usually trying to steal something. Both have happened on various boats in the fleet, so we check regularly."

"Thanks, private, that's what I want to know. Carry on."

They both crossed to the other side of the vessel and caught up with the others, by now partway down the starboard rail. On the way, Richard noted that one of the privates was regularly looking up into the rigging and masts and looking over the rail on the starboard side from time to time, obviously looking for anyone who should not be there.

All seemed very quiet on board, and Richard started to think that this routine would become dull over time when he heard unfamiliar noises coming from the aft hold. The four marines also noticed it and started to move quickly towards it. Richard then heard a blood-curdling scream and much shouting from the same area. He followed to the edge of the hold and looked over the side.

For some reason or other, the door to one of the cages was open, and Richard could see what looked like a bloodied body lying crumpled in an unusual heap just outside the gate. Further away from the doorway were four marines with their muskets at the ready, with fixed bayonets facing the cage entrance.

Richard ran around one of the ship's masts to the stairway to the hold and virtually dropped to the bottom, with the rest in his detachment right behind him. They at once raised their muskets in support of those already in the hold. The convicts were yelling obscenities, some at fellow convicts, others very much directed against the Marines. Upon reaching the lower deck, Richard said in a commanding voice, "What's going on here."

In response to his question, one of the apparent leaders of the convicts yelled, "None of your bloody business. If we wanted your opinion, we would have asked for it!"

Ignoring the remark, Richard glanced around, looking for any weapon that could have been used against the obviously dead convict. None were in sight, so he ordered the Marines, "Get that gate closed, now!"

Backed by their fellow marines, two handed their muskets to another marine, ran towards the gate, and managed to close it, just as a group of convicts rushed to the gate and tried to hold it open.

Motioning the other marines forward, Richard promptly yelled out to the convicts, "Leave that gate alone, or you will feel a length of cold steel!"

The convicts slowly moved back from the gate as the padlocks were fitted, although that did not stop them from calling out further obscenities.

Confident that the gate was now securely closed and locked, Richard approached the crumpled and bloody convict. He had not moved, but in case life was still present, Richard checked for a pulse at his neck and wrist. None, he was dead! Looking back at the marines, who had lowered their muskets by now, Richard said, "Get this man out of sight as soon as you can."

Four marines stepped forward, grabbed the man by his arms and legs and carried him past the cages and down to the stern of the Alexander. Richard was unsure how they usually dealt with such persons, but then he did not feel it was his business. He turned to one of the marines who had found the dead man and said, "Do you know what happened here?"

"We don't know for sure, Sergeant. We just found the man lying against the inside of the gate, so we opened it and pulled him outside. That is when you first saw us."

While all this was happening, the convicts near the gate were chanting, "Justice, Justice, Justice."

Not understanding what they meant by the words, Richard walked over to the gate, stood about three yards away, and asked no one in particular, "What happened to that man?"

One smart-alec said, "He died."

"That's bloody obvious. I want to know who killed him and why?"

188

Somebody else spoke out, "He was a snitch and a thief. He got what he deserved. We got our justice!"

Richard could see he was not likely to get anything useful from anyone inside the cage, so he said, not expecting any answer, "Anyone of you wants to come outside and tell me what happened?

No word was spoken, nor any movement occurred in response, other than the words one of the leaders spat out, "You have to be joking!"

Richard decided there was nothing more he could do, so he said to the marines standing behind him, "Two of you come with me, and the rest of you stay here and keep an eye on this rowdy bunch."

He climbed the stairs and, when he got to the main deck, asked one of the marines, "I need to report this to the lieutenant. Do you know where I'd find him?"

"If he is not on deck, he is usually in his cabin."

Richard found the cabin and, with one of the marines as his witness, detailed what he had seen and what had occurred. The lieutenant did not seem overly concerned and told Richard that he would take over the matter from there.

Richard was not expected to do anything more about the convict's death, so he returned to his squad of marines who had been expecting him. He said, "Well, that bit of excitement is over. Now, where were we? Ah, yes. Let's continue from where we left off."

This squad started getting to know Richard, so they felt more comfortable explaining what they were doing. In that regard, they offered further information without Richard asking all the time. As they passed the pulled-up gangway on the deck, it reminded them that they had to be very aware and careful of who and what came aboard the ship. They also had to be even more aware of who or what left the ship, as the opportunity for theft was never-ending. Somebody from onshore always seemed willing to risk their lives by stealing anything they could get their hands on. Something for nothing always seemed appealing.

By the time Richard and his squad arrived back where they started walking the ship's rail, the sun had set some while ago, and it was now dark. Then the ship's bell rang eight times, meaning it was now 10 pm, the end of Richard's second dog watch and the beginning of the first watch. He now had four hours off before he was due to attend his next watch.

On his way back to his shared cabin, he reflected on the excitement of the last couple of hours and then, now relaxed somewhat, felt tired and ready for a couple of hours of sleep. He entered his cabin, slumped down on his bunk bed, and before he knew it, he was out like a light.

Chapter 15

Elizabeth and her mother had discussed in detail how they could best live in such a small cabin without getting on each other's nerves. As William would be working most of the time, they thought that he would probably be sleeping when he was in the cabin. Both agreed that that would be advantageous because he would not be under their feet in such a small space.

The earlier talk with her mother had somewhat quelled Elizabeth's immediate concerns, and she was now looking forward to facing the expected challenges. She looked at her mother and said, "I think it would be wise to put some of our clothes away before Father gets back, don't you think?"

"Yes, dear. Which is your trunk? Ah yes, I remember, yours is the dark green one. Let's start there."

They had forgotten just how heavy these fully packed trunks were, but with a lot of effort and noise, they managed to pull down the trunk off the top of the others and move it into the middle of the cabin. All three trunks had padlocks fitted.

Ann could not remember where she had put the keys for the trunks, although she did remember putting them in a safe place, wherever that safe place was. She rummaged around in her hold-all again, finally finding them caught inside a folded scarf. "Found them!" she called out with a sense of relief.

Moving to open the lock on Elizabeth's trunk, Ann said, "Remember, we will only be able to put a small amount of what we have into those drawers, and if we want to make it as easy as possible, we will have to choose very carefully what goes in them. So, I suggest that our better clothes stay in the trunks, and we put only the daily essentials into the drawers."

Elizabeth replied, "That's what I was thinking. I tried to sort out my trunk in that order, although we have less room than I thought."

Elizabeth and her mother then spent some time sorting out clothes from all three trunks, although it was sometimes challenging to sort out the necessary priorities. Eventually, with Ann occasionally having to be very firm with Elizabeth, the job was done, and they put the three now slightly lighter trunks back against the far wall. While they did this, Elizabeth noticed that the room was moving slightly, something she was unfamiliar with, and reminded herself that she was aboard a ship tied up alongside a wharf. "I wonder what it will feel like in the open sea?" she thought.

"Mother, seeing as it is not wise for me to move around the ship alone, can we both go and look outside?"

"Elizabeth, I know you are keen to learn more about this ship, but I would not feel happy going out there by ourselves. Not yet. We need your father with us, at least until we learn the ropes."

Elizabeth slumped in her seat on the edge of the bed and said nothing. "This is going to be boring," she thought.

Elizabeth sat on her mother's bed for some time, thinking about what she could do, finally deciding to grab one of the blankets, climb onto the top bunk and lay down. It took a while for her to go to sleep, but she finally succumbed. The slight rocking movement of the ship seemed to help.

In the meantime, William remembered that the captain had said he had a couple of important matters to attend to, so he decided to use the time to familiarise himself with the Scarborough. Firstly, he noticed that there were no signs of any convicts aboard. Not knowing the current situation, he decided to ask somebody so that he was more aware of what would happen and when before talking to the captain.

Looking around at everything in sight as he walked the deck, he came across a couple of sailors scrubbing the foredeck. "I don't want to interrupt you, but I have a question?"

"Maybe! Who are you?"

"I am the surgeon on this voyage, and I am getting myself familiar with the ship."

Relaxing somewhat, the eldest sailor responded, "Ah, if that is the case, we may need your help sometime. What do you want?"

"I understand that the Scarborough is supposed to have convicts aboard, but I have not seen any sign of them. What's the story?"

"We only know what we have heard, but we believe they will arrive in the next few days. We don't know any more than that."

"Thanks."

William turned and continued his tour of the top deck and said to himself, "That's good. It gives me time to set myself up."

William had never been on a big ship before, so virtually everything he encountered was new. Still, he understood and accepted that what he looked at had little to do with his medical responsibility.

He guessed that at least an hour had passed since he left the captain, so he walked to the stern to see if the captain had returned. While doing so, William wondered whether Ann and Elizabeth had yet finished sorting out the cabin. "It is going to be interesting living in such a small space," he thought, "but I will leave that up to the women."

William knocked on the captain's cabin door and waited for a reply. Margaret answered the door and asked him to come inside, saying, "I assume you are looking for my husband. He should be here any minute if you want to wait."

"Yes, thank you. I will."

Margaret did not even get the chance to close the door as her husband caught it before it closed fully. "Hey, don't close it in my face!"

Margaret laughed as she let go of the inside handle and said, "William is here."

William waited for the laughter to die and then said, "Sorry to bother you, captain, but I need someone to show me around so I can prepare to work, particularly as I believe the convicts will join us soon. Have you got a place I can work from and call my own?"

"Yes, we have sorted out a place for you, although it is in a rather strange place. Space is at a premium, as you would understand. I will get someone to show you where it is." The captain stuck his head out the door and called out to the 1st mate, who looked over upon hearing the captain's cabin door open and said, "Could you show the surgeon where he is going to work."

"Yes, captain, right away."

The 1st mate promptly took off towards the aft hold as William exited the captain's cabin, so he had to run to catch up with him. Feeling that the 1st mate was not in a chatty mood, William decided to stay quiet and follow.

They descended the steep stairs into the hold, and then the 1st mate moved towards the vessel's port side to what looked like a workshop. He stopped outside the doorway and asked William to step inside. William was becoming more and more concerned that it looked like a wholly unsuitable place as it looked like it was the carpenter's workshop. The 1st mate then moved over to the left wall to a closed door, which he opened with a flourish and said, "This is yours. Not very big, I am afraid, but this is the best I could do."

William was somewhat shocked at what he saw. It was tiny, especially compared to his old surgery, and he was unsure how it would work. There was a low bench, which would have to do as the base of a bed, a large table that could be used at a pinch as an operating table, a cupboard on the wall, perhaps for instruments, and a single chair. All this was in a tiny space, barely large enough to hold what was already there. Sitting down on the hard bed base, he looked around, and after the first shock of it all, William started to realize that with careful planning, it could work, especially if he was well-organised. But there would be virtually no space for anyone else.

There was nothing else in the room but the bare essentials, so he started thinking about all the other items he would need, such as a bowl and a jug for water, bandages, swabs, and other such medical supplies, and where they would come from. Unless he got off the ship and bought them himself, there was no other way he could think to get the stock of such essentials. "Maybe the captain can help," was his first thought, "Or maybe someone has already thought of it, and they are already on board?"

As William had been away from his wife and daughter for a while, he decided to see how things were going in their cabin and catch up with the captain later.

"How is everything going," was his immediate question as he entered the busy-looking cabin. There were still some clothes on the beds, a few bedding items on the floor, and one trunk that needed to be put back in place. Those small number of things that still needed to be sorted made the cabin look much smaller. William mentally noted how vital tidiness would be because he accepted that he was not naturally a tidy person.

Ann and Elizabeth were standing in the middle of the cabin when William entered, and upon hearing William's question, they just looked at each other, unsure what to say.

Elizabeth was the first to respond, "We are nearly there; you just came back a little too soon, that's all."

While William was standing in the cabin, he noticed a slight rocking movement of the ship, the first time he had noticed it since he had come on board. He asked them, "Did you feel the ship move?"

Ann, who was now picking up the bedclothes from the floor, said, "Yes, we have both been feeling it occasionally. I guess we will feel a lot more movement when we get to sea."

Surprised that this was the first time he had noticed any movement, William said, "That is the first time I have noticed it. Well, it looks like you have just about everything under control here, and I must go and see the captain again. I will see you both later."

Elizabeth was staring at the extra clothing items on her bed, wondering where to put them. Every inch of space in the wardrobe and in the tiny drawers had been filled, but she needed to put the items in her hands somewhere. They had also put some things under the two lower beds, but some space remained. She posed the question to herself. "How can we use that space without shoving clothes between everything else?" Then it came to her. "Mother, we have a couple of extra pillowcases in the trunks somewhere, don't we?"

Ann stopped what she was doing and replied, "What do you want any more of those for? We have enough here for the beds?"

"Why don't we put our extra clothes inside a couple of those and put them under the beds? The clothes will be handy there and stay clean and tidy at the same time.

"That's a thought. I think a couple of extra pillowcases are tucked down the back of your father's trunk. If you don't make too big a mess, I will let you get them."

Elizabeth opened her father's trunk, found two pillowcases, put her extra clothes inside and found space under her mother's bed.

Within about twenty minutes of being interrupted by her father, Elizabeth and her mother had completed sorting out the clothes from their trunks. Ann sat on the chair, thankful to get off her feet, while Elizabeth sat on her mother's bed, both reasonably satisfied with their handiwork.

"Well, that job is done," said Elizabeth.

"Yes, but I am unsure whether it will stay that way. Time will tell."

"Mother, do you think it would be proper for us to look around the ship?"

"No, I don't think so. Not at this stage. It may be possible when everyone gets to know each other, but, in any case, I will always prefer that I go with you," her mother warned her.

Disappointed at hearing this, Elizabeth said, "Oh, Mother, do you really think so?"

"Yes, I do. You are not used to being alone in the wider world, particularly on a ship where the majority are men. You must deal with that over time, but don't worry; it will happen. You just must be patient."

Elizabeth was unhappy with what her mother had just said, so she sat silently on the edge of the bed with her head in her hands. Finally, becoming increasingly bored at the lack of activity, she decided to grab a blanket and climb up to her top bunk. She tried to read but found the lack of light made that very difficult.

William went back to his tiny surgery to look at it to see how the small space allocated to him could best be utilized. It was obvious that more complicated surgery, where a second person was needed, would be complex because of the lack of space. He saw that there was enough room for one person to be on each side of the table but not enough room for them to pass one another, so who did what would require serious planning. He was hopeful that at least one other person aboard the ship had some medical experience and could help him when needed. If nothing else, he thought, "It will be a serious challenge."

William left the temporary surgery and went directly to see the captain, who, unfortunately, was not there. His wife, Margaret, thought her husband had gone down in the hold to check on the large cages specially built for holding the convicts. William thought this was an excellent opportunity to check out the area before the convicts arrived, so he went below for a good look.

He climbed down the steep stairs through the main hatch, and upon arriving at the bottom, he could hear the captain's voice aft somewhere. The captain was obviously busy, and while he was there, William decided to look around while waiting.

He noted that there was more than one cage, each with a gate at the front and heavy hardwood timber slatted walls that ran from the floor to the bottom of the upper deck. Walking around the closest cage, he noticed it was one of four, all very similar in size and design. The prominent iron reinforcements at each cage's major joins and corners added a sense of solid security. They certainly looked very substantial to William, and he doubted that anyone could easily escape.

As William came around the back corner of the last cage, he came upon the captain standing alongside what looked like a carpenter, pointing to and discussing something along the back of the hold's partition. William paused as he waited for an opportune moment to intervene. By the tone of their voices, they seemed very intent on something important. He waited, stood some distance away, and looked at everything of interest within his view. He noticed a few iron rings securely attached to the hull frame on the starboard side, about two feet up from the deck. Before he had the opportunity to study the port side, he heard the captain's voice, "Oh, hello, William; I see you have come to join us."

William came to with a start and replied, "Yes, sorry to interrupt, but I am just making myself familiar with what is here, as I expect I will be down here quite regularly. I also have a question about the surgery, but I will wait until you are finished there."

"Right, I will be with you shortly."

William continued to walk around the entire hold, appreciating that the four cages took up most of the available space. He also noticed a pile of hammocks in each cage, plus a couple of extra heavy timber cross pieces with large hooks attached for one end of each hammock, assuming the other end would connect to the cage framing. He wondered how many convicts would be in each cage.

The captain's voice rang out from the other side of the hold, "William, would you mind coming here."

William replied, "Coming."

The captain was still with the carpenter, who was first introduced to William before he spoke, "Each of those cages will hold about fifty convicts, which will create conflicts within that group in such a small space. We are considering building a couple of small, single isolation cages back here that could be used when needed. I wondered how big they would have to be from a medical point of view?"

William had never been asked such an unusual question before, so he paused for a few seconds and thought about the convict's basic needs before answering, "Assuming the stay would only be for a few days, I think it should be at least long enough for someone to lay down in, and high enough to stand up in. In other words, about 6 feet long and 6 feet high but only about 3 feet wide. That is off the top of my head, of course. If you wanted to use the space strictly as a punishment, you could reduce the length to, say, 4 feet. Is that the kind of information you are looking for?"

"Yes, it is. Interesting, but not a lot different from what we were thinking. Thanks for your thoughts, but I realize they are not completely within your surgeon's role."

"No problem, captain."

The captain turned to the carpenter and said, "Follow those. I think the longer version would be best."

"Yes, captain, I will get onto that right away," the carpenter replied as he walked towards the stairs at the other end of the hold.

"Now, William, you wanted to ask me something."

"Yes, it is about the equipment I need for the surgery. Things such as bandages, swabs, water bowls and a jug. If I gave you a list of what I need, could you make sure they are on board by the time the convicts arrive?"

"That is a good question. I will certainly try and get what I can, although I cannot guarantee that they would all be available that soon, as the first of the convicts are expected here in three days."

"That soon?" replied William with a surprised look on his face.

"Yes, that soon. Considerable preparation still to be done before then."

"Thanks for that. I will get you a list as soon as I can."

William left the hold and returned to his surgery to write out that list, knowing that time was against him. He finally finished the list and took it to the captain's cabin. Unfortunately, the captain was not there, so he left it with his wife, emphasising how urgent it was.

Elizabeth was trying to read a book that Margaret had lent her but could not get into it, so she was sitting there, but not for long, as her mother shortly called out.

"Elizabeth, it is time to eat. We will need to go to the galley and get our meal."

As the day was nearly over and it was getting darker, William returned to his cabin, entered the door, and just about collided with his daughter, who just happened to be standing just inside the door.

William shouted, "Shit!"

"Sorry, Father," exclaimed Elizabeth.

"That's all right, but you certainly made me jump." Then, after composing himself, he continued, "I think it is about dinner time, isn't it?"

William had noticed where the galley was during his earlier inspections, so he led Elizabeth and Ann, simultaneously asking his wife, "Are you happy with how your day went?"

Ann was not sure how to answer the question. On the one hand, she was reasonably happy how the two of them had finally put everything away, but on the other, she was still not feeling very happy with the tiny and cramped quarters. "We finally managed to get most of the important items in their place," was all she was willing to say.

The closer they came to the galley, the more people seemed to come from everywhere. There did not seem to be any order as to who ate when, although a queue had started developing, so they tagged onto the end. They noticed that those who had already got their meal either squatted down against a wall or took it away to eat elsewhere. There were no specific eating places provided.

As far as Elizabeth could see, she was the only other woman or girl around, except for her mother. She was feeling somewhat overwhelmed by it all, so she followed closely in her mother's footsteps, all the while looking down at the deck and her feet. She shuddered as she felt the many pairs of eyes looking at her, which made her feel even more uncomfortable and out of place. "I am not sure I can stand much more of this," she thought.

The three of them finally arrived at the head of the queue and were handed a wooden bowl full of soup each from one of the cooks and a piece of hard brown bread by another. Elizabeth looked at hers with concern; although it looked unappealing, it smelled nice.

William led the other two away from the galley and said, "I think it would be wise to return to our cabin and eat there."

Ann and Elizabeth quickly agreed as both were finding the environment very uncomfortable, particularly the constant stares.

The family had always eaten their meals sitting on chairs at a large table, so sitting on one chair and a bed was not comfortable nor to their liking. Nevertheless, they continued to eat in silence until Elizabeth said, "Hey, this tastes a lot better than I thought it would, although the bread is so hard you have to dip the bread in the soup even to eat it."

William finished well before the others and said, "Yes, it was quite good, although it is not up to the standard of Ann's cooking," cocking his head on an angle as he looked in her direction.

Ann eagerly responded, "Now you appreciate my cooking. Has it taken you nearly 20 years to realize that?"

"No, dear, I have known it for years. I just have not mentioned it."

"Isn't that typical of a man?"

"What! We are not all the same, you know."

"I don't know about that. There are many similarities in most men."

"That is what I thought you would say," William replied with a sigh. "Anyway, that is enough of that. I have had enough for today, so I am going to bed."

Elizabeth found the interaction between her mother and father rather fascinating in that she had rarely heard them speak to each other in that way before. "I wonder if most men are very similar?" she thought, "No doubt I will find that out in time."

All three tumbled into bed, and after a busy day and the gentle rocking of the ship, they quickly fell asleep.

Chapter 16

It had been a while since Richard had been aboard a ship, so he was not used to the regular four-hourly watch system. This meant that he needed to sleep relatively lightly so that he did not oversleep for the start of his next watch. He knew he would get used to the routine over time, but he also knew it was not easy in the early stages of adapting to his new work routine and timeline. This had been in the back of his mind just before falling asleep, resulting in a fitful night. He had heard the bell from the bridge every half an hour, and what he was really waiting for were the seven bells indicating that it was thirty minutes till the start of his next watch at midnight.

He was half awake when he heard the bell ring seven times, so Richard slowly put his legs over the side of his bunk and, with some effort, managed to stand up. This was harder than he remembered, as he had gotten used to the larger, more comfortable household bed and the longer time to sleep. He grabbed his uniform off the end of the bunk and put it on while trying to make sure all looked neat and tidy. His boots, for one reason or another, did not want to go on. It felt like his feet had grown a couple of sizes, but with extreme effort and sitting down on the lower bunk, he finally managed to squeeze his feet into them. "This is not a good start," he thought.

Richard left the cabin, climbed the stairs to the top deck, and looked around, noting the weather. There appeared to be a 10-knot wind coming from the west, which was enough to move the ship around as it tugged at its anchor. Looking out to sea, even though it was nearly midnight, the white curls on the top of the choppy waves made them very obvious under the bright moon. The cool breeze helped him clear the fog from his sleepy eyes as he moved to the bow.

He walked forward to where he could hear muffled voices, assuming they were coming from the watch he was about to replace. He recognised the Sergeant's voice talking with four marine privates as he walked up to them and said, "Good evening, Sergeant. It looks like you lot are ready to go."

"Too bloody right," one of the privates said, then, remembering whom he was talking to, said, "Sergeant".

"Anything of interest tonight?" Richard said, asking anyone who wanted to answer.

The sergeant replied, "Nothing, really. All is very quiet."

"Thanks. I guess I had better get going."

Richard left those at the bow and returned to the usual meeting point for the middle watch further astern. He expected to find the same marines he had left earlier in the evening but was surprised to see a couple of new faces. As he walked up to the group, the ship's bell rang eight times, indicating the start of his watch.

Several marines nodded as Richard approached while they slowly formed into the required two lines.

Richard stood before them and said, "Hurry up, you lot. We do not have all night. Corporal, get these men organised." The men quickly added a spring to their step and promptly formed up. While this was going on, Richard thought, "I assume they will eventually get it right."

"A couple of new faces here tonight, Corporal. What's the story?"

The corporal, who had only just finished trying to get the squad into line, hesitated before he said, "There are a few sick, so we have to swap a couple of men around to make up the numbers."

"Thanks, Corporal, but let me know of any changes in the future before we form up."

"Yes, Sergeant."

Richard walked up and down the two lines inspecting the condition of uniforms and equipment. He nodded at each marine as he acknowledged each improvement from his last inspection.

"Well done to those of you who have tried to improve standards, although a couple of you still have more to do. I will not punish anyone tonight, but I will at our next watch if standards do not improve. I have nothing to report tonight so you can move off into your squads. I will move between the squads to see how each is working."

"Stand easy," Richard ordered.

The men promptly sorted themselves into one of the three squads and moved into their designated positions. Richard decided to descend into the hold and join those overseeing the convicts. He had not heard much noise other than the odd cough coming from that area, so he assumed most would be asleep.

Arriving at the lower deck, Richard walked around the cages without disturbing anyone. He wanted to see how things looked without any excitement or emergency. He first noted that most were sleeping in hammocks strung between anything strong enough and just far enough apart for a little elbow room. At certain angles they looked like rows of sardines, although no two were the same. He also noticed considerable laundry hanging from various points inside and outside the cage walls. Obviously, most convicts wanted their belongings always close at hand so they could keep an eye on them.

Whilst there was a moderate breeze blowing up on the main deck, there was not very little air movement down below, and Richard found himself holding his breath from time to time as he moved around the hold. The acrid smell was, at times, overpowering. There was minimal movement amongst the convicts, although the odd ones were whispering to one another. A couple of buckets in one corner were used as toilets, which proved to be the case as he passed each of them, Richard's nose confirming it. A rough lid was supplied, but this did not always get appropriately put back into place.

The four marines in this squad did not feel it necessary to move around, so they stood whispering in one corner of the hold. They had discovered many times before that waking the inmates in the middle of the night only created unnecessary difficulties. Keeping noise to an absolute minimum was the key.

After carefully walking around all four cages, Richard quietly walked over to the other marines and was just about to ask one of them a question when a loud cry of pain came from the furthest cage. It sounded both piercing and deadly at the same time. All five of them rushed past the two nearest cages to get to the one at the back, and because the noise of their boots on the wooden floorboards added to the volume of noise and confusion, they were yelled at as they passed each cage.

"Who the hell is that?"

"Get out of here!"

"Bugger off. I am trying to sleep!"

Richard was the first to turn the back corner of the cage where he thought the blood-curdling noise had come from. Everyone on the deck was now wide awake, and the sound of nearly two hundred convicts all talking and calling out at once was extreme. He thought the sound he had heard was deadly, but he was not ready to come upon what was before now him.

"Bloody hell!" yelled Richard.

The boy, who looked no more than twelve, was dangling by one leg from the beam used to tie off one end of the hammocks. The leg was twisted at such an angle that the foot pointed in an unnatural direction. The boy was not moving, either unconscious or dead, because it looked like his head had hit the deck hard enough to open the skin on his skull. Blood was slowly seeping across the deck from the wound.

The convicts sleeping in the injured boy's area were discussing how to remove him from that upside-down position. Many solutions were being offered. Confusion about what to do next was obvious, which meant nothing positive was being achieved.

Richard could see that no progress was being made, so he decided to take the lead, yelling in his loudest voice through the bars, "Stop! Hold everything."

The marine privates had followed Richard closely, so they were just behind him when he yelled out. He turned to the closest one and said, "You stay here and keep an eye on this. We are going inside."

"I am not sure that is a good idea, Sergeant!"

"This is an emergency," replied Richard in a firm voice, "Let's go!"

The four of them rushed around to the other side of the cage, one marine unlocked the cage door, and the others tried to enter. Unexpectedly, a small group of convicts surged towards them, blocking the doorway.

"Where the hell do you think you are going?" yelled one of the convict leaders.

Assuming that those on this side of the cage were unaware of what had happened, Richard urgently explained, "A boy has been badly injured over there in the back corner, and he needs medical attention. Now!"

Richard turned to one of the marines still outside the cage and said, "You stay here, lock the gate, and we will go inside."

"Not so bloody fast! This is our cage," the apparent leader retorted defiantly.

Richard replied in a commanding voice, "Whatever you say!" and then, with a change in tone, said, "Just let us in so that we can get that boy to the surgeon?"

The leader momentarily considered his options and said, "All right. Follow me."

Richard and the two privates followed the leader closely as they weaved through the excited convicts. They ignored most of the comments made by any convicts as they were not very complimentary. The convicts' leader called out as they approached the boy, "Out of the way! Coming through."

By the time they got to where the boy was originally dangling, the other convicts had cut the rope off the boy's leg, and he was lying on the ground with his foot still at a very awkward angle. It was evident that he was either still unconscious or he was dead. Thankfully, someone had tied a rag around his head to stop the bleeding.

Richard bent down and checked the boy's pulse. It was still there but very faint.

Taking charge of the situation, Richard called out to no one in particular, "We need one of those hammocks to carry the boy to the surgeon?"

A close-by convict piped up, "Take the boys'. I'll get it."

Richard turned to the two marines and said, "Let's very carefully get the boy onto that hammock. Try and keep that foot at the same angle it is now."

With a couple of convicts holding the boy's leg at the right angle, all three marines slowly lifted the boy onto the hammock. The boy stirred and groaned slightly as they did so.

"Easy now," said Richard.

With one marine on each end of the hammock and Richard holding the leg as best he could, they slowly moved to the other side of the cage. The convict leader made the pathway clear, occasionally needing a solid arm to do so.

Upon arriving at the gate, the marine outside unlocked it, and the hammock and its contents slowly exited the cage. The gate was quickly closed and made secure. The other two marines helped get the boy along the narrow passage towards the surgery. They entered the small area to find the surgeon absent, so they carefully lowered the boy onto the table. He was only half conscious, but his moans and groans were undoubtedly genuine.

Not knowing where the surgeon was, Richard instructed the Marines, "You four split up and see if you can find the surgeon. Once you find him, bring him here."

The bleeding from the boy's head wound had stopped, but his leg was still deformed. Richard shuddered just thinking about it. Although he was used to seeing wounded marines, seeing a misshaped leg like that on such a young boy was another thing altogether. Richard knew the boy was on this ship because he had probably been sentenced to seven years for stealing something as small as a loaf of bread.

The boy seemed to be coming to, but Richard was unsure what to do, although he realized that excessive movement of the damaged leg would not be helpful. So, he put his hands reassuringly on the boy's shoulders while, at the same time, talking to the boy in a calming tone. He did not want any violent or unnecessary movement.

After about ten minutes, the surgeon and an assistant arrived, quickly looked over at the boy, and the surgeon said, "You cannot do any more here, Sergeant. You can leave him with us."

Richard looked again at the boy as he left the surgery, saying, "I hope they can fix that leg."

The surgeon spoke to the boy, who was now awake but groaning with the pain, "Let's reset that leg of yours. This will be extremely painful, so hold this cloth between your teeth. Now hold very still."

The surgeon took hold of the boy's foot and ankle while his assistant held the boy's thigh. They had not done similar procedures as a pair before, but they both understood what needed to be done. Unfortunately, the ankle and knee joints were out of place, requiring strength and skill to return them back to normal.

The surgeon said to his assistant, "Now. Hold the leg as tight as you can and hold it still. Ready? Now!"

William pulled and twisted the leg as the boy let out a terrible sounding noise, not really a scream, as it was muffled by the cloth between his teeth, but blood-curdling, nevertheless. The boy at once went limp; the surgeon looked over and was sure he had only fainted.

"Just as well under the circumstances," thought the assistant.

The boy's leg looked better than before. The knee looked normal, but the foot was still at a strange angle.

The surgeon spoke once again, "We will have to have another go. Hold the lower calf just there."

"Now, Ready? Pull. Twist. Now!"

Luckily, the boy was unconscious this time, so they were no moaning noises from him. Nevertheless, the grating sound emanating from the leg was something both the surgeon and his assistant personally felt. The angle of the foot now looked a lot better. The boy would have extreme difficulty walking on that leg for quite some time and may always have a limp, but there was no way of knowing the long-term outcome. Rest was needed so the leg could naturally heal over time. How that would be achieved in a convict holding pen was beyond anyone's imagination. The boy was returned to the holding cage. Hopefully, his fellow adult convicts would assist him in the healing process.

Before he knew it, Richard's watch ended when the ship's bell rang eight times, showing it was 4 am and time to get some more sleep. On the way to his cabin, he noticed Michael, the other sergeant, getting the men on his watch sorted out. "Thank Christ, my watch is over," he said to himself, "I don't want to have to go through that again."

As Richard settled down in his bunk, he remembered that the fleet was about to set sail for New South Wales in the next few days, and the excitement was building. He could not wait to get back into the routine of life sailing on the high seas. Sitting around with the ship at anchor was starting to get to him.

Chapter 17

Elizabeth was up bright and early the following day, even before her father, who was usually an early riser. She tried her best not to make any noise, as she did not want to wake her parents, who usually were light sleepers. After dressing and sorting out her earlier unfinished tidying, she sat on the only chair and started to ponder her future. Such a long trip on a ship in a tiny space would indeed be a challenge, but she reasoned that the entire adventure and the outcome were something to look forward to.

While she realized that her longer-term future, in a place some 11,000 miles away, was challenging to visualize, maybe the trip and the time taken to get there were easier to think about. Then she remembered that the first load of the convicts was due to come aboard later today. She also thought about the responsibility and heavy workload her father would probably have from then on.

William woke while Elizabeth was sitting there thinking about her future, then he asked with a croaky voice, "Elizabeth, do you know what the time is?"

"I just heard the ship's bell ring six times. Does that tell you anything?

"Not really, as I am still trying to work out what the various watches on board are and what the actual time is when each bell rings."

William was reasonably comfortable, so he was firstly not in a hurry to get out of bed, and then suddenly, he also remembered that the convicts would arrive later today. He quickly jumped out of bed and prepared for what he expected would be a hectic day.

Ann, stirring slowly upon hearing the voices, was only half awake when William left for the surgery. Then, in a sleepy voice, she said,

"Sorry, I slept in. I hope your father will not be late, as today is important."

"Yes, I know. It will be interesting for everyone."

Concerned about what her daughter might think, Ann said, "You do know you will have to stay well away from them, don't you?"

"Yes, Mother, I know."

Elizabeth was now aware of the dangers of being too close to such convicted criminals, particularly the violent ones. The whole process nevertheless fascinated her, and she wondered what this exciting day would bring.

Ann was unsure how much Elizabeth was listening to her advice, so she made a mental note to keep a close eye on her all day.

Ann and Elizabeth left their cabin with the view to look around the ship before the convicts came on board, which they believed would start later in the day. They felt they could now venture further as they had been on board for a while. First, they decided to stay on the upper deck, which seemed the safest place. They walked past sailors, plus a couple of marines looking resplendent in their red uniforms with striking white belts. They each carried a musket and certainly looked very much in control.

Elizabeth certainly was impressed by how strong and manly the marines looked, even to the point of being unable to stop staring at them.

Ann, noticing what was happening, quickly commented to Elizabeth, "Hey, what did I tell you about being careful? It also applies to sailors and marines, you know. Don't stare. It could lead to something you don't want."

Elizabeth quickly turned her head away, then, looking at the ground, said, "Sorry about that. I will try and do better."

Ann, remembering what it was like being a teenager, said to herself, "This is going to be more difficult than I thought."

They continued to stroll around the deck, looking at everything they saw, although most of it was utterly foreign to them. These sailing ships were indeed an alien world. A couple of sailors were doing something with one of the long ropes. They had laid it along the entire length of the deck on the starboard side, and Ann and Elizabeth waited a couple of minutes to see what they were doing that for. It became rather obvious when they laid a new length of rope alongside the old one and then cut it to the same length.

While Ann reasoned what they were doing, Elizabeth had not yet worked it out, so she asked one of the sailors, "What are you doing with those ropes?"

The sailor she spoke to said, "Ah, that's a secret, Miss."

The other sailor piped up, "Take no note of what he is saying, Miss. He is pulling your leg. We are replacing the old rope by cutting the new one to the same length."

Elizabeth replied, "Ah, I see what you mean."

Both sailors smiled and nodded in response, and the first sailor acknowledged saying, "It's our pleasure, Miss."

Ann, noticing how the conversation had flowed, quickly grabbed Elizabeth's hand and led her to the other side of the ship. "What do you think you are doing?"

With a quizzical look, Elizabeth replied, "I haven't done anything!"

Ann was not sure how to respond to such an innocent reply. In fact, she was at a loss for words, so she just said, "We will talk about this later. Come on; we are going back to the cabin."

While Elizabeth and her mother had been walking the top deck, William promptly went to his surgery, hoping the supplies he had earlier ordered had arrived. To his relief, he noticed a couple of wooden boxes on the bed and, upon looking inside, found much of what he was looking for. He quickly removed all the items one by one so they could put them away in some logical order, hopefully remembering where he had put everything when he urgently needed them. Finally, after about an hour of consistent work, the job was done, and he sat down on the chair, feeling that most things in his tiny surgery were now under control.

William left the surgery and decided to have another look in the hold where the convict cages had been built, with the view to understanding a little more about the conditions they would be living in. Looking around the ship's hold from the top of the ladder, he thought, "Not a lot of room for nearly 200 men."

William had just left the hold to find out when the convicts would be arriving when he heard a commotion on the wharf. He walked over the starboard rail and was somewhat surprised at what he saw. The two carts carrying about twenty convicts each had arrived, both having low wooden cages attached, which made them look more like pig's transport. The convicts in one of the carts were shouting at one another as they pushed and shoved within the very restricted space. They were obviously very annoyed at something which was not apparent to William. He stood there and watched, wondering what type of injuries may result from such incarceration and who may need immediate treatment.

A sergeant of marines and his men stood ready to usher the convicts to their holding cages. The small doors to the two cages were opened one at a time, with each convict exiting carefully as they were all shackled at their wrists and ankles. Climbing down to the ground was extremely difficult under these restrictions, and some fell as a result. The clunking noises of the chains made during the process were loud and confronting, especially if you were unfamiliar with these processes and typical convict conditions. William leant on the ship's rail and took it all in, at the same time thinking that this was just the beginning. At this rate, there were at least eight more wagonloads to come.

The Marines had to yell at the convicts to form a line as they seemed extremely reluctant to do anything they were told. Pushing back against all authority seemed to be their philosophy. Finally, the first twenty or so were marched, as best as one could do in chains, up the gangway, across the deck, down the steep stairs into the hold and the first cage. William moved over to the edge of the hold to watch. It took a while, as climbing down the steep stairs in chains into the hold was a slow process. While the odd one missed a step, they caught themselves, and none fell to the deck below. The first 20 were locked into the first cage, and the marines returned to the dock to get the next group.

William noted that a few of the convicts now in the cage were wearing bandages, and he wondered if any of these wounds were serious. "Time will tell," he thought.

After the first load of convicts had been bustled into their cage, William decided to climb down into the hold and closely assess their health. He stood in the shadows, trying to keep well out of sight, with the view not to make any hasty judgements. He noticed a pile of hammocks in the middle of the cage, slowly getting smaller as each convict picked the one he wanted. He noted that a couple of more prominent men were enforcing their dominance over the others, usually raising their voices while pushing and shoving as they did so.

The general health of the convicts varied considerably. They were dressed in a variety of clothing, some reasonably dressed, others with barely anything on their backs. All their clothing was old and very dirty. Dried blood was showing on two or three of them, assuming older injuries that had not yet been cleaned up or healed. One convict had a rough stick he used to help himself to walk, and he strongly favoured his left leg. Their general demeanour seemed to be what one would expect for convicts living in such crowded conditions, although there was one who appeared to be very much at the bottom of the health pile.

William noticed that one of the apparent leaders in the group was aware of his presence and kept looking over at him as he went about his bossy business.

As the convicts in the cage sorted themselves out, the second group came down the stairs and were ushered into the same cage. As the ship was expecting nearly two hundred convicts, each of the four cages would have to hold roughly fifty men. This first cage looked over full to William's eyes, but he assumed the current chaos would soon end as they eventually worked out who went where and with what. He looked carefully at the second bunch; they looked in similar health to the first lot. He sighed, hoping that the general health of the balance of the convicts would not noticeably get any worse.

William returned to his surgery, and even though he had sorted out most of the essential items earlier, he wanted to make sure everything was ready. He did not want to be unprepared for any emergency. The quantity supplied was somewhat limited and was less than what he first ordered, so he hoped that they would be enough in the short term. He was completely involved in what he was doing, so he missed the knock on the door.

The first mate, whom William had not yet met, knocked a second time, this time much louder, making William suddenly look up and say, "Oh! Sorry, I did not hear you."

"That's all right; I am the first mate. The captain has asked me to ask you a question."

"No problem. How can I help?"

"On board, there will be about 200 convicts, plus about 60 others, including crew, which is about 260. Do you think this space you have here will be sufficient?"

"It will be tight, but I think I can make it work. Of course, it will depend on the number of health issues and accidents, and as I know that space is at a premium, this will do for now."

The first mate was somewhat surprised at the answer but was glad that there was no need to find more space, so, with a sigh of relief, he said, "Thanks for that, as I did not know what I would have done if you had wanted more space."

"Just as well, then. Anything else?"

"No, sir."

William was not sure that he should have answered the question that way, but now committed, he would have to make the most of the situation. So, he went back to double-checking his surgery supplies while putting to one side those that he thought would not be needed in the short term.

It was much later in the day when William returned to the hold, and the convict cages, to find that most of the convicts had now come aboard. He once again quietly inspected those he could see so that he could treat any major health problems that were obvious before the end of the day.

By this time, the noise coming from the convicts was considerably louder than earlier as each jockeyed for what they each thought was their rightful place. Each cage was slowly developing its leaders as its power struggle continued. The dynamics in each cage were interesting, and William was trying to take note of whom he may have to deal with in the future. The quieter and weaker ones would probably require the most medical attention, but this would be difficult unless it was carried out with the tacit approval of the cage leaders. He left the hold and returned to his surgery, now reasonably confident he could cope. However, the conditions the convicts lived in would make life difficult for everybody, including himself.

When Elizabeth returned to her cabin, she was unsure what to do, so she climbed up on her top bunk and lay down for a while. As she lay there, her mind quickly wandered from one subject to another, but she kept thinking about the two tall marines she had seen earlier. She had not seen two such strong and handsome-looking men in one place before. She started to visualize how it would feel to be clutched in the powerful arms of such a man, and that thought made her tremble, a strange but pleasant feeling. This was something she was not familiar with. Only recently had her thoughts turned to boys and men, and the whole idea of having anything to do with sex with anyone was just plain terrifying. Elizabeth had not had much contact with the opposite sex until now, as nearly all her education had been by private tutors at home, and her mother had been very strict about where else she went.

Elizabeth snuggled under her blanket, thinking about how cosy and comfortable it would feel in someone's strong arms. The feeling of closeness and intimacy was comforting. With that warm thought in her mind, she drifted off to sleep.

Elizabeth did not know how long she had been asleep when her mother called out, "Elizabeth, it is time to get something to eat."

Not fully awake, Elizabeth replied, "How long have I been asleep?"

"About 2 hours, I would think."

"Just a minute, Mother, I am still half asleep. By the way, where is Father?"

"He is busy, so we will get ours now."

Both left their cabin and headed to the galley to get their meal, assuming William would get his own later.

On the way, Elizbeth kept an eye out, hoping to see one of those handsome marines she had seen earlier. By now, she was starting to realize that it was necessary to be very discreet when out amongst these men, even though she felt it rather challenging to achieve the modesty required. It did not come naturally, but she understood such modest behaviour was necessary.

Elizabeth also noticed the commotion coming from the other side of the bulkhead and then remembered that the convicts were still being loaded. Although the bulkhead was of heavy timber, the foul language was sometimes undeniable, which, in most cases, was very foreign to her ears.

Upon hearing the same language, Ann said, "Hurry up, Elizabeth. Shut your ears to that terrible noise."

They arrived at the galley just as the meals were being served; they quickly got theirs and retreated to their cabin. All the while, Elizabeth was trying to look around very cautiously, hoping to see one of those marines—no such luck. "Damn!" she said under her breath.

Now feeling more organized and in control of his job, William left his surgery and returned to his cabin. He smelt the food cooking on the way, so he changed direction towards the galley and then realized how hungry he was. He gathered his meal and took off towards his cabin when a sailor came rushing around the corner, smashing into William, which caused his meal to shoot out of his hands and fall against the wall. The bowl hit the floor with a bang, and the meal slowly slid down the wall. As the bowl hit the floor, so did William. The momentum of the sailor running into him caused William to hit the floor bottom first, and then the rest of his body flew backwards until he was lying flat on his back.

The sailor stumbled, regained his feet and kept going, until he, with his hands in front of him, ran into the wall. At the same time, he yelled out, "Bloody hell!"

William was so surprised that he lay still for a few seconds, saying nothing. Then, sitting up, he too yelled out in similar words.

The sailor, now fully aware of what had just occurred, returned to where William lay on the ground, offered him a helping hand, and said, "Sorry, sir, I did not see you."

William took the offer of the hand and slowly stood up, saying as he did so, "That's all right. No real damage, although my meal is no longer fit to eat."

They both, seeing the funny side of what had just occurred, started to laugh while at the same time pointing to the smear down the wall and the rest of the meal lying on the floor.

Once they had both settled down, the sailor said, "Sir, I was on the way to see you. The captain wants you right away at the top of the rear hold. I will take care of this mess."

William left the sailor to clean up and went up top to meet the captain, wondering what the hell the emergency was all about. Another group of convicts were now going down into the hold and into their cage as William walked over to the captain.

"Captain, you wish to see me."

"Yes, that's right. We have a problem that needs your attention. Come with me."

The captain followed the last convict down the stairs into the hold with William right behind. William noted that all four cages now looked exceedingly full, and this last lot had yet to be allocated theirs. "It is going to be a tight squeeze," William said to no one in particular.

The captain happened to hear what was said and replied, "It certainly is, and I think it is going to cause problems. Come this way," as he led William to the cage on the other side of the hold. They came upon a convict lying on a blanket just outside the closed cage gate, and by the look and the colour of his face, William's first impression was that he was dead. He quickly tried to find a pulse, but there was none, so he said to the captain, "What is the story here?"

The captain shrugged his shoulders and said, "I don't know. The Marines have asked questions but are not getting useful answers. It could be murder as he was heard arguing with another convict shortly before he was found. I need to find out how and why he died, so can you look at him? You may find out what happened."

Unusually, the convicts were far quieter than usual, with no yelling out, which they often did when confronted by anyone who happened to be close to their particular cage.

Considering the next best step, William said, "If he could be bought to my surgery, I may be able to find out what caused his death."

The captain turned to the sergeant of marines and gave the necessary instructions. The dead convict was wrapped in canvas, and two marines carried him away from the cages and to William's surgery.

"Put him on the table and leave me alone. That's fine."

William did not want to be interrupted, so he closed the door and carefully walked around the table, looking at everything he could see without removing any of the convict's clothes. He turned him over and checked again. Nothing was obvious at this early stage, although he noted that the man was just skin and bones, with very hollow cheeks.

William continued to inspect the convict as he slowly removed his clothes, one by one. There were no apparent signs of bruising or abrasions that could have occurred in any struggle before his death. He also noticed that his skin was very dry to the touch, all his ribs were prominent, and his eyes were sunken back into his head. After further investigation, William concluded that the man probably died from extreme malnutrition, that then led to a heart attack. He decided to inquire from those in the cage who knew the deceased before making his final decision. He left the surgery and headed off to the convict cage where the dead man had been found, hoping to find at least one convict willing to supply relevant information.

William climbed into the hold and then asked a couple of attending marines to go with him and show him where the body was found. It was unnecessary to enter the cage as the sides were not closed in, just closely barred, so conversation with those inside the cage was possible without entering.

The marines pointed to where the body was found and stood well back at William's request as he walked up to the cage. He recognised some of the men inside from earlier, hoping they would not refuse to talk to him. As he approached the barred cage, the extreme hierarchy within the enclosure once again showed its ugly head.

"What the hell are you doing here?" was the first remark hurled at him.

William thought it best to tell the truth, so he replied, "As I must write up a report on that earlier death, I just want to ask a couple of questions. I don't think it is anybody's fault."

"All right, if you must," was the arrogant reply.

The two men that William recognised came to the walls of the cage and said, "We don't know much. He refused to eat anything. He did not want to leave England. That's all we know."

"Fine, I understand. That's all I need."

With that information confirming what he suspected, William returned to the surgery and entered the details he had found out in his log. His view was that the convict had died due to a lack of food that was self-inflicted and that there was no other cause other than his general run-down condition. William quickly dressed the body, which was later picked up by a group of sailors and taken to who knows where. William was happy that that part was not his responsibility. The convicts behaved reasonably over the next few days as they settled into their cramped quarters while more stores were bought aboard.

Chapter 18

The fleet (First Fleet) that was assembled to sail to New South Wales eventually came together off Portsmouth harbour and finally sailed on the 13th of May 1787, a Sunday as it happened. The eleven vessels, under the command of Captain Arthur Phillip, left the South of England bound for a continent on the other side of the world. The fleet comprised two naval vessels, HMS Supply and the flagship, HMS Sirius: plus six convict ships and three supply vessels. Approximately 1400 persons sailed on the fleet, with nearly 800 male and female convicts, with several dozen under 14 years of age. The balance comprised sailors, marines, officials and their families.

The HMS Hyaena, an armed frigate escort vessel, accompanied the fleet briefly before returning to port. The fleet continued its 8-month voyage. The weather that day was fine; so many convicts were allowed on deck under the watchful eye of the Marines as they watched their homeland slowly disappear over the horizon. A small percentage of convicts would return to England after their detention period ended, usually for seven years, while the rest would become permanent residents of New South Wales and sometimes elsewhere within the continent. The beginning of a true adventure and the unknown future for all had begun.

The First Fleet, less the Hyaena, which had by then returned to Portsmouth, arrived in Teneriffe in the Canary Islands three weeks after they departed from England. Fresh vegetables, meat and fruit were taken aboard during their one-week stay in Santa Cruz harbour. During this first stage of the voyage, two convicts tried to take over the Scarborough by force, but they failed, received 24 lashes for their efforts and were transferred to the Prince of Wales. The firm punishment swiftly dealt with proved to be a deterrent for further such behaviour, particularly for the next few months.

The First Fleet left Teneriffe on the 10th of June, setting off to cross the Atlantic Ocean on the way to Rio de Janeiro on the eastern coast of South America. On this leg of the voyage, many on board the ships found the hot and humid conditions near the equator difficult to bear, particularly with the constant vermin and parasitic infestation problems. The climatic conditions forced the ships to pump out and clean their bilges regularly to minimize disease. Water also became scarce on all the ships at one stage, which required strict rationing for everyone. Tropical rainstorms were a constant concern during the passage to Rio, and therefore, the convicts spent much of their time below decks, although this allowed rainwater to be captured.

The fleet arrived in Rio de Janeiro on the 5th of August, nearly three months after leaving Portsmouth, and it stayed in port for some four weeks. Further water and other supplies were purchased and stored on board, ready for the next leg of their long journey. The officers and other gentlemen of the fleet were treated very well during their stay, right up until the fleet left on the 4th of September. It took an additional six weeks or so to cross the South Atlantic to South Africa.

The First Fleet arrived in Cape Town, in Table Bay, on the 13th of October. The ships were stocked with further supplies and took on much livestock, including cows, horses, sheep, pigs, goats and a range of poultry. Some female convicts were moved onto other transport vessels so that the livestock could be boarded. The convicts were fed a range of meat, vegetables and fruit while anchored in the harbour to improve their strength and general condition for the next stage of their long voyage.

After about a month in Table Bay, the fleet left to complete the last leg of its voyage by crossing the Indian Ocean, along the south coast of Australia, and finally, to the east coast. The fleet experienced a wide range of sailing conditions, sometimes becalmed, other times experiencing violent storms. Supplies ran short again, including water and wine, the latter considered essential on an 18^t century sailing ship. They eventually sighted Van Diemen's Land (Tasmania) on the 4th of January 1788 and then headed north towards Botany Bay in New South Wales.

It was nearly three months after leaving Table Bay that the fleet finally came to their destination, and although the ships varied in size and sailing speed, they all arrived in the waters off New South Wales within two days of one another. This was amazing as the voyage from Cape Town was considered long, with every one of the 11 vessels having a vast range of weather and sea conditions to contend with. Finally, HMS Supply, the lead vessel, complete with Captain Phillip aboard, arrived at Botany Bay on the 18th of January, 1788. The rest of the fleet followed within a couple of days. Everyone aboard the fleet was overjoyed to find themselves and all their possessions at what they all thought was their final destination.

A group of natives (Aboriginals) were seen as the various ships in the fleet approached the shore. A few ship's officers and other senior members of the fleet stepped ashore later during the day of their arrival. They experienced several friendly interactions with the locals. After a few days, the Governor, Phillip Gidley King, in conjunction with other senior fleet officers, decided that Botany Bay was not the ideal place for a settlement. The Governor's party sailed some 12 miles to the north, to a place Captain Cook had named Port Jackson, to ascertain if it would be more suitable. They returned three days later and advised all captains that they were convinced it was a far better anchorage and place for a new settlement.

The entire fleet only sailed north the short distance to Port Jackson. They had found a far larger harbour with many safe anchorages, which they thought was one of the best harbours in the world. Such a harbour was considered far more suitable for a large fleet and a potential penal settlement.

Chapter 19

Elizabeth, in company with her mother and father, watched with wonderment as the Scarborough entered Port Jackson on its way to Sydney Cove. The eleven individual ships in the fleet were making their way to their various anchorages, and Elizabeth watched in awe at what unfolded in front of her.

Elizabeth, in her enthusiasm, said, "Father, Mother, this is amazing. Have you ever seen such a sight?"

Her mother, thinking more about the difficulties ahead of her, replied, "Yes, dear. It is."

William, not wanting to dampen Elizabeth's enthusiasm, said, "Now that that long voyage is over, this is the new beginning."

"When can we go ashore?" gushed Elizabeth.

"Not yet. There is a bit to do before that can happen. For a start, where would we sleep?" replied William.

"Yes. I see what you mean. All in good time, I guess."

Elizabeth stood at the ship's rail and gazed in amazement at everything within her sight. The Scarborough finally anchored very close to the shore, which allowed Elizabeth to get a close-up view of her future home. The shape and colour of the various trees were very different from what she was used to, which made the whole countryside, in her eyes, unique. While the family were watching the proceedings, her father had been asked to go and see the captain, who was still watching the rest of the fleet proceed to anchor.

William found the captain still near the helm, even though the ship was now anchored. "Captain, I understand you wish to see me."

"Yes, that is so. I have just received a message asking you to go with the first load of convicts, who are about to go ashore, to stand by while they clear scrub and trees. There will be a squad of marines with them, and from a safety medical safety point of view, it is thought best that you go as well. Any problems with that?"

"No problem. I will need a few essential items to take with me. When are they leaving?"

"Very soon. The convicts will be up on deck shortly."

With that, William rushed to the surgery, gathered what he thought he might need, put them in a canvas bag, and returned to the upper deck. By this stage, a line of convicts was standing along the port rail, waiting to climb down the rope ladder into the cutter. William waited as this process took place and, while doing so, noticed the eagerness of individual convicts as they prepared to be finally going ashore. They knew that there was hard work ahead of them, but their manner informed William they were happy to do anything to get off the damn ship.

Over the next few days, the entire group of convicts, marines and others returned to the ship each night after a hard day's work. William, although treating minor cuts and abrasions at times, was glad that there were no significant accidents, even though one large tree came down amongst a group of convicts, somehow managing to miss them. The most challenging part of William's days so far was the climb up the rope ladder onto the deck at the end of each day. He found the ladder's movements very difficult to control, particularly as his knees were feeling fatigued by that time of the day.

Over the next few days, other groups of convicts were also sent ashore to clear various areas so that tents and other shelters could be erected. The shoreline was becoming a hive of activity, and everyone was finding it very hot from such hard work. Some tents were eventually pitched, and a few from the ship's company stayed there overnight, unofficially the first to spend the night at their new home.

The whole process fascinated Elizabeth, and her mother finally allowed her to watch the proceedings from the ship's rail if she stayed well clear of the working men. Although the last eight months' voyage had been an absolute eye-opener for her, Elizabeth found the entire process of preparing the site for a settlement fascinating. So, she spent much of those early days watching from a safe distance. A few of the ship's sailors spent their spare time fishing over the side of the ship, and fortunately, they managed to catch a variety of well-received fish.

Unbeknown to William, Governor Phillip, under instructions from King George 111, was preparing to send a party to settle New Norfolk (Norfolk Island). Lieutenant Phillip Gidley King was appointed the Governor of the new settlement, who would be responsible for the first group to settle the island, made up of a small group of convicts, soldiers and free persons.

Shortly after King's appointment, William was invited to join King and travel to Norfolk Island with his family as the island's first surgeon. While he was extremely surprised by the suggestion, he felt somewhat privileged to have been asked.

Upon receiving the invitation, William found an ideal quiet time to speak to Ann as she stood at the rail looking out to sea. "I know we have been expecting to settle here in New South Wales, but I have been requested to join a team of convicts and settlers going to Norfolk Island. Captain Cook gave glowing reports about it, and after thinking about it, I think it is worth serious consideration. What do you think about going there?"

Ann was amazed that William would even consider such a proposition, and, in the first instance, she was not sure that she had heard right, so she said, "What was that you said? Are you really suggesting we leave here and go somewhere else? Norfolk Island, did you say?"

"Well, I know it is somewhat of a surprise, but I think it is worth giving the idea serious thought."

As cautious as ever, Ann said, "How long have we got to make a decision?"

"The ship sails in two days, so I need to reply by tomorrow morning at the latest."

"Goodness gracious me!" Ann exclaimed.

"Sorry, Ann, for springing this on you, but I was only asked about an hour ago."

"Well, how about you answer a couple of questions first?"

"That's fair. I will answer what I can."

"The most important one is: Why are they going there when we have not gone ashore here yet?"

William thought carefully about the question for some seconds, then said, "I understand that there are three official reasons. The first one is that a few foreign ships are sailing around these waters, and they don't want them to settle on any island close to here. The second reason is that they believe the island has flax and tall trees that could be useful to the Navy. Finally, it has also been said to have very fertile soil, which could easily grow extra food as a backup supply source for here."

"Oh. I see. It is essential, then.

"That's what I have been told. By the way, I have also been told the climate is not as hot and dry as here. You might prefer that."

Ann had numerous questions running around in her head, but she knew William would get very annoyed if she asked too many, so she just said, "One more question. Who is going to this island?"

"I was told that there would only be a small group of convicts and other persons going in the first instance, less than 30, I believe, with others following later."

"Can you give me a little time to think about this? It is a big step, you know, and nothing like what I was expecting. It probably does not matter where we go, really, as we are starting from nothing regardless."

William, understanding the enormity of the question that Ann had to consider, left her alone by walking to the other rail, which just happened to be towards what was happening on shore. Various loads of building supplies were being loaded into cutters and taken ashore, some of them looking very unstable as they were heavily overloaded. He stayed there for a while, taking it all in, when he heard a woman's footsteps approaching.

Ann sidled up to William and stood beside him, saying nothing, as she was still not 100% convinced that going to Norfolk Island was for the best. Elizabeth was her prime concern. William waited patiently.

Ann was the first to speak, and although unsure whether she was making the right decision, she said, "All right, if you think this move is the best for all of us."

Usually undemonstrative, William gave Ann a small hug and a peck on the cheek, saying, "Thanks. I don't think you will regret it."

Now that the decision to go to Norfolk Island had been made, William quickly advised Governor King and then the captain of the Scarborough, as he would require help from the latter to get his possessions onto HMS Supply.

Elizabeth was completely unaware of what her parents had just decided, as she had spent considerable time at the ship's forward rail watching the comings and goings of men, equipment and animals on the way ashore from several vessels. She was dreaming of what the future might hold, particularly taking note of the handsome marines who moved about as resplendent as ever. She did not wander away from the ship's bow, which seemed the safest place and was consistent with her mother's warning. After a couple of hours watching the spectacle, she thought it was now wise to return to their cabin.

Elizabeth came around the corner of the passage and found her mother, who had just opened their cabin door, leaving.

Ann was caught somewhat by surprise, and then she said, "Ah, I was hoping to catch up with you."

Following her mother inside, Elizabeth said, "Oh, is it important?"

"Yes, very important and fairly urgent,"

Elizabeth looked closely at her mother, trying to get a sign of whether she should be concerned.

Ann said, "Sit down on the chair, and I will tell you what it is all about. It is nothing to worry about, so you can get that worried look off your face."

Elizabeth, saying nothing, sat down on the bottom bunk bed very slowly, still worried about what this was all about.

"Now, Elizabeth, I know you have been watching what has been going on over the last couple of days, understanding that this will be your new home, but that is not entirely correct."

"What do you mean? Not entirely correct."

"Well, your father and I have made a significant decision that may take some getting used to."

The worried look that had started to leave Elizabeth's face returned as she said, "Some getting used to. What do you mean?"

Ann was finding this process very difficult to deal with, and she was not sure how she should answer the question, so she paused for a few seconds and then said, "Mm. In the first instance, we will not be going ashore here but transferring to another ship."

"But this is where the settlement will be, right?"

"Yes, it is. But we will not be settling here. We are going to settle on Norfolk Island."

Elizabeth, by this stage, was not sure she was hearing right and said, "Not settling here! I thought that is what we came halfway around the world to do. And Norfolk Island, where the hell is that?"

Ann was now worried that her daughter might not be willing to go unless she was given much more information, so Ann decided to tell her the whole story, at least the parts she knew.

"The settlement here will have hundreds of people, both convicts and others, so it will take considerable time and effort to set up fully. Because other countries are sailing around these parts of the world, the government thinks that it is important that they do not develop a base close to here. In addition to that, it is felt that Norfolk Island will be able to supply much-needed flax and timber for ships, and the island will also be better able to supply extra food for those living here."

"Hang on a minute, but what about me?" was Elizabeth's immediate response.

"I know that is of no real interest to you, but it is why another colony is going to be set up there. The important thing for you to think about is what it is going to be like for our entire family, and that includes you. There is no one living there now, and I am told it is a very beautiful place. Because not many are going there, it should be a better place for a family like ours and a better opportunity for your father. The weather is also supposed to be very nice, probably much better than here. You do realize that regardless of whether we were here or there, we will be starting from nothing."

"Well, I guess it does not matter where we are as long as we are together. And happy, of course," was Elizabeth's reply.

Surprised at Elizabeth's positive reaction, Ann said, "Are you sure you are happy to go? "

Elizabeth paused for a few seconds before she spoke, "Well, it is not what I was expecting, but I guess I cannot see any harm in it."

Ann, relieved that there would not be any argument, said, "Right, that's it then. We are going. We must start packing up our things immediately, as we will be leaving on the Supply in a few days."

"On one of the Navy ships?" replied Elizabeth with an expectant tone in her voice. "Who's going?"

"Yes. There will be some convicts, a few marines, some free persons, the new Commandant and us. It will certainly be a new experience. We still have a little time left before dinner, so let's get those trunks over here," Ann said as she pointed to the three trunks stored at the end of the cabin.

Not aware that his wife had already spoken to Elizabeth, William came through the door into the cabin with the words, "There you are, Elizabeth. I have been looking for you. I thought you were up on deck near the bow."

Ann jumped in, saying, "I have just been talking to Elizabeth, and everything is fine. We were just about to get the trunks so that we can start packing them."

"Ah, so you have beaten me to the punch. Everything is good then."

"Yes, we just need to get ready," Ann said in an upbeat tone.

Surprised that it had been easy to convince Elizabeth to go to Norfolk Island willingly, William said, "Elizabeth, are you quite happy?"

"Yes, Father, that's fine."

"Great! Now let's get down to it. What do you want me to do?"

The family found ways, unusually so, to work together as a team as they began to get their possessions back into the trunks, leaving out only the essentials needed for the next couple of days. A new adventure was ahead of them. Another ship and another voyage beckoned.

Chapter 20

Richard was glad to see their final destination, Port Jackson, finally came into view, although he was somewhat disappointed that they had not unloaded in Botany Bay because it all looked good from what he saw.

The rest of the crew and passengers on the Alexander had experienced plenty of difficulties with the convicts during the long voyage. Richard thought it would be advantageous for everyone to finally get back onto dry land. He watched the ship turn into the entrance to Port Jackson and was amazed that the harbour was so big, as it seemed to go on forever. They sailed into the inner harbour at the same time as several other ships of the fleet, so big was the harbour entrance.

With the obvious rattle of the anchor chains going down the side, Richard sighed, thankful they had finally arrived at their destination, particularly after such a long and arduous voyage. He was not on any ship watch but understood there would be much to do over the next few weeks. The Alexander was not carrying a great deal of general cargo, as its main cargo was convicts, which reminded him that they would need considerable oversight until a form of containment on shore could be built.

Richard's immediate superior, the lieutenant, had not done much on this voyage as he had delegated most of the work to his two sergeants, one being Richard. Richard had not heard what the plan was after they anchored, so he decided to chase up the lieutenant and find out what would happen. Luckily, the lieutenant was walking across the deck at the stern. Richard promptly followed him. Catching up, he said, "Excuse me, lieutenant. Do you know what the arrangements are about getting the convicts ashore?"

"Yes, Sergeant, I have just found out. They will all stay on board until some form of security can be worked out on shore, although I think it may be just chains in the short term. Then, starting tomorrow at daybreak, some will go ashore to help clear areas so they can put up tents. You lot will be making sure they stay on the job, of course. I will let you know more before the morning watch starts. Any questions?"

"Not really, lieutenant. That's what I thought. Thank you, sir."

The next day, Richard woke up on time as the morning watch would start in about three-quarters of an hour. Richard's first thought was that he should quickly get something to eat, realizing that today may be a long one. In any event, he felt pretty hungry as he had not eaten much over the last twelve hours.

It was still dark when Richard got out of bed and prepared for his watch, which started at 4 am. "This is indeed going to be an interesting day," he thought. Getting dressed in his bright red uniform, he thought that he had better make himself respectable as he realized that this day was a historical one. He also noticed that there seemed to be a little more movement and excitement throughout the ship, which he could hear and feel through the timber walls.

Richard arrived on deck just before eight bells to find his troop already lined up and ready to get to work. By now, the Marines knew exactly what standards their sergeant wanted and were doing precisely what he required. That meant the inspection procedure this morning was over very quickly. The convicts would assemble on deck by 5 am to be transported ashore and ready for work by sun-up.

Knowing that today would be the start of constructing a brand-new settlement, Richard thought it wise to update his troop on what to expect.

"Gentlemen, could I have your attention? Today is important because a few convicts will be going ashore today to start clearing land so that tents and other accommodations can be put up. They will be transported on one of the cutters, and obviously, we will be responsible for ensuring they all get ashore and back here again. A few may use this as an opportunity to escape, so be on your guard. There will also be a considerable quantity of supplies being put ashore from the store vessels, so some of the convicts will be helping with that. Are there any questions?"

"Sergeant, what is the routine if we see a convict trying to escape?"

"No different from usual; first, give them reasonable warnings, and if you have to shoot, don't shoot to kill unless you have to."

"Any others?"

The men remained silent.

"I am not sure how many are going ashore, but it could be several boatloads, so you will need to split into your usual three groups. One squad to stay on board, one group to ride on the cutters and the other to stay on shore with the convicts. We will be a bit thin, Particularly on shore, but I know you can handle it. I will stay on the ship until the last load goes ashore, and then I will follow you there. Is that clear? Oh, I have just thought of something. Many convicts will have axes and saws that could be used as weapons against you, so stay far enough away from them so you can use your weapon if necessary."

There were nods and a general murmur of consent, so Richard continued, "When the lieutenant gives the order, we will do as I have just outlined, and, in the meantime, the usual routine applies. Dismiss!"

The various groups worked out their routines and moved to their positions, with the first squad accompanying the convicts in the cutter moving to the ship's rail.

The lieutenant approached Richard as they moved away and asked, "Sergeant, did you manage to get the message across?"

"I think so, lieutenant, we will wait till you give the order to get the first load of convicts on deck, and it should be relatively easy from there."

"Very good. Continue, Sergeant."

"Sir."

As Richard moved around the main deck, he could see and hear the sailors preparing the cutter, finally leaving it tied up alongside, ready to receive the first load of convicts. He was also aware of the many voices coming from the hold; the convicts were obviously excited to get out of their cages and keen to go ashore.

The ship's captain oversaw this whole process as it involved most individuals on board the ship, including sailors, marines and convicts. Although the captain was present, the first mate was more directly involved in preparing both the convicts in the hold and the cutter alongside.

Richard decided to go into the hold and watch the proceedings there. His usual squad of marines were on the same deck as the convict's cages, although the excitement and the noise emanating from the pens was obvious. A few overseers stood alongside the nearest cage to the stairs, from where he assumed the first group of convicts would be selected.

The lieutenant descended the ladder and came up to Richard, and said, "Sergeant, I would suggest that you make sure your squads are in place, as the whole process will be starting shortly. Oh, by the way, I will be staying on board, so you go with the last cutter trip and stay ashore."

"Sir."

Richard walked over to the squad already in the hold and said, "You lot to stay on board for this watch, and we will change things around on later watches."

Happy that they would not have to stay on board the ship the entire time and get the opportunity to stand on dry land, the squad leader said, "Thanks, Sergeant, that's great."

Richard climbed up the ladder and found the other squad on the top deck and gave instructions, "You go with the convicts on board the first cutter, with one squad staying on shore with the unloaded convicts and the other squad coming back to pick up the next load. When the last load has gone ashore, the squad on the cutter will then stay there. Is that clear?"

Richard waited a minute or so for his instructions to be sorted between the two squads and then said, "Once the cutter is ready to receive you, the first squad can board, with the other squad boarding after the convicts."

The one corporal within the group said, "No questions, Sergeant, leave it with me," as both squads moved towards the ship's rail.

Richard decided to move over to the side of the hold and keep an eye on both the convicts coming out of their cages and watching what was happening on the top deck.. Nothing of concern seemed to be happening in the hold, so he walked over to the rail where the cutter was tied alongside.

The cutter had no mast, although he could see where one could be fitted. It was about twenty feet long, and the six sailors rowing were already seated. Richard estimated that it could carry no more than six in the bow and another six or eight in the stern at the most. It would have to make several trips, especially as a small squad of marines would take up some of the space.

Thinking about that space problem, Richard changed his original instructions, so walking up to the waiting marines, he said, "Because of the lack of space on the cutter, only two of you stay onboard for each trip, and the six of you stay onshore. Does that make sense?"

"Yes, Sergeant."

With that clarified, Richard returned to the top of the ladder that went down into the hold and noticed the first load of convicts was exiting the first cage. They continued onto the deck and across to the port rail and slowly climbed down the rope ladder and into the cutter one by one. All the convicts found this extremely difficult as they were chained by their ankles, giving them just enough length to step from one rung of the ladder to the next. As all eight marines had already got aboard by this time, the cutter could not take a full complement of convicts this trip. Six marines would stay on shore to watch those convicts staying there because the number of convicts ashore would grow with each trip.

The ferry process continued for some time as at least half of the convicts aboard the ship went ashore. Finally, the last load finished loading, and Richard just managed to find a space for himself. The cutter looked very low in the water and felt sluggish as the rowers manoeuvred it. Luckily, the harbour was relatively calm.

The convicts were well-behaved, probably because they were more than happy to get out of their cages. But this was not to last long. Richard and the other two marines were in the cutter's stern with five convicts and about six in the vessel's bow. One of the convicts in the bow seemed overly excited by his newfound freedom because he was climbing up onto the bow, waving his arms and shouting.

Richard yelled from the stern of the vessel, "Hey you," pointing to the man in the bow, "Get off there and sit down."

There were no others in the bow other than convicts, so the convict carried on with the others laughing and encouraging him. Richard yelled out again, "Sit down. Now!" In defiance of instructions, he continued with his dangerous antics, as he was now singing and acting up in response to the encouraging cheers of his fellow convicts.

Understanding that most could not swim, Richard was afraid he could easily fall overboard, so he quickly decided to move to the bow and get the man down. Standing just behind and between the six rowers, Richard called out, "Watch out. I am coming through," the rowers stopped rowing, and he rushed between them towards the bow.

The other convicts in the bow moved out of the way to let Richard through as he yelled, "Stop that." Unfortunately, just as he said that the convict, who had been standing on one leg, found that his leg chains were not long enough to allow him enough movement to keep his balance, so he lost his footing and fell. He yelled out as he tried to grab the railing but could not hold on, so he disappeared over the bow and quickly out of sight.

Richard promptly looked over the front of the vessel and then over each side, but the convict was nowhere to be seen. Richard yelled out to the rowers, "Back up!" Everyone in the boat was looking for the convict by this stage, but there was no sign of him. The rowers slowly rowed backwards while Richard kept his eyes on the sea over the bow.

As they did so, he yelled, "Has anyone seen anything?"

Other than a few murmurs, there was no positive response.

"Damn it!" Richard called out to no one in particular.

Turning to the rowers again, he said, "Row forward a bit."

The cutter moved slowly forward; Richard and everyone on board was scanning the water, but there was still no sign of the convict, not even a ripple.

The cutter stayed still for a few minutes while everyone on board took in what had just happened. Richard finally concluded that as the convict had quickly gone under the water, probably owing to the weight of the chains and probably could not swim, and as no one had seen him, there was not much more anyone could do.

Richard called out to no one in particular, "Does anyone know his name?"

"Yeh, it's Stuart McKenzie," someone called out, "Stupid Scottish bastard."

Richard returned to the vessel's stern and called out, "Can anyone see him? Does everyone agree he has gone for good?"

Richard did not want to leave the area but did not know what else he could do. The convict had obviously disappeared under the water, and unless a miracle had occurred, he would now have drowned.

After receiving a murmur of agreement, Richard reluctantly said to the rowers, "All right, let's carry on."

As the cutter continued towards the shore, Richard started thinking, "I wonder if he could have fooled us, and he is still alive?" Then, answering his own question as he looked behind the cutter, he thought, "I doubt it. Too late now anyway."

The cutter came closer to the shoreline, then finally lifted its bow as it glided up the beach. By the time it came to a complete stop, an onshore overseer came to the boat and took charge.

Richard's squad jumped out of the cutter into about a foot of water and watched as the overseer organized the convicts. They had trouble getting over the gunnel with their leg irons, but eventually, all were standing in a group.

Richard watched the various convict work gangs clear the land, using saws, axes and shovels that had come ashore from the store vessels the day before. By the end of the day, a large area, probably two acres, had been cleared of scrub and small trees. As the sun lowered towards the horizon, various groups of convicts started returning to their respective ships. The return trips were conducted very much as the outward journey was, other than no one falling overboard.

There had been no significant incidents during the day except for the odd minor accident, so the convicts, all but the one now missing, assumed drowned, arrived safely back onboard.

The lieutenant met Richard as he climbed over the ship's rail and said, "I hear you had trouble with one convict falling overboard on the way out?"

"Yes, Lieutenant, I did, and I will give you details in writing as soon as I can."

"That's good. Now, Sergeant, I have received orders that you have been assigned to HMS Supply that is not stopping here but going on to Norfolk Island. I don't know why they have picked you, so you may be able to knock it back."

"I see, sir. I have heard about that island. Captain Cook visited it, didn't he? Sounds interesting. How long have I got?"

"The Supply is leaving in a couple of days with a small group of convicts, a couple of marines, plus a few others. Just over twenty to set up a small settlement, I think."

"You have caught me by surprise, Lieutenant, but quickly thinking about it, it does sound interesting."

246

Richard confirmed his decision the following morning, then spent the next few days doing his usual watches and preparing to affect the transfer onto HMS Supply. He was looking forward to the new challenge. It would undoubtedly differ from the last eight months, mainly as it was a small party.

Chapter 21

Elizabeth and her mother repacked their trunks with difficulty, for it seemed they could not find room to hold as much as they had previously. Ann was particularly frustrated at the entire process and, in the end, decided to put a few things into a separate sack that could be carried by hand. Elizabeth finally managed to get all her things packed into her trunk, even though it took much time and effort to achieve.

Finally, they sat back on Ann's bed and looked at their handiwork, happy it was now done, although neither looked forward to ever having to do that again.

The family's last day aboard the Scarborough eventually ended, and the entire family turned in early, as they were expected to be ready for travel and be at the ship's rail at dawn.

Elizabeth lay in her upper bunk thinking about everything of importance that had occurred on their eventful voyage since leaving Portsmouth over eight months ago. She felt she had learned a great deal during the long journey and was now beginning to understand what it meant to be an adult in the big wide world. The people she had met and the situations she had to deal with outside of her earlier experiences gave her additional knowledge that she was thankful for. As her sixteenth birthday had come and gone during the long voyage, she felt ready for even more exciting experiences and felt very much like an adult. The fact that she was not going ashore here was not what she thought would happen, but the magical island she was heading for tomorrow beckoned.

William woke up earlier than the other two, and the first thing that Elizabeth knew about the new day was her father calling out, "Come on, you two, time to get up."

Elizabeth was finding it very difficult to wake up, as she had stayed awake for some time last evening thinking about her future. Then she realized this was the beginning of an entirely new chapter, so now it was time to get moving. She jumped out of bed and quickly dressed, remembering to put on the extra petticoat her mother recommended.

The trunks were now fully packed and sitting in the middle of the cabin awaiting transport to the Supply. However, they did not have to wait long before a loud knock on the door, which for some strange reason, made them all jump. William opened the door to two solid sailors who said, "We have come for your trunks, sir."

"Good," he said, pointing, "There they are. There are four of them."

One by one, the trunks were taken through the door, up the stairs to the main deck and over to the starboard rail. They were very heavy, but with the help of a third sailor, they managed to lower each of them over the rail and into the cutter. The captain of the Scarborough came over and thanked them for everything, mainly for what William had achieved as the ship's surgeon.

Elizabeth looked around the now very familiar deck for the last time, thinking that, while she was somewhat sorry to leave, the excitement of an upcoming adventure was far more powerful.

One by one, Elizabeth and her family climbed down the rope ladder to sit in the cutter's bow. While all three still found climbing down rope ladders challenging, their limited experiences made it more manageable. Finally, the six sailors took hold of their oars, pushed the vessel away from the ship's side, and started rowing across the bay. Elizabeth looked around, unsure of where they were going, as she thought the Supply was on the other side of the bay. Feeling concerned, Elizabeth asked no one in particular, "Where are we going?"

One of the sailors answered, "Miss, we are going to pick up a few more from the Alexander," pointing to another ship not far away.

Feeling foolish for not thinking of such an obvious explanation, she said, "Oh, I see."

Five minutes later, the cutter glided up alongside the Alexander under the rope ladder while several people watched their arrival over the rail.

While one of the rowers held onto the ladder, a marine in his unmistakable red uniform came over the side and climbed down into the cutter. He helped in the loading of two more trunks, now taking up much of the deck space. Then two convicts followed, both in irons, so their descent was slow and deliberate until they finally sat down on the seats at the stern.

Nothing happened for the next couple of minutes, with Elizabeth wondering why. Then, finally, another red leg came over the rail, and then the rest of the other marine came into sight as he climbed down the ladder.

"Hmm, broad shoulders," was Elizabeth's first thought.

The marine took no notice of Elizabeth and her family in the bow of the cutter as he was looking for a seat in the stern, as five trunks already took up all the available space. Being the last aboard, he found that the only seating available was on top of the trunks, so he planted himself facing forward.

The marine sergeant, whose name was Richard, then, without looking around, spoke to the rowers, "That's it, no others coming. Let's go!"

The sailors pushed off from the ship's side, swung the cutter around and rowed off towards the Supply. Only then did Richard look towards the cutter's bow, noticing the three persons sitting there. No uniform was his first observation; then he noticed that two of them were women, one relatively young and the other one older. He turned his head away as he reminded himself that it was rude to stare.

William listened to the noise of the oars dipping into the water and the creak of oars against the hull for a minute or so as the cutter moved away from the Alexander. He had watched the marine sergeant sit down on their trunks, and as no one had yet said anything, he thought it best to speak over the rower's heads and introduce his family. "Sergeant, are you going on the Supply to Norfolk Island?"

Richard replied, "Yes, sir, all four of us," pointing to the other three.

"I'm William Johnson. I am the settlement's surgeon, and this is my wife and daughter, Ann and Elizabeth."

Elizabeth had continued to stare into the bottom of the boat to this point, but upon hearing her name, she looked up. Her first thought was, "So this is what the marine with the broad shoulders looks like." She quickly looked away as she had discovered during the last eight months that it was not wise to gaze too long at any male.

In reply, Richard said, "I am Marine Sergeant Richard Clarke. Glad to meet you, sir, and your family."

William thought it wise to get to know every one of the small numbers of settlers sailing to Norfolk Island, regardless of who it was, so he said, "Good to meet you, Sergeant."

While all this was happening, Ann could feel Elizabeth's reaction to meeting this handsome marine, so she put her hand on Elizabeth's arm and held it there for a few seconds. Elizabeth knew exactly what her mother was thinking, so she looked away towards the Supply, now not far away. Her first thoughts and observations, however, continued.

Richard was aware of what Ann and Elizabeth were thinking, but he thought it wise to ignore them, as there would be plenty of time to get to know them later. So, he turned his attention back to the two shackled convicts and then to the Supply.

The cutter came alongside the Supply with the stern of the cutter closest to the rope ladder, giving Richard the opportunity to grab hold of the ladder and scamper up. The two convicts slowly dragged themselves up the ladder and over the ship's rail, with the second marine following closely. Elizabeth watched the proceedings with interest.

A sailor poked his head over the rail to see who or what else needed to come aboard and said, "Sir, would you and the ladies like to come aboard before the trunks?"

"Yes, that will be fine."

One of the rowing sailors then said, "Please stay seated. We will move the bow closer to the ladder." They then pushed the cutter along the side of the Supply so that the ladder hung directly over the bow.

"There you are, sir, ladies first perhaps?"

Feeling it was her job the go first, Ann grabbed hold of the rope ladder, stood on the bottom rung and started climbing. The closest sailor turned around in his seat and put his foot on the bottom rung so that the ladder did not move around so much. She climbed, with difficulty, up the ladder until she got to the rail when a strong arm and hand appeared under her elbow.

A strong voice said, "Let me help you, madam."

Ann looked up to see who was offering to help. It was that good-looking marine that Elizabeth had been eyeing, so she just looked back down at the rail and then said, "Thank you."

Safely onboard, Ann stood a few feet away from the ladder while Elizabeth climbed up. She heard her grunt a couple of times as she took the last couple of steps to the top. As she climbed, Elizabeth heard a voice offering her mother help, but she did not see who it was. She reached the top and looked over the rail to find herself looking straight into a marine's face. That marine!

"Hang on, miss. I will help you," she thought she heard, although she could not be sure. She hesitated with both her arms hanging over the rail. Then she exited her gaze and replied, "Oh, thank you."

The marine offered his hand, put it under her elbow, and then offered his other hand and said, "Just climb over the rail, miss; I have got you."

It took a little while for the surprise of coming face to face with that marine again to subside, and then she remembered his name, Richard Clarke. So then, Elizabeth, even surprising herself, said, "Thank you, Sergeant Clarke."

Richard helped Elizabeth over the rail and onto the deck. He held onto her hand until her feet met the deck, holding it a little longer than her mother thought necessary.

Elizabeth found the situation far more difficult than she could have ever imagined. While feeling an embarrassing glow spread across her face, she looked away and promptly stepped over to her waiting mother. Within no time, William climbed onto the deck and over to his family, completely unaware of what had just occurred. Elizabeth, the earlier glow slowly leaving her face and still feeling somewhat unsure of herself, fumbled around until she found her mother's hand, which she gripped tightly. She continued looking down at the deck while hearing voices in the background,

William looked around the deck, hoping to find someone to welcome them aboard, but there appeared to be no one nearby other than a couple of sailors hanging onto the cutter's ropes. The three of them waited a few minutes, expecting to be met at the rail, but no one appeared.

Turning to Ann and Elizabeth, William said, "Come with me. We will try and find the captain's cabin." Knowing that the captain's cabin is usually towards the vessel's stern, William headed off in that direction.

William knocked on what he thought was the captain's cabin, the door opened, and an officer in full uniform stood before him. Although they had travelled to Port Jackson on a cargo vessel, William reminded himself that he was aboard one of His Majesty's vessels, and things would now be different.

"Ah, the surgeon and his family, I assume. Sorry I could not formally welcome you aboard, but something important came up at the last minute. We have been expecting you."

"Yes sir, I am William Johnson, and this is Ann, my wife, and my daughter, Elizabeth."

"Glad to meet you. I am Lieutenant Henry Ball, the captain of the Supply. I assume you will be looking for your quarters. As this is a Naval vessel, we have limited special accommodation, but we have squeezed you into a spare room off my quarters. It is often used by any wife that may be going with her captain husband, and as I am alone, it is yours. Please follow me."

"Thank you very much, sir."

They followed the captain into his quarters and then off to one side, where they found a small room fitted out with a set of bunk beds and one separate bed and not much else.

"This is yours. Not very luxurious, but I think it should be workable, seeing the voyage to Norfolk Island only takes about two weeks. I will get your trunks delivered as soon as I can."

"Yes, this will be fine. We are used to being in small cabins. We will only be needing the three smaller trunks here. The bigger one can be stored elsewhere."

"Fine, I will organise that. Relax and make yourselves comfortable."

"Thanks, captain."

Elizabeth and her family were tired by now, so they sat on the single bed and looked at one another, unsure of what to say or do. Hopefully, the trunks would arrive soon.

Meanwhile, Richard had no sooner helped Elizabeth over the rail and onto the deck when the private marine who had arrived with him called him over to the opposite rail. One of the convicts they had just bought to the ship was making life difficult by not wanting to move towards the forward hatch.

"Sergeant, give me a hand, will you; this one is not co-operating."

Having helped Elizabeth come aboard, Richard had forgotten all about the two convicts they had carried over from the other ship, and the private's words suddenly reminded him of his duty. So, he rushed over to help.

Not wanting to start things off on the wrong foot or cause instant friction, Richard said to the convicts in a measured tone, "Listen here. You have managed to get yourself onto this ship which is going to Norfolk Island. I think you are lucky. Don't get yourself in any more trouble, or you will end up in solitary."

Richard could see the convict favourably considering what he had just said, so he relaxed his objection. "Thank goodness for that," thought Richard.

The marines escorted the two convicts to the storeroom set aside for them and locked them inside with the other seven male convicts already aboard. Richard thought it was time to find their quarters, probably situated near where the sailors slept.

Now that the immediate convict problem had been solved, Richard thought again about the young lady who had just come aboard. He noticed that she was tall, slim, had brown hair, was very pleasant-looking, and had a tanned complexion. He had no idea how old she was. She could be anywhere between fifteen and twenty for all he knew. "Interesting!" was his first thought, but then he got to thinking more about the bigger picture and his future on Norfolk Island.

Elizabeth and her family did not have to wait long before their three trunks arrived, carried by six burly sailors. "Please put them down there," was Ann's instruction.

Elizbeth noticed there was no dressing table in the cabin but an empty bookshelf that could be used at a pinch, although the shelves were rather narrow. So, she said to her mother, "We could put some items of clothing on those shelves, although they will not hold very much."

"Good idea. Let's get those trunks open."

Now somewhat uninterested in the domestic proceedings, William said, "I will go and find out who else is coming with us to Norfolk Island. See you two later."

William left the cabin, went through the captain's quarters without seeing him, and went out on deck. Having never seen a naval ship like this up close, he decided to look over the main deck. It appeared to be better organized than the previous ship as everything seemed to be in its place or ship-shape, but then William realized that it was, after all, a Royal Navy ship. It seemed somewhat smaller than the Scarborough and only had two masts. It also had a small number of guns on the main deck, which somewhat limited the deck's open space.

After finishing his informal inspection of the main deck, William thought he should seek out the captain and learn more about the settlement party. Unfortunately, he could not see him on the main deck, so he went below. This vessel had no stairs, so the descent to the lower deck was by an attached wooden ladder. William was still having difficulty going up and down ladders, although he found this one easier as it was stiff, made from wood, and solidly attached.

Arriving at the bottom of the ladder, the captain called out from the other side of the vessel, "William, I see you are getting yourself familiar with the Supply."

"Yes, sir."

"Settling in all right?"

"Honestly, I have left that up to the women."

"Good, I would probably have done the same."

That said, the captain returned to inspecting a load of offloaded supplies from the supply vessels. From William's observation, there was a substantial quantity and variety, probably enough for many months. Thinking about the future, William guessed that the entire settlement would need sufficient supplies to last till the next ship, and that would not be for quite some time.

William, not wanting to interfere with the captain's inspection, asked, "Captain, sorry to bother you, but can you spare me a few minutes?"

"Yes, providing you are quick."

"How many are going to Norfolk Island?

"Twenty-two in total, including your family."

"What about supplies? Is this some of it?"

"Yes. I believe we have taken aboard about six months' worth of the basics, including seeds and, of course, medical equipment for you."

"Thanks. Oh, one more question, if you don't mind. Who is going to be in charge?"

"Lieutenant Philip Gidley King has been appointed Commandant and is expected on board shortly."

"Thank you, captain."

With that information, William's curiosity was satisfied, so he climbed the ladder to the top deck and returned to his cabin. By the time he arrived, Ann and her daughter had sorted some of their belongings and stored them on the tiny shelves.

While Elizabeth was helping her mother, she could not get the thought of the tall, handsome marine out of her mind. "What was his name again? That's right, Richard," she thought, reminding herself not to forget that. She knew he was also going to Norfolk Island, which meant there would be plenty of opportunity to get to know him better later. That pleasant thought stayed with her for some time until she realized that she did know if he was married or not. "Hmm, that's possible, I guess," were her final thoughts.

"Finished?" was William's first question as he noisily entered the cabin, which promptly interrupted Elizabeth's pleasant thoughts.

Ann replied, "For now, I guess. I may change it later, though."

William had forgotten to ask the captain what the dining arrangements were on this ship, mainly as this was a naval vessel and the routine would be different than what they were used to. He left the cabin to find out.

William returned shortly and told Ann and Elizabeth, "They will deliver meals to us here as there is not enough space to eat in the crew area. The galley informed me they are nearly ready for dinner now. Unfortunately, there is no table in here, although I might be able to find one."

Their meal arrived a little later with a knock on the door, and, considering that the ship was at the end of a very long voyage, the meal was better than they had become used to.

No sooner had they finished their meal when Elizabeth heard a little more movement and noise than usual outside their cabin. Then she heard the captain's main cabin door slam shut.

With curiosity getting the better of her, Elizabeth said, "Father, do you mind if I go outside and see what is going on?"

William, fully aware that he will now have to allow his daughter a little more freedom said, "That will be all right, providing you stay just outside the captain's main door."

"I promise," replied Elizabeth as she ran out of their cabin, across the captain's cabin, and out the main door. She slowly closed it carefully to avoid making herself too obvious. She stood on the doorstep, taking in what was going on. There were two marines near the portside rail standing at attention, about ten sailors in a line doing the same, and then the captain walked up and took a position in front of them, all facing the port rail. They all looked extremely smart in their formal uniforms.

This was not something that Elizabeth had ever seen before. Still, she was more interested in that marine, Richard, looking very manly in his brilliant red uniform, musket in hand, than what looked like formal proceedings.

Then she heard it. A rather piercing whistling sound that would rise and fall in level and pitch. Then she noticed that the two sailors had a unique form of whistle in their mouths, which was obviously making that strange sound. Within a few seconds, a man in a naval uniform came over the rail, stood to attention, returned a salute, and shook hands with the captain. The noise stopped. Elizabeth had never seen or heard of such a formal procedure before, so she was now very curious as to what it all meant.

The two officers moved away from the rail and started coming her way. Thinking quickly, she realized that they were probably coming into the captain's cabin, so she promptly turned around, opened the door, and sprinted towards their cabin. Elizabeth was trying to do all this without making too much noise and at the same time moving as fast as possible.

Elizabeth was just about to open the door to their own room when she heard a voice behind her, "Elizabeth, I would like to introduce you to Lieutenant King, who is also going to Norfolk Island." She stopped, hand still on the doorknob, unsure what to do.

Then, that voice again, "Elizabeth."

She slowly turned around, not sure how to react, particularly as she was now standing before two naval officers in full uniform.

William had stayed particularly alert as he knew that Elizabeth was outside the captain's cabin door, so as soon as he heard a close male voice, he moved towards their room's door. He tried opening it, with difficulty at first, as Elizabeth's hand was still on the doorknob. The movement made Elizabeth lift her hand, and she turned towards the door. Her father quickly entered the captain's cabin from just behind her, moved beside her, and said in a firm voice, "Good afternoon, captain."

Elizabeth quickly turned around and faced the two naval officers, with the captain saying, "Good afternoon, William. I want to introduce you and your family to Lieutenant Philip King, the new Commandant of your settlement party going to Norfolk Island."

"Thank you, captain. I will just call my wife."

William turned around and called out, "Ann, could you come here a minute, please."

Ann, not feeling she was in any fit condition to receive anyone, only moved to the doorway but said nothing.

The captain said, "Commandant, I would like you to meet William, your party's surgeon, his wife, Ann, and his daughter, Elizabeth."

William replied, "A privilege to meet you, sir," upon which Ann and Elizabeth nodded their head in silent agreement.

The commandant offered his hand to William and said, "I am also pleased to meet you and your family. We will, of course, be working very much part of a team once the settlement has begun."

"Very true, sir, very true."

William, aware that there was no need for them to stay in the presence of the commandant, excused himself and his family and went back into their room.

Once the door was closed, Elizabeth said to her parents in a quiet voice, "He seems nice."

"Yes, he does," was Ann's brief comment.

Lowing his voice to a whisper, William said, "You could be right, but I will reserve judgement for a few weeks. Time will tell."

Richard had just completed his watch, and for some strange reason, he was far more tired than usual. Then he remembered that he was not sleeping as well as usual and therefore found it challenging to get his mind on the job at the beginning of the watch. He had joined one of the existing marine squads, although his primary role was keeping an eye on the convicts when on duty. His companion marine, who was also going to Norfolk Island, had joined one of the other watches so that they will be living in separate worlds for the next two weeks. He realized that things would change dramatically once they got to the island.

Richard woke up early for his next watch, which began at 4 am, remembering that later this morning was the commencement of the voyage to Norfolk Island and a brand-new settlement. It was the 15th of February 1788. Regardless of anything else, Richard envisaged that this was going to be a true adventure. Then, of course, there was that young woman he met yesterday, and who knows where that may lead.

Putting those thoughts behind him, he climbed to the main deck and joined the other watch members. As the Supply was a naval vessel, it carried marines as a normal part of the ship's complement, and Richard had joined one of those squads. The routine was somewhat different from what had occurred on the Alexander over the last eight months, so it took a while to get back into a naval vessel's standard procedure. The fact that the Supply was carrying nine male and six female convicts also altered the usual routine.

The six female convicts were allowed more freedom than the males, particularly as they were allowed on deck during the day and were rarely put into irons. The men were also given time on deck but subject to more oversight. Both groups were housed in different sleeping quarters, and both doors were locked overnight. It was expected that once the ship was away from the coast, both doors would be open during daylight hours. However, it was apparent to Richard that it would be necessary to keep males and females as separate as possible, more so at certain times than others.

As daylight slowly lit the waters around the Supply, the ship's activity quickened as it prepared to leave its anchorage and depart for Norfolk Island. All those who were going to create a new settlement were now well awake and looking forward to the short voyage and their exciting future.

The Supply slipped its anchor, swung around, and headed towards the harbour entrance and the open sea. Richard then joined the rest of his squad that first went down below decks to check on the health and well-being of the two groups of convicts. They were both still in their overnight accommodation, and other than general conversation, the men's storeroom was relatively quiet. Then they heard it - a violent scream coming from the other side of the ship where the women slept.

Running across the deck, Richard heard the words, "Listen here bitch, you keep your grubby hands off my stuff." As Richard got closer, he heard something heavy smack against the door and then a dull thud. Two other marines had also heard the noise and followed closely behind. There was considerable yelling and screaming coming from inside the room, although Richard could not hear exactly what was being said due to the general confusion.

Luckily, Richard had been given a key, so he quickly unlocked the door, then realized it would be wise to call out first. So, he yelled above the din, "What's going on? I am opening the door right now."

Richard opened the door but could not see anything in the darkness. Then he saw a woman convict lying flat on the floor, with the other women standing behind her at the back of the room. He bent down to find out if the woman was unconscious or dead. She was alive, although with a very shallow breath.

Not sure what had just occurred, Richard asks, "What happened here?"

"She just hit her head," came a reply from the back of the room.

"Right," Richard said.

He turned to the two marines behind him and said, "Carefully carry this woman out of here, make her comfortable over there, and I will get the surgeon. By the way, keep that door locked until I get back."

Richard promptly climbed the ladder, sprinted across the upper deck, and knocked on the captain's door. Luckily for Richard, the captain was there. He opened the door and asked, "Can I help you, Sergeant?"

"Yes, captain. I need the surgeon urgently to see an injured woman."

The captain turned around and yelled out in an urgent voice, "Mr. Johnson. Could you please come here?"

William had heard the rather urgent knock on the captain's door, so his ears were alert when he heard the captain's request. He opened their room's door, saw the marine sergeant at the door, and quickly crossed the cabin.

Standing alongside the captain, looking from one to the other, William said, "How can I help?"

Richard quickly replied, "Sir, I would like you to look at an injured woman convict in their quarters immediately."

While this conversation was going on, Elizabeth heard that somewhat familiar deep voice again. She stood up while staying at the back of their room but moved so that she could see through the open door. The captain and her father took up most of the doorway, but she could glimpse a red uniform. Her father then turned from the doorway and said as he did so, "I'll just get my bag."

Elizabeth turned and quickly returned to her seat, not wanting her father to see her looking through the door. Her father entered the room, grabbed his medical bag, and said, "I have a patient to see," and was gone.

Elizabeth got up, returned to where she was before, and stared through the open door. She could still not see clearly who was there, but then the captain moved to one side to allow William to leave the cabin. She saw who it was. I was that marine again, Richard, and then he, too, was gone.

William followed Richard as they rushed across the deck, down the ladder, and to the women's quarters. The unconscious woman was lying on her back alongside a partition wall. William quickly bent down and checked her vitals. She was breathing slowly, although she was still very white in the face. He checked her eyes, looked over the rest of her, and then rechecked her pulse.

William turned to Richard and said, "There is a bump on her head, so the fall probably caused her to be unconscious. I think she will be all right."

The woman started to moan slightly, upon which William said, "I would like to keep an eye on her over the next 24 hours. Is there a bed or bunk she could use outside of that room," pointing to the female convict's quarters.

Not knowing the Supply's layout well, Richard replied, "To be honest, I don't know."

William then realized that he had not yet organised any space as he would probably need an area to carry out his medical work during the two-week voyage. This affair reminded him to see the captain and sort something out. "You stay here and make the woman as comfortable as possible, and I will check with the captain." He did not have to go far, as he caught the captain crossing the upper deck towards the lower deck ladder.

"Captain," William called out, "Have you got a moment?"

"Not really, but how can I help?"

"A woman has been injured in an altercation in their room, and I need a bed for her. Can you help me right now? I will need a place to work later anyway."

"Yes, I see what you mean. Let me think for a minute."

The captain looked up towards the sky, trying to think of a practical solution to William's problem. Eventually, he continued, "This a relatively small vessel, so what you ask for is not that easy. However, I think the sail locker is only half full, and we should be able to move things around and organise some form of bed there. Come with me, and I will show you."

The captain led William down the ladder to the lower deck and towards the ship's bow. There was an open doorway leading forward with no door, so they walked straight into a triangular room. There were sails everywhere, but they could make some useable space by piling them up to one side.

"Do you think it would do if we made space on one side of this locker?"

William glanced around and said, "Yes, captain, I think something could be done."

"Good, I will send a couple of ratings right away. Just tell them what you want, and they should be able to organize something."

With that said, the captain left the sail locker.

William called out, "Thank you, captain," as the captain disappeared.

"Now, what can we do here?" William said out loud to no one in particular.

The ratings soon arrived to help William sort out the sail locker, and before long, a rough bed had been made up from a few planks of wood. The injured woman, who had now been carried in, was now breathing naturally and was resting on the makeshift bed. She still moaned occasionally and said a few rambling words that did not make much sense. The knock on her head had adversely affected her thinking. The injured woman stayed in the sail locker overnight and was discharged to the female convicts' room the next day as there were no apparent adverse symptoms.

The sail locker was now starting to look more like a sick bay, and all it needed was William's medical bag to make it workable. Even though the bed was very rough in its construction, at least it was usable, and William looked around and felt reasonably satisfied with his temporary workspace.

As the short voyage was well underway, all those destined to remain on Norfolk Island were looking forward to their new life on this tiny island in the middle of the South Pacific. A gale blew for the next two days, and the ship and all its inhabitants suffered accordingly, even though they were now used to this type of weather after their long voyage from Portsmouth. However, it felt worse than it was, as it took a little while to get their sea legs back after being in calm waters in Port Jackson for a couple of weeks.

Elizabeth felt safer in her room as the noise of the wind in the rigging and the creaking sounds coming from the ship's wooden timbers all added to the sensations felt with each of the ship's violent movements. Sometimes, it felt like the ship was going backwards as much as it was going forwards. At other times, the ship seemed to lift off the water, hang in mid-air for a couple of seconds and then smash back down with a shudder. However, while Elizabeth felt herself lifting off her bed occasionally, which made her a little queasy, she did not succumb to the raging sea.

On the other hand, her mother stayed in bed for nearly two days, and if she did get up, she quickly found she had to use the bucket. The associated foul taste was forever in her mouth, and by the storm's end, she had had more than enough. A sip of water, usually provided by Elizabeth, helped remove most of the foul taste from her mouth. After that, eating anything was entirely out of the question.

Ann was suffering but had found ways to minimise her adverse reaction to the ship's motion. It seemed to make a difference in the direction her head was facing compared to the ship's motion when lying down. A more comfortable position had been found using trial and error, although standing up in such weather was still a problem.

William had no real difficulty with the weather, except he had trouble keeping his footings as he crossed the deck towards his makeshift surgery. But, as climbing up and down steep ladders were required to reach the convicts, William found himself hanging on to each rung as though his life depended on it.

Everyone on board the Supply was waiting for the storm to end, particularly those travelling to Norfolk Island. In the main, they had had enough sailing since leaving Portsmouth and wanted to get to their future home and dry land.

Chapter 22

By the morning of the third day, the winds had finally died down, the seas were calmer, and the rain had stopped, so everyone on the Supply looked forward to a far more pleasant day.

Elizabeth had hardly left her room for the last couple of days, so, noticing that the ship's motion was no longer so violent, she got out of bed early, dressed and ventured outside into the fresh air. While the air was still cool, the sun rising from the glowing horizon supplied the necessary warmth. Elizabeth stood outside the captain's door, soaking up the sun's rays, when she heard footsteps. Looking in that direction, she saw a line of male convicts coming up from the lower deck and then across the main deck towards the ship's bow. One private marine was in the lead, with a sergeant following behind.

Elizabeth stopped breathing for a few seconds upon realizing the sergeant was Richard, the same marine she had glimpsed at the captain's door a few days ago. He was not looking over in her direction as he was too busy keeping the nine convicts in order heading towards the ship's bow. She was somewhat confused because she was unsure what to do if he looked in her direction. Could she smile without being too forward? Would a small wave be far too much? Should she be looking his way at all?

Then, the end of what could have been a magical moment ended as the door behind her opened. Elizabeth reluctantly turned as her mother appeared, who said, "There you are. I wondered where you had got to."

"I am just getting fresh air, and it is beautiful out here. How are you feeling?"

Elizabeth was trying to talk to her mother and, at the same time, keep an eye on the line of men. She watched Richard slowly move out of sight behind the masts and rigging.

Her mother replied, "Much better, thanks. How about you?"

"I'm fine. The storm did not bother me that much. I must be getting used to it."

"Aren't you lucky? What were you staring at?"

"Nothing," replied Elizabeth, with no absolute conviction.

"I don't believe you, Elizabeth. Was it that same marine again?"

"What, marine?"

"You know, the one that caught your eye on the cutter."

Trying to sound very casual, Elizabeth said, "Oh, that one."

"Yes, that one. You know who I am talking about."

Elizabeth knew she could no longer fool her mother, so she sighed and said, "Well, he is good-looking."

Ann was becoming somewhat alarmed at what she was hearing, as she knew things could get awkward once they arrived on Norfolk Island. While she had not discussed the question of "the birds and the bees" with Elizabeth in any detail till now, the matter was now becoming urgent. Ann, aware that her husband was not in their cabin at present, thought now might be a good time to sit down and talk seriously with her daughter.

Tugging on Elizabeth's sleeve, Ann said, "Elizabeth, look at me; I am over here."

Elizabeth slowly turned to her mother, who said, "Let's go into our room as I want to talk to you about something important."

They both entered the captain's cabin, crossed into their room and closed the door, upon which Ann said, "Let's both sit down on this bed."

Sitting on the bed, half facing one another, Ann said, "I am not sure how I will start this conversation, but here goes. You know I have spoken to you several times about the differences between boys and girls and men and women, but I have never gone into any real detail. I don't know; I'm finding this difficult!"

Elizabeth was now all ears because she knew something of interest was coming; although unsure where it would lead, she said, "Ah, don't worry, Mother, I won't feel embarrassed."

Pausing for a few seconds, not sure how to begin, Ann continued, "I think you are familiar with the external physical differences between men and women or boys and girls, but there are also other differences. What you see on the outside is only a part of the difference. Are you familiar with any of the words normally used, Elizabeth?"

"Mother, this is embarrassing."

"For you and me, to be honest, but I feel that it is important that we have this discussion. It could affect your whole future."

Elizabeth replied in an off-hand manner, "If you must."

"Now, how about answering my question?"

"What question?"

"Ah, Elizabeth, this is all too much! The question was whether you knew the words used to explain the differences between a man and a woman. There is no sense in me using words you don't know what they mean."

Elizabeth just grunted.

Ann thought it now best to change tacks and start the conversation from another angle. "You do know where babies come from. You saw babies being born on the trip out here during our stop in Rio, didn't you? You helped with one of those births if I remember rightly."

"Yes, Mother, I do know that much."

"Good. Do you know how they get there?"

"Mm, not really."

"Well, I won't go into too much detail, but a man and a woman must get together for a baby to be born. It starts very small and grows into a baby over about nine months. Now, I want you to remember that most men want to get with a woman, even when they do not want a baby. You must remember that a woman should not get together with a man before marriage. The woman may end up with a baby she does not want. Do you know what I mean, Elizabeth?"

"Umm, I think so."

Her mother went on, "When I say where a man and a women get together, it means a connection between the man and the woman in the area you are aware of that makes them different. It is that connection that you must be very wary of. Many men will take advantage of you and encourage you to agree, so be careful. Do you understand, Elizabeth?"

"I think so. You are saying that I should leave those close connections until I am married."

"Well, kind of."

Ann had difficulty explaining exactly what she wanted to say without saying too much, so she said, "The only physical connection a man and a woman should have before they are married is kissing. Nothing past that. Does that help?"

"So, kissing is all right, but nothing else?"

"Basically, yes."

Not sure what else to say, her mother continued, "If you have any questions about this, pick a time when your father is not around, and I will answer the best I can. All right?"

"Thanks, Mother, what you have said has helped."

"Good."

Ann sighed, glad she had managed to get through that conversation, even though she knew further discussions would be necessary. She was not looking forward to explaining any further details.

By this time, Richard had given the male convicts about an hour on deck and had taken them back to their room, which he believed was originally a sort of storeroom. The ship's crew had managed to string up just enough hammocks to hold the nine men. It was a tight fit, but at least they all had a place to sleep.

Richard had just finished his forenoon watch, and as it was just after noon, he decided to go and get something to eat. He thought the galley should be serving the mid-day meal by now, so he headed towards the crew eating area next to the galley. A few crew members were lining up to be served their meal, so Richard joined the end of the queue, right behind a marine private.

The marine turned and said to Richard, "Sergeant, I heard from someone that you had a different kind of posting and that you have not served on a ship for a while. Is that correct?"

"Well, yes, that is partially correct. I was part of a team improving and building Fort Cumberland for several months."

"That would have been a doddle, wouldn't it?"

"No, not really. It was quite a responsible job."

"Ah, come on! You don't mean that."

The line ahead moved on, so they shuffled closer to the galley.

Richard was starting to get a little short at the tone of the comments, so he said in a firm voice, "Listen here, private. Are you questioning what I was doing and what I am saying?"

"No, Sergeant, but you have to be honest; it was not a job for a real marine."

Richard's patience was wearing even thinner by this stage, his blood was starting to boil, and he was now seeing red. "That's enough of that private. If you continue like that, you will end up in the brig for insubordination. Do you understand?"

The private, realizing that he had overstepped the boundaries, said, "Sorry, Sergeant. I will say no more."

Richard finally got his meal, a stew that included vegetables and meat, although he did not recognize it. After that short altercation, Richard decided to eat alone, which meant he had to move away from the usual eating areas. Again, he had no idea what the meat was, but it tasted reasonable.

With a full stomach and feeling somewhat better, Richard was not currently on duty, so he decided to find a place to have a short snooze. Remembering that the sail locker on most ships was usually away from everybody else and a comfortable place to lie down in, he looked around in the usual places but could not find it. Then he remembered seeing a doorway in the ship's bow, so he moved forward. As he approached the open doorway, he noticed movement. Wondering who was inside, he stopped outside the room and asked, "Is anybody in there?"

"Yes, there is," was the reply as a head appeared in the doorway.

"Sergeant, it's you. How can I help you?"

Recognising the surgeon, he said, "Oh, Sorry to disturb you, sir, but I did not expect anyone would be here."

"Were you looking for the sail locker?"

"Yes, sir, I was. But don't let me disturb you."

"That's all right, Sergeant. You did not know that I have taken up half of the locker as a temporary surgery. Have a look inside."

Richard's curiosity got the better of him, so as William moved back into the locker, he poked his head inside the doorway and said, "Ah, I see, sir – a handy little place. I will now leave you alone. Sorry to disturb you, sir."

Richard's original idea of a short sleep was no longer a priority, so he left the ship's bow and returned to his sergeant's quarters.

The next morning, which looked like another fine day, Elizabeth again went outside the captain's cabin to take in the sun and the sea air. She noted that the wind was not that strong, and while looking upwards at the sails, she noticed several sailors up in the rigging and others hauling on ropes. From time to time, they would call out partly in English and partly in a language Elizabeth could not understand. Listening for a few minutes, she concluded that they were undoubtedly speaking English but also using sailing terminologies that meant nothing to her.

While standing there taking in the warm morning sun and gazing over at the slightly choppy sea, her thoughts turned to that marine, Richard. "I wonder where he is now?" she thought, "I will wait here for a while, and if I am lucky!"

Then Elizabeth heard a thump over to her left. She looked over and saw something moving on the deck, so she walked closer to what looked like a fish of some kind. She got within about three feet of it and was bending down to get a better look when it suddenly wriggled its body and flapped its tiny wings, all at the same time. Not expecting such violent movement or the flapping of wings, she leapt back in fright and let out a scream.

A sailor, who happened to be working close by, saw and heard the outcry, so he called out, "Don't worry, miss, it will not hurt you. It is just a flying fish."

Elizabeth stood there with her hands up to her face and a heart that seemed to be jumping out of her chest. She heard the sailor's comments, which helped the situation somewhat, but the initial fright was undoubtedly real enough.

The sailor walked over and said, "Are you all right, miss?"

"Yes, thanks; I will be fine in a few minutes. That certainly frightened me."

"We don't usually see flying fish this far from the equator, miss, but they are amazing."

By this stage, the fish had stopped all movement, so the sailor walked over to the fish and said, "Do you mind if I take this fish and have it cooked for dinner?"

Not wanting to touch the fish, Elizabeth said, "I have no use for it. Take it."

The sailor promptly grabbed the fish, which wiggled once again, so he held on tightly and then walked over and showed the fish to Elizabeth. She backed up as he came closer, as she did not feel comfortable near the wriggling fish. The sailor paused, smiled, and then walked across the deck and out of her sight.

By this time, Elizabeth felt she had had enough fresh air and returned to their room to find her mother sitting on one of the beds reading a book.

"Mother, you should have been outside. The sun was beautiful, and I saw a flying fish land on the deck. It is amazing to think that fish can actually fly and, at the same time, are also beautiful to look at."

Her mother nodded and said, "I saw a number of those fish flying and skipping across the waves on our earlier voyage to Rio. They are unusual, aren't they?"

"What are you reading, Mother?"

"Oh, just a book that I borrowed from the captain. It is entitled "A Voyage to the Pacific Ocean" by Captain James Cook. It is quite interesting."

"Can I read it later? Books are hard to find around here."

"Of course, dear."

After further rough seas, the Supply arrived at a small group of islands a couple of days later. One of the islands was very small in circumference, rose steeply to a considerable height, and looked somewhat like a sharply pointed pyramid. The captain of the Supply, Lieutenant Ball, named the bigger island Lord Howe Island and the very tall solid rock island Balls Pyramid. After circumnavigating the islands, the Supply continued its voyage to Norfolk Island.

While Richard was expected to do his appointed watches, the small number of convicts on this voyage made life somewhat easier, although the fact that there were men and women convicts on the same ship complicated things somewhat. It was essential to keep individual men and women apart as they would become sexually active if given half an opportunity. This fact became apparent to Richard as time passed, so he made special efforts to keep them apart wherever possible. What would happen once they all arrived on Norfolk Island was anyone's guess.

Richard had made several attempts to catch a glimpse of that attractive young lady, the surgeon's daughter, but up to this time, luck was not on his side. After a few days, he concluded that she rarely left her room, but thinking ahead, he realized that far more opportunities would be available once they were all on the island. "There is plenty of time," he told himself.

The next few days were pleasant for everyone on board the Supply as the weather continued fine, with sunny skies and light winds, although it made their progress towards Norfolk Island considerably slower.

Chapter 23

Norfolk Island lies isolated in the Western South Pacific Ocean, about eleven hundred nautical miles east-northeast from Port Jackson (Sydney Cove). The island was discovered, at least from the Western World's point of view, by Captain James Cook during his second voyage around the world on the 10th of October 1774. A party landed on the island from the Endeavor the next day, probably through the surf, into what was eventually named Emily Bay. No evidence was found of any earlier habitation, so after evaluating the worth of the flax and trees on the island, they sailed on. From his observations, Captain Cook made reference in his journal to its similarity to many parts of New Zealand.

The Supply came within sight of Norfolk Island on the 29th of February 1788, upon which the ship circumnavigated it three times, trying to find a safe place to land. During this time, the captain named one of the rugged offshore islands, Phillip Island, in honour of Governor Phillip. They anchored off an area of Norfolk Island that showed promise, as there was a cascade of water coming over the cliff's edge into the sea. However, due to the rough seas and the number of large rocks in the area, getting safely ashore was not an option. They continued looking.

Once Norfolk Island had come into sight, Elizabeth and her parents watched in anticipation as the ship got closer and closer. The island was surrounded by cliffs that looked hundreds of feet high, and the island appeared entirely covered by trees and other heavy green growth. The Supply continued to circle the island looking for a safe place to land, but an easy-to-reach beach without any dangerous surf or rocks seemed to elude them. It seemed like everywhere else was just high cliffs.

Elizabeth's first impression was how dark green everything was, and very different from the green-brown colour that seemed so typical of the New South Wales landscape.

While standing at the rail watching the island go by, Elizabeth said to her mother, "Look at that, Mother. Isn't it beautiful? Especially with all those tall, green and stately-looking trees everywhere. I wonder when we can go ashore?"

Not knowing what to say, Ann said, "I don't think anyone knows the answer to that question. We will have to wait and see."

The Supply once again rounded a headland on the island's southern side and came upon a large sandy bay in the distance, which appeared cut off from any approach from the open sea by a large reef. Although high cliffs surrounded the island, very few places looked like one could even try to land and then progress inland. The most likely one they had found to this point was behind the reef and onto what looked like a protected sandy bay.

While Elizabeth and her mother stood at the rail gazing at the island, Elizabeth noticed a red marine uniform over her mother's shoulder. Trying not to make it too obvious, Elizabeth watched the marine, but he was not looking her way, and she could not see any sergeant strips. Finally, alternating her gaze from the island to her mother and then to the red uniform, it became clear to her mother something was distracting her, who said, "What are you looking at?"

Swinging her head quickly back to watching the island, she said, not very convincingly, "Nothing."

Ann looked over to where Elizabeth had been looking, and saw the same red uniform, then the owner stood up, turned around and looked in their direction. It was, indeed, Richard, and both immediately recognized him. Elizabeth quickly turned to look at her mother, who unexpectantly raised her hand in acknowledgement.

When Elizabeth realized what was happening, she looked over towards Richard, but it was too late. Richard had nodded to Ann, turned the other way, and disappeared out of sight. It was evident that something urgent needed his immediate attention.

"Mother!" exclaimed Elizabeth, trying to keep her voice down, "What are you doing?"

Trying to sound very matter-of-fact, Ann said, "Just acknowledging his wave."

By this time, Elizabeth's face was becoming redder and redder with embarrassment. "This is too much!" was her only remark as she, with as much disdain as she could muster, turned away from the ship's rail and strode off towards their room.

Her mother glanced again in Richard's direction as she followed her daughter, but he was nowhere in sight.

Elizabeth lost no time getting to the captain's cabin door, which she promptly opened and, without looking around, nearly slammed it shut in her mother's face.

Ann hesitated outside the door for a few seconds before carefully opening it to see where Elizabeth was. She was not in sight, and Ann had heard their room's door slam, so there was no doubt where Elizabeth was.

Thinking about the whole episode, Ann decided that now was not a good time to disturb Elizabeth, so she went back outside the captain's cabin and onto the main deck. "Better leave things for a while," Ann said as she returned to the rail with the object of putting Elizabeth's feelings to one side. Staring at the island, she tried imagining them all on this small but beautiful island.

The Supply came as close as it safely could to the long coral reef, where the waves were constantly breaking. Someone on watch thought they saw a break in the reef that would allow a small boat to safely enter the bay. Accordingly, a small boat was sent over the side, and both Lieutenant Ball and Lieutenant King were rowed backwards and forwards while inspecting the reef. Eventually, an opening was found that looked large enough for the purpose, although it was difficult to see it from any distance. However, the gap in the reef did not look very deep, so it was thought it would be best only to cross the reef at high tide.

Captain King was losing his patience waiting for the tide to rise to its fullest, so he ordered a team of rowers from the ship's crew to test the water in the gap. The boat cautiously moved towards the opening, and from the rowers' viewpoint, it looked like there was sufficient depth of water to make the crossing safely. So, they lined the boat up with the opening and started their journey forward. The boat was just about to enter the narrow passage when suddenly, the bottom of the boat made a crunching sound as it lurched to one side. The coral had found its mark, but luckily the boat remained upright, and the crew immediately reversed out of the dangerous passage.

With all their might, they started to row backwards but soon realized that rowing against the wind in reverse would not work. Using all their experience with small boats, they decided to turn the boat around. This required the oars on one side to pull forward and those on the other to pull backwards. The boat started rocking from one side to the other, caused by the action of the waves as they tried to manoeuvre the boat in the very narrow passage. The bow finally smashed down on a coral ledge, and luckily, momentum carried the boat further around in the right direction. The rowers quickly finished the turning manoeuvre and rowed out to the open sea with all their strength. After realizing their error, they returned to the Supply and, on the captain's orders, waited for the full tide.

William had not been very busy during this short voyage besides the odd sprain and cut sustained by the crew and other minor injuries caused by the convicts fighting each other. He could not greatly help those who had suffered from seasickness, although all eventually found their way through that ordeal. The convicts always seemed to be challenging each other in their group, each trying to prove they were the top dog. This caused a few unusual injuries as arguments and minor fights occurred regularly, but thankfully, nothing serious.

Once full tide arrived, the rowboat was again sent off towards the gap in the reef, and they managed, due to the deeper water, to run through the surf and into the bay. There were dangerous outcrops on either side of the boat, but they cleared the reef during the interlude between the long swells. The fact that the rowboat was not carrying much weight on this trip helped it move through the reef smoothly and without any incidents. Using the same opening, which was much easier to see from the island side, they finally arrived back on board the Supply with smiles. They finally found themselves a calm bay, and the unloading could now begin.

Now that Norfolk Island had been reached and a safe landing point had been found, William was pleased that they would soon be on shore and be able to start constructing their new home. Like everyone else on the ship, he had kept an eagle eye on the coast, hoping to find a suitable spot. The Supply had continued to circle the island for a couple of days, looking for a safe place to step ashore. Now they could relax somewhat, as they had finally found one, even though it took extreme seamanship to get safely through the reef's gap.

Word quickly spread around the ship that the settling party would go ashore with all their belongings at high tide the following day, weather permitting.

As soon as word of finding a safe landing place reached Elizabeth and her family, Ann started to pack everything they would not need for the next day back into their trunks. She had to keep reminding herself that everything she was trying to re-pack had previously found room somewhere in the four trunks. She repacked once again. Elizabeth reluctantly helped her mother, but her heart was not in the process, and the two did not speak much. Both thought that this packing and unpacking was becoming extremely tiresome.

William gathered his medical supplies together and packed them away while at the same time taking extra items he had gathered while they were on the Supply. He reasoned that as they would not be expecting any further supplies for approximately six months, any extra medical items he could take with him would be more than handy.

In the meantime, Richard was going from the male convict's cabin to the female cabin, ensuring that all fifteen of them were ready for an early start the following day. There would be no time for any disorganisation and no time to look for any last-minute mislaid items.

Elizabeth was finding it hard to sleep her last night on the Supply because she thought about many disconnected things, including what had happened on the ship's rail when she was with her mother. She had a fleeting glance at Richard then, but her mother's reaction had spoilt everything. She could not understand why her mother had waved back to him.

Elizabeth's other major worry was her role once they arrived on the island. While young and fit, she appreciated that she only had limited lifetime experience. She concluded that helping her mother do whatever she did was the logical answer. "Time will tell," she thought.

The following day dawned fine, with only a slight breeze coming from the east. The ship had been a buzz of activity for a couple of hours before sunrise as a great deal needed to be gathered and ferried ashore. The two boats they were about to use, which would remain with them on the island, were specially selected to keep convicts on an out-of-the-way island. Each was relatively small, and they only had four short oars each, obviously not ideal for rowing long distances across open seas.

Elizabeth was awakened long before dawn by the noise caused by the general landing preparations and the fact that her father had got up extra early. While excited on the one hand, Elizabeth was still feeling apprehensive about what the day would bring. They were about to land and start a new settlement on a small island in the middle of nowhere. On the other hand, the unknown was making her feel sick to the stomach, and as soon as she heard her mother get out of bed, she moaned, "Mother, I don't feel very well."

"I don't know why. You should be excited as we will be going ashore shortly."

With a slight hesitation, Elizabeth replied, "I know what you mean, but somehow the huge step we are about to take scares me. I don't know what is going to happen."

Ann approached her daughter, put her arm around her shoulders and said, "I know what you mean, but we must be positive about the future. I am a little scared myself, so, as we are here, we must "soldier on," to coin a phrase. Have you put everything away where it should be?"

"I have checked everywhere, and I found nothing that is ours. I'm ready to go! Are you?"

"Yes, ready as I will ever be."

Ann heard a knock on the door. She opened the door to find two sailors, who said, "We have come for your trunks, Madam."

"There they are," she replied, pointing to the four trunks.

Elizabeth watched each of the trunks being taken outside and watched them being carried over to the portside rail. Their fourth and largest trunk was extremely heavy, so a couple of extra sailors were needed to get it into place. Several other trunks, boxes, barrels, and other bits and pieces were already stacked along the ship's side. Elizabeth stood outside the captain's cabin door and watched with interest as each item was hoisted over the side using a net, ropes, and a pulley system. They finally stopped loading that particular cutter, but much was still left on the deck, including their trunks. There would need to be many more trips.

Ann called out from their cabin, "Elizabeth, you had better stay here. Your father should be here shortly, and we must be ready."

Shortly after, William and the captain walked across the deck together towards them, seemingly in a deep conversation.

The captain said, "While I have you all here, I would like to thank you for helping during this voyage and wish the whole family the best of luck during your stay on the island. It will be a challenge, but it should also be rewarding at the same time."

The captain shook hands with William and nodded to both Elizabeth and Ann, upon which William said, "Thanks for those remarks, Captain. It has been a pleasure meeting and working with you."

William turned to his family and said, "Have we got everything? Ready to go?"

"Yes, ready to go," replied Ann.

While the two of them had been talking, fifteen male and female convicts had arrived at the side of the ship accompanied by three marines, including Richard, who had been watching Elizabeth standing there with her family out of the corner of his eye.

The arrival of the convicts made William reconsider if it would be wise for his family to move over to the ship's rail right away, so he said to Ann, "Stay here for a minute or two, and I will see when they want us."

While standing outside the captain's cabin door with her parents, Elizabeth caught Richard furtively looking over at her, although he was trying not to make it too obvious. Elizabeth tried her best not to stare, but the temptation was slowly getting the better of her.

Ann was more interested in what her husband was doing, so she was unaware of what was happening between Elizabeth and Richard. This continued for several minutes until William returned and disturbed the moment when he said, "They will be taking us on the next boat after the convicts. They are using two boats, so it should not be long."

The convicts and the other marine went over the side of the ship, with Richard staying on deck until all the others had disembarked. He glanced one last time at Elizabeth as he swung his legs over the rail and promptly disappeared out of sight.

Elizabeth impatiently stood alongside her mother for what seemed like forever, all the while resting her weight on one leg, then the other, waiting for something to happen. Finally, a call from one of the Supply's sailors, "Sir, you will be going next. We need to load your trunks first."

The four trunks were being loaded into a cargo net as the sailor spoke, so William and his family knew it was nearly time to say goodbye to HMS Supply.

William watched their trunks going over the side, then turned and called, "Come on, you two. It is our turn now."

Looking over the side of the ship down to the cutter, Elizabeth noticed no ladder, just a heavy rope net hanging down the side.

William called out, "All right, Elizabeth, you first."

Gathering her skirt and petticoat, she carefully climbed over the rail and found the first rope with her foot. Still hanging onto the railing, Elizabeth tried to find the next step with the other foot. She tried stepping down a couple more times, but it eluded her. She could not find the next step.

Then a man's voice called out from the boat, "It's further down, miss."

Elizabeth was so busy trying to find the next step that she did not hear the instruction, so her other foot kept seeking the next step down.

Calling out in a much louder voice, the sailor said, "Sorry, miss, but you must reach further down. It is a huge step."

This time Elizabeth heard the sailor, so she stretched her arms as far as she could and just managed to find the next rope step. She tried to put some weight on that foot, but the rope was loose and floppy, so it moved away under her weight. By this stage, she had to let go of the other foot, which put all her weight on her arms. She hung on as if her life depended on it, slowly lowering herself by her arms till the other foot took some of her weight. She paused for a moment or two, trying to get used to the fact that climbing down a rope net was neither easy nor very ladylike.

The earlier voice said, "That's it, miss, just do the others the same way."

Elizabeth slowly and deliberately climbed down, trying to hang onto her skirt whenever she could until her feet finally arrived on a firmer surface, which was an additional challenge as the cutter moved up and down.

The sailor offering her the earlier instructions happened to be closer to her as she landed at the bottom of the boat, so he offered his hand to get her off the rope net and safely seated. "There you are, miss. Safe and sound."

Both of her parents had been watching their daughter climb down the net, which, in turn, helped both to understand what needed to be done. Ann found it the most difficult as she was shorter than Elizabeth, and finding the next step down on the rope net alone was impossible. The sailor giving the earlier instructions climbed partway up the net, held on tightly to Ann's right arm, and half carried her down to the boat. They both eventually arrived at the bottom of the net rather undignifiedly, and Ann carefully took her seat. Ann slowly did her best to settle down from the ordeal and vowed to herself that she would never do that again.

By the time her parents had taken their seats, Elizabeth had regained her composure and, finally, her breath when she said, "That was an experience and a half!"

Her father said, "Yes, it certainly was."

Ann just sat there and did not comment.

Thinking about what had just happened, Elizabeth concluded that the last nine months had been an experience far beyond what she had expected. One thing was for sure; she fully realized she would not have experienced anything like this if she had stayed in Portsmouth.

Elizabeth watched as the rest of the goods were loaded into the boat, and to her eyes, making it look overloaded. She then looked over towards the island over the top of the spray, once again noticing the extreme greenness of the backdrop behind the curved bay they would be landing on. She also could hear the surf pounding on the coral reef that protected the bay, and although she had seen earlier cutters making the journey, she wondered how their boat would get through that. The previous boat had offloaded its cargo and was leaving the bay towards the reef and the crashing surf. She noticed the rowers stopped rowing just before they reached the reef entrance, waiting for about five seconds, and then they rowed like hell through the small gap in the breaking surf. They all received considerable spray on the way, but the boat came safely through the narrow gap and out into the open ocean.

"This is going to be interesting," Elizabeth said to herself.

Their boat cast off from the side of the Supply, and the rowers headed off toward the gap in the reef. As Elizabeth was now seated much lower than she was on the deck of the Supply, the size of the waves pounding on the reef from her level now looked formidable. The surf from this angle, viewed from only a few feet above the sea surface, looked immense, and the sound it made as it smashed onto the reef only made the spectacle even more intimidating. They rowed along the reef for a short distance before the rowers changed direction and headed towards the small gap in the reef.

As the cutter approached the reef, Elizabeth and her mother glanced at each other and saw the look of terror on both faces, showing each that this was pure madness. Elizabeth was now trembling with fear, and while she did not want to look at the reef and the towering waves, something drove her to do so.

Elizabeth then noticed that some waves hitting the reef were smaller than others, and obviously, it was necessary to time the run. The rowers stopped rowing for about ten seconds, and then one yelled, "Now!" Then, in an even louder voice, he urgently said, "Stop! Stop rowing!" The rowers knew precisely what was required, so they immediately stopped and started rowing backwards. Unfortunately, it had been a false start, and they would have to have another go. The boat rose and fell with the swell, and while the waves were not breaking over the stern of the boat, the spray from the top of each one drenched all those on board.

Elizabeth and her mother could not believe what they were seeing and hearing as they gripped their seat with both hands, at times hardly able to breathe. The look on their faces was of absolute terror as the boat's movement was such that they were both afraid of being tossed over the side. They hung on for dear life, afraid to relax their grip on the seat.

William, who was sitting on the seat behind them, was feeling the same thing, although he was trying to look as calm as he could.

The crew stopped rowing, with their oars now at the ready, waiting for the call to row again. Then it came, "Row forward. Now!" The rowers resumed their rapid pace as they headed off towards the gap in the reef, and, thankfully, the sea looked somewhat calmer this time as they approached the opening. It was not much wider than the width of the rowers' oars, but they continued to row at speed anyway as they half-surfed on a small wave through the gap in the reef into the much calmer waters inside the bay. They had made it!

Elizabeth was transfixed as spray from the waves hit her face, making it even harder for her to continue breathing. Finally, now inside the reef, she relaxed somewhat and felt like she could now take a much-needed breath. The boat continued towards the sandy beach as though nothing had happened. Elizabeth thought the calmness of the waters inside the bay seemed like absolute heaven compared to the movement and noise they had just been through.

Ann, now feeling very insecure due to that harrowing experience, turned to her husband and put her hand into Williams'. He grasped it tightly, and she said, "I thought I was going to die!"

William, trying to put on as brave a face as he could, said, "Well, we all made it, didn't we?" Then, to change the subject, he said, "Look at that beautiful smooth water and inviting beach."

Ann turned back towards the bow of the boat and the calmness ahead of them and said, "I am glad that is over." She was shaking and unsure that this was what she had signed up for when she had agreed to travel to the other side of the world.

Chapter 24

The boat continued across the bay until the boat slid smoothly and silently onto the inviting sand. The beach was several hundred yards long and curved in the shape of an open horseshoe. Large trees and the scrub came right down to the edge of the sand dunes with no obvious clearings, although it looked like those that had arrived earlier in the day had already started to make an opening.

Elizabeth and Ann slowly regained their composure as the boat approached the shore, helped by the calm water. It hardly seemed possible that such serenity existed only 200 yards away from the noise and violence caused by the waves pounding on the outer reef.

William and his family waited for those in the boat's bow to step ashore and followed the rowers off the bow. Then, standing on the soft sand and looking back at the reef and the Supply, Elizabeth said to no one in particular, "We are now on Norfolk Island."

Elizabeth then remembered that Richard had gone ahead of them and would probably be with the convicts, clearing spots for their tents. She looked all around for a red uniform but could not see any, and then thought, "He has got to be here somewhere."

Because of the small number of people involved, less than twenty-five, everyone pitched in doing what they could. As soon as they landed on the beach, William tried to find the limited quantity of medical supplies he had organised to be sent ashore. He found it under a pile of other stores, so he put it to one side a little higher up the beach and reminded himself to collect it later.

While all the male convicts were very busy clearing small glades just over the dunes, a few convict women helped on the tools where they could. The rest of the women were sorting out supplies under the supervision of the Commandant.

Elizabeth and Ann, not knowing what else they could do, joined in sorting the stores, particularly the food. By this stage, the second tent had been erected, and they started to transfer various items from the sand, over the dunes and into the tent. The sand was nearly white and very soft, and it took considerable effort to carry any decent load across the dunes. After several trips, Ann found that she needed to sit down and get her breath back, while Elizabeth continued while keeping an eye out for Richard. She saw him several times, but he was so busy that she could not catch his eye. At the same time, she had to keep reminding herself that it was not wise or ladylike to make her interest too obvious.

Slowly but surely, other small areas were cleared, and tents were erected in what looked like three small separate but adjoining campsites. Ann and Elizabeth helped where they could, particularly regarding foodstuffs, as they needed to be stored quickly and safely.

A small creek had been found along the beach's eastern end, and a couple of convicts had been sent to clear some land alongside. They removed a small area of scrub near the creek in preparation for planting seeds, which would be critical for supplementing their later food needs.

Since they were now alone on a relatively small island in the middle of the Pacific Ocean, the entire group seemed to work well as a team in establishing their new settlement. The convicts were not chained in any way, at least for today, and they were probably as free of constraints as they had ever been since leaving England.

Ann and Elizabeth had finished their part in organising food storage when a woman convict came up to them both and said, "I have been asked to organize to plant some seeds in a garden area. I have done this type of thing before, so would you two like to help?"

Ann looked over at her daughter and said, "Interested?"

"I have never done that, so let's do it."

The woman carried a rake and a few packets of seeds in one hand and a small spade in the other. She handed the rake to Elizabeth and promptly took off towards the Eastern end of the bay, with Elizabeth and her mother right behind. They left the beach and walked a short distance up the small running creek until they came to a flat area that had, by now, been roughly cleared of scrub.

The woman convict stopped at the edge of the plot and, in a friendly tone, said., "My name is Jane. What's yours?"

Although surprised by the introduction, Ann replied, "My name is Ann, and this is my daughter, Elizabeth."

Jane went on, "Well, let's see what they have given me," as she spread the packets of seeds on the ground. "Corn, cabbage, onions, carrots, potatoes and beetroot. Well, let's get going. There is still a fair fit of rubbish here so we will get that out first."

It was obvious to Ann that the simple dress the convict woman was wearing was far more sensible than the long dress and petticoats that Elizabeth and Ann were wearing. They both decided then and there to simplify their clothing from tomorrow on.

The sun was slowly lowering in the sky by the time all the seeds had been planted and watered, and it was now time to return to camp. The woman convict said, "I will try and water the seeds again tomorrow." As they walked up the beach back to the camp, they noticed that the Supply had slipped its anchor and was now well out to sea. They paused for a few seconds, acknowledging that they, and every other settler in the group, were now on their own.

Everyone else seemed to have gathered near the freshly erected flagpole. They quickly picked up their pace as it looked like they, too, were supposed to be there.

William had been looking all over for Ann and Elizabeth with no success, and he was pleased to see them hurry along the beach. As they approached the campsite, he said, "There you are. I have been looking for you two."

Ann replied, "We have just been over there," pointing to the other end of the beach, "Planting seeds."

While they were both talking, Elizabeth looked down at her filthy hands, not knowing what to do with them. She put them in the sand and wiggled them about, and they came out a bit cleaner. Then she looked up right into the eyes of Richard, who looked resplendent in his bright red marine uniform, who just happened to be standing directly in front of her.

Not knowing what to say or do, Elizabeth could feel herself turning red with embarrassment, and then she blurted out, "Oh, it is you!"

"Yes," was all that Richard had time to say when his name was called out by the Commandant, "Sergeant, would you come over here."

"Sir," was his reply as he nodded his head towards Elizabeth, and then he turned away and promptly moved towards the Commandant.

William started to follow Richard, and then he turned to Ann and said, "I have also been asked to join the Commandant."

William, the Commandant and Richard, walked over and stood before those gathered, all lined up in a rough semi-circle facing the freshly erected flagpole.

This was all very interesting from Elizabeth's point of view, but she had no idea what it was all about; she turned to her mother and said, "What's going on?"

Ann replied, "I heard this morning that there was to be some kind of ceremony this afternoon, but I am not sure what for."

By this stage, everyone in the settlement had lined up facing the flagpole, and then Governor King started to address the small gathering. He formally took possession of Norfolk Island in the name of His Majesty the King, the Queen, the Prince of Wales, and Governor Phillip and then drank from a small cup to the success of the new colony. It was the 6th of March, 1788.

Elizabeth took some interest in the proceedings and was just about to move away from the ceremony as she thought it was over when Richard walked to the front of the group, raised his hat above his head, and said, "Three cheers to the success of the new colony of Norfolk Island."

"Hip, Hip.

Hooray!" the assembled replied with gusto.

"Hip, Hip."

"Hooray!"

"Hip, Hip."

"Hooray!"

Elizabeth stood perfectly still, staring at Richard while trying not to make it too obvious. Finally, William broke the spell by striding over to where she and her mother stood and said, "Well, that is the end of a momentous day and a good start, don't you think?"

Getting no response from Elizabeth and noticing she was looking towards the flagpole, he turned to see what she was looking at and saw Richard furling up the flag. Elizabeth just stood there, transfixed as to what he was doing.

William turned to his wife, pulled her slightly to one side, and whispered, "What is happening here?" nodding towards Elizabeth.

Not sure what to say, Ann replied, "Nothing really, she is just starting to show interest in the opposite sex, and you must admit, he is not bad to look at!"

"Oh Ann, that is enough of that!" he said, more interested in what his wife had just said than what Elizabeth was doing. He then turned, called out, "Come on, Elizabeth," and walked over to the tent erected just for them. Elizabeth hesitated, then reluctantly thought it best to leave the area with her father, and her mother followed.

The entire settlement ate quite well that evening, but they were advised that things would be tighter from that day on as food would now need to be rationed. It was stressed that this was particularly important until some local food was found or caught or the recently sown seeds grew and matured to eatable size.

That night, Elizabeth lay on a blanket that had been spread over a few soft branches and leaves in the family tent, and in that regard, they were lucky. It became cool as the night wore on, and she wrapped the other end of the blanket over the top of her. Elizabeth was finding it difficult to sleep – there was just too much to think about. Over and above, the vivid memory of the harrowing trip through the reef, the fact she was about to sleep in a tent for the first time, and the knowledge that Richard had looked her right in the face and acknowledged her all added to a very eventful day. She felt that her awkward reaction when coming face to face with Richard earlier required her to find a better response in the future. "I'll just have to learn to relax more," she thought as she rolled over again onto her other side. Sleep, after tossing and turning for some time, finally overtook her.

Elizabeth awoke before dawn the following day to the sound of a sharp and heavy rain shower pelting down onto the canvas tent. It did not last long, but it was enough rain for water to seep under the sides of the tent toward her. She was lucky as the branches she was sleeping on were just high enough to keep her bedding out of it. She did not notice this until she got out of bed and when her foot landed in the cold water. She yelled out in surprise as she quickly withdrew it.

Upon hearing the noise, Ann asked, "What's the matter?"

"Nothing. I just put my foot in some cold water."

"Ah! Is that all? I thought a lion or something had jumped on top of you."

"Don't be stupid! Oh, sorry, Mother, I did not mean that."

"That's all right. It's time to get up anyway."

Elizabeth looked around the tent, but her father was not there. He had obviously left before the rain hit.

Over the next few days, the new colony spent considerable time and effort making themselves more comfortable by building rough tables and bench seats, putting up a few more tents, and erecting green screens where necessary. It was slowly becoming a small settlement.

The convicts were kept very busy, which had not only been designed to build the temporary settlement as soon as possible but to keep them out of mischief at the same time. Richard found that keeping the convicts doing what they were supposed to do was comparatively easy until, on one particular day, he heard a yell, "Hey, where's the bread gone?"

Richard turned around and saw one of the women convicts, who had been sorting out food for breakfast, had her hands wavering in the air. He rushed over to her and asked her, "What bread is missing?"

"Somebody has flogged the bread I just put on the table," she said, pointing to the table in front of her.

Richard looked around at everyone standing nearby and said, "Anybody see who just took the bread?"

Everyone looked at everybody else, but no one said anything and a couple of the convicts started to turn away as though uninterested in what was being said.

Now annoyed at the lack of response, Richard yelled out the command, "No one move. Stay just where you are!"

Richard called out to the marine private, who was not far away, "Private, I want you to search each of these three men looking for any bread."

The private moved towards the three men, and one of them started to back up. Once again, Richard yelled, "Stay where you are. Don't move. Private, search this one first," pointing to the convict who had just backed up.

The private checked the front of the man, who was standing rather awkwardly, then moved around the back, and then he said, "Look what I have found," holding up a chunk of bread that he had taken from underneath the convict's clothing. The offender looked around as though he was about to run away, then obviously thought better about it and stood still.

Richard felt somewhat naked in this situation as he had no weapon of any kind, as they all had just been too busy to carry one. Luckily, the private had grabbed the convict by the scruff of the neck and held him tight. He twisted and turned, trying to escape the grip, but to no avail.

Richard said, "Private, hang on to him tight and follow me," as he took off towards the Governor's tent.

Luckily, Governor King was sitting at a table writing his journal in his tent when Richard said, "Sir, we have a problem."

The Governor came to the tent entrance and, seeing the sergeant, said, "What do we have here, Sergeant?"

"Well, sir, this man has been caught stealing bread. We found it on him."

The Governor turned to the male convict and said, "What do you have to say for yourself?"

The convict mumbled something that could not be understood, so the Governor asked again, "Come on, man! What do you have to say? You have been accused of stealing bread."

The convict sheepishly looked down at the ground, gathered his wits, and said quietly, "Sir, I admit it. I will have to rely on your mercy."

The Governor, who was showing frustration by now, said, "Do you know what you have just done? This is a very serious offence. You will be severely punished. There will be no mercy, as you need to be taught a lesson. Lock him up, Sergeant, and I will deal with him later."

Richard said to the private, "Bring him this way," as they headed towards the small rowing boat left at the sand's edge for their easy use. Upon reaching the boat, he said to the private, who still had a tight hold of the convict, "Stay here. I will be back in a minute."

Richard quickly returned with two pairs of irons. One he promptly fitted to the convict's wrists, and the other pair were attached to one ankle of the convict and the heavy ring on the bow of the boat.

"He's not going anywhere," commented the private.

Not knowing for sure what would happen to the convict and when, Richard said to the private, "Keep an eye on him now and again until we hear when he will be punished. Then, you return to what you were doing and return later."

The convict tugged at the iron ring on the boat and then, without saying anything, forcefully sank himself onto the sand.

It was not long before Richard was advised what the punishment would be and when it would occur. He would receive twenty-five lashes at 3 pm this afternoon near the flagpole. Richard was instructed to find the leather lash that had been bought ashore for the purpose, but no one knew where it was. With the help of a couple of convicts, it was eventually found amongst a sack of ropes.

The Governor sent out a message to everyone in the settlement to attend the flogging, with no exceptions.

Elizabeth was leaving the kitchen area when she was told of the order. "A flogging!" she thought, "What is that all about?" She promptly went looking for her mother, who, she guessed, was hanging out clothes on the line.

Finding her mother, she said, "Have you heard about everyone having to attend a flogging at 3 o'clock this afternoon?"

"No, why is that?"

"I don't know the details, but everyone must be at the flagpole before 3 o'clock."

Not knowing anything about it, Ann said, "Well, it must be getting close to that now, so wait for me, and we will go together. Do you know where your father is?"

"No, I don't."

Unbeknownst to Elizabeth and her mother, William was advised to attend the flogging as he would be responsible for the convict's wellbeing. He quickly gathered his medical bag and headed towards the flagpole.

Elizabeth and Ann arrived at the flagpole a little late, as most of the settlement was already there, so they took their place behind everyone else. Elizabeth was unsure how she would react to a flogging as it was all new to her. However, she knew it was a common punishment but felt it was somewhat barbaric.

The commandant had asked Richard to find a suitable place for the flogging near the flagpole. He found two small pine trees about eight feet apart and cut off all the side branches, leaving just the trunks standing. This made it suitable for the convict to be tied by his hands and feet to the two trees so that he could not move away from the lash. Governor King had appointed two convicts to do the flogging, which would punish them for more minor indiscretions that they had previously committed. Unfortunately, they both had not been pulling their weight, and he wanted everyone to know that such laziness would not be tolerated.

Richard and the private went to the boat, unlocked the convict's irons, and marched him to the two flogging trees. Upon getting closer to the trees, he resisted by not moving his feet, so the two marines promptly grabbed him by the arms and dragged him along. As the two marines began to attach the manacles, the convict's legs gave way, and he slumped to the ground. He was yanked to his feet. Richard and the private then undid one end of the manacles holding the convict's hands together and attached the other end to one of the trees. They attached another manacle to the other wrist and attached it to the other tree. They then tied a rope to each ankle and tied it to the trees. The convict was effectively spread-eagled between the two small trees.

Richard did not find this process to his liking, but he knew that such punishment was essential in such a situation, so he gritted his teeth and got on with it. He had to accept that it was just a part of his job.

The entire settlement was now in attendance, including the Governor, who looked very formal in full uniform.

Elizabeth stood right at the back with her mother while her father waited not far from the convict. She looked at her mother, who grabbed her nearest hand and held it tight upon seeing her daughter's concern. Elizabeth had never seen such brutal treatment, and the apparent forcefulness by which Richard was performing his duties was extremely worrying.

The Governor turned around and faced the assembled group, and the murmurings promptly died. He paused for a few seconds before saying, "We are assembled here to witness the flogging of a member of this community who has not only broken the law but has broken the trust of every one of you present. He has stolen a piece of bread off the breakfast table. That lawless act must be punished if we are to survive as a colony here on Norfolk Island. Therefore, all such acts will be severely punished, which is a warning to all of you. Do not let your community or yourself down, or you will find yourself in a similar situation to this man. Accordingly, he will receive 24 lashes, as is his due."

Elizabeth was starting to shiver. She did not know why, but it was a strange feeling. She had noticed the harsh way Richard treated the convict and the firm tone of his voice. She was unsure how she should feel and did not know whether to be attracted or repulsed. She turned her head away.

Ann felt Elizabeth shivering, so she held onto her hand even tighter, then she turned to Elizabeth and said, "I know it is not nice to watch, but sometimes these things must be done. I don't like it either."

Elizabeth did not reply to her mother's comment; she just pursed her lips and nodded while still looking the other way.

Governor King looked at the two convicts who would give the lashing and said, "On the order, you will be giving 24 lashes in total. 12 lashes each, commencing with you," as he pointed to one of the convicts.

"Commence punishment, now!"

The Convict hesitated for a second or two, then raised his arm above his head in one sweeping motion and swung the lash with considerable force across the fellow convict's back.

Elizabeth was not watching, but she heard the swish of the lash going through the air and the slapping sound of leather hitting flesh. Both Elizabeth and her mother flinched in time with the ugly sounds.

No sound came from the manacled convict or the assembled settlers, only the sound of someone calling out, "One."

The assembled crowd, while only small, made a strange noise each time the lash contacted the convict's back. Perhaps each was personally feeling the blows and instinctually reacting accordingly.

The punishment continued until twelve lashes had been given, by which time the convict's back was starting to look ugly, with many red welts becoming obvious. While the convict had been stoic in his response, he started crying out each time the leather strips contacted his back.

William watched on, not in fascination, but concerned about the convict's wellbeing. While he knew that the convicts doing the flogging would change places for the next twelve lashes, William leaned over and looked closely at the face of the tied convict. He stood back and said, "Carry on."

The second convict was given the lash, who took over inflicting the flogging, and the punishment continued.

Elizabeth was finding it harder and harder to stand there and listen to the noises emanating from the lash itself and the groans of the convict. Some members standing there watching the punishment were starting to call out in response as the lash was given, although Elizabeth could not fully understand what was being said. She was not sure if they were of encouragement or of horror.

The numbers were being called out one by one: Thirteen, Fourteen, Fifteen, Sixteen, and then William called out, "Stop!" The convict giving the lashes paused and then lowered the lash as William went over to examine the bloodied convict. He had slumped down on the manacles and was now just hanging there, his head resting on his chest. The welts on his back had turned from red to now oozing blood running down his back and onto his clothing.

William examined the convict by checking his pulse, looking at his eyes, and concluded that he had just fainted. William had been reminded before the flogging began that it would not cease other than in exceptional circumstances. He called out, "All right to continue." A half bucket of water, which had been put there for the purpose, was emptied over the head of the convict. He slowly raised his head from his chest, and the flogging continued.

By this stage, Elizabeth was finding it more and more difficult and was now feeling lightheaded. That was her father's voice calling out, "Carry on". "How could this be," she thought out loud. Then the counting continued: Seventeen, Eighteen, Nineteen, Twenty. She looked over at Richard, who was standing a few yards in front of her, very upright, while intently watching the proceedings. "This is just not right," Elizabeth said to herself, not knowing what to think.

Upon hearing Elizabeth quietly muttering to herself, Ann squeezed her hand again. Her mother had seen various other forms of violence during her lifetime, so this was not affecting her to that extent, but she could understand how Elizabeth was feeling. Such violence was all very new to her.

The counting finally stopped at twenty-four, after which the marines unshackled the convict, who immediately slumped to the ground. He tried to stand up several times, but his legs kept giving way from underneath him, and he would drop back down to the ground.

A few settlement members started to leave, while others just stood there, seemingly fascinated by what they had just witnessed.

Richard had found the whole process difficult, particularly as Elizabeth and her mother watched from close by. He had been through such punishment previously when involved in similar flogging aboard His Majesty's ships. Both sailors and marines, especially if they had returned to their ship dead drunk while hanging onto somebody else's possessions, often found themselves at the end of similar corporal punishment.

By this stage, Elizabeth had seen more than she could stand, so she turned away from the grizzly spectacle and ran towards their tent with her mother in hot pursuit. She opened the flap and promptly dropped onto her bedding while tears ran down her cheeks. Finally, she curled up in the foetus position and sobbed uncontrollably.

Ann knelt beside her daughter, put her arm around her shoulder, and said soothingly, "That's it, have a good cry. It helps sometimes."

William quickly examined him and said, "I think he will be all right in time. Carry him gently to somewhere he can lie down, and I want someone to bathe his back in seawater. It will sting badly, but it will help his wounds heal."

By this stage, the Commandant and most others had left the scene, so William went to see his distressed wife and daughter. Upon entering the tent, he noticed that Ann was sitting on one of their trunks and

307

Elizabeth was sitting on her bed, so he said to both, "Sorry you had to see that. I know it seems unnecessary, but that tough punishment is done to convince others always to do the right thing. In this case, it was done because he stole bread. It seems cruel, I know, but it is supposed to work," as he put his arm around Ann's shoulders.

Elizabeth had composed herself somewhat by now, so she muttered, "It's so unnecessary." She was disgusted by the whole procedure and did not feel comfortable about Richard's involvement, although she knew it was part of his job. She slowly accepted that in real life, sometimes you just had to do something you did not want to do.

In the meantime, Richard organised convicts to carry the weakened, flogged convict to his shared tent, where they did what William had suggested, with the resulting screams when the salty water hit his now scarred back. Finally, it was over, but he hoped that that form of punishment would not be needed again as such unnecessary violence was not in his nature. He fully acknowledged, however, that it was just a part of the job.

Elizabeth was feeling better by lunchtime the next day, so she went to the kitchen area to help her mother prepare the mid-day meal. Ann noticed that the water barrel was nearly empty, and she needed some right away, so she said to Elizabeth, "We are nearly out of water, so could you fill that bucket over there?"

"Yes, Mother," Elizabeth grabbed the empty bucket and headed off to the stream that was not far away. The sun was shining, and it was a beautiful day, so she hummed to help keep negative thoughts away. Turning around a corner in the now well-worn but narrow path, she saw a string of male convicts approaching her, so she moved off the path to let them go by. They passed her one at a time and either nodded or said "Miss" as they did so. There were only about six of them, but they seemed to take forever to go by. Then, the last person came into sight. It was Richard who was escorting the convicts back to the camp.

As he walked along the path and was about to pass, he said, "Good morning, miss," and then stopped in front of her.

Surprised by both seeing him stop so close and hearing his voice, Elizabeth exclaimed, "Oh," and then, after some quick thinking, said, "Good morning, Sergeant."

By this stage, the line of convicts had moved forward a few yards, and then they heard Elizabeth's voice, upon which the last couple in the line stopped and turned around to see what was going on.

Knowing that the situation did not allow him to stay there talking very long, Richard said, "It is good to see you miss," then he turned and resumed following the convicts.

Elizabeth stood there for a minute or two before remembering her mother was waiting for the bucket of water. She hurried on, reached the creek, dipped the bucket in the water, half-filling it, and then ran back to the kitchen.

Ann was looking in her direction as she arrived at the campsite and said to Elizabeth, "Where have you been? Here, give me that water."

Elizabeth tried to look casual, saying, "Nothing, just getting the water."

Her mother had seen the convicts and the marine sergeant coming back to the camp from the direction of the creek, so she said, as she emptied the bucket, "Did you see the sergeant?"

"Ah, yes, I did pass him and the convicts on the path," she admitted reluctantly.

"Did you speak to him?"

"We just said good morning."

"Right. Now you'll have to get back to washing those pots."

Elizabeth was pleased that her mother was not asking any more embarrassing questions, so she returned to work with her pleasant thoughts, although she still found it hard to accept yesterday's violence. The day passed slowly as she could not stop thinking of the sergeant and what the future might hold if her parents did not get in the way of getting to know him better.

Chapter 25

Richard marched the convicts back to the camp, but he was not really thinking much about what he was doing as his thoughts were more about that girl he had met on the path, Elizabeth. He noticed that she was at least now willing to speak to him, so he reasoned that that was a good start and maybe there was a chance of getting to know her better. He made a pact with himself to find a more suitable time and place where that could occur, and he was still thinking about that when the party arrived back at the tent.

Richard called out to the convicts, "Halt," after getting their attention, he said, "Get a drink of water, and we will carry on where we were yesterday." While they were doing that, Richard noticed that a couple were arguing about something, which was starting to get out of hand. Voices were becoming raised, and the pushing and shoving had started, so Richard thought it best to intervene early. He called out in a loud voice," That is enough of that!"

By this stage, the two arguing convicts had grabbed each other's clothing, lost their footing, and continued their fight on the ground. Richard grabbed each by the collar and wrenched them apart. It required a great deal of strength, but it solved the immediate problem. They remained on their knees some four feet apart, panting heavily, with Richard standing between them while both glared at each other.

Richard felt that the whole matter was not severe enough for immediate punishment, so he said, "I don't know what you two were arguing about, but if you stop now and leave each other alone for the rest of the day, I will forget all about it. Got the message?"

Reluctantly, both replied, "Yes, Sergeant."

"Well, get up, and let's get back to work. Everybody!"

The working party moved to the clearing they had started yesterday, with Richard following close behind.

Other than the odd colourful remark hurled from one convict to another, the rest of the day went reasonably well. They finally finished work for the day and then, with less vigour than they had earlier, filed back to the camp for the evening meal. Nevertheless, it was an interesting and fulfilling day.

Everyone on the island now had a real sense of being a part of a team, and by starting a new settlement that way, they were all learning to get on with one another, although it was not always smooth sailing. Personalities occasionally seemed to get in the way, although the common goal continued.

The camp was, by now, enjoying a certain level of comfort as tables and benches had been made, storage compartments roughly put together, and a raised fireplace had been erected out of stone. However, the tents only served as sleeping quarters and places to escape the rain. The weather was reasonable and the temperature mild, although rain, in short bursts, came most days. The seeds planted early in the piece had grown well into mature plants, although there was not enough of it, and the bugs soon found out where there was easy food.

The following days for Elizabeth were starting to all roll into one another, mainly due to the routine of working long hours in the kitchen with her mother. The Commandant had given orders to restrict the quantity of food made available each day, as what stocks they had needed to last a long time. Although Ann did her best organising the food, those with bigger appetites started complaining. Several collecting and hunting parties went out to find local food on some days. The sea birds, who usually nest on the cliff tops, were easily caught and slaughtered as they had no real fear of men. They tasted rather fishy but added considerably to the settlement's overall diet. Fishing parties often travelled along the shore and tried their luck fishing off the rocks, often with good results.

The kitchen itself had been constructed on the edge of the camp so that the prevailing wind blew the cooking fire smoke away from the rest of the camp. There were no wild animals or other people on the island to be concerned about, so safety and security were not a problem. As it was now autumn, the days were becoming shorter and the temperature becoming cooler, particularly at night, although nowhere near as cold as the settlers had been used to in England.

Early one morning, Richard, who was also finding the smaller portions of food challenging to accept, crept around the back of the camp to the bush side of the kitchen. Peeking through the leaves, he saw Elizabeth adding wood to the fire. Rather than walking directly out of the bush and scaring her, he decided to whisper to her from behind the leaves.

"Elizabeth," he whispered.

No answer. A little louder this time, "Elizabeth."

Surprised at the sound of a male voice, she thought she had heard her name being called from behind her, so she quickly turned around to see where it was coming from. Elizabeth could not see anything at first, but then she noticed movement in the bushes and said, "Who is that?"

Richard replied in a quiet voice, "It's me, Richard."

Somewhat taken aback by the surprise of it all and looking around to see if anyone else was listening, Elizabeth said quietly, "What do you want? Can't you see I am busy?"

This was not the reaction Richard had expected, but then he did not consider himself an expert on the fairer sex, so he replied, "I just wanted to talk to you, that's all."

Suddenly, her mother's voice called from behind her, "Elizabeth, can you come over here for a minute and help me with this?"

Elizabeth swung around and replied to her mother, "Coming. Just give me a minute."

Not sure what to say or do, Elizabeth turned back towards Richard and said, "I can't talk with you now. Some other time."

"When?"

"I don't know, just not now." Then, with a swish of her skirt, she turned and hurried over to her mother.

Richard sank back into the bushes, turned and returned to the other side of the camp the long way round. "Damn," he thought, "That did not go how I had hoped."

Because there were only two marines in the entire camp, it became necessary for the Commandant sometimes to keep an eye on the convicts himself. However, it was becoming clear that once a task had been given, little, if any, supervision was now necessary. Moreover, there were only two small rowing boats left on the island, and, as the island was hundreds of miles from anywhere, it was thought that any escape attempt by boat would be perilous and, therefore, highly unlikely. In addition to that, the two sets of oars were kept in a separate store tent close to the commandant.

That night, Richard made a conscious effort to try and talk to Elizabeth whenever he could. Maybe the current convict supervision flexibility may make that possible, provided her parents did not get in the way.

Richard could not get the thought of what Elizabeth had said out of his head. She did not decline his attempt to talk to her, and she had said, "Some other time," and "I don't know, just not now."

Richard thought aloud to himself, "I think that was a positive reply?" With those thoughts and doubts still in his mind, he tossed and turned most of the night and woke up the following day still tired. It had been a long night.

Elizabeth was kept busy that afternoon until dark, helping her mother prepare the evening meal and clean up afterwards. She also kept thinking about what had happened earlier that afternoon and wondered where this was all heading. Richard obviously wanted to talk; it was just a matter of finding the time and place for that to occur. She had never felt this strange deep feeling inside her before and was unsure what it meant.

The next morning Elizabeth woke up early, still with what happened yesterday clearly in her mind. She tried to think of other things but could not get this tall, muscular marine out of her mind. While it felt good in specific ways, it felt frustrating in others. She lay under her blanket a little longer this morning, wondering what her next move would be. She felt something had to be done! But what?

Her father, William, was finding things comparatively easy on the island up to this point as his medical services had not been needed much, other than the flogging and the odd cut and sprain. However, he talked to Ann the day before about Elizabeth and was somewhat concerned about where this fascination may go. Ann said she would have a word with Elizabeth as soon as the time was right, but upon pondering the question, she realized that that needed to be soon. She considered that timing in such situations was vital.

Elizabeth heard her father get dressed, whisper something to her mother and leave before either she or her mother got out of bed. "That's strange," she thought, "He's not normally up this early."

Still in bed, Ann called Elizabeth, "I know you are awake, Elizabeth. I can hear you moving around."

"Just thinking, Mother."

"And I know what, or should I say, who, you are thinking about."

Elizabeth was unsure how to respond and said, "Well, yes and no."

Ann climbed out of bed, stood below Elizabeth, and, looking up at the top bunk, said, "Elizabeth, I do know what things go through a girl of your age's mind, you know. It is obvious to your father and me that you are interested in the sergeant, which is understandable. Do you remember what we discussed a while ago about what men are often like?"

"Yes, Mother, I do."

"Well, I just thought now would be a good time to remind you. You need to be careful and don't do anything that doesn't feel right. Understand?"

While she appreciated her mother's concern, she felt her mother was worried about something that did not exist, so she just said, "Yes, I do understand."

"Good," was her mother's short reply, although she was unsure that her inexperienced daughter knew what she was talking about.

Ann said, "Come on. Get up. We have not got all day, you know."

Richard found it difficult to get out of bed so early, but he knew he could not delay as the Commandant was a fanatic regarding punctuality. He did not usually dress in his uniform these days as it needed to be kept for more formal occasions. He also did not usually carry any weapon either, as there was no way for anyone to escape from the island successfully. His role was more of a supervisor these days and to keep the peace if needed. The other marine in the settlement took on a similar role on different shifts.

Richard had been informed by the Commandant the day before that he would be accompanying him on an exploration trip to the other side of the island. He had been told to wear his uniform and take a haversack and a bayonet, which may be useful. He arrived at the flagpole, the usual rendezvous point, just as the Commandant did, which was fortunate as he was slightly late.

"Good morning, Sergeant," was the cheery greeting, although Richard did not feel that great.

"Good morning, Sir."

"You ready to go, Sergeant? I am not sure how the day will go as it looks like it could rain. Maybe only showers if we are lucky."

"Are we going by ourselves, Sir?"

"No, we are not. But, oh, here comes William now."

Surprised by William's arrival, Richard said, "Good morning, Sir."

"Good morning, Sergeant. Are we all ready to go?"

Commandant King replied, "I think so. We all know how heavy the bush is so the going could be slow. Sergeant, put this food into your haversack; we will need it later. Let's go."

The three of them headed off towards the steep hills behind the flat area where their campsite was located. This part of the island was one of the few areas with no cliffs rising straight out of the sea, but there was an immediate rise to the top a few hundred yards behind it. They needed to cross the flat area and climb the steep valley to the two-hundred-and-fifty-foot-high plateau.

"Thank goodness it is not a hot day," were Richard's immediate thoughts as he pushed through the heavy bush on one side of the steep valley. After about twenty minutes, he stopped to take a breather, only to notice that William was finding the going tough and only about halfway up. He sat down on a fallen Norfolk Island Pine tree trunk while he waited for the other two to catch up. He then realized he was breathing heavily, proving the climb was more challenging than he first thought. Looking around, he guessed that he was about halfway to the top, and as the bush was not so dense where he was sitting, he could see the entire valley and the hills all around it. The countryside was unbelievable. It glowed from many shades of green on the sides of the valley, the light-coloured sandy beach in the middle distance, the white waves pounding on the bay's protective reef, and the contrasting deep blue of the sea in the far distance. Richard thought it looked just like a painting he once saw.

Eventually, the other two caught up and had to sit down for a while and get their breath back. Richard's only concern was the fitful sleep he had experienced the previous night, making the going this morning much more difficult.

Richard pointed to the scene below and said, "Look at that. Worth the climb. Wait until we get to the top!"

William, now able to speak far easier, said, "I agree with that."

After a few minutes, the Commandant said, "All right, you two, we can't sit here all day; we have a long way to go."

Richard got to his feet and said, "Sir, I forgot to ask you where we are going?"

"We are heading for Anson Bay on the island's northwest side."

Richard, now keen to explore more and get moving, said, to no one in particular, "Right, let's get going."

The small party headed off up the hill once again. This time they walked up the bottom of a valley, which was not so steep and was not any faster as the bush was considerably thicker than the hills on either side. At times Richard found that he had to use his bayonet to clear the way. He deliberately climbed a little slower this time so that the other two could maintain a similar pace.

They finally got to the top, turned around, and looked back over the valley that led onto the flat area that housed their tiny settlement. The campsite was not entirely visible as the tall Norfolk Island Pine trees limited their view. However, they could see Emily Bay, which looked as calm as ever, with Nepean Island just offshore and Phillip Island in the distance, surrounded by the choppy blue sea. All three stood there for a few seconds, taking it all in.

They moved off towards the northwest and Anson Bay, and while the bush was not so heavy in this area, they noticed that the pine trees were getting bigger and bigger. Coming upon one of the largest they had seen, the Commandant walked up to its massive trunk, trying to estimate its diameter, but then had to back up somewhat so he could see the overall size. Finally, he said, "Sergeant, please stand in front of the trunk and hold your arms outstretched to the side."

Richard did as he was requested as the Commandant stood back trying to estimate the diameter of the massive trunk, and then he said to Richard, "You are about six feet tall, aren't you?"

"About that, sir."

"That means the trunk is about nine feet across where your arms are, which means, if my mathematics is correct, it is about twenty-nine feet around. Some tree, don't you think?"

William walked further back from the base of the tree, trying to see the top and guess its height, but he could not see it from where he was standing, so he asked the Commandant, "Have you any idea how tall it is?"

"Well, I did look at this tree as we came up to it, and I think it is about a hundred and fifty feet tall. There would be a considerable quantity of timber in that tree, although I am not sure if the Norfolk Island Pine is suitable for ships masts as Captain Cook thought on his earlier visit. Come on. It will be a long day if we don't get moving."

They continued their arduous trek towards Anson Bay, sometimes up and down steep valleys, sometimes fighting through heavily wooded areas.

It had taken them over four hours to get this far, and the bay itself was not evident until they reached the cliff's edge and looked along it. The small sandy beach at the bay's edge was over two hundred feet down, and while it looked possible to climb down to the beach, it seemed extraordinarily steep and would be a dangerous descent.

After examining the whole area along the cliff's edge, the Commandant said to his two comrades, "We saw this bay earlier when we circled the island, and it was impossible to be sure from the sea how good this area would be as a landing point. I was hoping we could use this bay when this side of the island was in the lee, but looking at the cliff, I don't think it would be useable."

William replied, "I think you are right. That cliff is just too steep and high."

Richard, not to be left out of the conversation, said, "I could try and climb down to the bottom and then back up if you want me to."

"No thanks, Sergeant, that will not be necessary. I have seen enough from up here. Thanks for volunteering anyway. Let's have some of that food that you have in your haversack; I'm hungry."

All three felt better after eating, and as the middle of the day was now past, it was time to return to camp. The trek back was not quite as challenging as they tried to follow the track they had initially come out on, although that was not always so easy as they lost it several times. The sun was starting to set as they eventually came to the top of the cliff above their campsite. The red and orange hues in the clouds, which contrasted with the bright blue sky, and the silhouette of the tall pine trees in front of the sun created a magical scene.

They quickly climbed down the valley onto the flats at the bottom and, finding one of the now common pathways, headed back towards their camp. The Commandant was now in the lead, which they had swapped occasionally as they often had to push through the bush. Richard was the last in line at this point and was some way back when he heard a faint female voice. He could not see anybody down the track, so he stopped, and then he realized that the voice was familiar, and it sounded like it was coming from somewhere in front of the Commandant. He picked up speed as he walked towards the voice, and as he got closer, he was sure it was Elizabeth's voice.

By this stage, she was talking to her father and asking about the trek they had just been on, "That was a long day, Father. Are you feeling all right?"

"Fine. Yes, I'm fine," was the reply as he turned towards Richard, who had just joined them.

Speaking to Elizabeth, her father said, "You know Richard, don't you?"

At the sight of Richard and hearing his name, Elizabeth did not know where to look or what to say.

Her father continued, "The sergeant has worked hard all day and done a brilliant job. We are now back safe and sound. Is that not so, Sergeant?"

It was now Richard's turn not to know what to do or say, so he just mumbled something that sounded like, "Sir, it was nothing to do with me."

The Commandant, who by now realized that this discussion was nothing to do with him, turned to William and Richard and said, "Thanks to both of you. Everything went well," he turned and continued walking towards the camp.

Elizabeth felt far safer and more confident with her father present, so she said, "Of course, I know Richard. Hello, Richard."

He looked up into Elizabeth's face, the first time he had done so at such a distance since his earlier attempts from the bushes. Being so close, he felt she was more beautiful than he initially thought. His heart skipped a beat, but he smiled and replied, "Hello, Elizabeth."

Elizabeth's father felt like the two of them did not remember he was standing beside them as they stared into each other's eyes. Not sure if he was doing the right thing, he left them to it, as they were only a few yards away from the camp. He quietly said, "I will let you two talk for a little while. Don't be long, Elizabeth," as he moved off and continued walking down the path. Not sure that Ann would have approved of what he had just done, he turned a slight bend in the path into the campsite and decided to stop and wait for them to appear. He knew they were still not far away as he could hear their muffled voices, which made him reasonably confident all would be well.

As William had his back to the campsite itself, he did not realize how close he was to the kitchen area where his wife was busy preparing the evening meal. He was soon reminded when a loud voice called, "William, what are you doing standing there?"

Caught by surprise, he turned to Ann, put his finger to his lips and whispered, "Shush, keep your voice down."

This caught Ann entirely off guard; she looked around her and said quietly, "What are we whispering for?"

"Elizabeth and Richard are talking just down the path, and I am waiting for them to come into camp."

"Oh, I see."

No sooner had Ann finished her last comment when the voices from down the path grew louder. Not wanting to look like he was deliberately spying on them, William quickly turned around and walked toward Ann. The voices stopped as the two of them came around the corner and into view. Elizabeth came first, looking quite happy with herself, saw her mother and father and joined them at the kitchen table. Trying to look like nothing had happened, Richard came into the camp seconds later and turned away from the kitchen toward his tent. All three quietly watched him disappear from view.

Ann, unable to contain herself any longer, said, "I hear that you have just been having a serious discussion with the sergeant."

Not feeling as embarrassed as she usually was, Elizabeth casually replied, "We didn't talk about anything important."

William felt comfortable about Richard's interest in Elizabeth, as he had got to know him somewhat during the hike to Anson Bay. He quite liked him, and, as they were all going to live on this small island for some time, it seemed to him to be an acceptable arrangement. He left the kitchen to write in his journal on the completed expedition to Anson Bay, leaving Ann and her daughter to finish the conversation.

Ann was the first to say something, "Well, what do you make of that?"

"What do you mean?

"Your father seems to have relaxed his view of Richard. Haven't you noticed?"

"Well, he didn't make any objections."

"Exactly. What does that tell you?

"Does that mean he is not against me seeing him?"

"Yes, you may be right, but there will be limits. Remember what I have said to you before. Your father and I will discuss this and let you know tomorrow."

With a big sigh, she said, "Yes, Mother."

Elizabeth felt extremely relieved that both her parents had not objected to her seeing Richard again, and she assumed that the trip that her father and Richard had just taken may have had something to do with it. He had obviously impressed her father. For the rest of the day, she could not think of anything else than that meeting on the path.

Chapter 26

Now that he had had the opportunity to talk with Elizabeth, Richard could not get her out of his mind as he lay there on his bed. He knew that he had been attracted to her for some time now. But getting that close and having the opportunity to talk to her properly was something else. He had never felt this way about any girl before, and the experience was, on the one hand, fantastic, on the other hand, scary. After tossing and turning, he finally got to sleep, with the final thought being, "I just have to see her again."

The following morning, Richard, not at all feeling fully rested, found himself in a daze as he got ready for the day. He was unsure where or what he would be doing, so his mind turned to Elizabeth. Then he remembered that it was Sunday, and the usual daily work routine did not occur. "Maybe I can find an easy way of seeing Elizabeth again," he thought.

While a short religious ceremony occurred near the flagpole every Sunday, Richard did not usually attend, even though everyone was expected to. "I wonder if Elizabeth will be there today?" was his immediate thought.

With more effort with his appearance this morning than usual, Richard got ready for the day, tidying up his hair by cutting the extra-long bits with his bayonet. It was not ideal, but it looked considerably better than it usually did. Unfortunately, there was no barber on the island, so everyone had to do their best, which was difficult when you did not have a pair of scissors.

The service was held at ten every Sunday morning, so Richard casually wandered over a little early to the flagpole. He stood well back from everyone else as he was not sure of the usual routine, and anyway, Elizabeth and her family had not yet arrived. Moreover, Richard's tent was on the opposite side of the campsite to Elizabeth's, so standing there made any entrance from the opposite direction visible.

It looked like most of the camp had arrived, but still no Elizabeth or her family. Then he started to doubt himself. Did she usually come to the service? He thought he had seen her from a distance at other times, but maybe they did not come every Sunday.

The Commandant arrived and positioned himself in front of the gathered settlers, and it looked like he was about to start, but no Elizabeth. Then he saw her. "Wow!" was his immediate thought. She looked gorgeous in what looked like her best dress, and her hair was in a style he had never seen her wear before. He took a deep breath, held it briefly, and slowly released it. Her parents followed closely behind her, and all three stopped on the other side of the small gathering.

Now breathing more regularly, Richard slowly moved around to the back of everyone else and towards where Elizabeth was standing.

The Commandant started to speak, "Good morning, everyone. Thank you for coming."

Richard heard that part, but from then on, he had no idea what was being done or said as he turned his full attention back to Elizabeth. He stood about fifteen feet behind Elizabeth and her family and was having difficulty figuring out what he should do next. As the service had now started, he felt that a direct approach at this time would not be advisable, and, in any event, he would have to move very slowly and be quiet about it.

Then, for one reason or other, Elizabeth turned her head around and saw Richard right behind her. He smiled, gave her a tiny acknowledgement with his hand, and stayed right where he was because it did not feel like the right time to move. Elizabeth glanced at her parents, returned the smile and then a small wave. She had not expected to see Richard at the service as he did not usually attend, but it felt good that he had made an effort.

Her mother noticed Elizabeth turn her head and then the wave, so without looking, she assumed that Richard must be somewhere close.

Eventually, the last hymn began, and everyone except Richard joined in because he did not know the words. He felt completely out of place in this unfamiliar environment, but he had to stay there as Elizabeth's attraction was too strong to resist.

With the last "Amen," the service ended, and Elizabeth promptly turned around to see if Richard was still there. Thankfully, he was. She turned to her mother beside her and said, "Mother, if you don't mind, I would like to stay here for a while."

Ann turned to her husband, who had also heard the request and had seen her look over her shoulder. He had pre-empted the question, so he said, "That's fine."

Ann turned to her daughter and said, "That's all right, but only for a short while."

"Thank you, Mother."

Richard could see the conversation between the three of them, so he felt it best to remain standing where he was. William and Ann turned to leave, looked over at Richard, nodded, and moved off toward their tent. Elizabeth was left standing there, and Richard could not understand what was happening for a second or two. Then he realized that Elizabeth was not going with her parents. He quickly stepped forward, smiled, and said, "Good morning, Elizabeth."

"Good morning, Richard," she replied with the same formality and a return smile.

By this time, the rest of the congregation had dispersed, and the two of them were left standing there looking rather obvious. Richard felt slightly overwhelmed by the situation and could not think of what to say or do. Then he remembered that the flagpole was just over the sand hills from the beach, so he said, "Elizabeth, would you like to walk along the beach?"

Without seriously thinking about it, Elizabeth replied, "Yes, of course, but I will have to get back fairly soon."

Richard quickly led the way over the nearest sand hill and onto the beach. The first thing he noticed was that the bay was calm, except for the waves breaking on the reef, and that the tide was out. He led Elizabeth down the beach and onto the firmer sand at the water's edge and said, "I suggest you take your shoes off. The saltwater will ruin them."

They moved back up the beach a little, and both removed their shoes. "That soft sand between the toes feels good," was Elizabeth's immediate comment.

"Come on! This way," Richard called out.

They walked up the beach, taking in the breeze, the salt air, and the absolute beauty of it all. The light-coloured sand contrasted nicely against the clear blue water in front of them and the bright green foliage behind them. Being inside the coral reef made the water surface exceptionally smooth, and other than the slight slap, slap, slap noise as the tiny wavelets hit the beach, all was quiet.

Elizabeth was taking it all in and, at the same time, feeling amazingly at peace. She felt like it was meant to be. They were walking side by side along the edge of the water when they noticed they were getting closer and closer to each other. Their hands accidentally touched, and then one slipped into the other before each realized what had just happened. Elizabeth looked over at Richard and smiled. No words were necessary. She had never experienced such a feeling before, but it felt marvellous. They walked hand in hand till they reached the end of the curved beach, where they turned around and headed back.

Elizabeth let go of Richard's hand and started to jog back down the sand as she called out, "Come on, Richard. I must go back now. Otherwise, I will be in trouble."

"Wait for me."

About a hundred feet or so before where their shoes had been left, Elizabeth called out, "The last one to the shoes is a dirty dog," as she took off as fast as she could.

Not wanting to be outdone, Richard put all his effort into catching up and getting there first, but Elizabeth ran considerably faster than he expected and arrived just before him.

She turned to Richard and said, "So, who is the dirty dog now?" as she dropped to the sand alongside their shoes.

"That's cheating. You started long before I did."

Elizabeth could not help herself and said, as she burst out laughing, "You are just too slow."

Although both were breathing hard from the run, they continued laughing as they just stood there enjoying each other's company.

Finally, they both got their breath back, brushed the sand off their feet, put their shoes back on, and headed over the dunes to the camp.

Elizabeth's mother was concerned that her daughter had not yet arrived back at their tent, especially as it had been thirty minutes since they had left. She thought it best to go and find out what was going on. She walked back to the flagpole, but they were nowhere in sight. As the dune right in front of her was higher than anywhere else, she climbed to the top for a better look. Then she saw the pair of them walking up the beach towards her, so she promptly ducked down and slid back down the dune, hoping they had not seen her. She scurried back to her tent.

By the time Elizabeth and Richard arrived back at the flagpole, Ann was nowhere to be seen.

Elizabeth took Richard's hand and said, "Thanks for the walk. I enjoyed that."

"So did I. We must do that again."

"I would like that, but I must go now," she said as she reluctantly let go of Richard's hand and slowly headed towards her tent.

Elizabeth looked back as she left Richard and noticed he was standing there looking happy on the one hand but sadly alone on the other.

He raised his hand, smiled, and said, "See you tomorrow." She waved back. Richard then turned and walked to his side of the camp while glancing over his shoulder, as did Elizabeth, and with a wave from each, they disappeared out of each other's sight.

That night Elizabeth could not get that warm and comforting feeling of Richard's strong hands in hers out of her mind. She kept wondering where all this might end and whether she was doing the right thing getting so close to a soldier. It felt right, but how does one know what is right? That unanswerable question kept coming back to her every time she woke during the night. He was older than her, but then she reasoned that most men were older than their wives, which is nothing unusual. She tossed and turned most of what seemed to be a very long night, with a lovely warm sensation on the one hand and the fear of the unknown on the other. She eventually got a couple of hours of welcome sleep.

The following morning, Elizabeth woke early, long before her parents, and she noticed it was still dark outside. Unusually, she decided to take a walk before dawn as she could see the inviting cool light of the moon coming through the tent's canvas walls. She could tell there was little wind outside as the tent was not moving much, and the wind was not rustling the tree's leaves as usual. She quietly dressed and slipped through the tent's doorway. The moon was full that night, so she could easily find her way as she headed for the flagpole, walked through the clearing and onto the sandhills. She removed her shoes, allowing her bare feet to enjoy the cool sand between her toes.

Elizabeth could not hear any movement in the camp and was unsure what the time was, but it did not matter. She slid down the last dune onto the flat sandy beach, where she noticed the moonlight glinting on the smooth water in the bay. Even though there was very little wind this morning, she could hear the open ocean waves splashing against the coral reef some distance away. She could clearly see the spray sent up by each wave as the moon shined brightly through every one of them.

She walked to the edge of the soft sand and sat down. That view was amazing, but then her mind returned to yesterday and Richard. Even though the breeze was cool on her skin, she felt warm inside. She sat on the beach for some time, thinking about the recent past, the now and the future. Then, she noticed a slight glow over to the east, meaning her working day was about to begin. She stood up and reluctantly walked back to the camp where her usual role in the kitchen would be waiting for her.

While sleeping a little better than Elizabeth, Richard was not feeling particularly rested when dawn broke. He lay there thinking about the walk down the beach with Elizabeth and the feel of her hand in his. It was a small hand, and the skin was smooth and incredibly soft to the touch. He wondered whether all her skin felt like that. Maybe, just maybe, in time, he would find that out.

He decided to go to the kitchen and get something to eat for breakfast, which would give him an excuse to see Elizabeth. He even spent far more time than usual preparing himself for the day, even to the point of combing his hair. While he had a couple of fleeting relationships with girls in the past, he felt that his knowledge and experiences were minimal when it came to impressing the opposite sex. Nevertheless, he felt he now had an opportunity to get to know a girl he felt was right for him and that it would be foolish not to take advantage of the current situation. However, he fully realized that the settlement's minimal number of inhabitants made it essential to take things carefully if he wanted an agreeable outcome. The sun was now peeking over the horizon, and it looked like the start of a beautiful day, but he did not feel that comfortable or sure of himself when he walked to the kitchen.

Richard saw Elizabeth as soon as he got closer. She was preparing breakfast on the fire that had been built into a stone fireplace by now. He could not take his eye off her as he walked towards the breakfast line-up, but then, thinking of other things and not taking any actual notice of where he was walking, he tripped on what was left of a small tree stump. Richard tried his best to keep his balance but hit the ground with a thump before he knew it.

Elizabeth heard the strange noise, looked up and saw Richard slowly getting to his feet, at the same time shaking his head, obviously dazed. Her first reaction was to go to his rescue, but then she quickly realized that doing such a thing would not be in the best interests of any man, particularly a marine, so she just stood there watching.

Upon accepting his awkward predicament, Richard gathered himself together as fast as he could and joined the queue, trying to make it look like nothing had happened. Looking down, he saw grass leaves stuck to his knees, which he promptly brushed away, hoping no one had seen his fall or the resulting evidence.

Then Elizabeth heard her mother's voice, "Come on, Elizabeth; we have work to do."

Elizabeth had not heard her mother's comments as she was too busy watching the embarrassing proceedings continue before her.

 The lack of response made her mother call again, "Elizabeth, can you hear me?"

Elizabeth finally heard her mother's voice, turned to her and said, "What was that mother?"

Ann glanced over toward where Elizabeth was staring, and it all became clear. She saw Richard brushing himself off at the back of the line waiting for breakfast.

Not seeing Richard fall, Ann turned to her daughter and said, "Don't worry about that now. We have work to do."

Elizabeth finally came to her senses, heard her mother's instructions and went back to preparing breakfast, glancing from time to time in Richard's direction. It looked to Elizabeth like he had not seen her, but she did not know Richard was too embarrassed to look in her direction. Finally, they both looked up simultaneously, and their gazes met. They both smiled; Elizabeth gave a small unobtrusive wave, which Richard returned, although he did not feel at all comfortable standing there after his embarrassing fall.

It then became apparent to Ann that Richard was in the breakfast queue as he got closer to the serving table, so she called Elizabeth, "Elizabeth, do you mind coming here and serving for a while?"

"Coming," was her eager reply.

By the time Elizabeth arrived, Richard was next in line to get served, and he said sheepishly, "Good morning, Elizabeth."

"Good morning," came the confident reply while trying not to show too much familiarity, "How are you this morning?"

"Fine, thank you. And you?" replied Richard.

"I'm fine too. Do you want some porridge?"

"Yes, please," replied Richard in a more confident manner.

Richard was unaware of how much, if any, of his embarrassing fall Elizabeth had seen, but as she had not said anything about it, he felt a little more confident.

Just behind Richard in the line was a convict woman who realized what was going on but showed very little interest, so in a very impatient voice, she said, "Come on, you two. Enough of that. I am hungry!"

Elizabeth quickly served Richard and said quietly, "I will try and see you later," upon which Richard's heart skipped a beat as he took his meal and quickly walked away.

Elizabeth continued serving the last few in the queue, all the while trying to catch Richard's eye, but he did not turn around or look in her direction. He finally disappeared out of sight towards the other side of the camp.

Chapter 27

The general feeling within the newly set up colony on Norfolk Island was becoming increasingly mature as the weeks passed, and most members were finding their natural place within this highly varied group. The convicts were not treated much differently than everyone else, other than they were told what they would be doing rather than being asked. Supervision was fundamental, and a guard or supervisor was not always present, but the convicts would be checked on occasionally just in case anyone decided to abscond.

The two senior members of the settlement, Governor Philip Gidley King and Elizabeth's father, William, kept the whole settlement ticking over while preparing it to accept more convicts later that year. Finally, however, it was recognised that the tents they were still living in were only temporary and that more substantial longer-term accommodation was needed.

The settlement was initially set up just over the sand dunes behind Emily Bay, and as the ground was very sandy, it was not thought ideal for any substantial buildings. However, to the west of Emily Bay was another smaller bay, Slaughter Bay, where the ground was far firmer as it lay behind a beach made up mainly of large and small coral pieces. It was decided that this would be a much better area to build due to the more solid ground, and, at the same time, it was closer to the necessary building materials.

Once the decision had been made, most male and female convicts and freemen were sent to this next bay to clear an area of trees and bush suitable for more substantial buildings.

There were two types of building material available locally, wood from the many trees in the area that they had already felled, plus old coral and sandstone that could be cut into blocks. Once an area had been cleared, the slow and arduous task of collecting the required building materials began. Luckily, there was one experienced carpenter amongst the male convicts, so his expertise was taken advantage of by organising the cutting and preparing of the required timber. While the coral stone was quite soft, it was still necessary to find suitable material, cut it out of the bank, and shape it with a hammer and chisel. As this required many hours of manual work, everyone without other duties was expected to pitch in and help. Slowly, the piles of building materials grew, and the stone foundations of a couple of buildings began taking shape.

Elizabeth had earlier found her logical spot in the kitchen with her mother, and as she was not a physically strong person and knew what she was doing, it suited her just fine.

William found that he spent most of his time looking after the health of everyone, particularly treating cuts and abrasions from the coral, which would regularly cause badly infected wounds. Occasionally, someone would get in the way of a falling log or branch, injure themselves, and require medical attention. As a result, his expertise was regularly in demand, but not in a significant way. When not attending to any patients, he helped elsewhere, wherever he could be helpful.

Richard's role varied considerably. He was expected to help keep the peace, which sometimes tested his communication skills. He was no longer wearing his uniform as he only had one, so he had to make it last. This was particularly relevant as he often helped timber cutters and block makers. He had to be handy if fights or arguments became a significant problem, which usually required mediation. At times, more effective forms of punishment or persuasion were needed.

As everyone pitched in and helped, regardless of their usual role, the general informal tone of the place and the sense of being a part of a team became increasingly apparent.

Foundations started to be laid out with coral stone blocks, and a couple of building walls began to appear. The coral was also being ground up, fired in a pit in the ground, and made into a mortar with the addition of sand and water.

While all this building activity was ongoing, those not directly involved with construction work were inclined to fish or gather natural foodstuffs. Others tended the gardens, planted more vegetables, and generally coaxed them to produce much-needed fresh food. The animals bought onto the island also had to be looked after, although there were now fewer than when they first arrived. Unfortunately, a few original animals were slaughtered to vary the colonies' diet, even though as many as possible were kept for breeding. Fishing parties were regularly formed, and a good catch usually resulted. Occasionally, a party would scout the cliffs and find sea birds used to supplement what they had originally bought to the island. William kept reminding the Commandant of the importance of a varied diet, so every effort was made to achieve it. Ann did her best to assist.

While all the above was happening, Elizabeth and Richard found it difficult to see each other over and above brief contact near the kitchen. Both were becoming very frustrated by the difficulties they were experiencing and, in any event, were exhausted by the time the day was over. The only day that gave them any real possibility of seeing each other was Sunday, and Richard realized that Elizabeth's parents would have to agree before any regular meetings could take place.

One Sunday finally arrived after a hectic week, and Richard, although still aching from his weeklong physical exertions, decided that today was the day he would now talk to Elizabeth's parents. He was keen to move the relationship along if he could, and he felt that something had to be done! Both felt that their fleeting contacts were too short and infrequent.

Now clear in his mind what he needed to do, Richard waited till later that Sunday morning after Elizabeth and her family returned from the church service. He watched the family enter their tent from afar, waited about thirty seconds, and then, with much trepidation, headed towards their tent. As he approached, he heard voices that sounded like a serious conversation was taking place. He hesitated for about thirty seconds and, upon noticing a more extended break in the discussion, called out, "Excuse me!"

William heard the call and replied, "Who is it?"

"Sorry to disturb you, sir. It is Sergeant Clarke. Could I have a word with you?"

The tent flap flung open, and William stepped outside, saying, "Oh, I thought it might be you, Sergeant. How can I help?"

Although Richard had gone over what he would say many times since he had decided to talk with Elizabeth's parents, all that disappeared when the actual time came, he paused, trying to think of his earlier prepared words, but they did not come. So, he just stood there, saying nothing, as the embarrassment of the situation became more and more apparent. He felt his face redden.

Although he usually was forthright and spoke matter-of-factly, William felt Richard's extremely awkward moment and, in sympathy, said, "Don't worry, Richard, I think I know why you are here."

"Oh, thank you, sir," is all Richard could immediately think of. Then, after pausing, he continued, "May I have a word with you in private, sir?"

"Certainly, just give me a couple of minutes."

Elizabeth and her mother had heard Richard calling out earlier, so they immediately stopped what they were doing and listened to the conversation outside their tent. Both guessed why Richard had come calling and, as they had both expected something like this would eventually happen, they listened intently.

Elizabeth kept looking at her mother, trying to gauge her reaction to what was being said, but she did not give much away.

William finished the conversation, walked back into their tent, and, in a low tone, said, "That was Richard, and he wants to talk to me. We can guess what it is all about, so do either of you two have any objections?"

He stood there looking from one to the other, waiting for a response, but it was slow in coming. Elizabeth felt that she should wait for her mother's reaction before she took the next step, so she said nothing.

Although not surprised at what was occurring, Ann still had reservations. She looked at Elizabeth, saw a pleading look on her face, paused, and said, "All right. I guess this was bound to happen."

With that said, Elizabeth replied in a loud, enthusiastic voice, "Thank you, Mother. Thank you!"

Elizabeth was not entirely pleased with the slowness of her mother's reactions but at least was happy that she did not object. Elizabeth now felt she could be more open and show her feelings, although she did not know what her father would say to Richard.

Richard, who was standing a few yards away from the tent, heard the tone of Elizabeth's enthusiastic words, which made him feel more relaxed about the whole situation. He waited patiently for William to come back outside.

William opened the tent flap, walked over to Richard, grabbed his arm, walked him a short distance away from the tent, and then said, "All right, young man. What do you want to talk to me about?"

Richard had heard the joy in Elizabeth's voice a little earlier, so he assumed they had guessed what he was about to say, so he now felt more confident when he said, "Sir. You would be aware that Elizabeth and I seem to be getting along well, and I would like to get to know her better, but before I can do that, I would like to get your permission. Have you any objections to that, sir?"

William did not expect the question to be asked in such a formal manner, but it was what he expected. He was glad Richard had felt it best to get his permission rather than try and see Elizabeth behind his back. It confirmed his earlier opinion about who he was as a person. Moreover, William warmed to Richard during their joint trip with the Commandant to Anson Bay a few weeks ago, so he felt reasonably comfortable answering the question.

Not wanting to hurry his answer, William said, "Before I answer the question, I have a couple of my own. First, is this a longer-term relationship with Elizabeth, you are asking, or is this just a short-term passing interest?"

Being honest about how he genuinely felt, Richard said, "I want to have the opportunity to get to know her and I have every intention to be true to whatever it is that she truly wants. I can assure you, sir, that I do not intend to take advantage of her in any way."

"Good answer, Sergeant. One more question. Do you believe that you, being a marine in his majesties' service, will be a problem?"

"No sir, I do not. As you doubtless would have noticed, I, like everyone else here on the island, am now part of a team trying to create a decent settlement here on the island. I am the same as everyone else."

"Ah. I see what you mean. Well, seeing as you put it that way, not a problem."

"Well, sir. Do I have your permission to see Elizabeth?"

"Yes, Richard, you do. Providing you keep your promise to not take advantage of her, and you keep in mind what she truly wants. You do realize that I intend to hold you to your promises."

"Yes, I do. Thank you, sir; I mean William. Thank you very much. If that is all right with you?"

"No problem, we are both adults."

By this stage, Richard could barely contain himself. He had wanted this for weeks now, and it had taken considerable courage on his part to get where he was, and it made him extremely happy it had all ended well. He put his hand out, which William gladly took, and they firmly shook hands.

Meanwhile, Elizabeth, fully aware of what was happening outside, had slowly moved to the tent flap and, without touching it, peeked through the small opening.

Seeing what Elizabeth was doing, Ann whispered, "What are you doing?"

"They won't know I am here if I don't touch the tent."

Elizabeth could not hear what was said, but the tone seemed amicable, so she waited patiently for the expected positive outcome. She then saw the handshake; her heart jumped and, at the same time, missed a couple of beats. Then, finally, she took a deep breath, held it for a few seconds and then, with some difficulty, managed to breathe normally once more.

Not wanting to stay behind the tent flap any longer than necessary after seeing the handshake, Elizabeth could not contain herself further, so she burst through the flap and ran over to William and Richard. She wanted to hug them both, but who first? She hesitated just before getting there, not wanting to make such an immediate decision. Finally, she rushed towards Richard while looking out the corner of her eye at her father. She had her arms outstretched towards Richard before getting there, allowing her to wrap her arms around him eagerly. This movement caught Richard entirely by surprise, as Elizabeth's arms were around him before he even had an opportunity to raise his arms. She enthusiastically hugged him, arms and all.

Richard could only lower his head onto the top of Elizabeth's hair, which smelled like something he had never sensed or experienced before. "So, this is what heaven is like," was his immediate thought.

She finally let his arms go, after which he wrapped his arms around Elizabeth, savouring the moment. They stood there, embracing each other, not wanting to go any further because they remembered that Elizabeth's father was standing nearby. They slowly let each other slip from their arms and stood there, looking into each other's eyes.

William, somewhat taken aback by the intimate episode, that was not his usual style, said, "Hey, you two. I am still here, you know."

Elizabeth immediately turned towards her father and promptly hugged him, saying, "Thanks very much, Father. Thank you."

Ann, watching all this through the gap in the tent flap, waited until she thought it wise to show her face. Once all the hugging was over, she left the tent and walked over to the threesome, unsure what to say or do. She felt uncomfortable about how things had moved so fast and was unsure what to say, particularly as she did not want to squash Elizabeth's enthusiasm. However, as Elizabeth was thrilled and her face was glowing for everyone to see, Ann's automatic reactions were somewhat softened as she stood there looking at them both.

Ann, while not wanting to show her concerns so early in the relationship but at the same time fully aware of how her daughter was feeling, said, "Well, Elizabeth. I trust you realize that this is just the beginning. You barely know each other."

Elizabeth, somewhat deflated by her mother's comments, turned to her mother and said, "Everything will be fine, won't it, Richard."

Turning towards Ann, Richard believing he knew what she was getting at, said, "Thank you for your understanding, madam; there is no hurry."

Elizabeth could feel what seemed like a magnetic attraction between herself and Richard as her right hand instinctively inched its way toward his.

As Ann was standing right in front of both, she noticed the slight movement of Elizabeth's right hand. She did not want any further intimacy or complications right now as she thought it more important to discuss that in private and more detail with Elizabeth. Accordingly, she quickly called out in a firm voice, "Elizabeth! Now that that is sorted, I think it is time for you to come with me. We have a thing or two to talk about."

Elizabeth at once lowered her hand back to her side and, disappointedly, said, "All right, Mother."

She turned to Richard and said, "See you later, Richard."

Ann turned, gave Richard a small wave, and with Elizabeth following right behind, returned to their tent.

William, although fully understanding why his wife said what she did, felt that Richard had received somewhat of a cold shoulder. William looked Richard straight in the eye and said, "I think everything is going to work out fine, so don't worry too much."

Although unhappy with the final tone, Richard nodded to William in acknowledgement, shook his hand again, and took off towards his tent. While Richard was not completely happy with how things had gone, he was more than pleased with the result. He was at least now free to see Elizabeth.

Chapter 28

Both Elizabeth and Richard parted company in a state of confusion; on the one hand, her parents had sanctioned some form of relationship; but on the other, her mother seemed indifferent or even somewhat hostile. Both sat on their respective beds in their tents reflecting where all this was heading while, at the same time, now feeling much closer to each other since they had first met.

Ann thought it best not to say anything to Elizabeth at this stage as she felt it would be better for her daughter to think about things a little more before further discussions. She stayed out of Elizabeth's immediate way by leaving her in the tent to think about what had just happened while going for a long walk with William away from the campsite.

The next morning, all parties involved had slept on the previous day's events, and where they held doubts now felt a little better, although all realized that there were still matters to be resolved.

Elizabeth had gone to bed early, although she tossed and turned much of the night with both elation and doubt, in equal measure, entering her mind. She woke up early, her parents still in bed, so she decided to get up and go for another one of those early morning walks on the beach that she had enjoyed a few weeks earlier. There was no wind outside, and all seemed peaceful.

She headed towards the beach, across the dunes, and down onto the soft sand. The sky was starting to show signs of dawn, giving her just enough light to find her way. She tried to let the beautiful and serene surroundings clear her head and, at the same time, block any negative thoughts. Today, she decided, was going to be a good day.

This time the moon was setting in the opposite direction to the last time she did this, with the result that its light gave the whole bay, including the curve of the sand, the waves hitting the coral reef, and the smooth water, a completely different look. Standing at the water's edge, she gazed across the reef and out towards Philip Island, which looked majestic in the half-light. Luckily, and rarely, there was no wind this morning as she turned her gaze from one end of the bay to the other, noticing for the first time the few Norfolk Island Pine trees acting as a sentinel on the most exposed easterly point of the bay.

Elizabeth stood at the water's edge for some time, admiring the view; the sun started to make itself known as more and more light entered the bay. Finally, she told herself, "One of the most beautiful places in the world."

She turned away from the calm sea and started to walk back up the beach with the view of sitting atop one of the dunes. As she did so, she noticed a figure walking down the dunes and onto the beach about two hundred yards away. It was still too dark to see who it was, but the walk seemed familiar as the figure slowly approached her. She paused, trying to work out who it was.

Then it dawned on her. It certainly looked like Richard! Without thinking, Elizabeth impulsively ran up the beach toward him. He was looking out to sea, and disappointingly for Elizabeth, he had not seen her before she called out, "Richard, is that you?"

Richard was sharply awoken from his seaward gaze by a familiar voice calling his name from somewhere along the beach. He turned his head towards the voice and, to his amazement, saw a figure resembling Elizabeth running towards him. He could not make out the face as it was still half-light as the sun was still below the horizon. He waited for a couple of seconds as the figure got closer. He hesitated because he did not want to make a fool of himself again. He had to be sure.

He called out in a questioning voice, "Elizabeth?" Now feeling more confident, he took off running in her direction, not taking his eyes off her as he did so. However, he was still unsure, so he questioned more loudly, "Elizabeth, is that you?"

"Yes, it's me," was all that Elizabeth could say as they got closer and closer. They both put their arms out wide as they got nearer and met body to body with some force before wrapping their arms around each other. They stood there for a few seconds taking in the smells and the comforting feeling of being in each other's arms, not at all aware that they were, in fact, standing in cold seawater.

They eventually let each other go and stood back while gazing into each other's eyes. Then, they paused, and while still looking intently at one another, they slowly moved their heads closer and closer until their lips met, and then they pulled each other into a full embrace. Elizabeth and Richard felt their hearts gather speed, and a warm glow spread between them as they melded into one form, and their pulses raced as one.

Elizabeth had never kissed someone so passionately before, and the feelings within her were both strange and exciting at the same time. She hung on to Richard for some time; her lips pressed firmly against Richards until she felt she was running out of breath. She pulled back, took a deep breath, and quickly kissed him again while looking into his rugged face. Slowly, they let go of each other while looking into each other's eyes.

They then clasped hands, and in a breathless voice, Elizabeth said, "Richard, I am glad I caught you on the beach. I really missed you last night."

"Me too. I missed you," is all Richard could think of saying as he took a small step back while looking into her eyes and holding onto her outstretched hands.

Elizabeth stood there, doing precisely as Richard was doing, and then she said, "Let's go for a walk along the beach."

"All right. I think that it will be the start of a beautiful day."

They held hands as they walked along the firmer edges of Emily Bay towards Slaughter Bay, the next bay inside the reef, where Richard had been busy earlier in the week helping the convicts gather building materials. They walked along to the western end of Emily Bay, where luckily the tide was out, then around the rocky point and into Slaughter Bay. This bay was utterly different from Emily Bay as it was much closer to the coral reef, and there were only small patches of sand mixed in with chunks of broken coral, some quite large. This meant that they had to walk along the very top edge of the beach, which at times made it difficult for them to continue holding hands. However, the sun was rising above the horizon by now, and the beauty of it all was evident to both. They paused, hand in hand, looking out at the waves that always crashed onto the reef, only varying in intensity with the strength and direction of the wind.

The island was very much at the mercy of the Pacific Ocean as the nearest land was hundreds of miles away, and the nearest significant land mass was thousands of miles away. Finally, they arrived at the end of Slaughter Bay, where the land rose steeply to the cliffs surrounding the island. They turned around and headed back to the camp. As Richard had previously been in the area, he led Elizabeth slightly away from the coast and walked on the carpet of needles between the towering Norfolk Island Pine trees. Looking up in wonderment at the immensity of it all, they eventually reached the well-worn path that led directly back to the camp.

Neither Elizabeth nor Richard said much during the latter part of their early morning walk – they enjoyed being in each other's company.

They walked out of the scrub into the camp, still hand in hand, although Richard was the first to let go as he did not think it wise to show too much emotion publicly. They both paused, smiled at one another and went their separate ways.

Both Elizabeth and Richard found it difficult to concentrate on whatever they were supposed to be doing for the rest of the day. They both kept remembering the early morning light, the peaceful surroundings, the glint of light on the water, the warm feeling of holding hands, and, more importantly, that first enveloping kiss. They both floated through their daily work, barely remembering what they had achieved during the day.

Other than fleeting connections and words, they had little time together until the following Sunday. The rigid routine and hours worked made seeing each other during the week difficult. Richard had suggested to Elizabeth that he would see her again right after church and that they could go for a walk, to which she enthusiastically agreed.

Elizabeth spoke to her mother, and although she was still getting used to her daughter's budding romance, she reluctantly agreed to the Sunday walk.

Sunday took a long time to arrive for both, as the rest of the week seemed to last forever and ever. But then, Sunday finally came. The day was cloudy, but this did not dampen either Elizabeth's or Richard's spirit. Elizabeth had managed, using a little sleight of hand, to get together enough food for their lunch, so with a small bag over Richard's shoulder, they set off heading west.

Once out of sight of the camp, Richard reached over and took Elizabeth's hand, squeezed it, relaxed his grip, and held on. He could not remember ever holding such a small delicate hand before, and the smooth skin against his rough hand felt reassuring. They first headed to the western end of the flat area surrounding Emily Bay, then to the base of the Western hills that rose nearly 250 ft up to the island's central plateau.

Sometimes they found it impossible to continue holding hands as they pushed through the heavy bush, but their hands automatically found each other as soon as the going became easier. Richard found that he had to change hands occasionally and swap the small sack from one shoulder to the other. Finally, arriving at the bottom of the steep incline, and after pushing their way through dense bush to get there, they paused and looked upward. For some reason, the hillside had less bush at this point, although many Norfolk Island Pine trees stood proudly most of the way up the slope.

"How are you feeling, Elizabeth? Still want to climb up the hill?"

Elizabeth looked at the hill as a challenge, saying, "Of course, you just watch me."

Elizabeth let go of Richard's hand and surged forward, although she found the damp grass rather slippery and found she had to use her hands to maintain her footing and momentum.

Richard stood still until he realised this was turning into a race. For one reason or another, Richard's shoes did not grip the grass like Elizabeth's, so he found it challenging to maintain any continuous forward motion.

By this time, Elizabeth was nearly ten yards ahead of Richard, so looking back down the hill, she said, "Come on. What's holding you back?"

"Are you challenging me to a race to the top?"

Not answering the question, Elizabeth took off again, using her arms and hands as much as her feet and legs. The going was slippery, but she seemed to be holding her own as Richard tried desperately to get enough traction to get closer. He was not gaining on her at this stage, so he stopped and leaned back against a pine tree, hoping to get his breath back.

Elizabeth looked back and noticed that he had stopped climbing. She called out, "What's the matter? Is it too hard for you?"

"Just getting my breath back. My shoes keep slipping."

Elizabeth returned down the hill to where Richard was standing, and to his surprise, she quickly wrapped her arms around him and hugged him. Their lips found each other, and they embraced for some time, taking in every enveloping sensation as they did so. Then, as Richard was already breathing hard from trying to climb with slippery shoes, he, reluctantly, was the first to come up for air.

"Sorry about that. I could not breathe," he said.

They stood there, holding on and looking into each other's eyes, until they both remembered they were standing on the side of a steep hill, and the only thing stopping them from crashing down the steep hill was their leaning against a tree.

They loosened their grip and continued up the hill, and as Elizabeth was not racing anymore, they helped each other as they climbed. Finally, they reached the top and looked over their shoulders at the view below them. Elizabeth took Richard's hand, and they stood together as a couple, taking it all in. They could see Philip Island in the distance, the coral reef protecting both Emily and Slaughter Bays, the gentle curve of the golden sand of Emily Bay, and the blue, blue water of the Pacific Ocean. Their camp was only partially visible through the dark green of the Norfolk Island Pine trees.

After taking in the absolute beauty of the vista ahead of them, Elizabeth turned to Richard and said, "You did not say where we are going."

"Rocky Point. It is not that far away."

"What's there?"

"You will see when we get there."

Clasping hands once again, they happily continued on their way. It took another couple of hours or so to reach their destination as the going was, at times, quite tricky., They finally walked down the gentle slope towards the cliff edge, dodging many pine trees on the way. The grass was very green and thick underfoot, reminding Elizabeth of a rich carpet. Many large and elegant-looking Norfolk Island Pine trees covered the area. Upon looking up into the lower branches, Elizabeth noticed a smallish white adult bird alongside a much more petite fluffy chick. There was no nest as such, just a join in the branch, and in fact, they saw many other adult birds and their chicks sitting on the bare branches in the same way. Obviously, they did not have or need a nest.

Elizabeth then noticed that many of the trees in the area had the same bird on their branches, some by themselves, some with larger chicks. Higher up amongst the tops of the trees, she was amazed by the number of birds circulating in and around the branches, most calling out as they went. They were very slim, delicate birds, streamlined and with a racing-looking set of wings. It was a beautiful sight, reminding Elizabeth of elegant dancers swinging and twirling around a dance floor.

Elizabeth's neck was getting sore with the constant movement necessary to take in the expanse of this marvellous sight, and little had been said as they both gazed upward. They then looked downwards towards the ocean, its intricate whitecaps obvious underneath the now clear blue sky.

Richard broke the silence as he again reached for Elizabeth's hand and said, "Is that not a sight worth seeing?"

Elizabeth turned to Richard and said, "Absolutely. Absolutely, it is,"

They walked close to the cliff's edge while gazing at the expanse of the Pacific Ocean and the rich colours that the sun was creating. With the warmth of the sun's rays on their faces, Richard gently tugged on Elizabeth's hand, guiding her to sit on a large, exposed smooth rock. Richard followed suit, edging closer alongside her as he did so.

With the bird noises in the background and the occasional bird swooping close to them as it headed out to sea, they sat comfortably hand in hand, both feeling warm and contented and, in the moment, with not a care in the world.

Postscript

Norfolk Island, the destination in this adventure story, has a long and varied settlement history commencing a few weeks after Sydney, Australia, was colonised in 1788. A small band of individuals was sent there by Governor Phillip. It included male and female convicts, soldiers, free settlers and officials, who commenced setting up a settlement on the shores of Emily Bay on the south side of the island.

This book, "When Times Were Tough," ends within weeks of that First Penal Settlement landing over 235 years ago. Since then, there have been two further settlements, as the island was abandoned twice after the first settlement.

That first convict settlement period continued from 1788 until it was closed in 1814 when the population rose to nearly 1100 individuals, the majority being convicts. These convicts were sent to the island, partly as punishment for further crimes committed in Sydney and partially to remove those that did not fit within that settlement. When it was decided that the cost and inconvenience of an island so far from Sydney could no longer be justified, many individuals, families and convicts were transferred to Tasmania. The settlement was closed only 26 years after it was first settled.

The island remained vacant from 1814 till 1825 when Captain Turton used the decaying remnants of the First Penal Settlement to build the Second Penal Settlement. Once again, a small band of convicts, soldiers and free persons started to rebuild and extend the island's facilities. This time, the authorities decided to send the "worst of the worst" convicts from Sydney, and their fate on the island was extreme. It was proposed that the minimum stay would be ten years and release would only be after receiving a report of the last "5 years of consecutive good account."

The conditions on the island for the convicts were extreme, and many bloody mutinies and resulting deaths occurred. However, many well-behaved convicts completed their sentences during this period and started farming on the island as free settlers. As male and female convicts served their jail time on the island, many eventually married and had children. By 1845 there were about 1400 prisoners on the island, plus hundreds more soldiers and free settlers. During 1846 alone, seventeen individuals received capital punishment over a period of 7 weeks. Such was the violence during this period.

In 1852, Bishop Willson took his third trip to the island and reported that, on Monday, just before his arrival, 39 men from Kingston and 14 from Longridge had been flogged over two days. Such was the merciless and shocking situation on the island at that time. However, convicts during the later years of the Second Penal Settlement started to be sent to Port Arthur in Tasmania, and the numbers on Norfolk Island slowly dwindled.

During the later years of Norfolk Island's Second Penal Settlement, discussions took place as to whether the island would be more suitable for the residents of Pitcairn Island, who were finding it challenging to remain on their even more remote, tiny island. The relocation was finally agreed to, and Norfolk Island was abandoned as a penal colony in 1855. On the 8th of June 1856, 193 Pitcairn Islanders landed on the island.

The island was effectively ceded to the Pitcairn Islanders at that time, and the question of who owns the island has been debated and argued ever since. While the island achieved internal self-government during the early 1980s and a local Legislative Assembly was instituted, it was unilaterally removed by the Australian Government some forty years later. The Third Settlement continues to this day, although some on the island may suggest that since much Australian legislation now applies, it is a new ball game and the Forth Settlement has in fact commenced.

www.ingramcontent.com/pod-product-compliance
Lightning Source LLC
Chambersburg PA
CBHW020257120726
47904CB00001B/237